RANGER'S APPRENTICE

THE EARLY YEARS

BOOK 1: THE TOURNAMENT AT GORLAN

Also by John Flanagan

Ranger's Apprentice

THE EARLY YEARS

Book I: The Tournament at Gorlan

John Flanagan

PHILOMEL BOOKS

PHILOMEL BOOKS
an imprint of Penguin Random House LLC
375 Hudson Street, New York, NY 10014

Copyright © 2015 by John Flanagan. Published in Australia by Random House Australia in 2015.
Map copyright © by Mathematics courtesy Random House Australia.

Library of Congress Cataloging-in-Publication Data is available upon request.

Printed in the United States of America.
ISBN 978-0-399-16361-6
10 9 8 7 6 5 4 3 2 1
Edited by Michael Green. Design by Semadar Megged. Text set in 13-point Adobe Jensen Pro.
This is a work of fiction. Names, characters, places and incidents either are the product of the author's imagination or are used fictitiously, and any resemblance to actual persons, living or dead, businesses, companies, events, or locales is entirely coincidental.

Araluen, Picta and Celtica

FOREWORD

THE EVENTS DESCRIBED IN THIS BOOK FOLLOW DIRECTLY from the short story "The Hibernian," published in Book 11 of the Ranger's Apprentice series, *The Lost Stories*.

For those who have not read "The Hibernian," it describes how Halt and Crowley first met as younger men when Halt came to the Kingdom of Araluen as a fugitive from his homeland of Hibernia. Halt was the rightful heir to the throne of Clonmel, but his younger twin brother attempted to kill him and seize the throne. Saddened and embittered by his brother's behavior, but unwilling to fight his own flesh and blood, Halt chose instead to leave Hibernia behind.

He arrives in Araluen at a time when Morgarath, Baron of Gorlan Fief and the Kingdom's foremost knight, is engaged upon a carefully planned attempt to seize power. One of his first steps is to weaken and destroy the Ranger Corps, an elite special forces unit who are the eyes and ears of the Kingdom and the most powerful group supporting the existing King. Over a period of several years, Morgarath has organized for the more senior Rangers to be falsely accused of crimes and forced to abandon their posts or flee the country. He has replaced them with his own sycophants and toadies.

Morgarath is an influential figure and has gained King Oswald's confidence, convincing him that his son, Prince Duncan, has been conspiring to murder him. Oswald takes refuge in Castle Gorlan, under Morgarath's protection. As time passes, Morgarath's protection becomes increasingly oppressive and the King finds himself a virtual prisoner.

Crowley, a recently commissioned Ranger, trained in the traditional skills by an old Ranger named Pritchard, is disillusioned by Morgarath's scheming. Shortly after he meets Halt, he decides to reform the Ranger Corps. He plans to recruit the few remaining members of the original group and seek a royal charter from Prince Duncan. Crowley discovers that, like himself, Halt has been trained by Pritchard, one of the first of the Rangers to be driven out of the Kingdom by Morgarath. This seals their friendship. The bond between them is reinforced when Halt joins Crowley to fight off an attack by half a dozen of Morgarath's soldiers.

With Morgarath's men hot on their heels, Halt decides to join Crowley in his search for Prince Duncan. Together, they set off on their quest, with the ever-present threat of Morgarath's enmity behind them.

1

IT HAD BEEN RAINING FOR A WEEK.

Not heavy rain, but a steady, persistent, soaking rain that finally overcame the protective oil in their woolen cloaks and worked its way into the fabric itself, making it heavy and sodden.

And cold.

As they had done for the previous few nights, Halt and Crowley were camping out in the woods. Halt suggested that they should avoid towns and villages until they were sure they were clear of Morgarath's sphere of influence, and Crowley initially agreed. Halt, after all, had more experience of traveling as a fugitive than he did. Now, however, he wasn't quite so sure about the decision.

They were sitting under a rectangular oilskin sheet that they had spread between four trees, with the lower side angled so that the rain would run off it. The ground beneath them was saturated and they had constructed low cots from tree branches to keep them off the wet earth. Each cot consisted of a rectangular frame, with a series of short crosspieces, and leafy boughs laid across it to form a rough mattress. Each day, they would disassemble the frames and carry the longer timber pieces with them, lashed in a bundle.

A few meters away, their horses were tethered. The animals huddled together, sharing their body warmth and keeping their hindquarters turned to the wind and rain.

Halt shivered and pulled his cloak more tightly around him. As he moved, a runnel of water ran off the cowl and landed on his nose, continuing its downward passage to drip off the end. Seeing it, Crowley laughed.

Halt turned an accusing eye on him. "What do you find so amusing?" he asked coldly.

Crowley, also huddled inside his cloak, nodded his head toward his friend. "You sitting there, hunched over and dripping, like an old man with a runny nose," he said. Unfortunately, the shrugging movement dislodged a stream of water from his own cowl and the drops ran down his nose. He sniffed, the smile dying on his face.

"You find it amusing that I'm soaked to the skin and dying of cold?" Halt asked.

Crowley made as if to shrug, then realized that such a movement would send more water running, and restrained himself. "Not amusing, perhaps. But certainly *diverting*."

Halt turned, very carefully, to face him. "And from what does this sight divert you?" he asked, with careful attention to his grammar. When Halt was in a bad mood, he invariably paid careful attention to his grammar.

"From the fact that I'm also sitting here with water running off my nose, cold, wet and miserable," Crowley said.

Halt considered that. "You're uncomfortable?"

Crowley nodded, sending more water cascading. "Totally," he said.

"Some Ranger you turned out to be," Halt told him. "I thought Rangers could face the worst discomfort in the line of duty with a smile on their lips and a song in their heart. I didn't realize they would sit around whining and complaining."

"Facing discomfort doesn't mean I'm not entitled to whine and complain about it. Besides, only a few minutes ago, I was laughing and cheerful." Crowley shivered, and pulled his cloak tighter. More water ran off it. "These cloaks are good up to a point. But once the water has soaked into them, they're worse than nothing."

"If you were sitting here wrapped in nothing you'd soon see the difference," Halt replied. Crowley grunted, and a brief silence fell over the campsite, broken only by the persistent patter of rain on the leaves and the occasional stomp of one of the horses' hooves.

They were faced with another cold supper. The air was so moisture laden that getting a spark to take from Halt's flint and steel to ignite a handful of tinder would be beyond his capabilities. And even if he could manage that, there was no dry firewood. Usually, they traveled with an emergency supply of tinder and kindling, but they had run out of both two days previously.

Pity, Halt thought. Even a small fire would have provided some warmth, and the flames would have given them a psychological boost as well. He reached for the pack on the cot beside him and found a piece of beef jerky. He bit some off and began to chew methodically, his jaws working on the tough, flinty meat. Maybe the exercise of chewing the jerky would warm him, he thought. The meat was certainly tough enough to require considerable effort from his jaws. Slowly, the smoked meat flavor began to release from the jerky and fill his mouth. Then, of course, he realized how very hungry he really was, and how little opportunity he would have to relieve that hunger.

He took a deep breath and let it out slowly. Being cold and hungry was miserable. Being wet was equally so. Being all three was well nigh unbearable.

"I've been thinking . . . ," Crowley began, leaving the sentence hanging for a few seconds.

Halt shook his head. "And here am I without pencil or parchment to record this momentous event."

Crowley raised an eyebrow in his direction. At least, he thought, that didn't send water cascading down his face. He raised his other eyebrow as well, just to make sure. No cascade, so he relaxed them both.

"I think we might have crossed the border out of Gorlan Fief," he continued. Halt grunted, a noncommittal sound.

Crowley took that as a signal to expound on his theory. "That river we crossed late this afternoon, I think that might have been the Crowsfoot River, and that's the border between Gorlan and Keramon Fiefs."

"Equally," said Halt, "it might have been the Salmon River, and as I recall from the map, that's still kilometers inside Gorlan."

But Crowley shook his head. "The Salmon is much narrower—much faster running. And it's farther west, closer to Redmont. So unless our navigation is well off the mark, we wouldn't have come close to it."

"Well, you were the one doing the navigating," Halt said.

Crowley gave him a hurt look. "My map reading and sense of direction aren't wonderful. But I'm rarely twenty or thirty kilometers offline."

"Rarely, of course, implies that sometimes you are," Halt pointed out. But Crowley stuck to his point.

"Not this time. And as I say, the Salmon is narrower and faster running."

Halt decided to concede. "So, if you are right, what point are you making?"

Crowley shifted as cold water ran down inside his cloak. Halt was right, he thought, it might feel miserable sitting huddled in a soaking cloak, but at least it still kept most of the water out—and it did allow some body heat to be retained, damp as it might be.

"My point is, if we've moved out of Gorlan Fief, we might be able to look for an inn in a village and spend a few nights."

"You think Morgarath would stop at the border between the two fiefs?" asked Halt.

Crowley stuck out his bottom lip. "Perhaps not Morgarath himself," he admitted. "But if he sent some of his men after us—and we don't even know for sure that he has—they might well decide to turn back once they reached the limits of the fief. Particularly in this sort of weather. They won't be enjoying it any more than we are."

"It's possible," Halt said. "So do you have a village in mind?"

Crowley nodded. He'd been studying the map before the light failed. "There's a village called Woolsey," he said. "I'd guess it's about ten kilometers away and a little off the beaten track. It's big enough to have a tavern or an inn. And if it doesn't, we could always look for lodgings with one of the villagers."

Halt said nothing, considering the idea. Then a problem occurred to Crowley.

"Of course, we'd need money," he said. "Usually when I'm traveling, I pay with a chit that can be reclaimed from the Corps. But I can hardly do that now."

Since their confrontation with Morgarath, and the fight with his men, they had decided that Crowley should relinquish his identity as a Ranger. Morgarath's men would be looking for a member of the Corps. So far, Morgarath was probably unaware that Halt had joined Crowley. To this end, Crowley had set aside his mottled Ranger cloak and was wearing a simple wool cloak in a dark gray color. Halt's cloak was a forest green. Both colors were adequate for concealment, and not as instantly recognizable as Ranger cloaks.

"I have money," Halt said, and Crowley looked at him with relief. "But it's Hibernian. I'm not sure if innkeepers here will accept it."

"Is it gold?" Crowley asked and, when Halt nodded, he continued. "They'll accept it."

"Well then," Halt said, "tomorrow we'll head for Woolsey village. It'll give us a chance to dry out our clothes and our gear. And the horses will benefit from spending a couple of nights in a stable."

"Or even a week?" Crowley suggested optimistically.

Halt turned a baleful eye on him, peering at him through the multiple drips of water that were now running from his cowl.

Crowley shrugged. "A couple of nights is good."

"Let's turn in," Halt said, yawning. It had been a long day and the thought of a dry bed on the morrow was an attractive one. He lay down carefully and, shivering slightly, wrapped the soaking wet cloak around him, pulling the cowl high up over his head. A gust of wind shook the tarpaulin above them and water cascaded down on three sides. He shivered again.

"To blazes with Morgarath's men," Halt muttered. "I want a nice roaring fire tomorrow night."

"And a hearty beef stew," came Crowley's muffled voice.

"And a hearty beef stew," Halt agreed.

2

I T   W A S   L A T E   A F T E R N O O N   B Y   T H E   T I M E   T H E Y   R E A C H E D
Woolsey. The rain had eased to a steady drizzle but still refused
to stop completely.

They rode down the single street of the village, huddled in
their cloaks. The two horses plodded stolidly through the thick
mud that covered the street, their hooves making sucking,
squishing noises as they alternately placed them down, then
dragged them free of the clinging, wet ooze.

Crowley pointed to a building halfway down the street,
larger than those surrounding it. It was the only two-story structure in the village, and a painted signboard above the entrance
swung erratically in the wind.

He peered closely at the sign. "The Yellow Parrot. That does
sound jolly."

"What's jolly about a yellow parrot?" Halt shot him a sidelong look.

Crowley considered the question. Truth be told, he had spoken simply for the sake of saying something, but he wasn't going
to admit it.

"Well," he said eventually, "parrots are amusing creatures.

They talk, don't they? They say things like 'Polly wants a bread crust.' Or, 'Who's a pretty boy then?' And they're colorful, so they brighten things up."

"What's amusing about a bird wanting a bread crust? Or claiming to be a pretty boy then? After all, the bird doesn't actually know what it's saying, does it?"

"It knows it wants a bread crust," Crowley said. "I mean, when it says that, and you give it a bread crust, it eats the bread crust, doesn't it? So obviously, it knows what it's saying."

Halt nudged his horse so that it stopped, while he turned to look at his companion. Crowley twitched the reins and his horse halted as well.

"Are you always so insufferably cheerful?" Halt asked.

"I suppose I am," Crowley admitted. "Do you always travel around as if there's a big, black thundercloud hanging over your head?" He liked Halt, despite their short acquaintance. But the Hibernian did tend to be a bit of a Gloomy Gus at times, he thought.

"What did you say?" Halt demanded.

Crowley realized that he must have unwittingly muttered the words aloud as he had the thought. Hurriedly, he shook his head. Raindrops scattered around him as he did.

"I didn't say anything."

But Halt was glaring at him. "You called me a Gloomy Gus," he accused.

Crowley shrugged. "It's a term of endearment in this country." He tapped his horse with his heels to start moving again. Squish, suck, squish, suck, ooze squish, went the hooves.

Halt set his own horse in motion, its hooves spraying mud and water in the air as he hastened to catch up with the Ranger.

He was feeling somewhat out of sorts, he realized. But that was because for days they had been traveling with their bows covered by waterproof leather cases to protect the strings. Wet conditions could play merry havoc with a bowstring, reducing its tension and rendering the weapon almost useless. And Halt never felt comfortable when he was in unknown territory without ready access to his bow. It made him feel vulnerable, and that made him feel irritable and ill at ease.

Over the pervading smell of rain and muddy ground, he detected a hint of woodsmoke. He glanced up to see it curling away from the inn's chimney, weighed down by the rain and the driving wind so that it never rose more than a couple of meters above the roof.

"Now that's more cheerful than a yellow parrot," he said.

Crowley had already swung down out of the saddle. He tethered his horse to a ring set beside the door of the inn and waited for Halt to join him. Then, together, they pushed through the door, stooping slightly to go under the low lintel.

After the chill of the rain and wind outside, it was delightfully warm in the taproom. It was a wide, low-ceilinged room, with a wooden plank that served as a bar, set on barrels running along the wall facing the doorway. Other barrels, large and small, were ranged on their sides behind the bar, set on racks so that their spigots were within easy reach of the innkeeper and his serving maids. The room was half full of men. Farmworkers and laborers, Crowley guessed, seeking refuge from the miserable weather. They fell silent for a few moments as they assessed the newcomers. Then the low buzz of conversation began once more and they turned back to their ale and their meals.

At one end of the room was a large fireplace, with a roasting spit that was hinged to swing right into the hearth itself. There were several ducks on the spit, their skin glistening with fat that fell, dripping and hissing, into the coals. The room was full of a pleasant smell of roasting duck, rich ale and woodsmoke that eddied around the low ceiling, the chimney not quite up to the task of clearing it away.

Halt and Crowley made their way through the tables to the bar, where the innkeeper assessed them briefly.

Woodsmen, he decided. Possibly hunters. Not soldiers, at any rate. Soldiers in this area could mean trouble, he had learned over the past few years. They tended to take without asking and could be loud and demanding, bullying the villagers and farm folk and creating ill feeling and tension among them. And, while they drank a considerable amount, they often paid short measure and frequently started fights.

Soldiers were bad business.

Deciding that Halt and Crowley posed no potential threat, he took his hand away from the heavy, studded cudgel he kept under the bar and reached for two pint tankards hanging overhead.

"Ale for you, my friends?"

The two men nodded. The red-haired one spoke.

"That would be very agreeable, innkeeper." He unfastened his cloak and threw the cowl back. Already, steam was beginning to rise from the cloth, generated by the heat in the room.

"And we'll be needing a room. With a fireplace," the dark-bearded one said. He had a pleasant, lilting accent that was unfamiliar to the innkeeper. The innkeeper set down two foaming tankards and the newcomers took grateful sips. The redhead smacked his lips in appreciation.

"That's good ale," he said and the innkeeper inclined his head in appreciation of the comment.

"I'm known for it," he said. Then, turning his gaze to the darker-haired man, he said, "None of my upstairs rooms have fireplaces." The man's eyebrows came together slightly in a look of disappointment. "But I have an annex out the back with its own fireplace. There's no access to it from in here. It opens onto the stableyard."

The disappointment faded from the man's face.

"That sounds just the thing," he said. And as he thought about it, Halt decided that it was. A separate entrance, concealed in the stableyard and not visible from the main street, would give them a good degree of privacy and security, just in case Morgarath's men came looking.

They negotiated a price. Initially, Halt asked for one night, but seeing Crowley's expression, he relented and made it two.

"One night will hardly be enough to get our things dry," Crowley pointed out, and Halt had to agree.

The innkeeper, conscious that travelers would be few and far between in the current weather, offered to include their meals and the deal was settled.

"Your horses can go in the stable," he said. "Plenty of room there for them."

Halt finished his ale and set the tankard down on the counter.

"We'll bring them in now and rub them down," he said. He never liked leaving his horse untended for too long—particularly after a long journey in cold, wet weather.

"They can wait two minutes while we finish our ale," Crowley said.

Halt looked at him, one eyebrow raised. "You can finish that in two minutes?"

Crowley regarded the large, almost full tankard in his hand. "I can finish this in one," he said. "I figured you'd hold me up."

He finished his ale and, reluctantly, they went out into the weather once more, leading their horses through the stableyard gate and into the high-roofed stable building. It was clean and airy and there was only one other animal in it—a mule that regarded them with faint interest. They unsaddled the horses and dried them off, rubbing them down with handfuls of clean, dry straw. Then they put them in two adjoining stalls, and while Crowley forked hay into the two mangers, Halt went out into the yard and filled two buckets with clean water. Returning, he noticed that the mule's water bucket was only half full and the water was green and scummy. Sighing, he took it down from the peg and returned to the pump, filling it with fresh water.

As he replaced the bucket, he noticed Crowley grinning at him.

"What now?" Halt said, an irritable tone in his voice.

"Oh, you pretend to be so grim and grumpy," Crowley said. "But there you go, fetching fresh water for a mule you've never seen before. You amuse me."

"Well, I'm always glad to lighten your mood. Although it doesn't seem to take much to amuse you."

Halt made a final check on his horse and tack. His saddle blanket was wrinkled over the rail and he spread it out evenly so that it would dry more quickly. Then he jerked a thumb toward the stable door. "Let's see what our lodgings are like."

Carrying their saddlebags and bow cases, they crossed the muddy yard and opened the door to the annex built against the rear wall of the inn. They were pleasantly surprised when they entered. The room was large and well ventilated and the walls were solidly built from timber, with mud and plaster sealing any cracks left by irregularities in the logs. In the end wall, a fire was already burning. The innkeeper had sent one of his serving maids to lay it and light it. Already, its warmth was filling the room and the yellow, flickering flames sent out a welcoming and comforting light.

Crowley moved to stand by the fire, rubbing his hands together appreciatively. "Well, I must say, we've certainly fallen on our feet here!" he said.

Halt nodded briefly. "I've stayed in worse."

Crowley shook his head, grinning at his companion. "Try not to overwhelm me with your boundless enthusiasm."

Halt, realizing that the room really was quite comfortable and he might have been a little more effusive, grunted an unintelligible reply.

There were two beds in the room, each with three thick woolen blankets and a straw-filled pillow. There were no sheets, but compared to the branch-lined cots they had slept on for the past five nights, this was little short of luxury. A rough linen towel was folded over the foot of each bed and a washbasin and large water jug stood on the plain pine side table.

There were two wooden armchairs, set either side of the fireplace, and a small table with three straight-backed chairs set around it.

Hastily, they stripped off their cloaks, spreading them over the chairs in front of the fire to dry, then did the same with their jerkins and shirts. Soon the room was full of the pervasive odor of damp, drying wool, as steam rose from the sodden garments.

They both had dry shirts in their packs—although dry wasn't quite accurate. The spare shirts were damp, as was everything they owned. But after they'd been held in front of the fire for a few minutes, they were comfortable enough.

Halt tied the fastening at the neck of his shirt, then redonned the wide leather belt that carried the scabbards for his saxe knife and throwing knife—one on each hip. He looked around the room, now littered with drying clothing spread on every available surface.

"Well, we've got the roaring fire we wanted," he said. "Now let's see about that hearty beef stew."

3

THERE WAS NO HEARTY BEEF STEW. BUT THERE WAS A RICH mutton broth—big chunks of tasty meat in a hearty broth of vegetables. And there was fresh crusty bread to mop up the scraps. They ordered a bowl each, and two more pints of ale to drink while they waited.

"Find a table," the innkeeper said, making an all-encompassing gesture around the room. "Millie will bring your food."

Without prior consultation, they both moved toward a table against the wall, at the far side of the room. It was well out of the immediate line of sight of anyone entering the tavern, but enabled them to keep a constant watch on new arrivals. The table was well away from the fire, and the nearest oil lantern was several meters away, so they were partially hidden in the gloom.

For Halt, it was second nature to remain unobtrusive. He had spent several months traveling through Hibernia, avoiding recognition and staying away from the search parties his twin brother sent after him. Crowley's training as a Ranger must have left him with the same sense of reticence. Pritchard had taught Halt that Rangers never sought to stand out from the crowd, preferring to blend in with the background.

Millie, a pleasant-faced girl of about twenty-five, brought them bowls of mutton broth and two wooden spoons. She set a board down in front of them, with a warm loaf on it and a knife. A small crock held rich yellow butter.

Crowley took a sip of the broth and smiled contentedly. "Oh, that's good!"

Halt followed suit and nodded agreement. The soup was hot and rich, and the heat of it seemed to spread through his tired, cold body. He even imagined he could feel the heat spreading down through his chilled and weary legs.

Suddenly conscious of how hungry they were, after days of cold food and hard rations, they set to willingly, rapidly lowering the level in their bowls. Millie strolled past their table and indicated the near-empty bowls.

"More?" she asked. "It costs no extra for a top-up."

Crowley instantly scooped the last of the mutton out of his bowl and crammed it in his mouth. Then he handed the bowl to the girl, nodding enthusiastically.

"Mmmm. Yeff pleafe," he mumbled round a mouthful of hot mutton and bread.

She smiled and took the bowl, then glanced interrogatively at Halt. "How about you?"

He shook his head. The bowl was still a quarter full and that would do him. "Not for me," he said.

She pointed to his tankard. "How about more ale?"

This time they both shook their heads, without any pause to consider the question.

"We're fine," said Crowley. "Thanks." He smiled at her and she returned the smile with some interest. He was a good-looking young man, with a cheerful, cheeky light in his eyes.

She glanced at his companion. He was a different kettle of fish, she thought. His eyes were brown, deep-set under heavy eyebrows. His face was thin and the beard was dark. There was something vaguely frightening about him, although she sensed no danger to herself from the man. Rather, she felt, there was potential danger for anyone who might cause him trouble.

She realized her smile had faded as she studied the dark-bearded man and she hastily readjusted it. It was professional good sense to smile at customers, she knew, even the ones who had a somewhat frightening aspect to them. She moved away toward the kitchen door, Crowley's bowl in her hand.

"I'll bring you your broth," she said.

She was halfway to the kitchen when the entrance door banged open, letting in a swirl of wind and rain and setting the smoke that hung about the rafters drifting uneasily. A stocky figure strode into the tavern, arrogance in every inch of his bearing.

The room fell silent as all eyes turned to the doorway. The atmosphere was instantly heavy with distrust and apprehension.

The newcomer was no farmworker or itinerant traveler. He was wearing a sword at his side, and as he pushed back his black cloak, it could be seen that his black leather surcoat was adorned with a gold slash running from his right shoulder to his left waist, shaped like a lightning bolt. A tight-fitting leather cap covered his head. A smaller rendition of the yellow lightning bolt was on its front.

He wore high riding boots—again in black leather—with his trousers tucked into them. The heels clacked loudly on the floor as he advanced a few paces into the room, allowing the door to close behind him. He looked around, taking in the fourteen people sitting at tables and the innkeeper and his two serving girls behind the bar.

If he was aware of the dislike radiating from the inn's customers, it didn't seem to bother him. He was probably used to creating a negative impression wherever he went, Halt thought. The newcomer's left hand dropped to rest on his sword hilt—a crude reminder of the fact that he was armed.

Crowley leaned closer to Halt and said in a low voice: "Black and gold. Morgarath's colors."

Halt nodded. He had seen them before, when they had visited Castle Gorlan.

Eventually, the innkeeper broke the awkward silence that had gripped the room.

"Can I help you, traveler?" he asked mildly. The newcomer's face creased with a scowl.

"It's Captain," he said abruptly. "Captain Teezal, in Lord Morgarath's service."

He waited for the innkeeper to amend his method of address but no amendment was forthcoming.

"And . . . ?" said the innkeeper calmly, waiting for the soldier to voice his business. The scowl on Teezal's face deepened. He was used to cringing deference when he spoke to people he considered to be his inferiors—which included most people he met. But he could see no sign of deference from the innkeeper and he was forced to continue.

"And," he said, placing sarcastic emphasis on the word, "I'm searching for two renegade Rangers—criminals who've broken Lord Morgarath's law."

"This is Keramon Fief," the innkeeper pointed out. "The lord here is Baron Carrol. Baron Morgarath has no jurisdiction here."

"Lord Morgarath has been offended by these two men. I'm sure Carrol would want to assist him in apprehending them."

The innkeeper shrugged. "I'm sure Lord Carrol would, if they were here. Which they're not."

Teezal glared at him, his hand opening and closing on the sword hilt. "Do you have any guests at the moment? Have there been any travelers passing through?"

Halt, scanning the room unobtrusively, saw several of the other guests look instinctively to the table where he and Crowley were sitting. Fortunately, Teezal was concentrating his attention on the innkeeper, who was shaking his head.

"None. Just locals here."

At his words, Halt saw the other customers hastily avert their eyes from him and Crowley. The innkeeper appeared to be a man of some influence in Woolsey.

"I'll take a look around," Teezal said brusquely.

The innkeeper shrugged. "Suit yourself. But there are no Rangers here, renegade or otherwise. Come to think of it," he added, "I've never heard of a renegade Ranger."

Teezal, who had turned away, swung back on him.

"They've offended Lord Morgarath and broken their oath. They've also injured several of his officers. As a result, they've been dismissed from the Ranger Corps. These are dangerous times and disloyalty must be punished."

The innkeeper made a compliant gesture with one hand. "I'm sure it must," he said. "Go ahead and look around if you want to."

Teezal locked eyes with him for some seconds, trying to stare him down. The innkeeper held his gaze confidently. With men like this, he knew, it was best to remain firm and uncowed. Any sign of weakness or uncertainty would only increase Teezal's arrogance and overbearing attitude.

Eventually, Morgarath's man switched his gaze away from the innkeeper and turned to walk among the tables, studying the men seated there. Other than the serving girls, there were no women in the room. His heels clacked loudly on the floorboards as he moved slowly between the tables, stopping from time to time for a closer look. But the inn's clientele were obviously farmers or farmworkers. They wore farmers' smocks and thick working boots, caked with mud. On several tables, felt hats, rendered shapeless by years of rain and sun, were evident.

His inspection finished, Teezal grunted discontentedly.

Then he noticed the two figures seated at the back of the room, in the shadows. Quickly, he walked toward them, his left hand opening and closing on the hilt of his sword. He stopped a few meters from them, reaching up to the oil lamp that hung from the rafters and tilting it so that its light shone more directly on the two men.

These were no farmers, he could see. They wore leather vests and woolen trousers tucked into knee-high leather boots. Fortunately, however, Halt's and Crowley's cloaks were currently spread across the backs of chairs in front of the fireplace in their room. Even without the distinctive mottled pattern, they would have raised his suspicions. And of course, their bows and quivers were in the room as well. Outwardly there was nothing to show that they were Rangers.

"Names?" he asked curtly.

Crowley smiled disarmingly. "Morris," he said. "William Morris of Keramon."

"I'm Arratay," Halt said briefly. He thought it best to keep his answers as short as possible, to conceal his Hibernian accent. Crowley obviously realized what he was doing, as he took the lead in the conversation.

"We're foresters, in the service of Baron Carrol," he continued pleasantly. He was grateful that the innkeeper had mentioned the local Baron's name a few minutes prior.

Teezal sniffed. "Foresters? A fancy name for poachers if you ask me."

Crowley shrugged. There was no point answering such a statement.

Teezal waited several seconds for a reaction. When none was forthcoming, he turned abruptly away, releasing the lantern so that it swung wildly back and forth, casting its yellow light in a wide arc.

His heels clumped heavily on the boards as he strode to the door, ill temper obvious in every line of his body. He swung the door open, then turned back to the room, speaking to those present.

"I'll be in the neighborhood," he said harshly. "If anyone sights these two renegades, he'd be well advised to come find me."

Silence greeted his statement. He let his gaze sweep the room once more, then abruptly went out, slamming the door behind him. A concerted release of pent-up breath swept the room as the customers relaxed. Gradually, conversations restarted and the atmosphere went back to normal.

Crowley and Halt rose from their table and moved to the bar. The innkeeper was still looking at the entrance where Teezal had left.

"Thanks for that," Crowley said, then added, "Not that we're the ones he's looking for, of course."

"Of course," the innkeeper replied, the vestige of a smile touching his lips. "But really, we don't owe Morgarath and his men any favors. He's been throwing his weight around lately and we're getting heartily sick and tired of him interfering in this fief."

"I can imagine," Crowley said.

The innkeeper shook his head in frustration. "After all, we've got enough on our hands with Duncan and his band causing havoc in the district."

4

Both Halt and Crowley took an involuntary step back at the words. They exchanged a quick glance, then Crowley asked:

"Duncan? You can't mean Prince Duncan, the King's son?"

The innkeeper regarded them with renewed interest. "The same," he said. "He's been in the north for the past few months, with a gang of armed men—none of them the type you'd care to run into on a lonely country road."

"Doing what?" Halt asked.

The innkeeper switched his gaze to him. "Anything they please. Robbing, plundering, raiding farms and running off sheep and cattle. Sometimes they move into a town or village for a week or so and terrorize the locals, demanding food and drink and lodging and paying nothing for it."

"And they make sure they take only the best," added another customer, a farmer by his clothes, who had risen from a nearby table to join the conversation.

"But . . . he's the King's son!" Crowley protested. "He's the heir to the throne!"

"Then eventually, we'll have a robber and a thief for a King," the innkeeper said.

The farmer nodded agreement. "The gods know what the old King makes of it all. He must be disgusted."

Halt turned to Crowley. "This is the Prince you said a man would be proud to follow?"

Crowley shook his head, totally bewildered. "I . . . don't understand," he said slowly. "I know Duncan. Not well, admittedly, but well enough to know that this is unlike him."

The farmer nodded sympathetically. "I know what you mean. Up until a few months ago, I'd heard nothing but good about the prince. But now this . . ." He let the sentence hang.

"There's another thing," the innkeeper added. "He and his men have been raiding across the border."

"Into Picta?" Crowley asked, barely able to believe his ears.

The two villagers nodded. "Aye. They raid and burn, stealing cattle and horses. If anyone tries to stop them, they kill them."

"But that's madness!" Crowley said, his voice rising. "We have a treaty with the Scotti!" He knew how long and hard the King had worked to establish that treaty. Duncan had actually handled some of the negotiations. Now the prince's actions, if they were hearing the truth, would endanger the fragile peace that existed between the two countries, provoking retaliatory raiding and killing.

"It seems he cares nothing for that," the innkeeper said. "I suppose he assumes that if the Scotti start raiding back, he'll be safe behind the walls of Castle Araluen. We'll be the ones who'll bear the brunt of the trouble he's caused."

"I don't believe this," Crowley said in a low voice. "I can't believe it. Why would he do such things?"

"Power," said the farmer succinctly. "A man gets a little power and he starts believing he can do whatever he pleases. "

"But . . . Duncan? It's so unlike him. I can't believe it!"

"So you keep saying," said the farmer. "But it's the truth."

Crowley made a hasty gesture of apology, aware that he might have offended the man. The farmer shrugged. He understood the stranger's consternation.

"Any idea where he is at present?" Halt asked.

The innkeeper looked toward one of the tables in the middle of the room. The other customers had all been following the conversation and now he addressed one of them, a burly, gray-haired man. "Tom? What say you? You were up toward the border this week, weren't you?"

The man he addressed nodded confirmation. "Aye. That I was. Last I heard, Duncan and his men were in Lendsy village. Been there several days, I heard. I left quickly. I had no wish to run into them. No need to either," he added.

"Where's this Lendsy village?" Halt asked.

The innkeeper pursed his lips, then answered. "A day's ride from here. Longer if the streams are flooded and the bridges are washed away. It's to the northeast, a few kilometers from the border."

Halt took in the information and placed a hand on Crowley's forearm. The Ranger seemed stunned by what he had been hearing.

"Come on," Halt said. "We need to talk." He looked at the innkeeper and the farmer. "Thanks for the information."

The innkeeper shrugged away the thanks and held out his hand.

"We didn't introduce ourselves," he said. "My name is Sherrin."

Halt took the hand. "I'm Halt."

A smile touched Sherrin's lips. "I thought you told Teezal your name was Arratay, or something."

Halt smiled in his turn. "I thought you told him you had no lodgers," he replied. Then, turning, he led Crowley toward the door. They had a lot to discuss.

The annex was warm and a little stuffy, and redolent with the smell of drying wool. Halt checked his cloak where it was spread over an armchair by the fire. The fabric was still slightly damp, but it was a big improvement on its former state.

"Be dry by morning," he said. "And a good thing. We'd best be on our way."

They had planned on staying for two nights. But Teezal's appearance, and the news they'd just received, dictated otherwise. Crowley was staring into the flames of the fire, his face set in grim lines.

"There has to be some mistake," he said. "Prince Duncan isn't a thief or a bully. He's a fine young man and he'll make a great king."

"A wise man once told me, don't believe anything you hear until you've seen it with your own eyes," Halt said.

Crowley looked up at him. "Who said that? Pritchard?" It sounded like the sort of thing their old mentor might say.

Halt affected to think for a few seconds, then gave a slight smile. "No. I think it was me, actually. I can be very wise at times."

"This is no time for joking," Crowley said. "If this is true, our plans to revive the Corps are finished. I was depending on a royal warrant from Duncan to give me the authority. If he's turned rogue, he won't be likely to give that sort of permission."

His heart was heavy. He hadn't realized how much he was depending on Duncan's warrant to reform the Rangers. The idea had sustained him over the past weeks. Now he knew that Morgarath's enmity would spell an end to his time in the Corps. Without Duncan to overrule the Baron, his plan was finished before it had even begun.

"Then I suggest we ride north and see what's actually happening," Halt said. "Unless you simply want to give up here and now."

There was an element of challenge in the last few words and Crowley reacted immediately to it, looking up at Halt with an angry frown.

Redheads, Halt thought. Quick to anger, quick to forgive.

With an effort, Crowley forced down the anger.

"You're right," he said. "We need to see for ourselves."

Sherrin gave them a hearty breakfast of thick, nourishing porridge laced with honey. He also provided a large pot of coffee and Halt downed three cups in quick succession.

The innkeeper raised his eyebrows. "Pity you don't like coffee," he said mildly.

Halt shrugged. "We've been traveling on hard rations and cold water with all this rain. I'm making up for lost opportunities."

They settled their bill with Sherrin and were on the road a few minutes after sunup. The clouds were breaking up, creating large patches of clear sky above them. In light of the drier weather, they had unpacked their bows, checked their strings and restrung the weapons. With the long yew stave settled comfortably over his left shoulder, and the fletching of the arrows tickling the back of his neck from time to time, Halt felt more at ease than he had for the past week.

They rode in silence. There was no point in discussing Duncan any further. Halt knew that any such conversation would mainly consist of Crowley repeating the fact that he couldn't believe the turn of events. And, since there was no point to that topic, they remained silent.

They had to detour several times to bypass bridges that had washed away or fords that were still running too deep to cross safely. The countryside around them steamed with the rainwater evaporating under the sun. It made for humid conditions and by midmorning they had discarded their cloaks, rolling them tightly and tying them behind their saddles. At noon they stopped for a quick meal. Sherrin had provided them with a fresh-baked loaf of bread and slices of cured ham. They had also brought with them a supply of dry firewood and kindling from the stack in his stable. Halt built a fire and boiled water for coffee.

He ate and drank with relish, enjoying the fresh food after the hard bread and dried beef they had been eating for days. Crowley didn't seem to notice the difference. He picked idly at his food and barely touched the coffee. His thoughts were elsewhere.

By midafternoon, they realized they were getting close to Lendsy village. They had passed a fork in the road and descended into a small valley. Now, as they rode up to the ridge at the far side, Halt raised his head and sniffed experimentally.

"Smoke," he said. "Do you smell it?"

Crowley sniffed as well, then shrugged. "We must be nearly there. I imagine they have their kitchen fires alight."

They crested the rise at that point and looked across a shallow valley. Above the next ridge, a thick pall of smoke rose into the air. Halt shook his head, frowning. "That's more than a few cook fires," he said. "Come on."

He urged his horse into a canter—no sense in galloping and arriving with their horses exhausted. Crowley was a few strides behind him and their horses' hooves thudded dully on the damp mud and leaf mold that covered the road surface. Then they were into the trees at the bottom of the ridge and weaving their way along the narrow path, riding in single file.

As they rode up the far side of the valley, the trees thinned and once more they became aware of the smell of woodsmoke. Halt reined in as he reached the crest. The land here was an undulating series of ridges and valleys and he looked down now into the valley that stretched out before them.

The trees had been cleared here for farmland. He could make out two farmhouses and, beyond, a huddle of buildings that had to be Lendsy village. That was the source of the smoke. Several houses, and a larger establishment that was probably the village inn, were burning fiercely.

"Look there!" Crowley said, pointing. Beyond the burning inn, a makeshift barricade had been thrown up—consisting of several carts and assorted furniture from the houses. It formed a half circle, its back secured by one of the larger houses. A small group of half a dozen men sheltered behind the barricade, thrusting desperately with spears, pikes and, in two cases, sickles on long poles, to repel a larger group who were trying to climb the barricade. For the moment, they were being forced back. But there must have been at least three times as many attackers as defenders and it was only a matter of time before they overran the defenses.

The attackers were armed with axes and long swords, with small wooden shields studded with metal. As they watched, Halt caught a glimpse of a swirling garment in red-and-blue checks. Tartan, he realized.

"That's not Duncan," he said. "They're Scotti warriors!"

5

HALT CLAPPED HIS HEELS INTO HIS HORSE'S SIDES AND IT sprang forward, going from a standing start to a full gallop in the space of a few meters. He let the reins fall across his horse's neck and unslung his bow, reaching with his other hand for an arrow from the quiver angled over his right shoulder.

Shooting from horseback with a full-sized longbow wasn't an ideal position, but he held the bow at a forty-five-degree angle as he nocked the arrow, his hands moving surely in spite of the horse's plunging movement. Guiding the animal with pressure from his knees, he raced down the gradually shallowing slope toward the village. As he drew closer, he could see several huddled forms lying in the road. None of them wore tartan, he noticed.

He could sense Crowley a few meters behind him. He glanced back and saw that the Ranger had also let his reins drop and had an arrow ready on his own bowstring.

Closer still and he could make out more detail as they swept into the space between the first of the village buildings. Several of the defenders behind the barricade were women, he realized. One of them was thrusting with a heavy spear at an attacking

Scotti warrior. The clansman grabbed the weapon behind its iron head and jerked it toward him, dragging the woman forward over the barricade.

As she fell, off balance, he tossed the spear aside and raised his huge broadsword over his head for a killing stroke.

Halt heard the unmistakable thrum! of a bowstring from behind him, then an arrow flashed past, its fletching hissing in the air.

The Scotti threw up his hands, the broadsword falling to the dirt beside him. He clawed at his back with his right hand, trying to reach the arrow that had impaled him. Then he pitched forward, landing on the barricade, then tumbling off onto the road.

Another Scotti was striking with a sword at a villager armed with a sickle tied to a pole. The makeshift weapon was clumsy and unbalanced, and the villager was hard pressed to ward off the powerful strokes from the raider. As they watched, the pole spun out of his hands and he was left defenseless.

Halt shot and the second Scotti went down. The villager looked up, startled, searching to see where his salvation had come from.

The two riders were barely fifty meters from the desperate battle. Halt decided that was close enough. He reached down with his right hand for the reins—his bow was in his left. He dragged on them and pressed his left knee into the horse's flank, bringing it to a skidding, sliding stop, side on to the barricade. Crowley mirrored his actions and the two of them sat their horses, side by side in the middle of the village high street.

Now the Scotti were aware of the danger to their rear. A group of them disengaged from the barricade and formed a line facing the two bowmen. There were ten of them and their small circular shields were pressed together to present a barrier to any further arrows.

But not an impenetrable barrier. The shields couldn't cover the raiders' entire bodies and the two archers were expert shots who could pick the smallest target and hit it at this distance— virtually point-blank range. Halt shot again and one of the men in the middle of the line went down with a cry of agony, an arrow through his thigh. Then Crowley sent another arrow hissing on its deadly way and a Scotti warrior reeled back out of the line with an arrow transfixing his forearm. His weapon fell to the muddy road. As he staggered back, one of the defenders behind the barricade, momentarily forgotten, leaned out and brought a long, heavy staff crashing down on his skull. His knees folded up under him and he went facedown in the mud.

A huge Scotti, apparently the leader, bellowed with rage as he saw his men wounded. He pointed his broadsword at the two mounted men and shouted a command. His warriors responded with an incoherent cry of their own and began to advance, shields up and weapons raised.

Three more of them went down in the space of five seconds— two with leg wounds and the third with an arrow through his shoulder. Aside from the pain of the wounds themselves, the sheer force of the arrows at this range, propelled by eighty-pound longbows, knocked them backward. Another arrow slammed into one of the shields and its owner was forced back several paces. It was too much to expect them to continue to advance in the face of such withering shooting. The arrows came thick and fast and men screamed in pain and rage. One man turned and ran, followed almost immediately by another. Then the entire group had broken and were retreating at full pace to the north, those who were so far untouched by the arrow storm helping their wounded comrades to hobble with them at the fastest pace they could manage.

"That's enough," said Crowley, lowering his bow. He had no wish to shoot at men who were retreating and, effectively, defenseless.

Halt nodded agreement. "They'll keep running until they reach the border."

They turned their horses and began to walk the remaining fifty meters to the barricade. As they approached, the villagers straggled out from behind the tangle of tables, chairs, handcarts and the other paraphernalia they had thrown up to stop the attackers.

A ragged cheer went up as the two riders stopped and dismounted.

A tall, heavily built man in his mid-thirties stepped forward. He was one of the better armed and equipped among the villagers, with a single-bladed battleax in one hand and a large wooden shield on his other arm. He wore an iron helmet, a simple piece in the shape of an acorn.

He leaned his ax against a nearby handcart and greeted them, right hand outstretched.

"Can't tell you how glad we are to see you," he said, smiling broadly. "We were on our last legs here. You arrived just in time. I'm Yorik, headman of the village."

Halt deferred to Crowley, motioning for him to step forward. The Ranger did so, shaking the headman's hand and grinning at the other villagers who were clustering around.

"Glad to be of service," he said. "My name's Crowley, and this cheerful chap with me is named Halt."

Halt nodded a greeting as Yorik appraised them keenly. He took in the cowled cloaks, the dual sidearms—saxe and throwing knife—and, of course, the mighty longbows both men carried.

"Judging by the way you shoot," he said, "you're King's Rangers."

Crowley nodded. "I am. He's as good as." He gestured around the village, taking in the still figures lying in the street and the burning and smoldering buildings. "What caused all this?"

Yorik's face clouded over. "Prince Duncan caused it. He went raiding with his men over the border and stirred up the Scotti. Then he moved on before they could retaliate, leaving us to face the music. Curse his criminal hide," he said bitterly. Then a look of sudden fear swept over his face. These were King's Rangers, after all, and likely to owe their allegiance to Prince Duncan as a member of the royal household. "Forgive me," he said, dropping his gaze. "I spoke without thinking."

Crowley shook his head. "No forgiveness necessary," he said. "We've been hearing some strange tales about Duncan. Sounds like they're true."

Yorik nodded warily. He still wasn't totally sure of his ground.

Halt entered the conversation. "We heard he'd been throwing his weight around—stealing and helping himself to anything he fancied."

Yorik seemed a little reassured by the note of censure in Halt's voice. "Aye, that's right. And when he'd taken everything of value, he moved on. We were glad to see him go—until the Scotti turned up, of course. Duncan has twenty men-at-arms with him. They would have made short shrift of these brutes."

He gestured at the two dead Scotti lying in the street.

Already, the other villagers were beginning to dismantle the barricade and return the items of furniture to the homes they had come from. Of course, the inn was totally destroyed, so several pieces that had come from the taproom were left to one side. Yorik looked gloomily at the smoldering wreckage of the inn. As they watched, a final section of the roof collapsed in on the rest. Sparks flew in a shower, then settled slowly.

"We'll give you a hand clearing things away," Crowley said, and he and Halt joined the villagers in their work, returning the carts and furniture to where they had come from, and laying the bodies of those villagers killed in a row by the side of the road. The dead Scotti were piled separately, and with considerably less care.

"We'll bury our people later," Yorik told them. "The Scotti we'll burn."

Crowley dusted off his hands and looked around. The barricade had been dismantled and removed. The funerals, he sensed, would be a private matter for the villagers, where outsiders like him and Halt would be intruding.

"Thanks for your help," Yorik said. "If you hadn't turned up, we'd have been finished."

Crowley and Halt shrugged diffidently. There was nothing to say, really. It was an awkward moment and Yorik smoothed it over with his next words.

"Come join my wife and me for a glass of cider and a bite to eat," he said. "She's the best cook in the village."

They followed him toward one of the larger houses—a single-story wattle-and-daub structure with a thatched roof.

"I thought the Scotti might try something like this," Yorik said. "So I'd posted lookouts along the road to the border. They caught one but the second got here in time to give us warning. We managed to throw up the barricade before they arrived." He glanced down the road to where two men were lifting one of the still figures sprawled in the rapidly drying mud. "Not that it did young Merrick and his brother any good," he added heavily.

Crowley dropped a consoling hand on his shoulder. "Still, you held them off long enough for us to get here," he said.

Yorik nodded gratefully. "That's true. You certainly taught those murdering Scotti a thing or two."

He opened the door to the house and they went inside ahead of him.

"Maeve," he said, "we've guests joining us."

His wife was the woman Crowley had saved with his first shot. She nodded a greeting to them and began to set food on the table.

"You're welcome in our home," she said warmly.

There was a cold roast of beef on the table and a crock of yellow pickles stood beside it. Maeve was cutting thick slices of bread while Yorik poured three mugs of cider. She smiled and gestured to the chairs by the table.

"Seat yourselves, Rangers," she said.

"I'm actually not a—" Halt began, but Crowley cut him off.

"You ride and shoot and fight like a Ranger and you were taught by one of the best of the old breed. Let's just take it as read that you are one."

Halt shrugged in acquiescence and reached for a piece of bread, piling several slices of beef on it and spreading a generous helping of pickles over the top. He bit into the food and sighed contentedly.

"So tell us about Duncan," Crowley said.

Yorik paused, gathering his thoughts. "He and his men turned up here four days ago. Around noon, wasn't it, Maeve?"

"Aye," said Maeve. "Close enough to noon."

"They marched into the tavern across the way, kicking everybody else out and helping themselves to the best wine and ale that Tilson had in the cellar."

"They seemed to have an eye for the best," Maeve said heavily.

Yorik glanced at her, nodded agreement and helped himself to bread and beef before he continued. "Young Jemmy Mandell was driving his father's prize sow out to the green when they arrived. They took her and slaughtered her, right in the street. When the boy tried to stop them, they beat him something savage. Then they started roasting joints of pork over a fire, laughing all the while. Thought the whole thing was right amusing, they did."

"And Duncan said nothing about this?" Crowley asked.

Yorik shook his head sadly. "Prince Duncan was laughing the loudest. He was cheering his men on. And he kept doing so while they stole and beat people and terrorized some of the womenfolk. He's the worst of the lot of them, if you ask me."

"It sounds like it," Halt said.

"When did they raid across the border?" Crowley asked.

"That was the day before yesterday. They headed out around midmorning. We thought they were gone for good. Then they arrived back next day and told us what they'd been up to. 'You can expect a return visit from the Scotti,' Duncan told us. 'They seemed quite annoyed when we left.'

"Then, yesterday, they finally left us in peace. Except, of course, that we knew the Scotti would retaliate. Which they did, as you saw."

"I doubt you'll see the Scotti again," Crowley told him. "They won't be too quick to follow a war leader who comes back from a raid empty-handed, with a third of his men dead or wounded."

"No. That's true," Yorik agreed. "Although I'd give them free passage through here if they'd go after Duncan."

"Where was Duncan headed when he left?" Halt asked.

"They went west. Nearest village of any size in that direction would be Kirkton-Lea. And God help them if Duncan decides to visit."

"Have you thought of sending to Castle Araluen to ask for the King's help?" Crowley asked. "After all, he'd hardly condone what Duncan is up to."

But Yorik shook his head. "Haven't you heard? The King is no longer at Araluen. There was an attempt on his life and Baron Morgarath insisted that he move into Castle Gorlan, where he could keep him safe."

Halt and Crowley exchanged a surprised look. They both had the same thought but it was Halt who expressed it.

"Or keep him prisoner," he said.

6

THEY SPENT THE NIGHT IN YORIK'S BARN—THERE WASN'T enough room for four in the headman's house. The following morning, they set out on the road to Kirkton-Lea.

"Sometimes I get the feeling that we'll spend the rest of the year trailing Duncan from one village to the next," Halt said ill-temperedly.

Crowley's gaze was fixed doggedly on the road ahead. The more he heard about Duncan's exploits, the more he believed there was some terrible mistake being made.

"I want to talk to him myself," he said. "I can't understand why he would turn like this."

Halt shrugged. "Why do I sense Morgarath's interfering hand in all of this?" he asked.

Crowley looked at him in surprise. "Morgarath? Why would he have anything to do with Duncan?"

Halt shook his head thoughtfully. "Morgarath is hungry for power. Having Duncan discredited, and possibly disinherited, would work in his favor. And now we find that the King is in Castle Gorlan, under Morgarath's dubious protection. That's terribly convenient for our favorite baron, isn't it?"

Crowley looked a little surprised. "I hadn't thought of it in those terms," he said. "But there could be something in what you say."

Halt laughed scornfully. "I wouldn't be surprised if he hadn't cooked up the assassination plot in the first place. I have an uncomfortable feeling about Morgarath. And if I've learned anything over the years, it's not to ignore that sort of feeling."

Halt and Crowley paused on a small wooded knoll overlooking the village of Kirkton-Lea. They had sunk into the long grass at the edge of the small copse of trees. Their horses were tethered farther back in the woods behind them. Since Duncan was accompanied by at least twenty armed men, they had both thought it wiser to spy out the lay of the land before entering the village.

They could hear raised voices from the inn, with an occasional burst of ribald singing and, once, the sound of breaking furniture and a startled woman's scream.

"Nobody on the streets," Halt observed.

Crowley nodded, his brow furrowed by a frown. "Staying indoors, most like, to keep out of harm's way."

"Let's take a closer look," Halt said, gesturing toward the rear laneway running behind the houses on the left-hand side.

Without waiting for Crowley's reply, he rose to a crouch and ghosted through the long grass, moving instinctively from one piece of vestigial cover to the next, using bushes and small trees to conceal him as he went. Crowley allowed Halt to establish a lead of thirty meters or so, then rose in his turn and slipped through the waist-high grass after him, barely seeming to disturb the long stems, only remaining visible for seconds at a time.

For the purpose of this exercise, he had resumed his camou-flaged cloak, and the mottled green-and-gray material helped him blend almost completely into the landscape as he passed across it.

When he reached the lane at the outskirts of the village, Halt continued to move stealthily, going deeper and deeper into the cluster of buildings, now using the lean-tos and barns for cover. Better to keep moving at a constant pace than to stop and start continually, he knew. Variations in pace would almost certainly draw the attention of any eyes in the vicinity, whereas a constant, steady movement was more likely to go unremarked.

He glanced back once or twice but saw no sign of Crowley, even though he knew the redheaded Ranger would be following him.

From the knoll, Halt had marked a house that stood opposite the tavern. He reached it now and flattened himself against the rear wall, listening keenly for any sound of people moving within. For a few seconds there was nothing, then he heard a man cough and a low murmur of conversation inside—too low to make out the words.

If people were whispering inside their own homes, he thought, that indicated they were nervous. He peered round the corner of the house, looking down the littered alley to the front door of the tavern opposite. Without the bulk of the building to block the sound, the noise of shouting, roistering men was once more apparent. Scanning the sidewall of the house, he could make out one window facing into the alley. Most likely it would be covered with oiled cloth—glazed windows were a rarity in country villages. But the cloth would show a shadow moving outside, so it would be wise to move past the window in a crouch.

There was a large barrel at the far end of the alley, set to collect rainwater runoff from the roof, and several broken pieces of farm equipment lying around as well. He heard a slight movement beside him and turned to find that Crowley had arrived. Halt indicated for the Ranger to take a look. When he did, Halt leaned close, so that his mouth was almost against Crowley's ear.

"We'll move down to the main street to take a look," he breathed. "The water barrel will give us cover in case someone comes out of the tavern."

Crowley nodded assent and Halt continued. "There's a small window halfway down the alley. Keep below the sill level as you go past it."

Again, Crowley nodded. Then, without further discussion, Halt moved out from behind the house, crouching low as he half ran down the alley. As he reached the window, he crouched lower still, staying well below the level of the sill. As he ghosted past the window, he heard another mutter of voices from the inside. This time, he thought he could make out the word Duncan, and he was sure it was spoken in tones of contempt.

He took up a position behind the water barrel, where he could see through the triangular gap left between it and the wall by the tapered top of the barrel. Crowley joined him, standing a little taller so he could peer over Halt's shoulder. The shadows were deep in the alley, and as long as they didn't move, Halt was confident their cloaks would keep them concealed from a casual viewer.

They had been in position for several minutes when the door of the tavern was flung open and four men staggered out. Halt's heart lurched initially, but the men were looking into bright sunlight and the chances that they would see the two crouching figures in the shadows of the alley were slim.

They were all dressed in red surcoats over chain-mail shirts and they all wore swords at their belts. Short swords, noted Halt. Not long weapons such as those carried by knights or cavalrymen. These were simple men-at-arms then. Their mail coifs were folded down over their collars. None of them wore helmets.

Their red surcoats were dirty and stained with mud and food. On their right breasts, they carried the insignia of a red, stooping hawk in a white circle.

Crowley touched his shoulder gently, the contact barely noticeable.

"Red hawk," he breathed. "That's the symbol for the heir to the throne. These are Duncan's men, all right."

The four men were carrying tankards, beer slopping out as they moved. Obviously, they had been drinking for some time. There was a bench set against the wall of the tavern and they sank onto it, legs sprawling out toward the street, raising the tankards to their mouths to drink deeply. In the few seconds that the door had remained open to emit them, the sound of shouting and singing had intensified, only to be cut off again as the door shut.

"Not fair," one of them slurred loudly. "It's our turn to relax, not to keep watch. Tiller's playing favorites again."

Two of the others grunted agreement. The fourth man looked scornfully at the one who had spoken.

"Shut up and drink your ale. If he hears you complaining, you'll be in for it."

Scowling, the first man finished his ale, then viciously tossed his empty tankard into the street, where it bounced and rolled before coming to a halt.

"Let him try something with me," he said, with the belligerence of the drunk. "I'll soon show him what's what."

The others laughed derisively at his boast and he glared at them, his temper surging at their ridicule.

"I tell you," he continued angrily, "I'm sick of this. I've seen precious little in the way of loot. Tiller keeps it all for his favorites. I'm of a mind to cut loose and leave this band, first chance I get."

Unfortunately for him, the door to the inn opened as he said the last few words, and a tall, bearded figure in a red surcoat emerged. Halt stiffened instinctively. The man's clothes and chain mail were of a better quality than those of the men-at-arms. For a second or two, he was facing them and Halt could see that he wore the red hawk symbol in the center of his breast, not offset to the right like theirs.

Plus the sword at his waist was at least a meter in length, and jewels glittered on its pommel. His right hand dropped to the hilt of the sword as he turned on the man who had spoken.

"Looking to cut loose, are you?" he shouted. "I'll cut you loose, you worthless piece of dog's droppings."

There was a hiss of metal on leather as he drew the sword and advanced on the men sprawled on the bench. The one who had spoken last lurched to his feet, his hands held out in supplication, panicked by the sight of the naked blade.

"Steady on, Tiller—"

"Duncan, you ignorant swine! Call me Duncan!" The tall man shoved the speaker viciously, sending him sprawling in the street. He was half turned away from the two watchers in the alley and his face was obscured. But his rage was all too apparent.

He whipped the sword over and struck the prone man across the legs with the flat side of the blade. The man howled in pain, then howled again as the blow was repeated, this time across his shoulders. He crouched, trying to protect himself with his hands as the taller man rained blows down on him repeatedly, his voice rising in anger with each stroke, the blows punctuating his words.

"I told . . . you ignorant fools . . . to stand guard on the road! Not sit out here drinking! Now . . . get . . . to . . . your positions!"

"Yes, Captain! Yes, Lord Duncan!" the other men chorused. They rose hurriedly from the bench and, staying well outside the reach of the long blade, moved down the main street. Two of them went north. The third helped the unfortunate fourth man to his feet, then they half ran, half shambled their way to the south end of the village.

Satisfied that they were complying with his orders, the tall man sheathed his sword with a gesture of annoyance. Then he turned back toward the entrance of the inn. For a moment, he was facing the two observers in the alley. Neither man moved, knowing that with the bright sun full in his eyes, it would be virtually impossible for him to see into the shadows where they crouched, unmoving. Then, with a muttered curse, he flung open the door of the tavern and went back inside.

Halt had been crouching, every muscle tense as he leaned forward to watch. Now he relaxed, letting out a long-held breath with a low sigh.

"Well," he said softly. "What do you make of that?"

For a moment there was no reply and he turned to look at Crowley, who was staring fixedly at the tavern door, shaking his head slowly. Then the Ranger spoke.

"That's not Duncan."

7

They retraced their steps along the back lane, easily avoiding the guards now in position at the south end of the main street.

They spoke no further until they reached the small glade where they had left their horses. Then, as they stopped to take stock of the situation, Halt turned to Crowley.

"What do you mean, it's not Duncan?"

The Ranger shook his head once more. "At first, I thought it was. It looks like him. He's about the right height and build. And the beard is similar. Even his voice sounds like the prince. But when he turned toward us, with the sunlight full on his face, I realized it's not him. It's an impostor."

"You're sure?" Halt asked, although the conviction in Crowley's voice was obvious.

"Positive," Crowley replied.

Halt set about making a fire, to boil water for coffee. He frowned thoughtfully as he struck a flint on his saxe knife blade and sent a shower of sparks into a small pile of dried tinder—courtesy of Sherrin's woodpile. He breathed gently on the smoldering tinder, setting a tiny tongue of flame licking the dry matter. Then he placed the flames in the kindling he had piled up in a cone shape. The flames grew stronger and ran up the dried saplings, quickly enveloping the entire pile. He added heavier sticks to the fire and soon had a fierce little blaze alight.

"The question is, why would anyone impersonate Prince Duncan?" he asked.

"You said it yourself. To discredit him. To turn the people against him."

"And who would benefit from that?" Halt asked. He had learned some time back that when a situation like this occurred, asking who would benefit from it usually provided a good direction as to who was behind it all. They exchanged a glance as he set the coffeepot down into the flames.

"Morgarath," they both said at the same time.

"As you said," Crowley said thoughtfully. "He's hungry for power. He's popular among most of the other barons. He's the Kingdom's champion knight, after all, so a lot of them look up to him. The only person who might have rivaled that popularity was Prince Duncan."

"But not now," Halt said.

"Not now. He's provoked trouble with the Scotti and he's becoming hated by the common people."

"Next question," Halt asked. "What do we do about it?"

There was a long silence, during which the two of them stared into the bright, leaping flames of the fire.

"I suppose we could drag that false Duncan—Tiller, wasn't he called?—out of the inn and ask what he's up to?" Crowley suggested.

But Halt shook his head. "Chances are, he doesn't even know

who's hired him. He's a cat's paw, after all. Besides, he has twenty men-at-arms around him. That might make the dragging a little difficult."

"Then we're going to have to find the real Duncan—assuming he's still alive."

"How do we do that?" Halt asked.

Crowley regarded him with a sidelong glance. "You're full of helpful questions, aren't you. How about coming up with an answer for a change?"

Halt shrugged. "You're the local expert. I'm just an ignorant foreigner."

There was another long silence, then Crowley spoke again.

"If Morgarath really is behind this, then all I can suggest is that we head back into Gorlan and nose around to see what we can find out."

"And if he's not?" Halt asked.

"Then we'll go with your plan," Crowley told him.

Halt raised his eyebrows as he tossed a handful of coffee into the boiling water. "Do I have a plan?" he asked mildly.

"You'd better have."

The two friends rode silently, retracing their steps toward Gorlan Fief. There was an unmistakable air of defeat about them. They had found the false Duncan, which at least established that Crowley's suspicions were correct and that the real Prince Duncan wasn't behind the raiding and pillaging that had been going on. But they had no leads as to where the real Duncan might be, or what had become of him. They were back where they had started—in fact, Halt thought, they were several paces behind where they had started, with no leads to follow and only the vague hope that they might find more information in Gorlan.

Although how we'll go about that defeats me, the Hibernian thought. After all, Morgarath was likely to clap them in a dungeon as soon as he set eyes upon them. Still, Halt couldn't think of an alternative, save for wandering aimlessly about the Kingdom hoping to hear some word of the missing Crown Prince. And that was no plan at all.

They were almost at the border of Gorlan Fief, close to the winding body of water known as Crowsfoot River. The path here was a narrow one, cut through the thickly growing trees of an old forest. In fact, the path hadn't really been cut at all. It had been worn by the passage of thousands of travelers over the years. They were riding abreast, which meant they took up the entire width of the path, when they heard drumming hoofbeats coming toward them, from the direction of the ford across the Crowsfoot toward which they were heading.

As they reached a long, straight stretch of the path, a rider came into view. He was traveling at a full gallop, waving his arms at them to clear the path for him. He wore a black leather vest, studded with metal disks, and woolen trousers tucked into thigh-high riding boots. A sword bounced at his hip and he was also wearing a long-billed, crested cap—the mark of a messenger or dispatch rider.

As he came closer, they could make out a gold insignia on the left breast of his jacket.

"Black and gold," Crowley muttered. "Morgarath's colors."

"Clear the way!" the rider shouted imperiously. "Dispatches from Lord Morgarath! Clear the way!"

He was closer now, and showed no signs of slackening his

pace. His horse was bigger and heavier than those the two Rangers rode and it appeared that if they didn't move aside, he would plow right through them.

"Notice how when you put a uniform on a man he tends to throw his weight around?" Halt said. Crowley didn't answer but they urged their horses to either side of the path, leaving room for the man to pass between them.

"Out of my way, curse you!" the messenger shouted, in spite of the fact that they had already made room. Perhaps it was the final, unnecessary demand that tipped the scales for Halt. He slipped his bow from his shoulder and, as the dispatch rider thundered past them, he reached to his right and dropped the end of the weapon over the man's head, so that the thick bowstring fastened around his neck.

"What . . . ?" the dispatch rider began as he felt the string draw taut across his neck. But at that moment, Halt heaved back on the bow, hauling the rider bodily out of the saddle and sending him crashing to the ground. There was a woof of exhaled breath as he landed flat on his back, then a dull thud as his head struck the compacted leaf mold and mud that formed the surface of the path.

Halt swung down from the saddle to study the fallen man. Crowley did the same. About twenty meters up the path, the man's horse seemed to become aware that its rider was no longer in place. It slowed to a trot, then a walk. Then it stopped, looking around curiously.

Halt and Crowley knelt beside the unconscious man.

"You didn't kill him, did you?" Crowley asked.

Halt shrugged. "I wasn't trying to. But he certainly is still."

At that moment, the man took in a great shuddering breath.

He twitched violently once or twice, but his eyes remained tight shut.

"No. Just unconscious," Halt said. "He should be out for an hour or more. He certainly caught his head a whack."

"So was this a good idea?" Crowley asked. He stood up.

Halt remained on his knees, rifling through the inside pockets of the dispatch rider's leather vest. "It certainly seemed like one at the time," he said. There was nothing of interest in the man's pockets. He stood and glanced down the path at the riderless horse. It was slowly picking its way back toward them. He walked to meet it, making calming, reassuring noises as he got closer, and patting its smooth muzzle. The horse pushed its head against him.

"Good boy," Halt said. "You can't help who you work for, can you?"

The horse shook its mane, seeming to agree with him. Halt grinned at it, then took its reins and led it to the side of the path, where he tied the reins to a sapling. He noticed the leather saddlebags hanging either side of the horse's rump, behind the saddle. He untied the fastenings that kept them in place and lifted them clear.

"He said he was a dispatch rider. Let's see what dispatches he was carrying."

He unstrapped the saddlebags and dumped the contents onto the path. There were half a dozen rolled scrolls in the bags, each one fastened with a black ribbon, which was itself sealed with wax, into which a signet ring had been pressed. Halt picked up one at random and peered at the seal. It was the now-familiar lightning bolt that denoted the man's allegiance to Morgarath.

"Looks like a love letter from Morgarath," Halt said. "Let's see what he has to say." He drew his throwing knife and worked the sharp blade under the wax seal, twisting it carefully so that the entire slab of wax popped clear of the scroll. He placed the small piece of wax carefully to one side, then tugged on the slip-knot holding the ribbon and unfolded the scroll.

"It might be a little difficult to reseal that," Crowley murmured.

"I'll manage," Halt said briefly, scanning the message written on the scroll.

"Well," he said, after a minute or so. "This is interesting."

"What does it say?" Crowley moved to peer over his shoulder.

"It's a list of twelve Rangers who are to be dismissed from the Corps and have their authority as Rangers revoked." He paused. "And you're the first name on the list."

8

CROWLEY TOOK THE LIST OF NAMES AND SCANNED IT QUICKLY, his lips moving silently as he read. He looked up.

"I know these men," he said. He tapped the list lightly with his finger. "All of these men are trained in the old Ranger skills. And they hold to the old Ranger code of conduct."

"And the new appointees don't?" Halt asked.

Crowley shook his head in disgust. "Morgarath lobbied to have his own choice as Commandant installed, a man named Stilson. He had no particular skills, other than the ability to toady to Morgarath. Since he's been Commandant, the Corps has become nothing more than a glorified social club. The members don't train, they don't practice their skills. They don't have any skills, as a matter of fact. They simply enjoy the prestige and power that comes with being a Ranger."

Halt frowned. "How does Morgarath come to have so much influence?"

Crowley shrugged angrily. "He's a senior baron—probably the most senior in the Kingdom. And he's highly respected. King Oswald began to depend on him for advice and counsel some years back. The King's old and unwell. Perhaps he thought Duncan was too young and inexperienced to act as an adviser. Morgarath gradually assumed more and more power as time went by and the King obviously became more and more accustomed to letting him have his own way with things. He was tired and sick and I suppose it just seemed easier to let Morgarath make most of the decisions."

"So why would he try to weaken the Ranger Corps?" Halt asked, although he thought he knew the answer.

"Because the Rangers are loyal to the King, first and foremost. They're a powerful force and if you were trying to assume power in the Kingdom, they'd be a major stumbling block. He began by having Nicholl, the Commandant, accused of treachery and disloyalty to the crown. It was a trumped-up charge, of course, but Morgarath produced witnesses who swore to Nicholl's guilt. He was found guilty and banished. Some of the other Rangers resigned in protest. Morgarath let them go, then installed his own puppet as Commandant. Since then, he's been gradually weakening the Corps. Today, there are probably only a dozen of the original group left."

Halt glanced meaningfully at the parchment in Crowley's hands. "Not even that, by the look of things."

Crowley nodded sadly. "No. It looks as if he's finally destroyed the Corps—and removed it as an impediment to his ambitions."

"Let's see what else he has to say," Halt said. Kneeling, he picked up another scroll and carefully popped the sealing wax clear of the ribbon.

He glanced quickly at the message on the scroll and shrugged.

"Nothing important here. Just an appointment for some

Baron Naylor to act as grand marshal of the tournament at Gor-lan." He looked up curiously. "What's that about?"

"The Gorlan tournament is the most prestigious in Araluen. It's held in the first week of Fourthmonth. Morgarath has been hosting it for the past ten years. He's won the Golden Spur tro-phy three out of the past four—"

"The Golden Spur?" Halt interrupted. Tournaments weren't a feature of life in Hibernia and he had no idea what a Golden Spur might signify.

"It's awarded to the grand champion of the tournament—the man who defeats all challengers in single combat. The winner gains enormous prestige."

"And our friend Morgarath is the current champion?" Halt asked, but Crowley shook his head.

"No. Last year the Spur was awarded to a young baron— Arald of Redmont. He knocked Morgarath out of his saddle on the third pass."

Halt grunted. "I think I like him already." He set the second parchment to one side, being careful to retain the small blob of yellow wax bearing Morgarath's seal, then pried the seal from another parchment roll. He read in silence for a few seconds, then let out a low whistle. He looked up at Crowley.

"Well, I think this tells us just about everything," he said, and handed the sheet to Crowley. The Ranger smoothed out the parchment, which had curled up on itself as Halt passed it to him. He read the first few sentences, then glanced to the bottom of the sheet, where Morgarath's seal was affixed once more, con-firming the identity of the writer. Then he went back to the main body of the message. This time, he read aloud.

To Sir Eammon of Wildriver
from Morgarath, Baron of Gorlan Fief, Lord of the Realm.

Eammon my friend,

I'm delighted to inform you that ill feeling against Duncan is growing daily. Our man Tiller is doing an excellent job of impersonating the prince. As we anticipated, the villagers in the north are already alienated by his raiding and looting. Before too long, I expect their resentment will turn to hatred against the real Duncan. At the same time, the nobles are becoming disenchanted with the prince as he continues to jeopardize the treaty between Araluen and Picta.

As a result, it's vital that you continue to hold Duncan in Castle Wildriver—and allow him no contact with the outside world. No one must know he is our prisoner.

The time will soon be right for me to convince the King to disinherit Duncan in my favor. In the meantime, Duncan is to be kept alive. If Oswald refuses to cooperate, we can control him by threatening his son.

I will announce my appointment as Oswald's heir and regent at the annual tournament. It's an appropriately prestigious affair and a large number of the nobles will be there. Many of them have already been persuaded to my cause. As for those who might oppose us, we'll have them gathered in the one place, giving us a chance to thin their ranks.

*Once my position as Oswald's heir is confirmed,
we will have no further need of Duncan.*

*Until then, allow no serious harm to come to
him, at your peril.*

M.

Crowley looked up from the written sheet.

"So now we know," he said.

Halt nodded. "The question is, what do we do about it?"

Crowley thought rapidly. "The tournament is six . . . no, seven . . . weeks from now. We're going to have to break Duncan out of this Castle Wildriver before then, and have him confront Morgarath. As Morgarath says, there'll be a large gathering of barons and knights and that will work in Duncan's favor just as much as it would for Morgarath."

"We don't want to rescue him too soon," Halt said. "If Morgarath hears he's escaped, he may well change his plans. But you're right. If Duncan appears at the tournament, he'll have the chance to sway the barons back to his side—particularly if we free the King as well."

"And it might be a good idea to drag the impostor along and have him admit that he's been the one stirring up the north."

"So it's simple. We take the false Duncan prisoner, we set the real Duncan free and we rescue the King from Castle Gorlan before the tournament begins," Halt said.

Crowley raised an eyebrow as he considered the tasks before them. "That's a lot to ask of just two men."

Halt smiled grimly and picked up the first dispatch—with the list of discredited Rangers' names on it.

"I think I know where we might find some help," he said.

Of course, their plans would be jeopardized if Morgarath learned that his dispatch to Castle Wildriver had been intercepted. While Crowley kept a careful watch over the unconscious dispatch rider, Halt set about resealing the scrolls they had opened.

He unfastened a small pouch he kept at his belt and took out the contents. There was a cylindrical plug of lead some three centimeters in diameter—about the size of the seal used to fasten the wax over the ribbons on the scrolls. He rerolled the parchment sheets and tied the black ribbons to hold them in place. Then he set about carving a shape into the flat, smooth end of the lead plug.

After making sure that the dispatch rider was still unconscious, Crowley looked curiously over Halt's shoulder and saw that he was using a thick, pointed bodkin to gouge a lightning-bolt shape into the end of the lead. It looked roughly like Morgarath's seal, he thought. But it wasn't exact.

"Do you think that'll fool them?" he asked.

Halt looked up briefly. "Think about it. If you received a message from Morgarath, carried by Morgarath's messenger, how carefully would you check the outside seal?"

Crowley pursed his lips. "Not too carefully. I'd just look to make sure it hadn't been broken. So long as it was in place, holding the ribbon securely, that would be all I'd bother with."

"Exactly," Halt said. He gathered the small tablets of golden wax he'd removed from the scrolls and, moving to the fire Crowley had lit, began to melt them again in a small mold. As the wax grew soft, then liquid, he poured some onto the first of the ribbons, sealing the knot. Then, before the wax hardened, he pressed the fake seal into the hot wax, leaving a fairly credible lightning-bolt shape impressed into it. He blew on the wax to cool it and harden it and studied his handiwork with a satisfied expression.

"That looks good," Crowley said.

Halt nodded. He was busy melting the remaining wax so that he could reseal the other two messages.

Crowley watched him, frowning uncertainly. "Where did you learn to do all this?" he asked suspiciously. He was a little scandalized by Halt's unabashed ability to forge a seal.

"Oh, I have many skills," Halt said. "Fortunately, I'm an honest man."

Crowley nodded. "So I can see."

Halt waited a few minutes for the wax to harden completely on the three messages, then replaced them all in the rider's saddlebag.

"Now all we have to do is wait for Sleeping Beauty to awaken," he said.

Crowley grinned. "Do you want to try giving him the kiss of true love?" he asked. "I've heard that'll do the trick."

Halt glowered at him. "I don't think so."

It took a few more minutes for the dispatch rider to begin to stir. He moaned once or twice, then raised his hand to his forehead. Halt shook him gently, then tapped him lightly on the cheek with his palm.

"Wake up, sir," he said, affecting a thick country accent. "You've had a terrible fall."

The man's eyes opened and he stared groggily at the bearded face looking down on him.

"What happened?" he said, his voice thick.

"You fell off your horse. You've been out cold for an hour or more."

The man looked around, confused and dazed. He saw his horse standing nearby, tethered to a tree. Crowley moved into his field of view, with a two-meter length of creeper he'd cut from a tree a few meters from the path.

"This creeper was hanging in a loop from a tree," he said. "It caught round your neck and pulled you from the saddle."

The rider nodded slowly. He had a vague memory of something around his neck, jerking him violently backward. Then suspicion clouded his face and he looked quickly to the horse again, reassured by the sight of the saddlebags hanging behind the saddle.

"Do you know what's in those saddlebags?" he asked, his voice harsh.

Crowley shrugged and managed a guileless look.

He's good at that, Halt thought.

"Lot of papers and such," said Crowley.

"Did you read them?" the man demanded. "It's a crime to open a sealed dispatch. You could be in big trouble."

Crowley shrugged, maintaining his open-faced, honest look. "No point to that. Us can't read."

Us can't read? He's laying it on a bit thick, Halt thought. The dispatch rider looked relieved. There was no reason for him to doubt Crowley's statement. They appeared to be simple foresters, and it would be surprising if they were literate. The man held out a hand to Halt.

"Help me stand," he demanded.

For a moment, annoyed by the arrogant tone, Halt was tempted to help him lie down again, by virtue of a fist to the jaw. But he managed a helpful smile and hauled the man to his feet, helping him keep his balance as he walked unsteadily to the horse.

The rider rested his head against the horse for a few seconds while he regained his balance. Then, with Halt's assistance, he climbed awkwardly into the saddle. He looked down at them, haughtily.

"You did well to assist me," he said. "A dispatch rider is an important person. I'll see you're rewarded."

And with that, he set his horse into a trot and rode slowly away from them. Halt and Crowley exchanged a grin.

"Since he doesn't know our names or where we come from, I imagine that'll be a little difficult," Crowley said.

Halt nodded. "It's the thought that counts," he replied.

9

THE HOPELESS, DESPAIRING FEELING THAT CROWLEY HAD experienced was gone now, replaced by a firm resolve. He spread out a map of the Kingdom on the ground and they knelt beside it, studying it.

"Castle Wildriver is here," Crowley said, pointing with the tip of his saxe to a spot on the map.

"I take it the river is appropriately named?" Halt said.

Crowley nodded confirmation. "The castle is built on a long island that splits the river. As it narrows, the two arms begin to run with increasing speed. It makes the castle difficult to access. It's a very defensible position. We'll have to work out a way to get across the river and into the castle itself."

"We'll come to that later. We've got nearly seven weeks before we have to set Duncan free. I think our first order of business is to find some reinforcements. Which of those renegade Rangers is the closest?" Halt smiled grimly. "I like the idea of renegade Rangers," he said, more or less to himself. "It appeals to my natural sense of rebellion against authority."

Crowley ignored the comment while he studied the list of

names and fiefs, mentally sorting through them to determine the most efficient path. "Leander," he said, after some seconds' deliberation. "He's in Dacton Fief, and that's in the northwest."

"Of course," said Halt, "we're assuming these men will have remained close to the fiefs where they'd been operating. They may have moved on."

Crowley considered the point with his head cocked to one side. "Possibly," he said. "But that letter from Morgarath seems to indicate that they have only just been dismissed—or are about to be. I assume that's just one of many letters he sent out. There will have been messages to each of the barons in those fiefs, telling them that their local Ranger is to be replaced. Presumably, they'll have been sent out under the King's seal. He's the only one who can appoint or dismiss a Ranger." He paused, then added dryly, "And we know how easy it is to forge a sealed message."

Halt assumed a look of wide-eyed innocence.

Crowley eyed him for several seconds, then continued. "But even if those men have already been dismissed, odds are they won't have moved on too far. And in any case, our best chance of finding out where they've gone will be from people in the fiefs they were appointed to."

"Very well," said Halt, "our first stop is Dacton Fief. If we get started now, we should be there by tomorrow afternoon."

Crowley nodded agreement and folded the map, placing it in one of his saddlebags. They re-saddled their horses, which had been unsaddled to let them rest and graze while the two men considered the situation. Within ten minutes, they were on the road.

Both of them were glad to put Gorlan, and the risk of being intercepted by Morgarath's men, behind them. After an hour of traveling on narrow back trails, they reached the high road to the west and set their horses to a slow lope. They traveled at what Crowley described as "Ranger pace," cantering for twenty minutes, then walking the horses, leading them, for ten so that the animals could regain their strength. Every two hours, they stopped for ten minutes by the side of the road to rest and eat and drink a little—hard rations like dried beef and fruit washed down by cold water.

By late afternoon, they were well on their way and they found a small clearing a hundred meters from the road, well screened by trees, where they set up camp. Halt spent some minutes scanning the road, watching for traffic passing in either direction. In that time, he saw one farmer, slowly leading a plow horse past them.

"I think we can risk a small fire," he said. "That road doesn't seem to be very well traveled."

During the day they had sighted plentiful wildlife along the road and had shot two fat plovers and a rabbit. Halt skinned and cleaned them while Crowley went looking for wild salad greens. He returned after twenty minutes with a broad smile. In addition to the bitter greens, he dumped half a dozen earth-covered lumps beside the fire.

"Potatoes," he said triumphantly. "There's a small farm about half a kilometer in that direction"—he gestured to the trees behind them—"and they have a very convenient potato field planted right up next to the tree line."

"Excellent," Halt said. The thought of potatoes with the

meat set his mouth watering. Salad greens were all very well, but potatoes added a sense of solidity to a meal, he thought. He was busy threading the plovers and the rabbit onto a green stick they could suspend over the fire. "Rub some of the dirt off them and we'll cook them in the coals."

One of the small pleasures of traveling and camping, he decided, was that, to compensate for the nights spent in the rain with no hot food, there were occasions like this, when they could take the time to enjoy a good meal. He placed the spitted rabbit and birds beside the fire, ready to rest the green branch on two forked sticks driven into the ground either side of the fireplace. Crowley passed him the potatoes, now with most of the earth removed, and he pushed them into the coals at the side of the fire, heaping the glowing charcoal over them. The rest of the dirt would come away with the skins when the potatoes were cooked.

"Nothing like a brace of murphies to set off a meal," he said contentedly.

Crowley frowned at him. "Murphies?"

"It's what we call them in Hibernia," Halt replied.

Crowley shook his head. "Strange people, Hibernians," he said to himself.

In spite of the mouthwatering smell of the roasting meat, and the fact that they were both ravenous after a long day, they didn't hurry the cooking. There was a temptation to simply char the meat over the flames of the fire and eat it half raw, but experienced campers as they were, they resisted the impulse, letting the flames die down to a solid bed of red-hot coals, then cooking the spitted meat over the fierce, steady heat they emitted, turning the spit regularly to ensure the meat cooked evenly.

As a result, it took another forty minutes for the meal to be ready. But they both agreed, through mouthfuls of delicious meat, bitter salad and creamy potato flesh smeared with melted butter, that the wait was worthwhile.

When they had finished eating, Crowley made coffee and poured them both a large mug. He watched quizzically while Halt scooped two large spoonfuls of wild honey into his. He'd noticed this strange habit before.

"Why do you do that?" Crowley asked.

Halt looked up, not understanding, and Crowley gestured to the small pot of honey that Halt kept in his cooking kit.

"Oh. I always do it," Halt said.

"I know," said Crowley. "But why? It seems to me you're just ruining the taste of good coffee."

"On the contrary," Halt replied, "I'm enhancing the taste of good honey."

Crowley shook his head. "Strange people, Hibernians."

They breakfasted early the next morning, before the sun was truly up. Halt had left a flour-and-water dough in the coals overnight and it had baked into a golden-crusted damper bread. They ate it with cold meat from the plovers and another pot of coffee to wash it down. Then they broke camp and took to the high road once more.

"I was wondering," said Crowley, with a sly little smile at the corner of his mouth, "why don't you put honey on your meat?"

Halt turned in his saddle to look at his companion. "Are you seriously asking that question?"

Crowley shrugged. "Well, yes. After all, you put it in coffee, which has a perfectly acceptable taste on its own. Why not put it on grilled plover? Or rabbit?"

Halt studied him for a long minute, then kicked his horse into a trot, pulling away from the grinning, redheaded Ranger.

"You're an idiot," he declared, throwing the statement back over his shoulder.

"Maybe," said Crowley in a lowered tone, "but I don't put honey in my coffee."

"Heard that," Halt said shortly.

Crowley grinned after his friend. "You were meant to," he said, and tapped his own horse to catch up. Life was good, he thought. They had eaten well. They had a firm plan of action, and he had a traveling companion whom he could tease anytime he liked.

Castle Dacton was an ugly, utilitarian building. Squat and slab sided, it was sited on a hill, as most castles were, which made it easier to defend as attackers would have to struggle up the slope for the last few hundred meters. The ground in front of the castle walls had been cleared. Again, this was the custom, as it allowed no cover for attackers, and lessened the chance of the castle being taken by surprise.

There was no mistaking its purpose. It was a building designed for defense, designed for battle. Unlike Gorlan, no attempt had been made to beautify the castle. Even Halt's old home in Hibernia, built from grim, uncompromising granite blocks, had a certain purity of line that gave it a simple attractiveness. This looked like a mass of stone plopped down on top of the hill, dominating the landscape, gloomy and threatening in appearance.

"Nice place," he said.

Crowley smiled. "It's not too stylish, is it?" he said. "But in over a hundred years, it's never been taken by attackers."

Halt glanced around. "Who'd attack here?"

Crowley gestured toward the glittering gray line of the sea, just visible to the west. "Skandians. And Sonderlanders from time to time. They were very big on raiding some twenty years ago. Got a bloody nose here at Dacton, however."

"So do we ride up, knock on the drawbridge and ask for Ranger Leander?" Halt asked, gesturing to the castle. But Crowley shook his head.

"Rangers don't live in the fief castles. We like to keep the barons at arm's length. It doesn't do to get too cozy with them."

"But you serve the barons, surely?" Halt said, and again, Crowley made a negative gesture.

"We serve the King. We answer to him and him alone. And sometimes, that can be a little awkward for a baron. In a way, we outrank them—but we never push the fact."

Halt nodded. The concept was a sound one, he thought. As he had said the day before, he had an innate suspicion of authority. "So where do we find Leander?" he asked.

Crowley indicated the small village that sprawled at the foot of the hill, overlooked by the massive castle. "We'll ask there. Leander will have a small cabin in the woods somewhere beyond the village. That's the way we do things."

They bypassed the squat, massive castle and rode into the village. In times of danger, Halt knew, the villagers would seek protection inside the castle walls. But in more normal times, the village gave accommodation for the workers who tended the surrounding farms, and provided the basic services that the villagers and castle inhabitants needed from day to day. A clear little stream ran beside the village and a mill was set on its banks, the running water being used to turn its massive mill wheels. There was the inevitable tavern and inn combined and a cluster of the usual thatched cottages around it.

As was the custom, the tannery was sited on the outskirts and Halt wrinkled his nose at the pungent smell as they rode past.

"So who do we ask?" he said.

"First person we see. Everyone will know where the Ranger's cabin is."

10

AT THIS TIME OF DAY, MOST OF THE VILLAGE'S INHABITANTS were in the fields, tending crops and mowing the hay. As a result, the main street was virtually deserted.

Then a little boy darted out of one of the cottages, shrieking with laughter, looking back over his shoulder and very nearly going under the hooves of Crowley's horse.

The horse shied and Crowley heaved on the reins, pulling it clear of the boy, who had stopped, petrified with fear. Crowley's horse, like most Ranger horses, wasn't as imposing as a battle-horse or a plow horse. But viewed from a ten-year-old's perspective, it seemed enormous.

Crowley settled his horse, patting its neck and making sure the animal was calmed down.

"You should watch where you're going, young fellow," he said, smiling at the boy. The boy knuckled his forehead apologetically. In spite of the smile, the figure towering over him seemed grim and forbidding.

"My apologies, sir!" he said, his voice coming out as a squeak. He looked to Crowley's companion and his nervousness increased. The second rider was black-bearded and had a bad-tempered look to him, with heavy black eyebrows framing his dark, piercing eyes. Again, the boy knuckled his forehead. Halt added to his discomfort by remaining silent.

"Sam Crofter! Where are you, you wicked boy?"

The boy glanced over his shoulder as the voice rang out through the street. An elderly woman emerged from one of the cottages, looking up and down the village before setting eyes on the boy. She hurried forward, limping as she tried to run and gather him in. Like the boy, she looked nervously at the two riders. They were cloaked and had their cowls up. And both of them were armed. They carried massive longbows and she could see the hilts of weapons at their waists.

She made surprisingly good speed in spite of the limp, and seized the boy by the ear. He wriggled and howled in protest.

"My apologies, your honors," she said. "I hope the boy wasn't bothering you."

As she said it, she gave his ear a good twist, evoking another howl from him. Crowley grinned at her. She was the boy's grandmother, he guessed, too old for the heavy work in the fields, and further disadvantaged by the twisted leg that gave her the limp. She would be tasked with looking after the boy during working hours, leaving her daughter free to help work the farm.

"He's not bothered us, mother," Crowley said easily. His tone was friendly, and realizing that the cowl of his cloak might make him look a little sinister, he pushed it back, revealing his honest, open features.

The woman seemed reassured by his friendly tone. Nonetheless, she maintained an air of reserve. Trust was all very well, her attitude seemed to say, but in these uncertain times, mistrust was better.

"Tell me, where would we find the local Ranger?" Crowley asked and the woman's eyes clouded with suspicion once more.

"Would that be the new Ranger?" she asked. "Or the real Ranger, who's been here these past ten years or more?"

Halt and Crowley exchanged a quick glance. So Leander had already been replaced. The woman's choice of words was interesting. She referred to Leander as "the real Ranger." That seemed to indicate that she regarded Morgarath's new appointee as something of a usurper. Not surprising, Halt thought. She was an older woman and was probably used to the old ways. Older people tended to resent and distrust change as a matter of course. In this case, he thought, the distrust was well placed.

"Ranger Leander," Crowley elaborated.

The woman's distrust faded a little. She studied them more closely. The boy, finally working his ear free of her viselike grip, scuttled away to their cottage.

"You're Rangers yourselves, are you?" she asked. Their clothing and equipment seemed to make it clear that they were. Plus their cloaks were drab and unremarkable—ideal for remaining unseen in the green and gray shadows of the woods. The new Ranger, whom she'd seen once or twice, favored a shiny satin cloak in rich green. Even among the green foliage of the forest, it stood out like a beacon.

"That's right," Crowley replied. It seemed easier than explaining Halt's uncertain status each time. The old woman nodded.

"Thought so," she said. "And you're of the old school." Obviously, she approved of what she referred to as "the old school." She jerked her head up toward the castle, which dominated the landscape. "That new man, Littlefoot, lives up at the castle.

Leander has always stayed down here, among us, where he could help if we needed it. Drank in the tavern here, talked to the children, listened to the men when they had trouble with a bear or a wolf taking their animals. The new man cares nothing for us. He wouldn't know one of us if he fell over us."

Halt was impressed by her confidence. Crowley had told him that the common folk sometimes viewed Rangers with suspicion, thinking they might be versed in the ways of the occult. Obviously, this woman was old enough to ignore such superstitious nonsense. She'd seen how Leander lived and operated and knew he was a man to be trusted.

"So Leander has moved on, has he?" he asked her.

"He has not," she assured them. "He's still in his cabin, although Baron Reemer has sent him several messages, telling him he has to move out." She let out a cackle of laughter. "Even went down to tell him personally at one time. Came hurrying back through the village, minus the fine feathered bonnet he'd been wearing."

Crowley allowed himself the ghost of a grin. "So where do we find his cabin?" he asked.

She pointed to the far end of the village. "Past the village, the road forks. Take the right fork toward the stream and you'll come to his cabin after fifty or sixty meters. It's among the trees, and not too easy to see until you're almost on it."

"Thanks, mother." Crowley gathered up his reins, which he had let lie loose upon his horse's neck. He clicked his tongue and his horse moved forward. The woman watched them go. After five meters, she called out to them.

"One thing, Ranger. Make sure Leander knows you're coming. Wouldn't do to surprise him."

Crowley turned back and nodded to her. "I'm sure it wouldn't," he replied.

They followed the fork in the road and came to the cabin. It stood in a clearing among the tall trees, a pleasant-looking little cabin, fashioned from pine logs and with a roof of slate.

"No thatched roof," Halt murmured. The vast majority of roofs were thatched in this part of the country. Slate and tiles were difficult to come by.

Crowley nodded. "Thatch burns," he pointed out.

The cabin seemed deserted. The door was closed and the shutters on the two windows facing them in the long front wall were both fastened. At least, Halt thought, peering more closely, they seemed to be. But now he looked, he could see that the left-hand shutter had been pulled closed but not fastened. There was a narrow gap noticeable between the two halves.

A small lean-to stood against the rear wall. Crowley indicated it. "That's the stable."

Halt surveyed the clearing in which the cabin stood. The trees towered over it on all sides. The cleared ground was some thirty meters across. There was a pump, with a leather bucket hanging from the handle, set close to the verandah that ran along the longest wall of the cabin, and a woodpile stacked under an open-sided, roofed structure that would keep most of the rain off it. An ax was driven into a sawn-off tree trunk that obviously served as a chopping block.

"Looks like nobody's home," Halt observed. The cabin definitely looked deserted, aside from that small chink in the shutters. As he spoke, they heard a short whinny from the stables.

"Someone's home, all right," Crowley told him. "That's a warning signal and a Ranger horse wouldn't make it unless there was somebody around to hear it. Have you noticed that left-hand shutter? It's not properly fastened."

"I noticed," Halt said. Pritchard had trained him to look for little anomalies like that. Noticing small details can help you stay alive, the old Ranger had been fond of saying.

"Keep an eye on it," Crowley said out of the corner of his mouth. He shifted his balance in the saddle, then called:

"Hullo the cabin!"

There was no reply. Halt saw a blur of movement in the narrow gap between the shutters, then an arrow split the air between them, thudding into a tree some five meters behind them, vibrating viciously. Halt's horse shied a few paces sideways. Crowley's, Ranger trained, stood stock-still.

Almost immediately, Halt moved to unsling his longbow from his shoulder, but Crowley threw out a hand to stop him.

"Don't!" he said, his voice quiet in spite of the urgency of his command. Then he added, "He's a Ranger. If he wanted to, he could have hit either one of us—and followed up with a second shot at the other."

Halt relaxed, letting his bow settle back on his shoulder. Still there was no word from the cabin. Nor could he see any further movement behind the shutters.

"We're friends," Crowley called toward the silent cabin. This time, a voice replied.

"That's what Reemer said, before I shot the fancy feathered bonnet off his fancy featherbrained head."

Crowley grinned. "Yes, we'd heard about that in the village," he said. "I take it he's all in favor of your replacement."

There was a tone of disgust obvious in the voice now. "Replacement? Usurper is more like it. That man is no Ranger.

He's one of Morgarath's stooges. Can't shoot. Can't stalk. Can barely sit his horse at a walk, let alone a gallop. All he's good for is drinking wine and swishing his satin cloak around his shoulders."

Halt smiled grimly at the description. He felt he could picture this new Ranger pretty well. "Both valuable skills," he said.

Crowley glanced at him, amused.

"So who are you two?" Leander demanded.

"We're Rangers," Crowley told him. "Of what's described as the 'old school.'"

"Step down and let's take a look at you," Leander ordered and the two men dismounted, stepping clear of the horses and standing shoulder to shoulder.

"If you're Rangers, one of you should be able to hit that leather bucket on the—"

He got no further. In the blink of an eye, Halt unslung his bow, nocked an arrow and sent it slamming through the middle of the leather bucket hanging from the pump, knocking it clear and sending it bouncing and rolling across the ground in front of the cabin. It was a demonstration of devastating speed and accuracy that only a master bowman could have accomplished. Halt looked at the gap in the shutters, a challenge in his eye.

"I was going to say on the pump," Leander said. "You seem to have beaten me to it."

"No sense in shooting slowly," Halt called to him.

There was a pause. "All right, so you can shoot like a Ranger. What are your names?"

This time, Crowley answered. "My name's Crowley. I'm from Hogarth Fief. This is Halt."

"Your name's familiar. Remember you from one of the

Gatherings a few years back. But I have no idea who he might be." There was a note of challenge, of disbelief, in the voice.

"Halt's from Hibernia," Crowley said hurriedly. "He was trained there by my old mentor, Pritchard. Surely you remember him?"

"Aye, I do. He was one of the best," Leander replied. "So what do you want with me?"

"We're looking for a few good men to help us," Crowley said, hoping to stimulate Leander's curiosity. The ploy was successful.

"Help you with what?"

"We're planning to bring down Morgarath," Halt said.

There was a long, long pause. Then the door of the cabin slowly opened and a stocky, clean-shaven man stepped out onto the verandah, a longbow held loosely in his left hand.

"Now that sounds like something I might enjoy," he said.

11

LEANDER SHOOK HANDS WITH THE TWO MEN AND INVITED them into his cabin. They sat at the table and Leander offered them ale.

"Do you have any coffee?" Halt asked.

Leander shook his head. "Coffee's hard to come by at the moment. The Baron is making sure I don't get any luxuries or supplies. The villagers are sneaking food to me, sparing me what they can. I'm not sure how much longer I can hold out here."

"Ale is fine then," Halt said, and the local Ranger poured three small tankards full.

They all sipped appreciatively and Halt looked round the cabin, with its long room serving as a sitting room, and a small kitchen space off to one side. Doorways led to two other rooms— bedrooms, he assumed.

"This is cozy," he said. The two Rangers glanced at him, then at the interior of the cabin itself. They were both accustomed to Rangers' cabins and so didn't find them particularly noteworthy.

"It's a standard Ranger's cabin," Crowley told him. "We all have them, pretty much in the same layout. As I said, we prefer to live separately from the castle and the baron in each fief. That way, we retain our independence."

Leander nodded agreement. "Unlike my replacement," he said, sarcasm obvious in his voice. "He likes to live in the Baron's shadow. I've heard he has a luxurious suite of rooms at the castle."

"Then why are they so keen to have you out of here?" Halt asked, indicating the cabin with a sweep of his arm.

Leander curled his lip scornfully. "The new man wants it as a hunting lodge," he said. "Not that he'd know anything about hunting. I've stayed on because this way I can keep helping the villagers if they need it."

"And by being here, you're a thorn under the Baron's saddle?" suggested Halt.

For the first time since they'd met him, Leander allowed himself the barest of grins.

"Yes. That too," he said. "Now what's all this about Morgarath?"

Crowley quickly explained what they had learned about Morgarath's schemes, and how they were determined to thwart him.

Leander listened carefully, then, switching his gaze between the two young men, he asked, "You're planning to do it yourselves? Just the two of you?"

"We've got a list of names—Rangers who've been discredited by Morgarath. We want to recruit them and spoil Morgarath's party," Crowley said.

"He's planning to make his move during the tournament at Gorlan," Halt put in, and Leander frowned thoughtfully, digesting this information.

"That's about seven weeks away. How many men do you think you'll need?"

"We've got the names of twelve," Crowley said. "But they're all Rangers, so that should make a pretty potent group."

Leander nodded slowly, considering. "Yes. I agree. Twelve Rangers would be a force worth reckoning with. But you'll need to get some of the other barons on your side as well. A lot of them will just go with the prevailing wind. And Morgarath is a well-respected figure. You need someone to counteract that."

"We're planning to approach Arald of Redmont Fief," Crowley told him. "From what we've heard, there's little love lost between him and Morgarath."

"Yes. I've heard much the same. And Redmont is one of the more powerful fiefs—maybe as powerful as Gorlan itself. Arald would be a handy ally. He has the prestige you'll need to sway a lot of the others to your side. This is going to be a matter of winning people over, as much as defeating Morgarath by sheer force of arms."

They sat in silence for a minute or two, while Leander pondered the situation. Halt fidgeted in his seat. He wanted to press Leander for a commitment right away. But Crowley caught his eye and shook his head. Better for the man to make up his mind without pressure. Finally, Leander looked up at them.

"So, how many men do you have so far?" he asked and the two men exchanged a glance. There was an awkward pause.

"Two of us," Halt said, eventually.

Leander looked at him and held up three fingers, a grim smile spreading over his face.

"Make that three," he said.

It took Leander ten minutes to pack the belongings he wanted to take with him. He strode out of the cabin door and turned to look back at the little building, a look of sadness on his face.

"I've enjoyed life here," he said quietly to Crowley—Halt had volunteered to go to the stable and saddle his horse. "It sticks in my throat to leave it for that idiot in his satin green cloak. I'm tempted to put a torch to it and burn it to the ground."

Crowley laid a hand on his arm. "Don't. You'll be coming back here before too long."

Leander nodded slowly. "Let's hope so."

Halt emerged from the rear of the cabin, leading a dun-colored horse. Leander took the reins from him.

"Thanks," he said. "You didn't try to mount him, did you?"

Halt frowned and shook his head. "Why would I do that?"

Leander exchanged a grin with Crowley and dismissed the matter. "Never mind," he said.

They mounted their horses and moved out at a slow walk. As they reached the first bend in the track, Leander stopped and turned back to look sadly at his neat little cabin. It seemed like a symbol of all that had been good and simple and straightforward in the world—all that Morgarath had been trying to drag down. Then, abruptly, he turned away and urged his horse to a canter, leaving the little cabin in the woods behind him.

They had already decided who would be their next recruit. His name was Berrigan, the Ranger in Weslon Fief. They had to traverse another fief to reach Weslon and, as before, they elected to stay away from towns and villages and to camp out.

It was strange to have a new member in their group. Halt and Crowley had grown used to each other's company over the preceding weeks, but it didn't take Leander long to fit in. At least now, Halt thought, they'd get more sleep, with another member to take his turn keeping watch at night.

As they rode, Crowley filled Leander in on the meager details he knew of Halt's origins, how he had come from Hibernia, after being instructed in Ranger skills by Pritchard, and how he had helped Crowley when he had been attacked by a group of Morgarath's soldiers. He had no idea of Halt's royal antecedents, of course, so he made no mention of that side of his history.

When he heard how the soft-spoken Hibernian had rejected Morgarath's offer to join his forces, Leander nodded approvingly. His respect for Halt increased. He had already seen an example of his speed and accuracy with the longbow. He had no doubt that he would show the same skill with his saxe and throwing knife. And he was impressed with Halt's woodcraft. The Hibernian had a natural ability to select a good campsite—one well screened from the trail through the woods, where they would have ample warning of someone approaching them.

He also admired both the other men's skill and ability at camp cooking. Leander was an indifferent cook at best—although cooking was one of the skills an apprentice Ranger was required to master. Leander had managed to pass his tests as an apprentice, but had then pretty well ignored the finer points. As a result, when he cooked game over a fire, he tended to scorch the outside and leave the interior virtually raw. He didn't have the patience that Halt and Crowley displayed and quickly realized that he would eat a lot better if he left the food preparation to them.

In return, he took on the menial chores around their nightly camp, preparing the fire, cutting firewood and cleaning their utensils after they had eaten.

On the third day after they had left his cabin, they crossed the border into Weslon Fief. Crowley pointed to the small stone column that stood by the side of the track, marking their entry into the fief.

"Another half day and we'll reach Castle Weslon," he said.

"Berrigan," Leander muttered, half to himself. "Think I remember him. He was the singer, wasn't he?"

"That's right," Crowley agreed. "He played the gitarra and sang. He was the one who composed 'Cabin in the Trees.'"

Halt looked up. "What's that?"

"It's the Ranger song," Leander told him. "It's sung at all our Gatherings."

There was a slight pause, then, without any discussion, both Leander and Crowley began to sing softly as they rode.

> "Going back to the cabin in the trees
> Going back to the creek beneath the hill.
> There's a girl used to live there when I left
> But I doubt she'll be waiting for me still.
> Never thought I'd be gone so many years.
> When I left always planned that I'd return
> But time slips away before we know
> That's just one more lesson that we learn."

They stopped singing after the second verse, but Crowley continued to whistle the refrain softly as they rode. Halt frowned at him.

"You're making a strange shrieking noise," he said.

Crowley looked round in surprise. He hadn't been aware that he was whistling and he didn't immediately equate it with the phrase *strange shrieking noise*.

"It's music," he said.

"Not from where I'm sitting," Halt said.

12

THE RIPPLING, FLUID NOTES OF THE GITARRA FILLED THE TAP-
room of the Jolly Frog tavern in Weslon village.

The villagers sitting around the room, nursing tankards of
ale and enjoying quiet conversations among themselves, beat
time with their free hands—some of them not even aware that
they were doing so. Most had stopped their conversations and
turned in their seats to watch the musician as his nimble, fast-
moving fingers seemed to fly across the strings, without effort or
tension.

The fingers of his right hand, curled up under themselves so
that it was difficult to see what they were doing, picked out a
complex rhythm on the strings, plucking the bass and treble
strings in a set order, then occasionally breaking the pattern for
a bar or two, and producing a sound that was bright and jaunty.

After eight bars of the introduction, the player began to sing,
his voice a light, attractive tenor.

> *"Jenny in the village, Maisie by the mill,*
> *Katy at the castle, Hannah on the hill,*

All of them are pretty, that is plain to see.
But Sadie in the stables, she's the one for me."

He bent his head over the instrument and played a variation on the opening. As a result, he failed to notice the three cloaked figures who slipped in through the door and took seats toward the back of the room. Most of the audience, their eyes on the singer, missed seeing them as well. Only a few of the patrons glanced at the men. But they saw nothing noteworthy about them and quickly looked back to the singer. Now, as he began the chorus, the drinkers joined in with him.

"Sadie in the stables, pitching out the hay
filling up the buckets, every single day.
She isn't very pretty, but I have to tell
I'm not very handsome. So she suits me well!"

The crowd fell silent as he began another verse, all of them now engaged with the song.

"Jenny said she loves me, Maisie said it too
Don't want to hurt their feelings, what am I to—"

The door crashed open, interrupting the song. The singer's voice stopped abruptly, although he continued to play the accompaniment for a few seconds more.

Four armed men, wearing studded black leather vests over chain mail, barged into the tavern. They wore short swords at their belts and flat-topped iron helmets on their heads. As they entered, they spread out in a shallow semicircle, covering the interior of the room, those at either end of the line turning their attention slightly outward, alert for any sign of rebellion from the villagers. A fifth man entered behind the men-at-arms. He was wearing an ornate cloak, made from green silk and with an oakleaf embroidered in gold thread over the right shoulder. It was a short garment, little more than a cape, actually. There was no cowl, but there was a high collar turned up, framing his rat-like face.

It was notable that this fifth man didn't enter until he was confident that the four soldiers had the room well and truly under control. His confidence boosted by their presence, he stepped forward and pointed a finger at the musician.

"Berrigan!" he snarled, his voice a little too high pitched to carry any real authority. "You have no right to be here. You're no longer the Ranger of Weslon Fief!"

"Let him sing," muttered a customer in a surly voice. "He's doing no harm."

Almost immediately, one of the soldiers stepped forward, his sword sliding free of its scabbard with a ringing hiss. He leveled the point at the speaker's throat.

"D'you want to argue with the Ranger, you scum?" he demanded.

The man, an unarmed farmworker, shrank back, dropping his eyes. "No, sir. Not me," he said, fear all too evident in his voice.

"Then hold your tongue or I'll cut it out for you!" the soldier threatened.

The singer placed his gitarra carefully on the table behind him, out of possible harm's way. He was wearing a double scabbard at his belt, and the hilts of a saxe knife and a throwing knife were visible. However, he made no attempt to reach for either of them. The pompous, overblown fool in the green cape didn't concern him. But the four soldiers were armed and ready for trouble. In fact, he sensed, they would welcome it, and he didn't want to give them any excuse to start what would be a very one-sided fight. If that happened, some of the villagers might try to take a hand on his side and they might be hurt. He didn't want that on his conscience.

"There's no need to threaten Isaac," he said calmly. The soldier glared at him and he returned the angry look steadily, until the man-at-arms muttered a low curse and re-sheathed his sword. Only then did the former Ranger of Weslon address his replacement.

"I'm doing no harm here, Willet," he said in a reasonable tone. "I'm just trying to earn a few coins to pay for my dinner. Surely I can do that?"

"Surely you can't!" the man named Willet replied. "You've been dismissed from the Ranger Corps. And you've been singing insulting songs about the King! We don't want your kind here in Weslon Fief!"

Berrigan shrugged. "I was under the impression that the people here were enjoying my music. And I certainly don't recall singing any disloyal song about the King."

"You sang about how the King has constant trouble with wind!" Willet shrilled and Berrigan couldn't help smiling.

"I assume you're referring to 'Good King Artur, the Terrible Farter'?"

The new Ranger nodded several times. "Exactly! It's insulting and disloyal. It could even be construed to be treasonous!"

Berrigan shrugged. "But as the title says, the King's name is Artur. He's not our King. It's just a silly doggerel song."

"That's where you're so clever! You pretend it's about another king. But I know you're referring to our King, and encouraging people to laugh at him!"

The former Ranger shook his head. "Not so. I've been singing that song for years."

"So," Willet crowed triumphantly, "you admit to the crime! And you admit to having committed it repeatedly!"

Berrigan sighed. He looked sadly at his replacement. "Willet, do you sit awake at night thinking up stupid things to say? Or does it just come naturally to you—on the spur of the moment?"

A couple of the watching villagers laughed. The men-at-arms swung round angrily, trying to see who was responsible. But the villagers had quickly composed their features. Willet glared at Berrigan for a few moments, his mouth working silently. The former Ranger watched him carefully. He sensed he may have pushed the ridiculous little man too far. Finally, Willet got control of himself. He thrust out his right arm, the forefinger pointing at the gitarra lying on the table.

"Confiscate that instrument, Corporal!" he snapped. "Smash it!"

As the leader of the small squad started toward the table, Berrigan stepped to block his way. And now his hand dropped to the hilt of the saxe at his waist.

"I don't think so," he said. His voice was low but there was an unmistakable note of warning in it.

The corporal stopped. He was armed with a sword. But he was facing a Ranger. Not one of the dilettantes like Willet, who had been appointed to the Corps in recent months, but a real Ranger, trained and ready to fight. He spoke out of the corner of his mouth.

"Men!" he ordered and the other three soldiers stepped forward to join him, their swords hissing clear of their scabbards. Now Berrigan was in a dangerous situation. He was outnumbered and he was yet to draw his own weapon. Slowly, the corporal unsheathed his sword and turned an ugly smile on the former Ranger.

"Step aside, singer," he said. "I'll give you two instruments for the price of one."

He drew back the heavy short sword, his eyes on the polished wood instrument on the table behind Berrigan. But before the corporal could act, Berrigan had drawn his saxe and stood ready to parry any blow the other man might attempt—either at the gitarra or at himself.

There was a deep-throated thrum! from the back of the room and an arrow flashed across the bar. It caught the flared cuff of the corporal's gauntlet, jerking his arm forward as it slammed into one of the heavy timber uprights supporting the ceiling of the tavern.

The sword fell from the man's grip as he struggled to free his hand, pinned by the arrow to the tough timber of the upright. His companions turned to see where the attack had come from. Three cloaked figures were advancing across the room toward them. One still held the massive longbow that had sent the arrow streaking across the room. The other two had saxes in their hands.

As the three soldiers started to move to meet the obvious threat, Berrigan acted. He drew his own saxe and brought the hilt thudding down on the shoulder of the nearest man-at-arms, between neck and shoulder bone. The man screamed in agony and dropped his sword, clutching at his shoulder. His companions, now thoroughly confused as to where their greatest danger lay, hesitated and turned back to the singer. One of them aimed a diagonal cut with his sword—the low ceiling precluded a vertical stroke.

Berrigan parried the blow easily with his saxe, and the sound of steel ringing against steel filled the room. Then he stepped forward and drove his left fist into the man's solar plexus. The soldier was wearing chain mail beneath his vest. But the force of the blow crashing into his ribs forced the air out of his lungs and he doubled over, falling to his knees with a weak grunt.

By now, Halt and Crowley were upon the remaining two soldiers. Crowley quickly slipped his throwing knife from its scabbard and parried a sword stroke with the two knives crossed in the classic defense. Then, as the other man's blade was trapped in the V formed by his saxe and throwing knife, Crowley jerked his knives to his right and twisted the sword out of the soldier's grip. It fell clattering to the floor. As the man stooped to try to retrieve it, Crowley hit him with a left hook to the jaw. The soldier, already bending toward the floor, continued the movement and fell to the rough boards, where he lay, moaning quietly.

The remaining soldier, realizing that he was now facing odds of four to one against him—instead of the original four to one in his favor—dropped his sword and held his hands high in surrender.

"Mercy!" he cried, seeing his doom in the dark, deep-set eyes of the man facing him. There was no sign of pity there and the saxe in the man's hand gleamed in the lamplight of the tavern. The soldier fell to his knees, his hands still raised in supplication.

Halt glared at him in disgust. "Oh, for pity's sake," he said.

For a second or two, he was unsure about what to do with this unarmed former bullyboy. Crowley solved the problem for him. He brought his saxe around in a backhanded blow, slamming the brass-bound hilt into the back of the man's helmet. The force of the blow was transmitted through the iron helmet almost undiminished. The soldier fell forward, facedown on the floor, his head spinning from the blow.

Willet, the new Ranger, watched wide-eyed as his men were reduced to moaning, groaning wrecks. Realizing that no one seemed to be paying him any attention, he scurried toward the door and ran out into the night.

But Halt saw him go and went after him.

Leander stepped up to the soldier pinned to the timber column, still struggling to free his hand. The arrow had closed the cuff of the gauntlet close to his wrist, so he was unable to slide his hand free of the glove. Instead, he was forced to struggle with the arrow, buried deep in the tough wood.

"I'd like my arrow back," Leander said. He gripped the shaft close to the head and gave a solid jerk. The broadhead came free of the wood and the corporal's arm, no longer suspended by the arrow, fell to his side. He glared at Leander as the Ranger slid the arrow back into his quiver. Then rage overcame him and he drew his broad-bladed dagger, striking up at Leander's midriff.

The blow never struck home. Leander dropped the bow and blocked the upward thrust with his left hand, turned over to seize the soldier's wrist. Then, almost without pause, he jerked the arm upward, using the corporal's own force to bring the knife high over his head. At the same moment, he slid his right hand behind the corporal's knife hand, continuing to force it up and back. Then, stepping forward so that his right leg was behind the other man's, he used both arms to continue twisting the knife hand up and back.

The whole sequence of movements, practiced hundreds of times in the past in mock combat, took about a second. There was an ugly wrenching noise as the soldier's shoulder gave way. The knife fell from his hand. He didn't notice. He was conscious of nothing but the searing pain in his shoulder. He collapsed, weeping, to the floor.

Berrigan looked around at his former attackers, now reduced to pitiful wrecks, either unconscious or disabled. The two cloaked men grinned at him.

"Who the blazes are you two?" he asked.

13

IN THE STREET OUTSIDE, HALT SAW THE FIGURE OF THE caped would-be Ranger scurrying through the shadows.

"You!" he shouted. "Stop or I'll put an arrow through you!"

In truth, he had left his bow inside the tavern. But Willet wasn't to know that. He froze in place, eyes closed, waiting in terror for the smashing, tearing pain of an arrow.

Willet heard footsteps approaching and opened his eyes to look into those of the dark-bearded stranger. Too late, he realized that the man was carrying no bow. He tried to bluster his way out of the situation.

"Stand back!" he said, his voice cracking with fear, which rather ruined the attempted bluster. "I'm a King's Ranger!"

"You're no Ranger." Halt's lips curled in a sneer. "You're a posing, whining prat."

His eyes fell on a familiar shape at the man's throat. It was a silver oakleaf pendant, the symbol of a Ranger's authority. Seeing this man wearing it was an affront to Halt's sense of justice and order.

"Where did you steal this from?" he demanded, seizing the chain and pulling Willet forward. "Where?"

"I confiscated it," Willet babbled. "It's mine by right. It was Berrigan's."

"It still is," Halt said, and ripped the oakleaf, chain and all, from Willet's neck. Then abruptly, he released him and the caped man staggered back a few paces. Realizing he was out of reach, he regained a little of his former dignity.

"Lord Morgarath will kill you for this!" he spat.

Halt allowed himself a hollow laugh. "That's as may be. But he won't leave you alive to see it. You've failed him. And you know how he treats failure."

Fear lit Willet's eyes as he realized the truth of what the stranger was saying. Morgarath was a pitiless, cruel taskmaster. Those who let him down weren't allowed to make the same mistake twice. He whimpered softly, unaware that he was doing so.

"If I were you," Halt said in a low voice, "I'd start running. And I'd keep on running till I reached Celtica. Maybe Morgarath won't bother with you there." He paused, seeing the message sink in, then stepped forward abruptly.

"Run!" he shouted suddenly and Willet, galvanized into terrified action, turned to do so—just as a well-placed boot, with all the force of Halt's right leg behind it, slammed into his backside, propelling him for the first few meters of the journey to Celtica.

"And there's something to help you on your way!" Halt shouted after him as Willet ran, limping and rubbing his bruised buttocks, down the main street of Weslon village.

"I think this is yours," Halt said, tossing the gleaming silver oakleaf onto the table in front of Berrigan.

The former Ranger looked at the little amulet and picked it up, a slow smile spreading across his face.

"Didn't realize how much I was missing this," he said. Then he looked up at Halt. Crowley had apprised him of the Hibernian's Ranger training while Halt had been outside. "Thank you."

Halt shrugged. "That can wait."

But the comment jogged a memory in Crowley's mind, something that had been occupying his thoughts over the past few days. "Maybe that can wait, but there's something else that can't," he said.

Halt looked at him curiously, but Crowley made a negative gesture. He'd tell the Hibernian what he had on his mind when the time was right. Crowley jerked a thumb at Berrigan, who was packing his gitarra into a hard leather case.

"We've filled Berrigan in on what we're planning," he said. "He's decided to join us." There was a note of satisfaction in his voice. In truth, he hadn't expected Berrigan to refuse, but it was reassuring to see the way both he and Leander had decided to throw in their lot with Halt and him. A refusal at this early stage would have seemed like a vote of no confidence in their plan.

"So now we're four," Leander said.

Berrigan grinned up at him, fastening the last strap on his instrument case. "A good, round number."

Crowley shrugged. "I'd like it rounder," he said. "Maybe three times rounder."

Their next potential recruit was Egon, the Ranger at Seacliff Fief. But before they headed to the east coast, Crowley led them westward. Halt noticed Crowley and the other two

Rangers having several quiet conversations and, from the way they had looked at him, he knew he was the subject. They had seemed to come to a joint decision. But still Crowley could not be drawn on the matter. Halt shrugged philosophically. He knew enough about his redheaded companion now to understand that Crowley was an inveterate showman. He loved to dramatize seemingly ordinary events, to make them more memorable. Obviously, he had a surprise in store for Halt and, equally obviously, Halt would just have to be patient to find out what it was.

And Halt, having a somewhat contrary nature, was determined not to feed Crowley's enjoyment by asking what was in store for him.

They rode west for a day and a half, eventually finding themselves riding up a long, winding access road surrounded by fenced paddocks and open fields. In the distance, trees marked the beginning of the forest.

The road was fenced on either side, and looking into the fields beyond the fence, Halt saw several mature horses grazing, and a couple of younger animals running and kicking their heels up at the sight of the four riders. The horses were all of similar conformation—shorter in the leg than a battlehorse or a palfrey, with sturdy bodies and shaggy hair and manes. He glanced at the horses his three companions were riding and saw that they shared these characteristics.

Interestingly, although the fields had been cleared, there was no sign of any crops growing. They were covered with rich, long grass, which in some places had been cut into hay, then rolled up in long bundles to be stored.

They crested a rise and saw a small, neat farmhouse at the

end of the road. Behind it was a much larger structure, longer and wider, and with a second story. A large double door opened into the top story, surmounted by a loading hoist, where a hooked rope swung in the light breeze. Now Halt understood the lack of crops in the fields.

"It's a horse stud," he said to himself. There were no crops planted because the horses were the crop. The well-grassed fields provided them with room for exercise and with food. The large two-story building was a stable. He looked at it with interest. There would be room in there to accommodate at least eight horses, he estimated. That was a relatively large number for such a small farm. The farmhouse seemed only big enough for two or three people at most.

The four riders walked their horses into the saddling yard in front of the house and stables and came to a stop. By unspoken agreement, they made no move to dismount, but sat quietly. Halt became aware of the buzz of flies and the flittering of crickets through the long grass on the other side of the paddock fence.

"Bob?" Crowley called out. "Are you home?"

He was facing the door to the house, expecting an answer, if it came, to be from that direction. There was no reply and he drew breath to call again, louder this time, when the sound of a large door sliding open in the side of the stable building turned all their heads in that direction.

A man stepped out of the stable into the bright sunlight. He held up a hand to shade his eyes so that he could see the four mounted men more clearly. Then a slow smile lit up his homely face.

He was quite small, probably shorter than the Rangers, who were all of a compact build. His lack of height was accentuated by the fact that he was severely bowlegged. Obviously, Halt thought, due to a life spent in the saddle. He couldn't have been more than thirty years old, but he was already almost completely bald, with only a few tufty fringes of brown hair around his ears. His skin was tanned the color of leather—courtesy of a life spent in the open air—and his smile widened as he recognized his visitors.

"Well, well," he said, "Rangers. Aren't you a sight for sore eyes. Step down, won't you, and come into the house."

Gratefully, the four men swung down from their saddles. They had been riding steadily for more than half the day, keeping to the Ranger forced-march pace. Halt's horse, Declan, sighed gratefully as his rider dismounted. He stood with his head drooping slightly. Halt glanced quickly at the other three horses. None of them showed any signs of weariness. They stood alert, their ears pricked, ready to move on at any time. He frowned. Declan was a fine horse, from one of the best breeding lines in Hibernia—a country famous for good horseflesh. Yet he thought back over the past week and realized that these shaggy, small horses that his friends rode seemed far more capable of cantering for hours every day without wearying.

"Coming?" Crowley asked.

Halt realized that he had been standing, studying the horses, for at least a minute.

Crowley ushered him past, through the doorway of the farmhouse. "I think you might be getting an inkling as to why we're here," he said, grinning.

Inside the farmhouse, which was small and neat and well kept, they sat around a wooden kitchen table while Bob served them mugs of cold, refreshing apple juice.

The Rangers drank deeply, washing the dust of travel from

their throats. When they were settled, Crowley caught Halt's attention and indicated the small, brown-skinned, balding man.

"This is Bob Saddler," he said. "Or as we call him, Young Bob."

Bob grinned and tilted his head, winking at Halt. He seemed to be an irrepressibly cheerful fellow, the Hibernian thought.

Crowley continued with the introductions. "Bob, this is Halt, our companion. He's from Hibernia, where he was apprenticed to Pritchard. You remember him, of course?"

"Of course," Bob said with alacrity. "He was a fine man. A fine Ranger too."

Crowley indicated the other Rangers. "And you know Berrigan and Leander," he said.

Bob nodded. He seemed to put a great deal of energy and enthusiasm into the action, his head bobbing rapidly up and down. Halt wondered if that was where his name came from.

"Yes indeed," Bob said. "Welcome, Rangers, to Saddler's farm."

Berrigan and Leander murmured greetings in return. Halt could sense a feeling of expectancy about the two of them, and about Crowley as well. He looked at them suspiciously but they all returned his gaze with innocent eyes. Too innocent. He was about to challenge them when he heard a soft giggle.

Turning quickly, he saw a swift movement at the door into one of the other rooms as someone, or something, pulled back out of sight. Bob noticed his reaction and sighed.

"All right, cheeky monkeys," he called in a stern voice. "Come show yourselves."

There was a pause, then two children appeared around the door frame—a boy and a girl who appeared to be around ten years old and who were smothering their giggles with their hands up to their mouths. It was obvious that they were brother and sister. And it was also obvious that they were Bob's children. They were miniature versions of him: small, with high foreheads and wispy brown hair. Their skin was tanned like his. But the most obvious similarity lay in their wide, mischievous grins, which became apparent when they lowered their hands. Halt—grim-faced, serious Halt—couldn't help smiling back at them.

Bob scowled at them in mock ferocity. They seemed totally unterrified.

"These are the twins," he said. "Little Bob and Roberta. We call them the Bobbities. Say hello to the Rangers, children."

"Hello, Rangers," they chorused, then dissolved into giggles again. The four Rangers, all grinning, returned the greeting.

"Is the beardy man come for a horse, Da?" asked Little Bob, indicating Halt.

His sister instantly added, "Can we watch?" and again, they dissolved into helpless giggles.

Bob shook his head at them. "That's enough now." He turned to the inner room and called, "Robina! Can you remove these terrible children of yours, please?" The Bobbities shrieked with laughter at his description of them. Then a woman came bustling out into the room. She was short like her husband, but plump and motherly where he was wiry. Like his, her skin was brown from hours in the weather and sun. And like the rest of her family, her beaming smile lit up the room. Her hair was a gray-blond shade. Fortunately, she had more of it than her husband did and it was pinned back in a bun.

"Greetings, gentlemen," she said.

Halt, raised in a royal court, instinctively rose from his seat to greet her. She looked, Halt thought, exactly like the sort of a person you'd want for a mam. Crowley and the others followed his lead, a little shamefaced.

"This is my wife, Robina. I call her Bobby when we're not being formal."

Halt made a gracious half bow in her direction and she giggled. The sound was surprisingly like the one made by her children.

"No need for that, Ranger," she said. The others, again following Halt's lead, mumbled greetings to her and she turned her smile on all of them. Then she made a shooing motion at her children, as if they were a pair of recalcitrant geese. "Now then, out with you two! Leave your da alone with the Rangers."

The children reluctantly allowed themselves to be ushered out. At the doorway, the girl looked back at her father.

"But can we watch the beardy man, Da?" she pleaded.

Bob mirrored his wife's shooing motion. "No. Now go do your chores."

The Bobbities departed. Their mother paused at the door, turned gracefully and dropped a perfect curtsy to the Rangers. Then, laughing aloud, she followed her children.

"Nice family," Halt said. His voice was a little wistful. His own early family life hadn't been the happiest. Then, out of curiosity, he asked, "Is everyone in the family called Bob?"

Bob Saddler frowned, puzzled. "No," he said. "Why do you ask?"

Halt shrugged. "No reason," he said mildly.

Bob's frown deepened, then he dismissed the matter. "Now, to business. That horse of yours, he's from Hibernia too, is he?"

Halt nodded. "Aye. He's from the Glendan strain in

Clonmel." He watched Bob carefully, to see if the name meant anything to him. He was gratified to see that it did, as the man's head went up and down several times in quick succession.

"Thought he had that look about him. Good horses in Glendan," he said. He turned to the other three. "Used a few mares from Glendan two or three years back, when we needed to add some speed to our horses."

Halt frowned, slightly puzzled by the words.

Crowley quickly explained. "Bob is the master horse breeder for the Ranger Corps," he said. "He supplies all our horses."

The smile left Bob's face. "Not anymore, young Crowley. These new men have no call for my horses. They want them tall and glossy and fine legged. Built more for show than speed and stamina."

"Speed and stamina," Crowley repeated. "That's why we're here, Bob. Our friend Halt needs a good horse."

14

EVEN THOUGH HE HAD BEEN HALF EXPECTING IT, HALT still reacted with surprise—and a little chagrin at the implied insult to Declan.

"I have a good horse," he said brusquely.

Crowley raised his hands in a defensive gesture, conceding the point. "True," he said. "I should have said, you need a better horse."

Halt went to reply, but Crowley held up a hand to stop him. "Declan is a fine horse, in his way. But Rangers need a different kind of horse—with different abilities. Our horses are fast—sometimes I'm not sure I know how fast mine is—but even more important, they're bred for stamina. They can move fast and keep it up all day if necessary."

"What we do, Master Halt," Bob interrupted, "is breed and interbreed different types of horse to bring out the qualities we want. I mentioned that we used some Glendan horses to improve the breed a few years ago. Our herd is based on the Temujai ponies from the Eastern Steppes. They're small, rugged and shaggy in appearance. But they have enormous stamina.

"Years back, we bred them with some Gallican Tireurs, to

bring some sturdiness and power into the herd. Then we used Hibernian horses for their speed. Every so often, we reintroduce some of the originals to maintain the qualities we sought in the beginning." He paused and glanced at Crowley. "Pretty soon we're going to need some more Temujai ponies to enrich the bloodlines."

Crowley nodded. "We have other fish to fry first."

Bob returned his gaze to Halt. The horse breeder's eyes were bright blue and they seemed to sparkle as he discussed what was obviously his favorite topic—the Ranger horse herd.

"So as a result, we've ended up with horses that are fast, but have huge reserves of stamina. And they're strong as well. No fine-boned legs that'll snap like a twig. And a decent Ranger horse can bowl over a big, slow-witted battlehorse if it wants to."

Halt raised an incredulous eyebrow. Battlehorses were big and powerful. Slow moving at first, they would gradually gather speed and momentum until they were virtually unstoppable. The idea of a pony-sized, shaggy horse, such as the Rangers rode, bowling over such a monster seemed highly fanciful.

Bob saw the look and tilted his head to one side. "Oh, I see you thinking that can't be. But let me tell you, it can. A Ranger horse gets up to speed and rams its shoulder into the battlehorse's ribs, just behind his fore shoulder, getting down low and then lifting. And bang! There's a battlehorse floundering on the ground."

Halt turned his gaze to Crowley. "Be that as it may, I have a horse. And Declan has suited me fine so far."

"So far," Crowley repeated. "But it's getting more and more difficult for him to keep up with our horses every day. He tires faster and takes longer to recover."

Halt pursed his lips. He'd noticed the same thing, particularly since they'd been traveling with the other Rangers. When he and Crowley were traveling alone, it wasn't quite so noticeable that Declan was having trouble keeping up—there was only Crowley's horse to measure him against. But it had become obvious that all of the three Rangers' horses could outlast him over a hard day's riding.

"Perhaps so," he said reluctantly. He was loath to admit that his horse was lacking in any way.

Crowley recognized the fact and continued in a gentler tone. "Declan's a fine horse, Halt. But our horses are purpose bred. There's probably no breed on earth that can match them for their combination of speed, intelligence and stamina."

"No probably about it," Bob put in. "And there's another thing: a Ranger horse can't ever be stolen. That can come in very handy."

Crowley glanced at him. "I assume you've kept up the breeding and training program even though the new Rangers don't seem interested in your work?"

"Oh yes indeed," Bob said forcefully. "Just because those namby-pamby fancypants don't know the first thing about good horseflesh is no reason to stop. I've kept breeding the herd, hoping that some of you would turn up."

Crowley grinned. "Well, here we are. And we plan to kick those namby-pambies, as you call them, right in their fancy pants—and get the Corps back on its feet."

"Or back on its horses," Berrigan put in with a smile.

Bob smacked his fist into his palm in exultation. "That's what I've been wanting to hear! I'll do all I can to help you!"

"Well, the first order of the day is to replace Declan," Crowley said. "Do you have any horses ready to go to work?"

Bob rose eagerly from his chair. "I've got four three-year-olds in the stable. Fully trained and fit and each one ready to meet his rider." He gestured toward the door. "Come meet your new horse, Master Halt."

Halt rose, the other three following, and Bob led the way out into the bright sunshine toward the stable.

As they entered the big, dim building, Halt heard the sound of hooves shuffling in the straw and one curious whinny. His eyes became accustomed to the dimness and he followed Bob to where four horses were peering curiously over their stalls at the newcomers. Crowley, Berrigan and Leander, understanding what was about to take place, and knowing that it would be a personal encounter for Halt, stopped just inside the doorway.

"Take a good look at them," Bob told Halt. "See if one of them might be the horse for you."

Halt paused and looked along the line of heads protruding from the stalls. All four were turned toward him, horses being curious animals. Four pairs of big, dark eyes watched him calmly as he walked slowly down the line of stalls.

Three of the horses were bay. But the third in line was a dappled gray. His eyes met Halt's as the Hibernian reached his stall and paused to study him more closely. There was something in those eyes that seemed to reach out to Halt. This horse was more than simply curious. There was a level of understanding and communication in those eyes that seemed to say, you'll do for me.

Halt went to move on to the fourth horse, but something stopped him and he turned back to the gray. It shook its head, rattling its mane the way horses do, and met his gaze once more.

Told you so, the eyes seemed to be saying.

Halt gestured toward him, turning to Bob. He saw that the breeder was already smiling, a look of satisfaction on his face.

"He talking to you, is he?" Bob asked. He kept his voice low so that Crowley and the others wouldn't hear.

Halt took a half pace back in surprise at the words. It had certainly seemed that the gray horse had been communicating with him.

Bob saw the look of surprise and nodded wisely. "They say that a Ranger horse can talk to its rider," he said. "Can tell him what it thinks, what it senses. Did you get that from him?"

"Well . . . not exactly," Halt said. He was sure he had been imagining those messages in the big, intelligent eyes.

Bob didn't press the point, but he reached out for the bar that closed the stall. "Would you like a closer look?"

"Yes. I think so," Halt replied. He was suddenly conscious that he had paid no attention to the fourth horse in the line. Then he dismissed the thought. The gray was the one that had seized his interest. Bob led the horse out of the stall and Halt moved round him, studying the sturdy body and strong bones, feeling the firm muscles in the shoulders and hindquarters, lifting a forefoot to study the hoof, pulling back the horse's lips to inspect his teeth.

He knelt and ran his hands over the horse's front legs, feeling the cannon bone, knee and ankle in each for any sign of tenderness or heat. Then he stepped back a little to assess its general conformation, checking that the croup wasn't higher than the withers, which was the mark of a "downhill" horse that would be prone to lameness in the front legs. The horse turned its head to watch him curiously as he did all this. It seemed to be vaguely amused by his attention to detail.

Halt put his hands on his hips and a smile spread over his face. "He's a fine one," he said. Shaggy coat and barrel-like body notwithstanding, there was something very appealing about this little horse.

Bob laughed, a strange, high-pitched cackle. "That's what he says about you!" he replied, shaking his head with pleasure. He looked back at Halt and added, "We say a Ranger horse chooses his rider, rather than the other way around. I think Abelard's chosen you, Master Halt."

"Abelard?" Halt said. The name seemed a little exotic for such a sturdy, workmanlike animal.

"Oh yes. Abelard. It's a Gallic name because his dam was from Gallica. Told you we'd included a few Gallic horses in our recent program."

"Abelard," Halt repeated, trying the name out. The horse shook its head in answer to its name. "I suppose I can get used to that."

Bob moved into the stall and brought out a saddle and bridle, quickly putting them in place on the gray. Abelard turned his head to watch him as he did so, as if checking that the girth straps were tight enough.

"Lead him out into the sun," Bob said. "Get to know him."

Halt took the reins and led Abelard out of the stable and into the sunlit saddling yard. The other Rangers followed. Halt noticed that they exchanged a strange, furtive look. They were smiling about something and trying to conceal the fact. He shrugged. Crowley loved a drama, he thought. He was undoubtedly enjoying the sight of Halt and Abelard bonding.

He went to place his foot in the stirrup, preparatory to swinging up into the saddle. Abelard turned his head around to watch him prepare to mount.

Bob put out a hand, resting it on Halt's arm. "Planning to mount up, are you?" he asked.

"Well, unless you think I intend to spend the rest of our time walking beside him, yes," Halt said sarcastically.

Bob made a small moue. "All right then," he said, removing his hand from Halt's arm.

Halt looked quickly around at the other Rangers. They were all watching him, with innocent looks on their faces. He had the distinct impression that they had been smiling broadly a second or so before.

"Is there anything I should know?" he asked Bob.

The breeder seemed to consider for a few seconds. "Let's see. I told you a Ranger horse can never be stolen, didn't I?"

Halt brushed the comment aside impatiently. He didn't see how that had any bearing on the situation.

"Yes. You did. A fine trait to have in a horse too," he said. "Now if you don't mind?"

Bob stepped back. Halt seized the pommel and used his bent left leg to propel himself up into the saddle. He settled himself, found the other stirrup with his right foot, and gathered the reins together.

At which point, the world went mad.

Abelard took off vertically, as if he had springs under his hooves. He shot into the air, arching his back, then came down on his forelegs. He jerked his rump up and down three times, moving in an arc to the left while Halt hung on for dear life. Then, suddenly, without warning, he reversed direction, spinning on his hind legs to the right, spinning in a wild circle three times. Halt was now jerking in the saddle like a rag doll, managing to keep his seat by sheer instinct—and a lot of luck. Abelard was moving too quickly for him to counter the horse's wild motions in any conscious way.

The saddling paddock whirled around him. The house, the stable, the drinking trough where Bob was leaning, watching. He was conscious of the blurred sight of his three companions and was sure they were all grinning hugely. He set his teeth grimly. He was determined that Abelard would not win this contest.

Unfortunately, Abelard was determined that he would. He reared back on his hind legs. Halt compensated by leaning way forward, burying his face in the short, shaggy mane. But in a fraction of a second, Abelard reversed the action, suddenly dropping to his forelegs and burying his head and neck between them.

The sudden, unexpected change defeated Halt. He shot forward, managing to kick his legs free of the stirrups as he went. He turned a half somersault in the air and crashed down in the dust of the saddling paddock, landing flat on his back.

The air escaped from his lungs with an explosive WHOOF! and he lay, groaning and winded, desperately trying to suck oxygen back into his empty lungs.

Slowly, as his breath returned, he rolled onto his stomach and got his knees under him, rising painfully to his feet, dusting himself off with his hands.

"Maybe I should try one of the other horses," he managed to wheeze.

15

As Halt dusted himself off, his three companions moved forward to join him. All of them were wearing huge grins, which they now made no attempt to conceal. From somewhere behind the house, he heard the sound of children giggling.

"Welcome to our world," said Berrigan.

Halt turned a baleful look on him. "You knew this was going to happen."

It was an accusation, not a question, and Berrigan shrugged diffidently. "Let's say I had a good idea it might," he replied.

Leander said, past a huge grin that threatened to split his face in two, "It's happened to all of us."

The baleful look now turned in his direction. "Your horses are constantly bucking you off into the dust? I can't say I've noticed."

Leander shook his head. "Not constantly. It happened the first time to all of us. Because we forgot to ask the right question."

"And that question is?"

"It's a lesson in not taking things for granted," Crowley said, joining the conversation. "Did Bob tell you that a Ranger horse can never be stolen?" he asked. Then he answered his own question. "Yes. He did. I heard him. Why do you think he told you that?"

"I have no idea," Halt said. "I thought he was just naturally garrulous." He turned to the breeder. "No offense, Bob."

Bob shook his head and spread his hands out, palm upward, in a gesture of acceptance. "None taken, Master Halt. Gammulous is a good description of me, I think."

Crowley continued. "He told you just before you went to mount Abelard, didn't he? In fact, he stopped you mounting to tell you. Didn't that make you think?"

"Think what?" Halt asked shortly, although he was beginning to get the glimmering of an idea about what Crowley was getting at.

"Didn't you wonder why a Ranger horse can never be stolen?"

"Perhaps you could enlighten me," Halt said.

Crowley turned to Bob and gestured for him to explain. Like the others, Bob was grinning broadly.

"It's a matter of training, Master Halt. The horses are specially trained not to let anyone ride them unless they've said the secret password to them."

"Secret password?" Halt said incredulously. This was beginning to sound like some far-fetched fantasy tale. He wondered if this wasn't a further practical joke that they were playing on him. But Bob was nodding, with no sign of any hidden smile.

"Each horse is given a private phrase, or password, if you like, during its training. When the horse is assigned to a rider, he's told the phrase and he has to say it to the horse before he mounts up."

"Every time?" Halt asked, his voice rising with his incredulity. "That could be a darn nuisance if someone was chasing you."

Bob shook his head patiently. "Not every time. Just the first time. After that, the horse knows you're allowed to ride him. Didn't you notice how Abelard turned his head to look at you just before you went to swing up into the saddle?"

Now that he mentioned it, Halt did recall that Abelard had done so. He'd assumed at the time it was just the horse's natural curiosity. Now it seemed there had been an ulterior motive behind the movement. He still wasn't totally convinced, but when he glanced around at the other Rangers, he could see they were nodding in confirmation of what Bob told him. And none of them seemed to be hiding a smile.

"Wouldn't it have been simpler if you had just told me about this before I tried to mount?" He addressed the question to Crowley, who considered it, and then answered.

"Well, yes. I suppose it would've. But it's something we do with all our apprentices—a kind of rite of passage, if you like. It teaches them never to take things for granted, and always to question the most obscure and seemingly unimportant piece of information."

"I'm not an apprentice, you know," Halt said. He could feel the heat of anger rising in his cheeks and worked to subdue it.

Crowley inclined his head, admitting that there was some truth in what Halt had said. "That's true. But you're not formally a Ranger yet either, are you? And this way, you'll know never to try to mount one of our horses without knowing the permission phrase, won't you?"

Halt said nothing for several seconds, merely glaring at his friend. Crowley seemed totally unabashed by the fierce look. He met Halt's eyes readily, smiling back at him, until Halt eventually realized that he wasn't going to shame or browbeat his friend into any sort of apology. With a sigh, he dismissed the redheaded Ranger and turned back to Bob.

"Very well. What's this magic phrase I have to say?"

"No magic," Bob told him. "Just good sense and good training. You say it once and you never need say it again."

Halt made a "hurry up" gesture with his right hand. "So what is it?"

But Bob glanced at the three Rangers, who were well within earshot, and beckoned Halt closer.

"It's private," he said. "Between you and Abelard. Although it might be a good idea to share it with one of your friends in case there's an emergency and one of them has to ride young Abelard."

At that moment, Halt had no intention of sharing anything with his three so-called friends and his expression said so, very definitely.

Bob, studying the dark-bearded man's scowling face, nodded his understanding. "Still," he said, "that's up to you. You may change your mind in the future. Good enough to do it then, I say. After all, a man's—"

"The permission phrase," Halt reminded him, an ominous note in his voice.

Bob nodded again. He could see that Halt's temper was stretched almost to breaking point. "Of course. Step a little closer, so the others can't hear." And when Halt stepped close to him, he put his mouth up to the Hibernian's ear and whispered: "*Permettez moi.*"

"*Permett*—" Halt began to say, incredulously, but Bob hastily silenced him.

"Hush! Hush! Don't tell the world about it. It's just for you and Abelard. Whisper it in his ear."

Abelard stood by expectantly. He seemed to know what was going on. Halt sighed and stepped up to the horse, who moved his head round so that his ear was close to Halt's mouth once more.

"Now," said Bob, rolling his right hand over in a "go ahead" gesture. Halt regarded him doubtfully, then, feeling a total idiot, leaned forward and whispered in Abelard's ear.

"*Permettez moi*," he said. The horse's head jerked up slightly and he made eye contact with his would-be rider. It seemed to Halt that there was an expression of acceptance, or understanding, in the big, dark eye next to his face. He glanced at Bob, who made a gesture for him to continue.

"Mount up," he said. "He won't try to buck you off now."

For the second time in five minutes, Halt swung up into the saddle. Quickly, he found his seat, settling his feet in the stirrups and bringing the reins together over Abelard's neck. The horse grunted and Halt tensed, waiting for a plunging, rearing attempt to hurl him out of the saddle. But none came. Abelard stood, solid and unmoving as a rock. Halt glanced at Bob, then at the three Rangers, who all nodded encouragement. Then Bob indicated the open gate that led into the larger field on the other side of the fence.

"Give him a run," he said.

Halt tapped his heels gently into the horse's flank. The effect was instantaneous and Halt delighted at the easy, flowing motion of the horse as he cantered through the gate and into the field. Abelard went from a solid, unmoving stance to a light-footed gait so smooth and even that his hooves barely seemed to touch the ground. Instead, he flowed across the field like a river through its bed, responding to every slight signal that Halt sent him through the reins or through the pressure of his thighs around the barrel-like body.

Halt urged him further, and Abelard went from a canter to a full gallop in the space of two strides. The response was amazing as he shot forward like an arrow from a bow, striding out in a full gallop that was as fast as anything Halt had ever experienced on a horse.

And yet, the rider had the distinct feeling that Abelard was holding more speed in reserve. They flew across the field, Halt's cloak streaming out behind them, matched by Abelard's long tail. Halt saw a fallen tree to their left and swung the horse toward it. Later, he tried to remember and it seemed that he had simply thought to go left and the horse had obeyed, without any physical command. But he knew that was fanciful. Abelard had sensed the minuscule shift in his position and understood instantly. He gathered himself, steadied, then leapt over the tree trunk, hitting the ground beyond with barely any impact and resuming the high-speed gallop.

They swung in a wide semicircle until they were heading back to the farmhouse, and the little group of figures waiting for them in the saddling yard. As they came closer, the slightest touch on the reins slowed Abelard to an easy trot. They rode back through the gate and Halt twitched the reins once more to stop the horse. Abelard shook his mane and whinnied in delight. He loved to run and he recognized that his new master was an expert rider, with a good, balanced seat and light hands on the reins.

The three Rangers' horses whinnied in reply and in welcome. Abelard stamped one forefoot in the dust. Crowley grinned at the expression on Halt's face—a mixture of surprise and delight.

He'd seen it many times before on apprentices when they had their first experience of the horse that was to be their constant companion.

"I guess he's one of us now," he said.

Halt spent the rest of the day working with Abelard, learning the many signals the horse had been trained to respond to. At the end of the day, Bob gave him one last piece of advice.

"There's something else you need to learn. Abelard has a smooth, even gait when he gallops. There's a point in every stride when all four feet are off the ground. It's maybe a second or so. If you're shooting from horseback, you have to learn to aim and release in that second, so that his movement won't throw off your shot."

Halt raised his eyebrows. "That sounds difficult."

Bob regarded him for a moment, his head tilted to one side.

"It is difficult," he agreed. "But that's why you're Rangers."

16

KING OSWALD LOOKED UP AS THE DOOR TO HIS CHAMBER was flung open, slamming back against the wall then rebounding with the violence of the movement.

He frowned. There had been no preliminary knock, no waiting for permission to enter, as might be expected of someone entering the presence of the King. Instead, Morgarath simply strode into the room, his attitude and expression showing all too clearly that he regarded this as an unwanted interruption to his day.

"You wanted to see me?" he said brusquely.

Oswald bit back an angry reply. There was no point in antagonizing the Baron of Gorlan, he knew. And in truth, he found Morgarath to be a rather intimidating figure. He seemed to dominate any room he entered, filling it with a dark energy. In part, that was because of his physical presence. He was a tall, powerful figure of a man. But there was more. There was a sense of self-assurance about him—self-assurance that bordered on arrogance. No matter whom Morgarath was speaking to, commoner or king, there was an underlying note of contempt and impatience—as was witnessed by his abrupt entrance and question.

Oswald took a deep breath. He wanted to be calm and, above all, he wanted to make sure his voice didn't tremble. It angered him that he should feel this way. He was, after all, the King of Araluen. But he couldn't help it. Morgarath created this sense of uncertainty and inadequacy.

"I'm worried about my son," he said finally.

Morgarath allowed himself a contemptuous snort. "So you should be," he replied. "He's killing and stealing in the northern part of the Kingdom. He's alienating the common people and he's antagonizing the Scotti with his forays across the border."

Oswald shook his head. "It's just so unlike Duncan," he said. "I can't believe that he would suddenly start behaving this way. He's always had a good relationship with our subjects."

Morgarath hid a scornful smile. That was precisely why he had instigated the program of stealing and raiding being carried out by a man named Tiller who was impersonating Duncan. If Morgarath's plan were to succeed, he needed to destroy the affection that the prince's subjects felt for him. He needed the common people to hate and fear the prince.

"People change," he said flatly.

But Oswald continued to demur. "Not Duncan," he said. "He's a good man. Always has been."

"Is this the same good man"—Morgarath laid sarcastic emphasis on the two words—"who tried to assassinate you only a few months ago? Or did that poison find its way into your wine by accident?"

"I've been thinking about that," Oswald replied. "The more I do, the more I think it was a mistake. Why would Duncan want to kill me?"

"Because," Morgarath said, speaking slowly and distinctly, as if to a not-too-bright child, "he wants you out of the way so he can be King."

"I can't believe it," Oswald said stubbornly. "Now I look at it, I think I acted hastily in letting you persuade me to move here to Castle Gorlan."

Morgarath shook his head. "I can protect you here," he said. "At Castle Araluen, you were at risk. If Duncan had made another attempt on your life, he might well have succeeded. After all, he has freedom of movement at Castle Araluen that he doesn't enjoy here. And he undoubtedly has cronies among the castle staff who would have assisted him in another attempt. It'd be far easier for him to put a dagger in your heart there than he could manage here, with my men constantly on the alert."

"I don't believe it," Oswald said.

"I can produce witnesses to swear that he was behind the attempt," Morgarath replied. In truth, he could bring witnesses to swear that the sun rose in the west if it suited his purpose.

But Oswald drew himself up and asserted himself. "Witnesses can be bribed to lie."

Morgarath's eyes narrowed. "Are you saying that I lied, Oswald?" he challenged. The lack of any title before the King's name was an obvious pointer to his anger.

Oswald swallowed angrily. He had come this far and he wasn't going to give in. But he knew there was no future in accusing Morgarath. He was alone in Castle Gorlan. None of his retainers had been allowed to accompany him—for his own safety, Morgarath had insisted. Oswald was all too aware of the uncertainty of his position. Effectively, he was powerless here, even though he might be King. At Castle Gorlan, Morgarath's rule was absolute and Oswald knew he needed to keep the

Baron's goodwill. The fact might gall him, but it was incontrovertible.

"No. Not at all. But other people, who wanted to mislead you, may well be doing so."

Morgarath noted the King's retreat with satisfaction. Oswald's next words, however, rapidly dismissed the feeling.

"That's why I've decided I need to confront Duncan myself," Oswald said, a note of determination creeping into his voice.

"Confront him? To what purpose?"

"I need to hear his version of events from his own lips. I know my son. I trust him. I'm sure there's a good explanation for all this—the poison in the wine and the raiding across the border. I want to accuse him face-to-face and hear what he has to say. If he lies to me, I'll know. But I want to give him the chance to defend himself."

Morgarath shook his head, expelling his breath in a long hiss.

Oswald continued, ignoring the man's obvious disdain for his words. "It's what I should have done in the first place," he said heatedly. Now that things were out in the open, he was gaining in confidence. "What kind of king goes scuttling off to hide in someone else's castle when there's a hint of trouble?"

"One who wants to stay alive," said Morgarath sarcastically. But Oswald was shaking his head and Morgarath felt anger mounting inside him. So the royal worm is turning, he thought. He'd wondered how long it would be before they reached this point.

"A king has to take chances," Oswald said. "And he has to trust his own judgment. That's why he is king. I'm sorry, Morgarath. I mean you no offense but it's time I took charge of things and started behaving like the King of Araluen. I appreciate your concern for me, but I can't hide behind your walls any longer."

You pompous fool, Morgarath thought. But he assumed a winning smile as he seemed to consider the King's words. Morgarath could charm a snake out of its skin if he wished, as an old saying went.

"And exactly what do you have in mind, your majesty?"

"I want you to send to Castle Araluen for a company of my own guard, then I'll ride north with them to confront Duncan, and settle this matter once and for all."

"So you'll simply find Duncan and say, 'Stop all this killing and stealing. You've been a bad boy'?' Is that the plan?"

Oswald hid his anger at the obvious sarcasm. He nodded once.

"That's about it," he said. "It's time for me to start acting like a king."

Morgarath paced around the room for some moments. He stopped at the window, looking down on the green parkland that stretched out below the castle. It was time to stop the pretense, he realized. He turned back to Oswald, who was waiting expectantly for his answer.

"I'm afraid the time for that is long gone, Oswald," he said.

The King took a step back, startled by the contempt in the man's voice. "What are you talking about?" he demanded.

"I'm saying your time to act like the King is long gone. Your time as King is long gone. You're going to disinherit your son in my favor. You're going to name me as your heir and as regent for the immediate future."

"How dare you!" Oswald exploded. "What makes you think I'd agree to such a threat?"

"Several things," Morgarath said in a silky tone. "For one, you're all alone here and I can make you do anything I want you to. And secondly, your son isn't in the border country, raiding villages and stealing cattle from the Scotti."

Oswald felt a cold hand of fear clutching his heart. As Morgarath continued, the grip grew tighter.

"Duncan, your oh-so-noble son, is currently being held prisoner by one of my followers. And if you don't do exactly as I tell you, you'll never see him again."

17

IN LATER YEARS, HALT WOULD LOOK BACK ON THE DAYS spent traveling with his new friends as a particularly happy time of his life. Up until this point, he had been a solitary person, suspicious of strangers and, as a result of the events that had led him to leave Hibernia, even his own family. But now, as they crisscrossed the country in search of other Rangers to join their band, he found himself in the company of men whose friendship and camaraderie he valued.

They were all driven by a common purpose and they were all men to be admired for their mastery of the Ranger's craft.

They shared the same skills, of course, and all of them were expert in each one. But some were more skilled than the others at certain disciplines. Crowley, for example, was an absolute adept in the art of moving silently and without being seen. Leander's ability to track and read and understand signs on the forest floor was far above that of his companions. Berrigan's accuracy with both his knives—the big, heavy saxe and the lighter, smaller throwing knife—was uncanny. Halt found himself asking the others for advice and tips on how to improve his skill in these areas, and he found his companions always willing to share their knowledge with him. As a result, his ability improved with each passing day. As he told himself, he was learning from the best.

Halt himself was by far the finest archer in the group. His speed and accuracy were unmatched by any of the others, and since they had left Saddler's farm he had practiced the extra skill Bob had mentioned—shooting while Abelard was moving at a full gallop—every day when they stopped to camp. Before long, he was almost reproducing the accuracy he showed when shooting from a standing position. The others were fascinated by this technique and they tried to copy it, with mixed results. Crowley was the most successful, but even he couldn't match Halt. Of course, the redhead didn't admit that this was due to any inferiority on his part.

"Abelard's obviously got such a smooth gait that it's easy for you to gauge his motion and adjust your shooting to it. He moves like silk," he said to Halt as they discussed it one evening. "Poor old Cropper"—he indicated his horse—"is such a tanglefoot it's a wonder he manages to stay upright when he's galloping."

Halt regarded Crowley's horse, who was watching them with an interested expression. He hadn't noticed any tendency for him to stumble or lurch unexpectedly when he was galloping. On the other hand, he had noticed a tendency for Crowley to try to rush his release when shooting from horseback. He didn't do it all the time. Three out of five times, his shots would fly true, which was a more-than-acceptable average. But Halt managed to do it five out of five times—and ten out of ten times.

He decided, however, to allow his friend this little conceit.

They were approaching Seacliff Fief, a small barony set on an island off the southeast coast. The island, and the castle built on it, was accessed by a flat-bottomed punt that spanned the narrow waterway separating it from the mainland. Crowley, who was in the lead, raised a hand to stop the others as they approached the little strip of sand where the ferry was beached. They were still inside the fringe of trees and, so far, they hadn't been noticed by anyone at the ferry station.

"Question is," he said in a low voice as they formed a semi-circle around him, "do we all go across, or just one of us?" He paused, then added in explanation, "We're becoming quite a noticeable group, after all."

Berrigan shrugged. "So people notice us. What harm does that do?"

"People notice. People talk," Halt said. "Word could get back to Morgarath that there's a group of renegade Rangers recruiting their former comrades. If that happens, he'll start to wonder what we're up to."

"He'll do that sooner or later anyway," Berrigan pointed out, but Leander joined in, agreeing with Halt.

"The later, the better. The more we can surprise him, the easier our task is going to be."

"You think it's going to be easy?" Berrigan asked, his eyebrows raised in amusement.

"I didn't say easy. I said easier," Leander replied doggedly.

Berrigan nodded agreement. "Fair enough. It's a good point, I suppose. So who gets to ride aboard the ferry?"

There was a pause, then Halt said, in a voice that brooked no argument, "Crowley. This whole business has been driven by him. He's the one to do it."

Seeing there was no disagreement from the others, Crowley prepared to ride out onto the sand. "Set up a camp back in the trees," he said. "I'll find you when I've made contact with Egon." Egon was the Seacliff Ranger, who had been on the list of those to be dismissed.

"Don't get seasick," Berrigan admonished.

Crowley regarded the narrow neck of water that separated Seacliff Island from the mainland. The surface was as still as a millpond.

"I'll do my best," he said. He urged Cropper forward and rode out into the sunlight.

They had all decided to do away with their camouflaged cloaks for the time being. The distinctive pattern marked them out as Rangers—or, to be accurate, former Rangers. They all wore long cowled cloaks in dull colors of brown or gray or green. But even without the camouflage pattern, a band of four cloaked men, carrying longbows and armed with saxes and throwing knives, would be easy to recognize as Rangers of the old school, whereas one man in a brown cloak might well be taken for a forester or gamekeeper.

Cropper's hooves made virtually no sound in the fine dry sand of the beach, aside from a light squeaking as the tiny grains were compressed and rubbed against one another.

Crowley was nearly up to the ferry master's small house, built on pilings above the high tide mark, before he was noticed.

"Da! Traveler coming!" It was a young voice and Crowley saw that there was a boy of about ten or twelve watching him from behind the railing of the small verandah that spanned two sides of the house. A deeper voice answered from inside, the words muffled and indecipherable. Then a door onto the verandah creaked open and a short but powerfully built man emerged into the light.

"Welcome, traveler!" the ferry master called. He stepped heavily down the four stairs that led up to the verandah, buckling on a thick leather belt as he came. Crowley could see a long-bladed dagger in a scabbard on the right-hand side, and as the man reached the first step, he casually took up a blackwood quarterstaff that was leaning against the railing.

As welcoming as the ferry master might seem, Crowley was still a stranger and, in these times, no stranger was accepted without some precaution.

"I'm looking to cross to the island," Crowley said. The ferry master regarded him for a few seconds, taking in the longbow and the shaggy-coated, small horse. He said nothing but Crowley sensed he had been recognized for what he was. Then the man glanced at the flat-bottomed punt pulled up on the beach and the island beyond.

"Then I'd say you're in the right place to do it," he said pleasantly. He gestured to Crowley to move toward the punt. "Wait while I get the boat in the water, then you can come aboard."

Crowley swung down from the saddle and led Cropper toward the water's edge. "I'll give you a hand moving her," he offered, but the ferry master shook his head.

"I can manage," he said.

Crowley took in the thick, heavily muscled arms and massive shoulders. He had no doubt the man could move the ferry by himself. The ferry master leaned his shoulder against a padded post at one corner of the clumsy vessel and heaved. The punt slid easily down the sand and into the water. Flat bottomed and wide beamed as she was, she floated easily in a few inches. Crowley dismounted and led Cropper aboard as the ferry master lowered the ramp. "That'll be one royal for the two of you," the ferry master said. Crowley paid and the man began to haul on the thick rope that drew the flat-bottomed craft across to the far beach.

After a few minutes, they glided into the shallows and the tapered bow ran up onto the sand, grating against it as it came to rest. The ferry master lowered the bow ramp and Crowley led Cropper ashore. He paused as he came level with the heavy-set man, who was leaning against the railing by the ramp.

"The Ranger Egon," he said. "Where would I find him?"

The ferry master considered the question for a second or two. There was a knowing look about him as he studied Crowley once more. The mention of Egon's name seemed to confirm his earlier supposition that Crowley was a Ranger.

"Most likely in the tavern," he replied eventually. "That's where he spends most of his time these days, since the unpleasantness with the new man." His tone was even, without any note of censure in it.

Crowley nodded, keeping his expression neutral. "How do I reach it?" he asked. He had never visited Seacliff before.

The ferry master gestured to an opening in the trees some thirty meters down the beach. "That's the track to the top. It winds up to the castle at the top of the hill. The village is a hundred meters from the castle and the tavern is there."

Crowley held up a hand in a gesture of thanks, mounted Cropper and began to walk him toward the track. After a few paces, he turned and called back.

"How do I . . . ?" he began but the man anticipated the rest of the question.

"Hit that gong on the tree there." He indicated a metal hoop hanging from a tree branch, alongside a heavy wooden mallet. "I'll come across to fetch you."

He moved to the hawser at the stern of the boat—although in truth, the bow and the stern were interchangeable, and depended on the direction of travel. Seizing the rope, he heaved and the boat slid smoothly into deeper water, the wavelets battering at the square bow as she slid forward. Crowley watched him go for a second or two, then turned back toward the entrance to the track.

He was frowning as he rode into the shade under the trees. So far, the dismissed Rangers they had encountered had shown a sense of rebellion and defiance. The news that Egon was likely to be found in the tavern this early in the day was troubling. It indicated that the former Ranger had simply given up when he had been replaced.

"Don't like the sound of that," he said softly to Cropper. The horse shook its head, rattling his mane and ears as horses tend to do.

Apparently, he didn't like the sound of it either.

18

THE VILLAGE OF SEACLIFF WAS SET ON A NATURAL PLATEAU at the top of the hill, alongside the castle itself. Crowley rode slowly into the village as he emerged from the tree line. Several of the villagers looked curiously at him as he passed. He nodded greetings to them and they responded awkwardly, a little embarrassed to have been caught staring. But he was a stranger, and in spite of the lack of mottled camouflage on his cloak, there was something about him that marked him as a Ranger.

And, since the position of Ranger in the fief had recently been usurped by an overdressed fop, Crowley's arrival might well signify trouble.

He could see the tavern halfway along the main street. There were several tables and benches set out in the open air in front of the building, with a canvas awning above them to provide shelter from the sun. The awning bellied and flapped in the light sea breeze, alternately filling with air like a sail, then drooping once more as the breeze gusted.

There was a solitary figure seated at one of the benches, his back resting against the tavern wall. A pottery jug and a pewter tankard were on the table in front of him and he turned an incurious gaze on the rider approaching down the street. As he came closer, Crowley took in the leather jerkin, the green woolen shirt and trousers tucked into knee-high boots. It was typical Ranger garb, matched by his own, and he was confident he had found Egon, former Ranger of Seacliff Fief. A cloak was lying, folded carelessly, on the table in front of him.

Egon wasn't a young man. His hair and beard were gray, turning white in places. His face was lined and showed the marks of a hard life. He must have been close to taking the gold oakleaf of retirement, Crowley thought, which would have made his dismissal even harder to bear. His advancing years were probably the reason he'd been assigned to Seacliff—a small fief where nothing much happened, other than the occasional raid by a Skandian wolfship. Seacliff was often a young Ranger's first assignment or an older Ranger's final one.

His clothes were rumpled and stained with the marks of food and wine. His hair was matted and untidy and his beard was untrimmed. Egon looked like a man who simply didn't care anymore.

Crowley eased down from the saddle, knotted Cropper's reins and let them fall across the horse's neck. That, if nothing else, marked him as a Ranger. Ranger horses were never tethered. There was no need for it. A Ranger horse would never stray and, as Halt had discovered, could not be stolen. And, in the event of the need for a quick departure, a Ranger didn't have to waste any time untying his mount.

Egon looked up at the new arrival, recognizing him for what he was. His lip curled in a sneer.

"What are you looking at?"

The words were slurred. The tone was aggressive. Egon had

obviously been here for some time. There were wet rings and spilled liquor on the table to attest to the fact.

Crowley removed his riding gauntlets and dropped them lightly on the table. "Mind if I join you?"

The other man snorted an unintelligible reply.

Crowley shrugged his bow off his shoulder, leaned it against the table and took a seat. Egon grunted again, peered into his tankard, frowned at it, then upended the jug over it. A small trickle of liquid ran from the jug to the tankard. The former Ranger glared at it through bleary, befuddled eyes, then rapped the tankard loudly on the table.

"Jervis!" he shouted. "Bring me more brandywine."

Crowley's eyebrow arched. Brandywine was a potent spirit. Had Egon been drinking ale, there might have been some explanation or excuse. But brandywine? And at this early hour? No wonder the man was slurring his words. He wondered if this might turn out to be a fool's errand. Egon, at first glance, seemed an unlikely recruit to their cause. He sighed. Everything had gone well to date. He'd begun to feel complacent, assuming that every former Ranger they approached would be willing to join them.

The door to the tavern swung open and a bald man, wearing a long apron over his shirt and trousers, emerged, looking with some pity at the disheveled figure slouched on the bench. He placed another jug down in front of him and took the empty one. Then he noticed Crowley, with a small start of surprise.

"Greetings, stranger," he said.

Egon snarled another incomprehensible comment at the words and hastily poured his tankard full to the brim.

"Good afternoon," Crowley said quietly. He was at the same

table as Egon, but sitting far enough away for the innkeeper not to assume that they were together.

"Can I get you something?" Jervis asked, gesturing to the jug in front of Egon.

Crowley shook his head at the offer of alcohol. "Do you have any coffee?"

The innkeeper couldn't prevent a look of relief touching his features. Two customers drinking ardent spirits this early in the afternoon could turn out to be trouble.

"I've got a pot just brewing. Be ready in a minute or two."

"I'll have a mug then. A big mug," Crowley said. He'd been riding since early morning and breakfast was a long time in the past. He glanced at Egon again. The man had his head sunk over his tankard and was muttering to himself. Crowley decided that before he spoke further to the man, he needed information. The innkeeper's pitying look seemed to indicate that he had some sympathy for the Ranger. In any event, there was no one else available to ask.

"Where's the privy?" Crowley inquired.

Jervis jerked his head toward the door. "Through the bar, out the back in the stableyard," he said.

Crowley rose and followed him back through the door. Egon watched him go, snarled something to himself and refilled his tankard.

Once in the taproom, the innkeeper pointed to a rear door that led to the stableyard. But Crowley shook his head.

"I wanted a word in private," he said, "without Egon hearing us."

Jervis raised an eyebrow at the mention of the name. "You know him, do you?"

Crowley dismissed the question with a negative gesture. "I

know his name. I know who he is. Or rather," he amended, "who he was."

"He was the Ranger of this fief," Jervis told him. "But then a new Ranger arrived out of the blue, with papers that said Egon was to be dismissed from the service and turned out of his cabin."

"On what grounds?" Crowley asked.

Jervis shrugged. "They said he'd stolen a necklace and a purse from a widow on the mainland, and when her fourteen-year-old son tried to intervene, Egon beat him half to death."

Crowley frowned. "And you believe this?"

Jervis shook his head sadly. "Egon's been the Ranger here for seven years," he said. "In all that time, I've known him to be a good, gentle man. The people of the fief loved and respected him. I can't believe he'd do such a thing. But the papers were given under the King's seal, so they must be true."

Crowley looked long and hard at him. Not necessarily, the look said. The innkeeper shifted uncomfortably. Denying the King's authority was a dangerous path to follow. Crowley let him off the hook with a further question.

"You say he was turned out of his cabin," he said and, when Jervis nodded in confirmation, he added, "So where does he live? And how does he pay you for the brandy he's drinking?" Brandywine was usually brought into the country by Gallican smugglers and was an expensive tipple.

"I let him sleep out in the stables," Jervis said, obviously feeling that the arrangement was an unfortunate one. "And the Baron pays for his drinks. I send him an account each week."

"That's generous of him," Crowley remarked, but Jervis shook his head, frowning.

"More self-serving than anything else. There was a lot of bitterness between them when he dismissed Egon from service. I think he decided it was safer to keep him well and truly drunk. That way, there's less chance of trouble. Egon may be getting on, but he was trained as a Ranger, after all."

Crowley took in all this information, rubbing his chin thoughtfully. Finally, he looked up at Jervis. "Thanks for that," he said, and turned toward the door again.

Egon was still sitting slumped at the table. He glanced up when Crowley reemerged. He snorted again—it seemed to be his favored form of communication—and reached for the wine jug.

"Put that down," Crowley said and, for a moment, the note of command in his voice made Egon pause. Then his misery got the better of him and he tilted the jug over the tankard. Crowley noted that he had to tilt quite a way now that the jug was nearly empty. He reached out and pried the jug out of the old Ranger's hand, placing it on the table out of reach.

"You won't find the answer to your problems in a jug of brandywine," he said quietly.

Egon went white with rage. Then his right hand shot to the hilt of his saxe and he drew the big knife with a ringing hiss.

But Crowley was younger, faster and sober. He caught Egon's hand and slammed it down hard onto the tabletop, catching his knuckles between the wood of the table and the hilt of the saxe.

Egon howled with pain and rage. He released the saxe, lurched to his feet and aimed a wild, swinging right fist at Crowley. The redhead swayed back and the fist passed harmlessly in front of his face.

"I'll allow that once," Crowley said. "And once only."

But Egon was beyond reason and, still wildly off balance, he aimed another jaw-crushing right hand at Crowley. This time, the young Ranger chose not to duck. He blocked the punch with a rigid left arm, then drove his own fist into Egon's solar plexus.

The punch only traveled thirty centimeters or so. But it was lightning fast and it had all of the force of Crowley's arm and shoulder and upper body behind it. It sank deep into Egon's gut and the breath hissed out of him. He doubled over, staggering, then began to retch, vomiting up the brandywine he had consumed that afternoon. The rank smell assailed Crowley's nostrils. He waited, watching like a hawk, ready in case Egon was foxing. But the older Ranger sank to one knee, continuing to retch, even though his stomach was now empty.

Slowly, he toppled over and lay on the dirt, knees drawn up, hands clutching his midsection. There was a rainwater butt nearby. Crowley took the brandy jug, tossed the remaining liquid out of it and filled it with cold water. He proceeded to throw that over Egon's head. He refilled the jug and repeated the dose, while Egon spluttered and snuffled.

The door jerked open with a bang and Jervis emerged, taking in the scene outside with wide eyes. He saw the discarded saxe on the table, looked down at the writhing, groaning form of Egon and shook his head.

"Drunk or not," he said, "I wouldn't try to take his saxe away from him." He looked at Crowley with a great deal of respect, mixed with a little fear.

"Does he have a horse?" Crowley asked.

Egon nodded, pointing to the rear of the building. "In the stable, with the rest of his gear."

Crowley smiled at him. "Would you mind fetching it for me?" he said. "I'll keep an eye on our friend."

Eyes wide, Jervis backed away from the redheaded stranger. After a few paces, he turned and dashed through the door. Crowley heard his footsteps pounding across the taproom, then the slam of another door. Egon groaned and Crowley turned to look down at him. The older Ranger was still doubled up, clutching his stomach.

"I'll . . . kill . . . you . . . for . . . that," he snarled, the words forcing their way past the skeins of drool and spittle hanging from his lips. The smile faded from Crowley's normally cheerful face.

"You already tried," he said, his voice low and dangerous. "And it didn't work out so well for you, did it?"

19

THE FERRY MASTER HAD BROUGHT ANOTHER TRAVELER across and decided to wait on the island for Crowley's return. He was lying comfortably against the side railing, dozing in the sun, when he heard the soft whinny of an approaching horse.

His eyes snapped open, then opened a little wider in surprise as he saw not one but two horses approaching. The first was Cropper, and the redheaded young Ranger was riding him. The second horse trailed a few meters behind Cropper. His rider wasn't sitting upright in the saddle, but was slumped over it, head hanging down one side and his feet on the other. He emitted a constant low moaning noise.

The ferry master stood and moved to where the ramp was let down onto the beach. The punt was floating in the shallow water at the edge of the little strait.

"We're going back across," Crowley told him.

The ferry master nodded absently, peering at the figure slumped across the horse, leaning down to see his face more clearly. "Isn't that . . . ?"

Crowley nodded briskly. "Yes. It's the Seacliff Ranger. I'm helping him find something he's lost."

"And what would that be?" the ferry master asked, genuinely puzzled. Crowley regarded him steadily.

"His dignity," he said.

The ferry master opened his mouth to say something, thought better of it, and closed it again.

"Right," he said. "Bring him aboard then."

Crowley rode up the shallow ramp onto the boat. Egon's horse followed docilely behind him. He dismounted and gestured to the comatose body over the saddle. "Help me get him down, would you?"

The ferry master took hold of one side. Crowley took the other and they heaved Egon down onto the deck of the punt. He slumped there, his head resting against the side rail, his arms clasped across his midsection.

"What's wrong with him?" the ferry master asked.

"He had a gastric attack," Crowley replied. He didn't explain that the attack had come from his right fist.

The man nodded somberly. "There's a lot of that going around."

Crowley paid him for their passage and the ferry master began to trudge back down the length of the boat, dragging it along the fastened hawser that ran from bank to bank. Once again, the punt slid out into deeper water, and the pok-pok-pok of wavelets under the bow began their regular cadence.

Crowley looked down at the gray-haired Ranger sprawling on the deck. He had the uncomfortable feeling that Egon was going to be their first failure and he frowned at the thought. Their numbers were small for the task ahead of them and the loss of even one man would make a big difference. Until now, it hadn't occurred to him that any of the dismissed Rangers would reject his plan. He had assumed they would all join him and Halt without any argument.

But Egon? He seemed to have lost his spirit and his sense of duty. Understandable, Crowley thought. He had probably been looking forward to his retirement. To be thrown out of his home, and to have his livelihood taken away at such a late time of his life, must have been a shattering experience.

"We'll give it one try to talk you around," he said quietly. "Then we'll have to move on."

"Pardon?" said the ferry master, as he trudged past Crowley on his endless task of hauling the rope from the bow to the stern, then repeating the action over and over again.

"Nothing," Crowley said. "Just thinking out loud."

The ferryman grunted and went back to his work. A few minutes later, the bow slid up the beach with the familiar grating sound of timber on sand. The current slewed the stern a little and the boat came to a halt. The ferryman approached Crowley and pointed to Egon.

"Want a hand to get him back on his horse?"

Crowley shook his head. "Just let me get him to his feet," he said and together they hauled the limp body upright, leaning him against the side rail of the ferry. The ferryman moved away to lower the bow ramp onto the sand. He'd taken three paces when he heard a loud splash behind him. He swung around to see Egon's head bobbing to the surface next to the stern of the punt, his arms thrashing wildly as the shock of the cold seawater revived him.

Crowley grinned at the ferryman. "Thought a little swim might do him good," he said.

Egon was already floundering his way toward the beach. He was in waist-deep water now and in no danger of drowning. Sodden and spluttering, he staggered up the sand and stood, glaring at Crowley and dripping water.

"I'll kill you for that!" he snarled.

Crowley raised an eyebrow. "So you keep saying."

He snapped his fingers at the two horses and they followed him down the ramp and onto the land. The ferry master watched with interest. He'd never seen a Ranger tossed overboard before—particularly by another Ranger.

As Crowley drew closer, Egon set his feet and took up a threatening stance, both fists raised.

Crowley stopped and smiled coldly at him. "Remember what happened last time," he admonished. Then he jerked a thumb toward the grass at the inland edge of the beach. "Let's go up there and talk. We've got a few things to go over."

And saying that, he turned his back on the sopping wet Egon and walked up the beach. The two horses followed him. Egon's horse actually turned an admonishing look on his owner. The gray-haired Ranger was left with no choice but to follow them.

Crowley found a fallen tree and sat down on it, gesturing for Egon to join him.

"So tell me about it," he said.

Egon hesitated, expecting an argument and not ready for the reasonable, sympathetic tone Crowley used. While he pondered, Crowley stood again, walked to where Cropper stood and took a small towel from his saddlebags. He tossed it to Egon.

"Dry off," he said, "and tell me what happened here."

Egon mopped the water streaming down his face, then toweled his hair and beard. He hesitated over the rest of his sodden form. A small hand towel would be useless there. Shrugging, he tossed it back to Crowley.

"Thanks," he said.

Crowley grinned. "Least I could do," he replied. "After all, I was the one who threw you in the sea. How's the gut feeling?"

Tentatively, Egon touched his hand to his solar plexus. He seemed to have sobered up somewhat. Possibly being tossed into cold seawater had that effect. "Bruised," he said, and added with a wry grin, "and empty."

"Sorry about the former. But the latter is probably just as well. Seemed like there was nothing in there but brandywine."

Egon had the grace to look ashamed. "True," he said. "I've been drinking a bit too much of that lately."

"Would that have anything to do with your being dismissed from the Corps?" Crowley asked.

Egon nodded, his expression darkening at the thought. "It would have everything to do with it," he said bitterly.

He paused, then, sensing that Crowley wanted him to carry on speaking, and that he might prove a sympathetic audience, he continued. "I've served the King as a Ranger for twenty-three years," he said. "Never a blemish on my character. Never had to be disciplined for anything. I had four commendations for bravery in that time, and every fief I served in respected me and honored me when I left." He stopped, not wanting to proceed.

"And then?" Crowley prompted.

"And then . . . this! Out of the blue, an accusation that I robbed a poor widow and beat her young son when he tried to protect her. No chance to defend the charges. No opportunity to say that nothing of the kind ever happened. No chance to appeal to the Ranger tribunal. Just a letter to the Baron telling him I was dismissed. My replacement was already appointed and I was to be cast onto the scrapheap. That's what I get for more than twenty years' loyal service. Thank you, your majesty! How wonderful it must be to be the King and to make such decisions!"

"It wasn't the King who dismissed you," Crowley said.

Egon turned an angry face toward him. "The letter was under his seal," he said belligerently, but Crowley shrugged the statement aside.

"The letter was written and sent by Baron Morgarath of Gorlan Fief," he said. "He's holding the King prisoner and has his son Duncan as a hostage. And you're not alone. You're one of the last twelve Rangers to be dismissed. If it makes you feel any better, I was sacked a few months ago too." He gestured vaguely toward the woods behind them. "And there are two more former Rangers back in the woods here who have received the same treatment."

The anger faded from Egon's face as Crowley continued to talk. It was replaced by a look of astonishment and shock. "But . . . why? What does Morgarath hope to gain from this?" he asked in a quiet voice.

"My guess is the throne," Crowley told him. "And his first step toward doing that is to dismantle the King's most potent force of loyal supporters." He paused, waiting to see if Egon would make the obvious step of logic.

"The Rangers."

Crowley nodded. "Exactly. He's broken the Rangers up, replacing real Rangers with sycophants and favorites of his own. It's been going on for some time."

"Pritchard said something along those lines," Egon murmured.

Crowley sat up at the name. "Pritchard? You've been in touch with him?"

Egon nodded. "We stay in touch. He's in Derry Kingdom in Hibernia." He paused as a memory struck him. "I remember you now. You're Crowley. You were his apprentice."

"I graduated a year or two before he left Araluen. He was one of the first to go."

"Like me, he was falsely accused of a crime," Egon said heavily.

"I never believed those accusations," Crowley said, anger evident in his voice. "But at that stage, I had no idea Morgarath was behind them. And Pritchard wasn't the only one. Some of the former Rangers have left the country. Some have been killed." He paused and looked pointedly at the older man. "Some of them started drinking."

Egon's eyes dropped from his. "All right," he said softly. "I suppose I deserved that. But what are you planning to do?"

"We're assembling a group of Rangers—twelve men like yourself who have just been dismissed—and we're going to stop Morgarath."

"Just twelve of you?"

"Twelve, if you'll throw in with us. And twelve Rangers will make a force to be reckoned with."

Egon gazed thoughtfully at his feet for a few moments. "You'll need more than just twelve of us," he said.

Crowley smiled at the word us. "We figure not all of the barons will be ready to side with Morgarath. A lot will, of course. But there are others who recognize him for what he is. We plan to approach some of them and get them on our side."

"Arald of Redmont Fief would be a good one to try," Egon said. "I've heard there's no love lost between him and Morgarath."

Crowley smiled. "So we've heard. We plan to visit him next," he said. "Will you be coming along?"

Egon didn't hesitate. His head nodded slowly, several times. "If you'll have me. I'm not so young anymore, you know."

"You can still shoot, can't you?" Crowley asked.

Egon allowed a grim smile to cross his lined features. "Just let me get a clear shot at Morgarath and you'll see."

"I'll see if I can arrange that," said Crowley. "Although there might be a queue." He stood and offered his hand to help Egon up. "There is one other thing . . ."

The older Ranger looked at him, understanding what he was about to say and preempting him.

"No more drinking?" Egon asked.

"No more drinking. Now come and meet the others."

20

THEY FOUND THE OTHER RANGERS CAMPED FIFTY METERS into the trees, in a small clearing. Egon was welcomed enthusiastically into the group. Nobody remarked on the fact that he was soaked to the skin, but Berrigan and Leander quietly found a spare shirt and trousers for him, and helped him set his wet clothes to dry by the fire, on a rack hastily constructed from thin branches.

Halt had shot a small deer during the day, as they traveled to Seacliff. He set a haunch on a spit over the fire, turning it from time to time and letting the juices and fat dribble onto the fire, sending flames flaring as they hit the red-hot coals. The smell of grilling meat was heavenly to the hungry men. Egon, however, eyed the roasting joint with a raised eyebrow.

"I thought only the King could take deer in the forest?" he said mildly.

Halt eyed him, straight-faced, as he turned the joint a quarter turn, setting more of the juices dripping into the fire and releasing more of the succulent-smelling smoke. "He wanted us to have it," he said. "He's a kindhearted King and he couldn't bear the thought of his loyal Rangers starving in the forest."

Leander had gathered some wild greens for a salad. He tore them into small pieces, then doused them with a mixture of oil and vinegar to produce a tart dressing. Berrigan had found a flat stone and was using it as a table to pound and knead a large lump of dough. He shaped it into a loaf and pushed it into the edge of the fire, raking a thick layer of hot coals over it.

When the food was ready, they piled thick juicy slices of venison onto chunks of the camp-bread loaf, then garnished it with Leander's salad. The rich taste of the venison contrasted pleasantly with the astringent taste of the salad and the warm bread was ideal for soaking up the delicious meat juices. All conversation halted for the duration of the meal and the silence round the campfire was broken only by the occasional grunt of satisfaction or pleasure.

Afterward, they cleaned their plates and utensils and packed away the leftovers for a later meal. There was half of the loaf remaining and they would toast that over the coals of the fire next morning to break their fast. Finally, replete and satisfied, they sat in a semicircle around the fire, their backs resting against the logs of several fallen trees. Berrigan had produced his gitarra and was strumming soft chords at random on it. Halt and Crowley were drinking coffee—as usual—while Berrigan and Leander shared a small flask of wine. They offered a mug to Egon but he shook his head decisively.

"Water will be fine," he said. Unnoticed by the others, Crowley eyed the exchange with a small nod of approval.

There was a pleasant lethargy settling over them, the result of a combination of a day's riding in the fresh air, a good meal under their belts and the warmth of the fire on their faces, contrasting with the crisp night air. Soon, it would be time to turn in and one of them would be assigned the duty of keeping watch for the next three hours. But for now, they could all relax and let their minds wander at will. So when Halt spoke up, there was a low murmur of protest from the others.

"We need to discuss something," he said.

Leander groaned softly. He was stretched out comfortably, his head resting against a log, his cloak warm underneath him and his chin resting on his chest. His legs ached dully from the day's exertions—not an unpleasant or painful sensation, but the enjoyable feeling that comes when one can finally relax after a hard day and let the muscles stretch out and loosen.

"Let's do it tomorrow," Berrigan suggested, stroking one more chord from his gitarra.

"Now," Halt said firmly. The others eyed him with mild irritation.

"I hate talking on an empty stomach," Crowley said.

Halt turned his steady gaze on him. "Your stomach isn't empty," he pointed out. "Your stomach is full of venison and bread and salad and coffee."

Crowley considered that point and yawned hugely. "That's even worse," he said. "I hate talking on a full stomach even more than an empty one." He smiled, hoping that he might have dissuaded Halt from whatever it was he wanted to discuss. Halt continued to eye him steadily, however.

Crowley sniffed with annoyance, pulling himself up to sit straighter. "Oh, all right," he said. "Let's talk if we must."

Egon glanced around at the faces of his new companions. As a new member of the group, he didn't think he should voice an opinion for or against Halt's suggestion. Time to do that would be when he heard what the dark-bearded Hibernian wanted to discuss. Berrigan and Leander, with great outward shows of reluctance, hitched themselves up into more attentive poses, their eyes on Halt.

Crowley made an encouraging gesture with his hand, indicating that Halt should proceed. "So," he said, "talk away."

Halt leaned forward, elbows on his knees, and let his gaze travel round the small semicircle of faces. When he was sure he had their attention, and that all protests and jokes were stilled, he spoke.

"There are five of us now . . . ," he began. He got no further.

"Well," said Crowley, "I'm glad that's settled. I was wondering, seeing how I have trouble counting past three. But if you say there are five of us now, that's good enough for me." He settled back down to slump against the log, pulling his cowl forward to shield his eyes.

Halt regarded him with enormous patience. The silence stretched out between them.

Finally, Crowley roused himself, grinning at his friend. "Oh, did you want to say more?" he asked innocently.

Berrigan and Leander hid grins. Egon, still not sure of the prevailing dynamic in this little group, watched without expression, but with great attention.

Halt sighed. Sometimes talking to Crowley was like trying to herd smoke, he thought. Retaining his patience with great difficulty, he resumed. "Now there are five of us," he repeated, and turned a warning glare on Crowley, daring him to interrupt. Crowley smiled guilelessly at him and he continued. "We've become a bit of an unwieldy group."

Berrigan frowned. "'Unwieldy'? How do you mean?"

Halt made a vague gesture with his hands. "We're without cohesive direction," he said. "By which I mean, nobody is directing our actions. We're bumbling along from day to day—"

"Can't say I've noticed a lot of bumbling," Crowley protested.

Halt shot a warning look at him but he could see that, for once, the redhead was serious and not trying to make a joke.

"Maybe not yet," Halt agreed. "But with five of us, we're bound sooner or later to disagree over a course of action. That could lead to squabbling and people taking sides. And if that happens, it could well break up the group."

"You're saying we need a leader," Egon put in, deciding it was time he took part in the conversation.

Halt nodded at him gratefully. "Exactly. We need to elect a leader—and give him the power to make decisions and the authority to have those decisions obeyed and carried through. Otherwise we're like a band of headless chickens."

"But dangerous chickens nonetheless," Leander said with a faint smile. Then, as Halt turned toward him with an irritable look on his face, he held up his hands in a defensive gesture. "All right! Point taken, and I do agree. We need to elect a leader."

He glanced keenly at the Hibernian. In his experience, when a person suggested that someone needed to be elected leader, they often had themselves in mind for the position.

"Are you offering to take on the job?" he asked and was relieved to see the shocked look on the bearded face.

"Me? By the ghost of Barry Boru, no! After all, I'm not even officially a Ranger yet!"

"Barry Boru," mused Crowley with a smile. "He sounds like an interesting person."

Halt's next words wiped the smile from his face.

"I'm suggesting Crowley for the job," Halt said.

Crowley sat bolt upright. "Me? Are you joking?"

"You. And no, I'm not," Halt told him. "You've been the driving force behind this whole affair. It was your idea in the first place and you're the one who's recruited the rest of us. Who better to lead us?"

"But . . ." Crowley searched for a good reason to refuse and thought he found one. "I'm younger than the rest of you—with the exception of you, of course," he added, looking at Halt.

Leander was shaking his head. "That's not altogether a bad thing," he said. "You've got a younger man's passion and drive for this task. You've shown us that."

"And you've got a younger man's energy to take the job on," Berrigan said, his face serious. "It's not going to be easy. I know I'd find it a daunting task."

"Shall we vote on it?" Halt suggested mildly.

"No! We need to discuss it further!" Crowley answered immediately.

Halt turned a wicked smile on him. "I thought you hated talking on a full stomach."

Crowley made an angry, dismissive gesture. "This isn't a matter for joking!" he insisted.

But then Egon coughed apologetically and they all turned to look at him. "I'm new to the group," he said quietly, choosing his words with care, "and I don't know any of you too well." He nodded toward Berrigan and Leander. "Oh, we've run into each other at Gatherings, of course, but I can't say we're close friends."

The two Rangers nodded. Berrigan smiled. "Not yet, anyway," he murmured.

Egon continued, acknowledging the comment with a small

nod. "The thing is, Crowley, it seems to me you're ideally suited to be our leader."

Crowley was still sitting bolt upright. A small frown crossed his face. "Oh? And why would that be?"

Egon glanced around at the other three before he spoke. He wasn't altogether keen to tell them about the condition he had been in when Crowley had found him. They had been welcoming and positive in their approach to him and he didn't wish them to think any less of him. However, he felt he had to continue.

"I was a bit of a mess when Crowley found me this afternoon," he admitted. "I was looking for my future in the bottom of a tankard of brandywine. I'd been doing that for some time now," he added sadly.

He stopped for a second or two while he gathered his thoughts, glancing nervously at the others. He saw no sign of condemnation or criticism in their eyes. Just interest. He shrugged. They were men who had seen a lot of life, he thought. They weren't likely to be horrified by an admission like the one he'd just made.

"I was angry. I was disillusioned. I had lost all faith in the King. Crowley tossed my jug of brandy away and I lost my temper rather badly. I drew my saxe on him."

Halt winced. "Oh dear," he said softly. He thought he knew what was coming. He had seen Crowley in action and he knew the redhead's reflexes were as quick as a snake's.

Egon glanced at him and nodded. "Oh dear indeed," he said. "After Crowley had taken away my saxe, and after he threw me into the sea off the end of the punt . . ."

His audience exchanged a glance. That explained why Egon had arrived at the camp dripping wet.

Egon went on. "After that, he sat me down and talked to me for a few minutes. That's all it took. A few minutes." He looked at Crowley, who gave a diffident shrug. "And in those few minutes, he explained to me what you were planning and convinced me that I should join you. He was able to put your case very succinctly and in a most convincing way. Perhaps the most compelling part of it was his total belief in what you're doing. That came across unmistakably."

He paused and the others nodded wordlessly. They had felt the same thing when Crowley had approached them.

"As I say," Egon continued, "I don't know the rest of you too well. But I doubt any of you could have convinced me so completely or so quickly. If for no other reason than that, I think Crowley should be our leader."

There was a murmur of agreement from the others. Crowley, embarrassed, looked down at his feet.

Halt nudged him with an elbow. "Isn't it nice to be loved?" He grinned evilly. Crowley glared at him but before he could speak, Halt raised his voice. "Let's vote on it! Crowley for leader. All in favor?"

"Aye!" the others chorused. Crowley opened his mouth to say nay, realized there was no point to it and closed it again.

Halt nodded. "And I say aye as well." He slapped Crowley on the shoulder. "Congratulations. Looks like you're our new commander."

21

They rode on the next morning. Crowley had overcome his resistance to being elected their leader. It was a bright, sunny day and the air was crisp and fresh. He whistled softly as he rode, a jaunty little tune about a blacksmith and his ladylove.

He and Halt were riding side by side. Berrigan and Leander rode behind them and Egon brought up the rear, riding some fifty meters back, keeping a watchful eye on the trail behind them. From time to time, one of the others would take a turn at being the rear guard. There was little likelihood of trouble, but there was no harm in being ready.

Halt glared at his friend as the whistling continued. "I had hoped that your new sense of responsibility would put an end to that painful shrieking noise you make between your lips," he said.

Crowley smiled. It was a beautiful day and he was feeling at peace with the world. And that meant he was more than ready to tease Halt. "It's a jaunty song."

"What's jaunty about it?" Halt asked, grim faced. Crowley made an uncertain gesture as he sought for an answer to that question.

"I suppose it's the subject matter," he said eventually. "It's a very cheerful song. Would you like me to sing it for you?"

"N—" Halt began but he was too late, as Crowley began to sing. He had a pleasant tenor voice, in fact, and his rendering of the song was quite good. But to Halt it was as attractive as a rusty barn door squeaking.

"A blacksmith from Palladio, he met a lovely lady-o . . ."

"Whoa! Whoa!" Halt said and, as Abelard obligingly came to a stop, he nudged the horse in the ribs. "Not you. Him," he said, pointing to Crowley.

In the future, be more specific, Abelard's withering glance seemed to say. I'm a horse, not a mind reader. Halt ignored him. Crowley was looking at him, eyebrows raised in interrogation.

"'He met a lovely lady-o'?" Halt repeated sarcastically. "What in the name of all that's holy is a lady-o?"

"It's a lady," Crowley told him patiently.

"Then why not sing 'he met a lovely lady'?" Halt wanted to know.

Crowley frowned as if the answer was blatantly obvious. "Because he's from Palladio, as the song says. It's a city on the continent, in the southern part of Toscana."

"And people there have lady-o's, instead of ladies?" asked Halt.

"No. They have ladies, like everyone else. But lady doesn't rhyme with Palladio, does it? I could hardly sing, 'A blacksmith from Palladio, he met his lovely lady,' could I?"

"It would make more sense if you did," Halt insisted.

"But it wouldn't rhyme," Crowley told him.

"Would that be so bad?"

"Yes! A song has to rhyme or it isn't a proper song. It has to be lady-o. It's called poetic license."

"It's poetic license to make up a word that doesn't exist and that, by the way, sounds extremely silly?" Halt asked.

Crowley shook his head. "No. It's poetic license to make sure that the two lines rhyme with each other."

Halt thought for a few seconds, his eyebrows knitted close together. Then inspiration struck him.

"Well then, couldn't you sing, 'A blacksmith from Palladio, he met a lovely lady, so . . .'?"

"So what?" Crowley challenged. In truth, he was more than a little surprised that Halt had come up with an alternative rhyme so quickly—and one that seemed to open up further opportunities for the story.

Halt made an uncertain gesture with his hands as he sought more inspiration. Then he replied. "He met a lovely lady, so . . . he asked her for her hand and gave her a leg of lamb."

"'A leg of lamb'? Why would she want a leg of lamb?" Crowley demanded.

Halt shrugged. "Maybe she was hungry."

"In any event," Crowley said, becoming more and more irritated by this conversation, "hand and lamb don't rhyme with each other."

"They assonate," said Berrigan, who had been listening with some interest to this discussion. "They have a similar sound. That's quite common in songs, you know."

Berrigan, of course, was a musician and could be considered to be something of an authority when it came to song lyrics. Crowley, feeling as if he were being backed into a corner, turned to him.

"Well, even if they do aspirate—"

"Assonate. The word is assonate," Berrigan corrected him, making it all too obvious that he was hiding a grin.

"Whatever! Even if they do . . . that . . . why would he give her a leg of lamb? He's a blacksmith, not a butcher."

"Maybe," Leander said slowly, "he gave her a cattle brand. That rhymes with hand, after all. He asked her for her hand, and gave her a cattle brand. That works," he added, looking at Berrigan.

"Works for me," Berrigan murmured.

"A cattle brand? Why would he give her a cattle brand?" Crowley had once seen a bear being attacked from three different directions by hunting dogs. He began to feel a great deal of sympathy for that bear. But Leander wasn't cowed by the scorn in his voice.

"Because he's a blacksmith, isn't he? And blacksmiths make things like cattle brands—you know, branding irons. So maybe she'd asked him for one so she could brand her cattle and he gave her one."

"That is idiotic!" Crowley snapped.

But Leander merely shrugged. "It's no sillier than calling her a lady-o. After all, we don't call ourselves Ranger-o's, do we?"

"And we don't ride horsey-o's," Halt said, rejoining the discussion with some relish. It wasn't often that he was able to get the better of Crowley in one of these arguments. Crowley had a quicksilver brain and tongue and Halt was enjoying this rare moment of ascendancy.

Crowley reined in Cropper and glared around at his three companions, who were all smiling fondly at him and obviously enjoying themselves far too much.

"Very well," he said sharply, "remember last night when you all elected me commander?"

He paused and they all nodded. "Because you said"—he

looked severely at Halt—"there might come a time when we couldn't agree on something and I'd have to make a decision?"

Halt nodded. That wasn't exactly what he'd said but it was close enough to, he thought.

"In that case," Crowley said, "I choose to invoke that authority now. As your elected leader, I make this decree. He didn't give her a leg of lamb or a cattle brand or even a slice of ham—"

"Oh, that's not bad," Berrigan interrupted but Crowley's withering glare silenced him almost as soon as he spoke.

"As leader of this group, I say she was a lady-o. Clear?"

The others exchanged a glance, wondering if they could keep this going a little longer.

Crowley raised his voice. "I said, is that clear?"

Halt, Berrigan and Leander all nodded.

"So this discussion is now officially closed. I declare it so in my position as your elected leader—who must be obeyed. Is anyone unhappy with that?"

"No, Crowley," they all said, eyes downcast like guilty schoolboys. Although he noticed that their shoulders were shaking with mirth. He took a breath, preparing to berate them further, when Egon spoke. He had ridden up to join them when they stopped in the middle of the track to debate song lyrics. There was a mild note of condemnation in his voice.

"Has it escaped your collective notice," he asked, "that there's a rider waiting for us?"

They all looked up in surprise. Egon was right. There was a rider sitting in the middle of the track, some thirty meters away. He was mounted on a shaggy black horse, wore a camouflaged cloak and had a longbow held across his thighs. Obviously, he was a Ranger. Halt and Crowley exchanged a guilty look. They had been so intent on their ridiculous discussion that they had failed to notice the rider. Perhaps, Halt thought hopefully, he had been concealed in the trees until a few minutes ago and had only just ridden out onto the track.

"Good morning," Crowley called. The newcomer touched his heels to his horse's flanks and walked slowly forward until he was only a few meters away.

"Good morning," he said. He flicked his cowl back from his head and twitched his cloak back over his shoulders. Crowley caught a quick gleam of silver at the man's throat—the silver oakleaf, symbol of a Ranger. The man had blond-white hair and a neat, carefully trimmed beard. His face was pale and his eyes were a piercing blue. He appeared to be in his mid-thirties—older than Crowley, younger than Egon.

"Can we help you?" Crowley asked and the man shifted in his saddle.

"Perhaps," he said. "I'm Norris, former Ranger of Holsworth Fief. I've heard rumors about a small group of other Rangers like myself, recruiting members to face Baron Morgarath of Gorlan Fief. I thought you might be them."

"And so we are," Crowley said, smiling a welcome. But the smile faded with Norris's next words.

"As I said, I thought you might be them—until I heard the utter tommyrot you've just been discussing."

"Oh," said Crowley, a little embarrassed. "I think you caught us at a bad time."

"I think so," Norris said. Obviously, a lively sense of humor wasn't one of his qualities.

"Crowley was just exercising his new authority as leader of the group," Halt put in, with a smile.

Norris turned his gaze to the Hibernian. "He's your leader?"

Halt nodded. "Elected him last night," he said.

Norris studied Crowley for some time and pursed his lips. "Was that a wise choice, do you think?"

Halt took a deep breath. In addition to having no sense of humor, Norris apparently had no sense of tact, either.

"Tell me," Halt said eventually, "do you understand the concept of a joke?"

Norris sat up straighter in the saddle, looking a trifle affronted by the question. "Of course I do!" he said. "I have an excellent sense of humor."

Halt's eyebrow shot up before he could stop himself. In his experience, people who claimed to have an excellent sense of humor usually had none at all.

"Well, what you heard was a joke. We—were—joking," he said, enunciating the last three words slowly and distinctly.

Norris looked doubtful. "Didn't sound very funny to me."

Halt shrugged. "You had to be there to appreciate it," he said.

"I was. I was right here!" Norris protested.

Halt shook his head slowly. "My point exactly. You were here. You had to be there."

Now Norris looked confused, so Halt decided to explain.

"That was another joke," he said.

"It wasn't very funny."

Crowley decided it was time he stepped in and smoothed things over. "So, Norris, tell us about yourself," he said in a friendly tone.

Norris, still frowning over Halt's professed joke, turned back to Crowley.

"I've been a Ranger for eight years," he said. "Served the last five at Holsworth Fief, close to here. Then a few weeks ago, I received a letter dismissing me from the Corps. It was delivered by a puffed-up twerp who had been sent to replace me. Said he was acting under Lord Morgarath's authority."

"Apparently Morgarath has decided to come out into the open and usurp the King's authority," Crowley replied. "Up until now, he's made it look as if those letters of dismissal have come from the King. Morgarath's next move will be to claim the crown for himself, I should think. We plan to stop him." He paused, then voiced a thought that had been running through his mind. "You said you'd heard about us?"

Norris shrugged. "Just general rumors. Word gets around, you know?"

Halt and Crowley exchanged a look. "We'd better pick up the pace," Halt said. "It won't be long before word about what we're doing gets back to Morgarath."

"True." The redheaded Ranger turned back to Norris. "So, Norris, can you put up with Halt's bad jokes long enough to join us?"

Halt snorted indignantly. "My bad jokes?" he said under his breath.

But Norris didn't hear him. He nodded, his face very serious. "I suppose so. If it'll give me a chance to get a shot at Morgarath." He touched the longbow lying across his knees.

Crowley held out his hand. "Welcome to our band."

22

MORGARATH WAS IN HIS STUDY IN CASTLE GORLAN, WITH an enormous, leather-bound book on the table in front of him.

The book was quite ancient and had been hand-copied by scribes. In addition to the text, there were illustrations in fine black ink. One such illustration was on the page facing the text he had been reading. It showed a heavy-bodied, ugly creature about the size of a bear. It was covered in thick, shaggy hair and had a low brow over small, slitlike eyes. The muzzle was long, and the open, snarling lips revealed long fangs like a wolf's.

The forelegs ended in humanoid hands—but instead of fingernails, they were equipped with thick, curved claws. The claws were sharp and dangerous looking, but not long enough to impede the creature gripping with the thick, stubby fingers.

The hind legs were squat and muscular, but longer than a bear's, with a pronounced angle at the elbow. It would appear that the creature could cover ground in a series of long, leaping bounds. According to the text, they could also walk with a strange, rolling, shuffling gait.

There was a light tap at the door and he looked up, frowning at being interrupted in his studies.

"What is it?" he said, his ill temper evident in the tone of his voice.

"It's Teezal, my lord. I have news from Dacton Fief."

Morgarath sighed. Teezal, he knew, wouldn't interrupt him unless the news was important. He pushed the book to one side and studied a sheet of parchment that had been underneath it. Dacton Fief. The name rang a bell. Then he saw it, in the list of twelve fiefs whose Rangers had recently been dismissed.

"Very well," he said. "Come in."

But this had better be important, the tone of his voice said clearly. Teezal entered, peering round the door before coming farther into the room. He was an obsequious dolt, Morgarath thought, although he was a pitiless killer and a skilled torturer, both qualities that Morgarath prized in a subordinate.

Teezal hesitated, turning his feathered bonnet in his hands, several meters back from the large table Morgarath used as a desk. The Baron of Gorlan made a bad-tempered gesture, summoning him closer.

"Oh, come forward! Don't shilly-shally there like a nervous bride! You've broken my train of thought now, so you might as well get on with it."

Teezal forced a smile onto his features. In his own right, he was a man who inspired fear and loathing in others. He was cruel and vicious and would kill without hesitation. Yet even a blackhearted monster like him harbored a deep-seated fear of his lord. Morgarath could fly off the handle without notice if he heard news he didn't like. More than one of his minions had paid with their lives for his terrible, unpredictable temper. He shuffled forward a few steps, making sure to stop while he was out of the tall, blond-haired man's reach. He glanced behind him, marking the escape route to the door.

None of this went unnoticed by Morgarath but he said nothing to ease Teezal's nervousness. He ruled by fear and he wanted his men to be frightened and uncertain in his presence. He held Teezal's eyes with an unblinking gaze. He saw the other man swallow nervously a few times. Teezal, uncertain as to whether he should speak, opened his mouth and realized his lips were dry. He moistened them, took a breath, hesitated.

"Were you planning on standing there all day gawking at me?" Morgarath said. His voice was deep and beautifully modulated. But the beauty was like that of a venomous snake. It held its own sense of threat.

"It's from . . . Dacton Fief." Teezal managed to force the words out. Again, Morgarath maintained a long silence, while Teezal's fingers gripped and ungripped the bonnet he held before his chest.

"Did you want me to guess what it is?" Morgarath said finally.

Teezal shook his head, then found his voice. "The Ranger . . . the former Ranger," he corrected himself, "has gone."

Morgarath glanced down at the list on his desk. "That would be Leander?"

Teezal nodded several times. "Yes, my lord. Leander it is. Or was," he added nervously.

"I seem to recall he was making life . . . difficult for his replacement—refusing to give up the Ranger cabin he had been living in."

"Exactly, Lord Morgarath. Not that the new man wanted to live in the cabin anyway. But Leander was unsettling things in the village attached to the castle. The people there weren't sure who the Ranger actually was."

"Then, presumably, it's a good thing that he's moved on." Morgarath's tone was silky and sarcastic. "Presumably, things are no longer unsettled, as you put it."

"No, my lord. I mean, yes, my lord. That's correct."

"Then why did you see fit to interrupt my important research"—he flicked a finger at the huge book he had pushed aside—"to bring me such totally unimportant news? Leander was causing a problem. Now he's gone. Why did I need to be apprised of this breathtakingly unimportant fact?"

Teezal could feel a trickle of sweat running down the back of his neck. Morgarath was smiling coldly at him. But the smile didn't reach his eyes.

"It was more . . . the manner of his going, my lord," he finally managed to say.

"Oh? Did a dragon swoop down from the clouds and bear him away?" said Morgarath, the sarcasm heavy in his voice.

Teezal, trapped by those eyes, shook his head. "No, my lord . . ."

"A griffin then? A griffin swooped down and took him."

"No, lord. It was the former Ranger Crowley."

As he said it, Teezal realized the absurdity of his statement. He had made it sound as if the former Ranger had swooped from the heavens and borne Leander away. He waited for a sneering retort from Morgarath. But now the Baron's face had darkened with rage.

"Crowley? That redheaded interfering fool from Hogarth Fief?"

Teezal nodded several times. "Aye, my lord. That's the one. Crowley."

"And do I take it that the arrogant Hibernian Halt was with him?"

Teezal hesitated. "He did have a companion, my lord. But whether it was the Hibernian or not, I couldn't say." It was better to profess ignorance than to offer Morgarath information that might prove false, he knew.

Morgarath grunted. "I'll wager it was. So Leander went off with them, did he?"

"Aye, my lord. And there's rumor that he's not the only one to join them. Word is that the Rangers Berrigan and Egon are also—"

"They're not Rangers. I dismissed them. They're renegades," Morgarath snapped.

"Of course, my lord. But as I say, it's rumored that they've joined together."

"To what purpose?"

Teezal hesitated, then shrugged unhappily. "I don't know, my lord. I've had no information about what they intend to do."

"Hmmmph." Morgarath stared at the window as he drummed his fingers on the table. So Crowley and several other Rangers had banded together, he thought. He wondered what they might have in mind. "Chances are, they'll simply become outlaws. I've always thought that the Rangers were not much better than outlaws anyway. In any event, there's not much they can do to bother me, is there?"

"No, my lord."

"No. Four or five of them won't pose any threat to my plans. We'll have to deal with them at some time, I imagine. But for the moment, I have more important matters to deal with than a few disgruntled renegades hiding in the forest and shooting deer. I'll deal with them when I've taken the throne."

"Yes, lord. I simply thought you should know," Teezal said,

suddenly nervous that he might have disturbed Morgarath for no good reason.

But the black-clad Baron nodded absently as he pulled the massive book back to the center of the desk. "No, no. You did well to tell me," he said.

Teezal heaved a mental sigh of relief. After all, as he had thought before, with Morgarath, you never knew. He glanced down at the book in front of Morgarath and let out an involuntary exclamation of horror.

"By the gods! What's that?" He pointed at the illustration of the grotesque beast.

Morgarath smiled. "It's called a Wargal," he said, looking down at the illustration himself. "Some people say they're mythical beasts. Have you ever heard of them?"

Teezal shook his head, his eyes riveted on the fearsome illustration. "Can't say I have, my lord."

"And yet this book says they existed in times past. They're simple-minded, semihuman creatures, strong as a bear and as vicious as a wildcat. They make fearsome soldiers, as they're afraid of nothing. They will keep attacking as long as their commander orders them to do so. They kill without remorse." He allowed himself an indulgent smile. "Rather like yourself, Teezal."

"How do you command them?" Teezal asked.

Morgarath turned back a page and consulted the text. "It says they communicate without spoken words. Their minds contact each other. And they can be controlled and commanded by a mind stronger than their own."

Teezal frowned. "How would a person manage that?"

Morgarath smiled sarcastically. "A person like you wouldn't.

But someone with a powerful, dominant mind"—he paused, then continued—"such as me, for example, can make contact and bend them to his wishes. It says here"—he tapped the text with one forefinger—"that King Prescott the Conqueror enslaved them to his will some three hundred years ago. They provided him with an unbeatable army and victory after victory—until he lost control of them."

"How did that happen?" Teezal said, fascinated.

"He became a drunkard, and the alcohol weakened his brain, making his mental signals uncertain and disjointed. The Wargal army rebelled, killing their human commanders, and deserted. It's said they disappeared into the Mountains of Rain and Night, and became lost in the wilderness up there."

Teezal nodded gravely. "I've heard tales about some terrible beasts in those mountains."

"And perhaps they were based in truth. Once we have the current problem settled, I might take the time to seek them out and bend them to my will. It'd be handy to have an inexorable force of killers who know no fear."

Teezal swallowed. The idea of the bestial creatures running amok and killing indiscriminately was a worrying one. Morgarath saw the concern in his eyes.

"Never fear, Teezal. I'll make sure they never attack you."

Teezal lowered his head in a small bow. "Thank you, my lord," he said in a low voice.

Morgarath looked at him for a second or two, then made a dismissing gesture. "Now go away and leave me to my studies," he said.

23

THESE DAYS, THE RANGERS HAD TO SEARCH FOR A LARGER campsite when they stopped for the night.

Halt and Crowley continued to share the lean-to tarpaulin they had been using since they began their journey. The others each had a small one-man Ranger tent, which they pitched in a semicircle facing the fireplace each night.

Their horses, being Ranger trained, didn't need restraining at night but were left to wander free and graze in the vicinity of the campsite. But the extra numbers meant that they needed to be more organized than they'd been before, so Crowley assigned camp tasks to each of them.

He and Halt volunteered to continue with the preparation of meals. And, since they were good cooks, the others agreed readily. The more menial tasks of gathering firewood, building a fireplace and fetching water were all assigned on a rotating roster to the others, as was the cleaning of pots and pans used for cooking. Each Ranger cleaned his own plate and eating utensils and all of them contributed to the pot by hunting.

The weather continued fine, although the nights were chilly. But camping outdoors was no hardship to such seasoned travelers and, in the evenings, after they had eaten, Berrigan would usually sit and coax pleasant melodies from his gitarra.

Norris, it turned out, was an expert fisherman and he loved to spend the last hour of daylight sitting beside a stream, with a long, limber fishing pole extended over the water. He had an uncanny knack of sensing where fish might lie and often supplemented their larder with fresh river trout or the occasional succulent salmon. When such opportunities arose, he was excused from the daily chores of setting up camp. The prospect of fresh fish for dinner more than compensated for the extra work the others had to undertake.

All in all, Halt thought, if it weren't for the deadly serious reason underlying their journey, it would have been a very pleasant interlude.

On this particular evening, Norris had managed to land a three-kilogram salmon for their supper. Halt and Crowley had wrapped the cleaned fish, liberally covered in butter and slices of wild-growing onion and lemon, in bark and large leaves so that it was completely sealed, then created an earth oven by shoveling red-hot coals from the fire into a small trench they dug next to the fireplace proper. They laid the wrapped fish into the trench, then covered it with more coals. Finally, they heaped earth over the layer of coals and left the fish to steam and roast inside the leaves while they sliced potatoes and fried them in butter in a cast-iron pan, with mushrooms and wilted wild greens to go with them.

The group sat round the fire when the meal was served, eating steadfastly, without too much conversation to slow down the eating process. Finally, Berrigan leaned back after his third helping, licked his buttery fingers and sighed contentedly.

"It's a pleasure to have you aboard," he said to Norris, who frowned, not understanding.

"Aboard?" he said. "Aboard what? We're not on a ship."

As has been stated, Norris tended to take things literally.

Berrigan simply smiled at him. "I mean it's a pleasure to have you around, if you can produce fish like that one."

"Oh. Thank you," said Norris. He smiled awkwardly. He wasn't a man who was used to compliments. Berrigan cleaned his greasy fingers on a convenient piece of cloth, realized too late that it was the hem of his cloak and shrugged. A few stains and smears on one's clothes never hurt anyone. In fact, he thought, as he looked down his nose at the irregular, greasy stain, it might well add to the camouflage qualities of his cloak. He glanced across the fire to where Leander was absentmindedly wiping his hands on the front of his shirt. Beside him, Crowley belched gently.

"We're a refined lot, aren't we?" Halt said. "We'd be a big hit at a formal dinner at Castle Araluen."

Crowley shrugged. "We're not at a formal dinner party. We're in camp. Camp manners and castle manners are two different things."

"So I've noticed," Halt said, then he belched as well. Raised in Castle Dun Kilty in Clonmel, he had been taught to behave with strict table manners and politeness in his youth and he was enjoying the freedom of being on the road with such an easygoing group. The belch was a long and resounding one and he smiled in satisfaction.

"Better out than in," he said.

Egon gave him a sidelong glance. "Not for those of us who are out here with it."

Halt considered that and nodded. He couldn't argue with it.

The beauty of cooking the salmon the way they had done was that there was no pot to clean afterward. The cast-iron pan in which they had cooked the potatoes needed cleaning and scouring, however. So Egon checked the water bucket and saw it was only a quarter full.

"I'll get water," he said, and moved off into the shadows, soon being lost among the trees. Even on such a mundane task as fetching water, Rangers tended to be as unobtrusive as possible, instinctively moving from one patch of shade or cover to the next. It was a lifelong skill that they practiced constantly, and unthinkingly. On more than one occasion, a Ranger's life had been saved by the practice.

"We should reach Redmont tomorrow," Crowley said. "I'll be interested to see how Baron Arald greets us." They were currently in Eagleton Fief and had spent the past two days inquiring about one of the dismissed Rangers—a man named Samdash. But they had had no success. People in the villages they had passed through had given them no word of the Ranger's present whereabouts. Crowley's inquiries were met with blank looks and stony silence. Finally, they had decided to abandon the search for Samdash and proceed to the adjoining Redmont Fief.

"Who's the Ranger at Redmont again?" Halt asked. He had been told, but he was full of delicious food and a little drowsy so the effort of searching his memory for the man's name seemed too much.

"Farrel," Crowley told him.

Berrigan looked up at the name. "He's a good man."

Leander nodded agreement. "One of the best. He'll be a great addition to the group. He's fought in more than one battle on the northern frontier when he was assigned to Norgate Fief. I hear he uses a battleax in close combat. Frightened the lights out of more than one Scotti warrior, I believe."

"Is that allowed?" Halt asked. "I didn't think Rangers were encouraged to use heavy, close-range weapons like axes and swords."

"Technically we're not. But who's going to tell a man with a battleax?" Berrigan said, his eyes half closed as he leaned back and enjoyed the heat radiating from the fire.

Crowley yawned hugely. "We should start thinking of turning in," he said, trying to remember whose turn it was for the first watch. The prospect of his bedroll was a very pleasant one. He looked up curiously as Cropper emerged from the trees and emitted a low-level grunting noise. "What is it, boy?"

Then understanding dawned and he started to his feet, his hand reaching for the saxe knife, where it lay in its scabbard on the fallen tree trunk he had been using for a backrest.

Before he could draw the weapon, however, an arrow hissed across the clearing and slammed, quivering, into the log, a few centimeters from his hand.

"Don't anybody move," a harsh voice said out of the darkness. "There are four of us and we all have arrows ready nocked."

Four indistinct figures moved out of the shadows under the trees. Crowley, his night vision ruined by staring into the glowing coals of the fire, squinted to see them more clearly. As they came into the circle of light thrown by the fire, he could see they were all dressed in Ranger cloaks and carried massive longbows.

As the speaker had said, each one of them had an arrow nocked on the string, drawn back about thirty centimeters. There was an air of competence and quiet confidence about them that told him they could draw fully and shoot in less than a second if necessary.

Slowly, Crowley moved his hand away from the saxe.

"Take it easy," he said, his voice calm and untroubled. "We're not your enemies."

"We'll decide that," said the speaker. His face was hidden in the shadow of his cowl, with only the lower third visible. Crowley, Halt and the others were caught at a disadvantage, lying relaxing against the trunk of the tree.

Halt studied the four figures. He rolled slightly to one side and used his fingertips to slide his throwing knife out of its scabbard, keeping it concealed beneath his body.

As he moved, the second figure from the right turned to cover him, the partly drawn arrow shaft pointing in his direction.

"Don't do anything stupid," the man warned him. His voice sounded younger than that of the original speaker but his features too were concealed in the shadow of his cowl.

Halt held his hands up in submission. "Wouldn't dream of it," he said mildly.

"Who are you?" Crowley asked.

The original speaker turned to face him directly, although his face was still hidden by the cowl. "That's funny," he said. "I seem to be the one with the bow. So I would have thought I'd be the one asking the questions." He paused a few seconds, letting that sink in, then continued in a harder tone. "Who are you?"

"My name is Crowley. I'm a former Ranger, as I'm guessing you are. And these are my companions, Halt, Berrigan—"

He got no further. The cowled man interrupted roughly. "Actually, I don't really care who you are. I want to know why you've been asking about me."

A look of understanding came over Crowley's face. "You're Samdash?"

The other man made a peremptory gesture with the point of his arrow. "You're fond of answering a question with one of your own, aren't you?" he said. "Yes. I'm Samdash. Now why have you been asking about me? Did Morgarath send you to hunt us down?"

"Morgarath?" Crowley said with a hollow laugh. "Far from it! I'm no friend of his. None of us are."

"So you say. Nevertheless—"

"Put your weapons down . . . now!" Egon's voice came from the darkness behind the four men. Samdash tensed and began to turn around, but Egon spoke again.

"No. Don't turn around or I'll shoot," he said calmly.

Samdash stopped the movement and cursed under his breath. He hadn't been told how many men were in the group who were asking about him. The villagers who had told him had been hazy on that point—five or six, they'd said. Obviously, he realized now, it had been six. But he didn't let his sense of frustration show as he spoke again.

"You do realize there are four of us and only one of you?" he said. "We could easily—"

He flinched violently as two arrows slammed in quick succession into a tree stump by his knee.

"You couldn't easily do anything," Egon said. "But I could easily take down two of you before you could turn—as you just saw."

In spite of himself, Samdash looked down at the two shafts quivering in the stump. That had been extremely fast shooting. Ranger-trained shooting, he thought.

"In addition, I'm behind you and in the dark, whereas you're outlined against the fire, where I can see you. Before your other two men could locate me, I'd have plenty of time to hit them as well." He paused, then added, "Of course, that won't be of much interest to you, because you'll be the first one to die."

Samdash ground his teeth together in frustration and anger. He had been careless, he realized. They had spent the afternoon searching for the small group who were asking after him, finally locating them by the glint of their fire through the trees. Then, instead of waiting and watching to ascertain how many of them there were, he had led his men forward impulsively. And now they had been outflanked. Taking a deep breath, he glanced sideways at his three companions.

"Ease your strings, boys," he said, "and lay your bows down as he says."

Four bowstrings were let down with a series of slight creaks. The bows were set on the ground and the arrows returned to their quivers. Crowley waited until the threat was removed, then rose slowly and walked forward. To Samdash's slight bewilderment, he held his hand out in greeting.

"As I was saying, I'm Crowley and I'm delighted to meet you."

24

So NOW THERE WERE TEN IN THEIR GROWING PARTY OF
former Rangers. Samdash's companions were Lewin, Berwick—
which he pronounced "Berrick"—and Jurgen. They were all
names on Crowley's list—Rangers who had been dismissed by
orders purporting to come from the King. Samdash, however,
was suspicious and, by dint of some judicious investigation, had
determined that Morgarath was probably behind their
dismissal. The four had banded together and their plan was to
travel to Gorlan Fief and turn outlaw, preying on the couriers
and traders serving Castle Gorlan.

"If nothing else," Berwick said, "we can be an infernal nuisance to Morgarath."

Crowley confirmed their suspicions about Morgarath's hand
in their dismissal. And he offered them a far more effective way
of getting their revenge. When the newcomers heard of his plan
to release Prince Duncan and face Morgarath at the Gorlan
tournament, they were eager to join Crowley's group.

There was one problem, however. Samdash was unwilling to
accept Crowley's leadership. They discussed it long into the
night, without reaching an agreement. A vote would have settled

it—after all, there were six in Crowley's group and four in Samdash's. But Crowley feared that if Samdash lost the vote, he would depart, with his followers.

"After all," Samdash said, after some time, "I've been leading this group for the past four weeks."

"And you led them straight into trouble tonight," said Halt, who had so far refrained from speaking. "You didn't take the time to find out how many men you were stalking. You just rushed in and let Egon get behind you. That's not good leadership. That's the sort of impulsive behavior that gets men killed."

Crowley looked quickly at Samdash, whose face was flushed with anger. He felt it best to say nothing, but to see how the other ex-Ranger reacted. Surprisingly, it was Jurgen who spoke next, and he agreed with Halt.

"The Hibernian's right. You're a good man, Samdash, but you're too impulsive to be a good leader. You're impatient to get things done and that leads to mistakes."

Samdash went to answer, but he was cut off by Lewin. Lewin had only been a Ranger for two years. He was one of the least experienced of the group. But now that the subject was raised, he was ready to add his contribution.

"I agree with Jurgen," he said quietly. "You take too many risks, Samdash. On top of that, Crowley and his men have a real plan to take the fight to Morgarath. We were simply going to be a nuisance to him. I say we stay with them, and accept Crowley as our leader."

Samdash, growing more flushed by the moment, looked to Berwick. Berwick was an older man. His beard was flecked with gray. He was steady and reliable and Samdash valued his advice. Berwick pursed his lips and shrugged. He knew Samdash wasn't going to like what he had to say, but he also believed that he should hear it.

"If it comes to a vote, I'll vote for Crowley," he said. He inclined his head toward the redheaded Ranger. "You've got a good head on your shoulders, young man. And you were trained by a great Ranger." He looked back at his former leader. "Sorry, Samdash, but he's the better choice."

"Well, that settles it, I suppose," Samdash said, throwing his hands wide apart. "Crowley is leader." He wasn't happy about it. His ego was bruised by his friends' rejection. But he realized that if he disagreed and left, he would be on his own. At least, by staying with the group, he would have a chance to strike back at Morgarath, and he wanted that more than anything else.

He leaned over and shook hands with Crowley, accepting his leadership. Crowley looked him in the eyes and judged that he was a man of his word. Samdash didn't like the way things had turned out, but he'd accept Crowley's orders.

"Thank you," Crowley said simply. There was no point in making a speech. It was best just to let matters proceed.

Shortly after, they turned in for the night. Lewin volunteered to take the first watch. Berwick went to fetch their horses, which they had left in a glade five hundred meters away. The two groups of horses greeted each other and then moved quietly to graze close to the camp. The Rangers doused the fire and settled into their blankets. Like the others, the new members of the group had one-man tents. Soon the little campsite was quiet, except for the occasional gentle snore from one of the tents.

They moved on the following morning, riding in two files along the narrow forest track that led to the high road to Redmont. Crowley was pleased to see that their new recruits made a point of splitting up, not forming a clique but mixing with the established members of the group. Round the middle of the morning, he dispatched Jurgen and Berrigan to hunt. The two rode off together, rejoining them a couple of hours later with half a dozen plump mallard ducks.

Halt and Crowley rode together, some ten meters ahead of the others, where they could talk without being overheard.

"I've been wondering, why didn't Cropper alert us earlier last night?"

"He would have if he'd caught their scent. But they came from downwind. By the time he heard them, it was too late."

"Do you think Samdash will be all right?" Halt asked. There was an edge of doubt in his voice. Crowley considered the question for some seconds before answering.

"I think so," he said carefully. "Though he does seem a little arrogant, and his ego took a blow last night."

"More fool him for letting Egon sneak up behind them like that," Halt said.

Crowley nodded slowly before answering. "That was careless. But then again, so was I. I should have posted a sentry to make sure we weren't surprised."

Halt shrugged. "We may have been at fault there—"

Crowley interrupted him. "Not we. I. I was at fault. I'm the leader. I should have known better."

"All right," Halt conceded. "But there's a big difference between being a little careless and planning an attack without proper reconnaissance or preparation. He just barged in without taking the trouble to see how many of us there were."

"Still, I'll need to bear it in mind for the future. But you are right. Samdash does act too hastily. He sees himself as a leader of men but he acts without thinking. And he had no real plan as to what he and his men might do in the future. Mounting nuisance raids against Morgarath's patrols wasn't going to achieve too much."

"The important question is, do you trust him?" Halt asked.

Crowley considered his reply for several seconds. "Yes. I do. When I explained what we had in mind last night, I could see he was impressed. He'd never thought it through that far."

"I'd be surprised if he thought anything through."

"I think you're being too hard on him. If he's given a detailed plan of action, he'll carry it out, I'm sure."

"If you say so," Halt said reluctantly. He respected Crowley's ability to judge character. The young Hibernian tended to make quick judgments based on first impressions and he knew they often turned out to be mistaken as time went by. Crowley, he knew, had a more measured view. That's what made him a better leader than Halt. So if he felt Samdash could be relied upon, Halt was prepared to accept his decision.

They stopped for a quick midday meal of bread and dried meat and fruit, then proceeded onto the high road, where Crowley pushed the pace up to a steady canter. He kept glancing around nervously as they ate up the miles to Castle Redmont. As its name suggested, the high road was built on elevated ground, with extensive views over the surrounding farm and forestland.

"I feel very exposed here," Crowley muttered to Halt. "We can see for miles, but that means we can be seen for miles. And we're becoming a rather noticeable group."

"Maybe we should split into two or three groups," Halt suggested.

Crowley shook his head. "After we're done with Baron Arald," he said. "I think we're relatively safe here in Redmont Fief."

They topped a rise around four o'clock and found themselves looking across a small, shallow valley to Castle Redmont. In the late afternoon light, it glowed a dull red. The party stopped to study the land, spreading themselves out on either side of Halt and Crowley.

"That's magnificent," Halt breathed, looking at the massive red-hued building rearing up above the surrounding countryside.

"It's quite something, isn't it?" Crowley said. He had visited Redmont as an apprentice. "It's built of ironstone. That's why it glows red in the westering sun. It's not as beautiful as Castle Gorlan or Castle Araluen. But I prefer it somehow. It's more . . . businesslike." He rode forward out of the line and turned so that he was facing the others.

"Halt and I will go ahead to talk to the Baron," he said. "And to see if the Ranger Farrel will join us. But there's no sense in letting the world know how many of us there are now. The rest of you head down to those trees"—he indicated a densely growing section of forest at the bottom of the slope—"and make camp there. We'll join you after we've spoke to Arald and Farrel."

There was a mumble of assent from the others. Samdash looked vaguely disappointed. He wanted to go with them into the castle. But he recognized the sense of what Crowley was saying and reluctantly agreed. He also knew he wouldn't have thought of keeping their numbers a secret. He would have barged in with all the others. He pursed his lips thoughtfully. Perhaps he was a little too impulsive, he thought, and, for the first time, he accepted the fact that Crowley was a better, more thoughtful leader than he would have been. But there was something that needed to be said.

"What happens if you're wrong about Arald and he claps you in the dungeon?"

Crowley smiled at him. "It's a good point. After we've made contact, and we see how matters lie, we'll send a signal from the battlements—there, above the main gate."

They all looked at the spot as he pointed to it. "We'll have someone wave a red flag there. So one of you stay up here to keep watch for it while the others make camp. If you don't see it within an hour or two, you'll know we've been captured."

"What should we do then?" Leander asked.

"Two choices," Crowley told him. "Either disband and go home or break into the castle and get us out. I know which choice I'd prefer you to make," he added, with a half smile. "Egon, I'll leave you to work out how that's done."

The others looked at Egon. Crowley had chosen him because he was the oldest and steadiest member of the group. He wouldn't run any silly risks. He nodded back at Crowley.

"I'll wait here for the signal then," Samdash said, determined to have some role to play. "I'll give it an hour after you've gone through the castle gate."

"Better make it an hour and a half," Crowley told him. "These days, there's a lot of searching and questioning going on at castles like Redmont. We could be left cooling our heels for some time."

Samdash nodded. "An hour and a half then," he agreed. "I'll time it from the moment you enter the gate."

"Very well." Crowley looked round the line of grim faces once more to see if everyone understood their role. Then he twitched the reins and faced Cropper toward the slope leading down into the valley. "Come on, Halt," he said.

As Halt urged Abelard forward to join him, Crowley turned

back in his saddle. "No fire," he said. "Let's not let the world know where we are. Make sure the camp is well hidden."

Cropper would find them, he knew. The others wheeled their horses and began to ride single file down the other side of the hill toward the trees. Only Samdash remained behind. He slipped from his saddle and led his horse to a small copse of trees, where he would be concealed by the shadows. There was a patch of sunlight and he selected a straight branch from the deadfalls lying around. He drove it upright into the ground, noting where its shadow lay. Then he made a mark at a point that he knew the shadow would reach in a little over an hour. Making sure he had a clear view of the castle and his improvised shadow clock, he settled down to wait.

Crowley and Halt rode down the gentle slope. The castle was set at the top of a hill, dominating the landscape, but in the foreground, they could make out the roofs of buildings that marked a village. Several thin spires of smoke rose from among them. Cook fires, Halt thought.

"That's the village of Wensley," Crowley told him, and he nodded. "And there's the Tarbus River, running between the village and the castle."

They could see the river twisting and turning, glinting silver gray in the late afternoon sun. There was a timber bridge across it and Halt could see that the center section was removable. If the village came under attack, the people could retreat to the safety of the castle, removing the center section of the bridge as they went to impede the progress of any pursuers.

"Looks like a good defensive site," he said.

"Redmont is one of the three great castles of the Kingdom.

Castle Gorlan and Castle Araluen itself are the other two," Crowley said.

They rode in silence down the main street of the village and from there to the bridge. Their horses' hooves clopped loudly on the planks. Halt noticed the sound changed to a hollow note as they rode across the removable section. Obviously, it was made from lighter timber than the rest of the structure.

From the bridge, the hill became steeper as they rode up to the castle. Unlike other castles Halt had seen, Redmont was a three-sided structure, with a tall keep in the center, inside the triangular walls, and towers at each of the three corners.

"Three walls?" he commented to Crowley.

"They needed less ironstone that way. It's not a common material. But it's virtually indestructible. You could shoot away with siege weapons all day here and barely make a mark on the walls."

The walls loomed above them as they drew closer. The road led to a huge drawbridge, set across the moat and currently lowered, with a heavy portcullis on the far side, in the gateway to the castle.

Two spearmen in half armor were on guard at the near end of the drawbridge. They stepped into the middle of the road to bar Halt's and Crowley's passage as the two horsemen drew closer. Crowley had re-donned his camouflage cloak for this encounter and now he produced his silver oakleaf insignia from under it, holding it up for the sentries to see.

"King's Ranger," he said, his voice full of authority. "I'm here on official business to see the Baron."

25

THEY WERE KEPT WAITING IN THE ANTEROOM OUTSIDE THE Baron's office for some twenty minutes. Crowley kept glancing at a water clock on the mantelshelf as the liquid slowly dripped away and the level lowered. Halt realized his friend was worrying about Samdash, sitting on the hill waiting for their signal that all was well.

Finally, Arald's secretary emerged from the inner room and beckoned them in.

"The Baron will see you now," he said.

The office was a large room, with a huge fireplace to one side and a low table surrounded by four comfortable-looking chairs on the other. In the middle, facing a window that looked out over the parkland, was Arald's massive desk—an oak table set on four thick legs, with his high-backed chair behind it and three straight-backed wooden chairs in front.

The Baron was writing as they entered. He looked up and waved his quill toward the chairs. "Sit down," he said. His tone was curt and decidedly unwelcoming.

Halt and Crowley exchanged a worried glance and took their seats.

Arald was a burly, broad-shouldered man and Halt guessed he was in his mid-twenties. He was handsome and clean-shaven, and looked to be well muscled—although it appeared that he might have a problem controlling his weight. He had a hint of a double chin and his tunic seemed to strain across his middle. There was a large bowl of sweets on the desk close to his left hand and he absentmindedly popped one into his mouth and chewed on it. A long sword in a red leather scabbard, chased with silver, lay sideways across the table, its two-handed hilt within easy reach of his right hand.

Arald glared at them for some moments before speaking. "I suppose you're two more of those useless fops Morgarath keeps sending to replace my Ranger," he said harshly. Then he frowned slightly. "Although I have to admit, you don't look like the others."

"The others?" Crowley asked.

Arald continued. "He's sent two so far—spineless couch lizards they were too. The first one came with a letter over the King's seal, accusing Farrel of attacking and robbing a party of traders on the border between Gorlan and Redmont, and dismissing him from the Ranger Corps. I sent that one packing back to Morgarath."

"You didn't believe the accusation?" Halt asked.

Arald glanced at him curiously, noticing the Hibernian accent. "No, I didn't—since Farrel was traveling with me at the time he was supposed to have committed the offense. I sent back a letter to that effect but the only reaction was another of those soft-handed idiots turned up, repeating the accusation and bearing a commission to take over as Ranger of Redmont Fief. Sent him packing too."

He paused, eyeing them suspiciously. "But if you came from Morgarath, you already know this."

Crowley cleared his throat, then said deliberately, "We didn't come from Morgarath." He hesitated, looking to Halt, not sure whether he should reveal their hand. The Hibernian nodded and Crowley continued. "In fact, we think he means to usurp the throne. We plan to accuse him of doing that at the annual tournament at Gorlan."

Arald had been leaning forward to talk to them. Now he sat back in surprise, studying the two faces before him. He saw a grim resolve in each and he inclined his head thoughtfully. "I was going to bring the charges against Farrel before the Council of Barons at the tournament to have them dropped. Sounds like you're preparing to do a whole lot more. Who's we and how do you plan to do it?"

"We are a group of former Rangers—all of us dismissed by Morgarath, who claimed to act on the King's behalf. We plan to enlist the aid of Prince Duncan and get him to issue us with a royal warrant in lieu of the King."

Arald made a dismissive gesture. "Duncan won't be any use," he said bitterly. "Last I heard, he was stirring up trouble on the northern border and doing his best to break our treaty with the Scotti."

"That's not Duncan," Halt said. "That's an impostor working under Morgarath's orders. We've seen him. The real Duncan is being held prisoner in Castle Wildriver. We believe that's how Morgarath is keeping the King under control."

Arald let out a low whistle of surprise. "Is he now?" he said. "How do you know all this?"

Halt and Crowley exchanged a glance, then Halt answered.

"We intercepted a messenger from Morgarath to the master of Castle Wildriver. He was carrying dispatches that detailed how Duncan was to be held prisoner until after the tournament. They also mentioned the fake Duncan and how he's working to discredit the prince."

Arald studied the two young men with a new level of regard. "You two have been doing your homework, haven't you? Do you still have those messages?"

Crestfallen, Crowley shook his head. "We resealed them and left them with the messenger. He was unconscious and never knew we had read them. We thought it best if Morgarath didn't know they'd been intercepted."

Arald absentmindedly popped another sweet into his mouth and chewed for a few seconds, thinking.

"Hmmm. Yes. You were probably right to do that. No sense in forewarning him. Pity, however. They would have been concrete proof of his scheming."

He reached for a small silver bell on the desk and pealed it several times. Almost immediately, the door opened and his secretary's face appeared around it.

"Yes, my lord?"

"Martin, ask Mistress DuLacy to join us here, would you? And send someone to fetch Farrel as well."

"Yes, my lord." Martin disappeared around the door's edge.

Halt was vaguely reminded of a jack in the box. Then he remembered something. He leaned toward Crowley and whispered, "Samdash."

Crowley raised a finger, acknowledging the reminder. "My lord," he said to Arald, "one of our men is watching the castle. If we don't signal that all is well, it'll trigger a rescue attempt from the rest of our men. We said we'd wave a red flag from the battlements near the gate."

"I'll attend to it," Arald said. At that moment there was a knock and Martin reappeared.

"Mistress DuLacy and the Ranger are both on their way, my lord," he said.

Arald nodded and, as Martin was about to disappear round the door again, he held up a hand to stop him. "Martin, go out onto the battlements over the drawbridge and wave something red, would you?"

Martin frowned. "Something red, my lord?"

Arald waved impatiently. "Yes. Yes. A flag. Or a tablecloth. Or your underpants. Anything so long as it's red. Otherwise we'll have a gang of Rangers breaking in on us."

Martin's expression made it clear that he had no idea what Arald was talking about. It was also clear that this wasn't unusual. "As you say, my lord."

Arald turned back to Crowley and Halt with a smile that seemed to say he enjoyed confusing his secretary. Then he went back to business.

"So what exactly did you have in mind?" he asked.

"We plan to rescue Duncan from Castle Wildriver," Crowley said, "and have him confront Morgarath at the tournament. We also think it would be a good idea to kidnap the impostor—the false Duncan—and have him confess."

Arald's eyebrows went up. "Ambitious," he said. "And exactly how many of you are there?"

"There will be twelve," Crowley told him. "All of us Rangers who have been unfairly dismissed."

"You plan to confront Morgarath and accuse him, with just twelve men?"

"Twelve Rangers," Halt corrected him.

Arald turned to eye the dour Hibernian for a few seconds. "Point taken," he said. "Still, twelve men, even if they are Rangers . . ." He let the sentence hang in the air, but Crowley was quick to reply.

"We had hoped to have your support, my lord. We'd heard you weren't fond of Morgarath."

Arald smiled, but it was a grim smile, and not at all humorous. "Not fond of him hardly sums it up. I believe he's a liar and a traitor. And I think you're right. He's trying to take over the throne. Unfortunately, a significant number of the barons admire him and look up to him."

"We'd heard that you also command a lot of respect among the barons, my lord," Crowley interjected.

Arald reacted with a diffident shrug. "Possibly," he said. "And if I could bring Morgarath before the Council of Barons with proof of what he's been doing—"

At that moment, there was a light tap on the door and he didn't finish the sentence. He glanced across at the door. "Come in," he called.

The door opened and Halt's heart turned over as he found himself looking at the most beautiful woman he had ever seen. She was tall and slender and graceful. He estimated that she would stand half a head taller than he. She wore a simple and elegant white gown, with the silver laurel branch brooch of her Diplomatic Service insignia on the right shoulder. Her hair was long and ash blond, falling below her shoulders, and her face was exquisite. Her eyes were blue and had a half-amused look to them, as if she watched the world about her and enjoyed what she saw. She looked now at the two strangers sitting with the Baron.

Halt rose to his feet instantly, knocking his chair over backward, sending it clattering on the bare floorboards of the office. Hastily, he bent to retrieve it and his cowl fell forward over his eyes, so that he was groping blindly for the chair. Finally, he composed himself, shoved the cowl back and righted his chair. Crowley had also risen to his feet, but not in the same precipitate rush as Halt. Halt faced the new arrival, who viewed him with an amused look. She held out her hand.

"I'm Pauline DuLacy," she said. He seized her hand, realized he had done so with excessive zeal and released her. He essayed a half bow but only managed to look as if he were studying her feet.

"Halt," he finally managed to croak.

She inclined her head gracefully. "Halt?" she said. "But I wasn't doing anything. Why should I halt?"

Halt opened his mouth, closed it, opened it again and searched for words.

Fortunately, Crowley found them for him.

"Halt is his name, Mistress DuLacy," he said.

Pauline DuLacy raised an eyebrow in poor Halt's direction. "Indeed?" she said.

"He's Hibernian," Crowley said, as if that explained everything.

"Ah," said Pauline DuLacy, as if it did.

Crowley reached out a hand for hers and, when she took it, he bowed over her hand, touching it lightly to his lips. "And my name is Crowley, Mistress. Delighted to make your acquaintance."

"How very gallant, Master Crowley," she said. She glanced back at Halt, who was still watching her, red-faced and with his mouth slightly open, cursing himself for a clumsy, stumbling social dolt.

"Crowley is a former Ranger," Arald explained. "Another one of those dismissed by Morgarath."

Pauline turned back to Crowley with a look of understanding. Then she glanced at Halt once more. "And Master Halt—are you a Ranger as well?"

Again, Halt sought for words, and again, Crowley rescued him—although Halt wished, with a stab of jealousy at Crowley's ease, that he hadn't.

"Halt is as good as a Ranger, my lady. He was trained by Pritchard."

"Was he now?" Arald interrupted. He looked at Halt with a new level of respect.

So did the beautiful Mistress DuLacy, Halt noted, and felt his tongue well and truly tied in a knot once more.

"Pauline is a senior Courier," Arald explained, although her clothes made the explanation unnecessary. "She's the head of the Diplomatic Service here in Redmont." He allowed that to sink in, then said, "Pauline, these Rangers think Morgarath is planning to take over the throne."

The woman looked at him, then at the two cloaked figures before him. "I couldn't agree more, my lord," she said.

"And they want to stop him," Arald continued.

Pauline now smiled at them with a new warmth. Halt's heart lurched.

"I think that's an excellent idea," she said.

26

"TELL US WHAT YOU FOUND AT CASTLE GORLAN, PAULINE," Arald said. Then, turning to the Rangers in explanation, he added, "Pauline went undercover to the castle a week ago, disguised as a traveling noblewoman."

"A rather ditzy one, it must be said," she added, smiling. "I find men tend to feel no threat from a twittering blonde—and because they're not on their guard, you can learn a lot from them."

Both Halt and Crowley regarded her with new admiration. It would take a lot of courage to penetrate Morgarath's lair in disguise. Pauline and the Baron seemed to think there was nothing special about it.

"It was obvious that someone important was being kept prisoner in the castle—in the top floor of the eastern tower. I didn't see who it was, but I saw food being taken in, and servants came and went. And the tower is heavily guarded. I'd say that indicates a high-ranking prisoner. But a prisoner, nonetheless. I assume it's the King but I have no definite proof."

"Of course, Morgarath maintains that he's protecting the King after that failed assassination attempt," Crowley said. "That would explain the high level of security."

Pauline nodded. "That's true. It's a clever ploy. And I believe Duncan was the one behind the attempt on the King's life."

Halt shook his head. "No!" he said abruptly and, as Pauline turned her dazzling smile on him, he found he was once more lost for words. "I, er . . . I mean . . . well, that is . . . ," he stumbled. Once more, Crowley came to the rescue, and once more, Halt glared at him.

"We've discovered that Prince Duncan is also being held prisoner by Morgarath," Crowley said.

Pauline's eyebrows registered her surprise. "At Gorlan? I saw no sign of him."

But Crowley shook his head. "At Castle Wildriver. There's an impostor moving through the north, leading raids across the border, throwing his weight around in border villages and generally destroying Duncan's reputation."

"Halt and Crowley plan to rescue Duncan, capture the impostor and confront Morgarath with them both at the tournament," Arald explained.

Pauline inclined her head slightly to study the two cloaked men. "That's taking on quite a lot."

Halt went to speak, found he couldn't and cleared his throat instead.

Crowley glanced at him with amused surprise, then replied. "We have help, mistress. There will be twelve of us, I hope, all former Rangers. And we're hoping for support from those barons who are loyal to the King and who are willing to side with Baron Arald."

"With so many of the barons present at the tournament, along with their retainers and knights, Morgarath will hardly be ready to use force," the Baron said. "Of course, he'll have all his knights and men-at-arms present—it's his home ground, after all. But I doubt he'll be confident enough to try to do anything by force of arms. He'll have no confirmed idea yet as to how many of the others will stand by him—particularly if Duncan appears unexpectedly on the scene."

Pauline nodded and steepled her fingers together, thinking over what Arald had said. "Yes. I agree. He'll avoid direct confrontation as long as he can. It's not his style. He prefers subterfuge and deception wherever possible."

"What I need you to do, Pauline, is find out how many of the barons will be prepared to take our side," Arald said. "Send out your agents. Use your contacts. Get on the road yourself. I hope that the majority of the barons will be loyal to the King and to Duncan, but I want an idea of who won't be."

"It's a lot to do in the time we have left," Pauline said.

The Baron nodded. "I understand. Do what you can. Any information you can get will be valuable."

"Invaluable," Crowley amended, and she smiled at him. Once again, Halt felt a surge of anger at his friend.

There was a tap at the door and Arald looked toward it. "Come in," he said.

The door opened to admit a broad-shouldered man in a Ranger cloak. He carried a bow and there was a quiver slung around his back. On his belt, a heavy battleax was thrust through an iron ring, opposite the double scabbard that all Rangers wore. He wasn't the typical Ranger, Halt thought. He was taller and more heavily built than most. Perhaps that explained his predilection for the battleax.

Arald smiled a welcome. "Ah, Farrel. Come on in. Here are two of your confreres." He indicated Halt and Crowley and the newcomer eyed them critically.

Crowley held out his hand in greeting. "Crowley," he said.

Farrel took his hand, nodding recognition. "I remember you," he said. Then he jerked his head toward Halt. "Don't know him."

"He's Halt, and he's from Hibernia. Old Pritchard trained him in Ranger skills. He's not officially a Ranger yet, but he's already annoyed Morgarath considerably."

Farrel's face registered interest at that. "Is that so? What did he do?"

"Well, for a start, he fought off half a dozen of Morgarath's men who were attacking me," Crowley said.

Farrel nodded approval. "That's a good start."

Halt shrugged. "That was after Morgarath had the hide to offer me a job," he said.

"What did you say to that?" Arald put in.

Halt turned to him to answer. "I told him where he could put it," he said, then instantly flushed as he remembered Pauline was in the room. He turned to her. "My pardon, Mistress DuLacy. I didn't—"

She waved his apology aside. She was already laughing. "I imagine that angered him more than beating up his soldiers," she said.

Halt nodded. "I think you're right."

Farrel had been regarding the newcomers and his eyes narrowed in thought. "Are you the two who are going round recruiting Rangers who've been dismissed?"

Crowley nodded. "That's right. There are ten of us now. Eleven if you'll join us."

"Count on it," Farrel said. He glanced at Arald for confirmation and the Baron nodded.

"And twelve once we speak to Truscott, from Eisel Fief," Halt added.

But Farrel shook his head. "Truscott is dead," he said sadly. "He resisted the attempt to have him discredited and dismissed. He was found murdered in his bed."

Crowley's shoulders slumped in disappointment. "A pity," he said. "He was a good man."

"He was a very good man," Farrel agreed.

Then Crowley squared his shoulders once more. "Still, eleven Rangers is a good start."

Farrel nodded. "Or, in Morgarath's case, we might be a good finish."

27

AT ARALD'S INVITATION, THEY FETCHED THE OTHER MEMBERS of their party and dined in the castle that night. The Baron's chef was a smooth-faced young man named Chubb.

"He's an artist in the kitchen," the Baron averred, patting his own belly. "Gives me a lot of trouble keeping the weight down."

It was apparent that Chubb had the same problem. Obviously, he spent a lot of time sampling his own wares. The other Rangers all chorused their approval of the magnificent feast he set out before them. The central piece was a splendid turkey pie, with golden-brown, glazed pastry concealing a savory mix of turkey mince, spices and vegetables.

The Baron's wife, a beautiful red-haired woman introduced as Lady Sandra—"Never mind the lady, just call me Sandra," she said—joined them for the meal. She was a charming and gracious host and the Rangers were all captivated by her. Farrel was present as well, and was introduced to his new comrades. Most of them knew him already, of course, if not personally, then by reputation. Farrel was known as a fierce, highly skilled warrior, an adept with the battleax in addition to his Ranger training, and they all felt they were lucky to have him along as part of their band.

When he first arrived, Halt scanned the dining room for a sight of Mistress Pauline. But the beautiful Courier was nowhere to be seen.

Arald saw Halt's quick look around the room, and the flash of disappointment, almost instantly masked, and guessed the reason. "Pauline is getting ready for her mission," he explained quietly to the young Hibernian. "She'll be sending out letters to her agents and informants and planning her own itinerary."

"Of course." Halt nodded, showing no sign of his disappointment. He had hoped to make a better showing in front of the beautiful, graceful woman. He felt he had left her with the impression that he was a bumbling, tongue-tied clod. Now, he thought gloomily, she would retain that picture of him.

For once he would have liked to talk about his past, and impress her with the fact that he was the son of the royal family of Clonmel, and an heir to the throne. That would have dazzled her, he thought. Then, sadly, he realized that it wouldn't have impressed her in the slightest. A woman like Pauline would judge a man on his own merits, not his parents. He realized that Jurgen was asking Arald a question and turned to listen.

"Will you be defending your title at the tournament, my lord?" Jurgen asked.

Arald ate a large chunk of pie and wiped his greasy fingers on his bright yellow doublet. His wife raised her eyes to heaven. For five years, she had been trying to break him of that habit.

"I suppose so," he said, spraying pastry crumbs across the table. "Have to give Morgarath a chance to win it back, won't I?"

Halt regarded him with interest. Arald was a little overweight, as he had noticed. But he was also burly and broad shouldered, and there were muscles underneath that doublet.

"You defeated Morgarath in single combat?" he asked. He knew that Morgarath was regarded as one of the most accomplished knights, if not the most accomplished, in Araluen. But this smiling, good-humored, slightly chubby young baron had defeated him.

Arald shrugged diffidently. "Good luck more than skill," he said. "I got lucky and he tended to underestimate me. Never a good idea to underestimate an opponent, even if he's me." He laughed aloud.

Halt glanced around and saw Lady Sandra watching her husband shrewdly. She didn't join in the laughter and, from her expression, Halt guessed that Arald was making light of his own abilities. In his experience, people who attributed their success to luck often had a lot to do with making their own luck.

The dinner broke up around ten o'clock. Crowley apologized to the Baron for the early finish to the night. "We want to be on the road just after dawn, my lord," he said.

Arald nodded his understanding. "I've never known a Ranger to sleep in much past sunrise."

The others all chorused their thanks as they trooped out of the dining room—making much of the fact that Chubb's banquet was a welcome change after Halt's and Crowley's rough camp cooking—although in truth, they all enjoyed the meals that their two comrades served up each night.

"I'll see you at Gorlan on the third day of next month," Arald told Halt and Crowley as they bade him good night. He gripped both their hands firmly and looked deep into their eyes. Theirs was a dangerous undertaking, but he saw no sign that either of them would flinch from it.

Chubb hurried up to them as they were about to go, with a white cloth bundled around a large section of turkey pie. "It'll be fine to eat cold on the road for your lunch tomorrow," he said and they took it gratefully.

Arald watched the two men descend the stairs, their soft boots making virtually no sound on the flagstones. Then, as they went through the high doorway and out into the castle yard, he returned to the dining hall, where he had a flagon of good wine to finish and where Sandra was waiting for him.

"They're a good group of men," she said and he glanced keenly at her. He respected her opinion in such matters—always had, he realized.

"You think so?"

She nodded. "Well trained. Loyal. Expert archers. Eleven men like that will make a group to be reckoned with."

"They are Rangers, after all," he said. "Real Rangers, not like the pretenders that Morgarath has been palming off on fiefs for the past few years. I'm particularly impressed with their leaders—Crowley and Halt," he added.

Sandra took a sip of her wine. "Crowley is their leader, isn't he?"

Arald acknowledged the statement. "He's been elected as their leader. But the others look up to Halt just as much as to him. They'll obey Crowley. But Halt is the sort of man you follow instinctively."

"Even you?" She smiled, but he took the question seriously.

"Yes, given the right circumstances, I'd follow him. He's a natural leader."

The door flew open and Pauline DuLacy rushed into the room, slightly flushed and a little out of breath after running up two flights of stairs. She looked quickly around the dining room, saw the empty chairs pushed back from the table and the servants clearing away the remains of the meal, and her face fell.

"They're gone?" she asked.

"A few minutes ago," Arald told her.

She looked around, as if wondering whether there might be time to catch up to them, then realized that she hadn't seen them crossing the castle yard as she ran toward the keep. They'd be well ahead of her on the way to their camp in the forest, she thought.

"Oh . . . I wanted to say good-bye to Halt," she said, then added quickly, "and to Crowley as well, of course. Halt and Crowley."

The Baron and his lady exchanged a knowing look. So that's the way the wind blows, thought Arald. Over the years, he'd seen at least a dozen bold young knights try to impress the beautiful Courier. She had politely fended them all off. But now this bearded, beetle-browed Hibernian seemed to have sparked her interest. He wondered if he should mention the fact that Halt had been looking for her, then decided that, if he did so, his wife might hit him with the wooden serving ladle that lay close to her right hand.

"Of course," he said, hiding his smile. He noted with relief that Sandra moved her hand away from the heavy ladle. "But we'll see them all at the tournament." She nodded, a little distractedly, he thought.

"Yes. Of course," she said. "Well, I'd best get back to my office. I still have a few orders to send out with tomorrow's post."

She gave a perfunctory curtsy and exited, closing the door behind her rather abruptly, so the room echoed with the noise of it.

"Well, well," Sandra said. "Pauline and the Hibernian. Who would ever have thought?"

Arald smiled. "I saw it coming," he said smugly, patting his stomach with both hands in a contented way.

His wife looked at him, eyebrows raised in disbelief. "Of course you did, dear," she said.

He wondered when she had become so sarcastic.

Half an hour after daybreak, the Rangers were on the road again. This time, as Halt had suggested, they broke into three groups, leaving a gap of ten minutes between them, to avoid raising the curiosity of anyone who saw them.

Halt and Crowley rode together at the head of the first group. After some minutes of companionable silence, Crowley glanced sideways at his friend and said in an overly casual tone:

"That Mistress DuLacy is quite a woman."

Halt looked quickly at him and grunted something that Crowley took to be agreement.

Hiding his grin with some difficulty, the red-haired man continued, in the same overly casual voice. "I thought that when this is all over, I might call upon her." He stared straight ahead, but when Halt said nothing, he stole a glance at his friend.

Halt wore a stricken expression. The thought of his friend Crowley—witty, urbane and totally at ease with women—paying court to the stunning young Courier was too much for him to bear. Had it been any other man, he might have offered to fight him. But Crowley was a friend—more than a friend, in truth. Halt had come to think of him as a brother. In fact, he held him in a higher regard than his real brother, who had tried to murder him to gain access to the throne.

"Good thinking," he managed to croak. "Wish you both well."

Crowley looked at him again, startled by the break in his voice. Halt wore a miserable expression that tore at Crowley's heart. He leaned over and seized Halt's forearm.

"My friend," he said sincerely, "I was joking! That's all."

Halt shook his head doggedly. "No. Really. Why would I care if you . . . saw her," he said, his voice thick with emotion.

Crowley shook his arm. "Do you think I'd do that? I can see how much she means to you, Halt. And I rather think," he added thoughtfully, "that she returns the feelings."

Halt looked at him quickly, suspicious that Crowley, ever the trickster, was joking now. But Crowley met his gaze steadily, and nodded.

"Did she . . . say anything about me?" Halt asked. His spirits fell when Crowley shook his head. Then rose again with his answer.

"No. Not in so many words. But it was pretty obvious that she was interested in you. Didn't you see the way she looked at you when you told Arald about Morgarath offering you a job?"

Halt shook his head. "No. I didn't notice." All he could remember was that he had inadvertently used a rather crude expression in front of her. He flushed now as he thought of it.

"Well, take my word for it," Crowley said, "she was pretty impressed. And amused. And that's always a good thing with women."

Halt rode on, facing forward, his mind racing.

"And trust me," said Crowley, who had kissed two women in his entire life—and one of them his mother—"I *know* about women."

Halt felt a warm glow suffuse his breast at his friend's words. "Yes," he said happily. "I should think you do."

The conversation about Pauline was interrupted as they rounded a bend in the road. Crowley reined in Cropper, Halt matching the action with Abelard.

"Does that person look familiar?" Crowley asked.

Halt leaned forward to peer more intently at a figure sitting on the side of the road, leaning back against a tree. He was wearing a cloak like theirs, but with the cowl pushed back to reveal his white hair and beard. A gray horse was cropping the long roadside grass a few meters away from him. It wasn't tethered or hobbled, which marked it as a Ranger-trained horse.

There was something very familiar about the seated figure. For a moment, they stared at him. Then recognition dawned. "Pritchard!" they both said at once and, clapping their heels to their horses' flanks, set off at a gallop to greet him.

28

THEY RACED PELL-MELL ALONG THE ROAD TO WHERE THE figure sat, calmly waiting and watching them. Reining in in a cloud of dust, Halt and Crowley flung themselves down from their saddles and rushed toward him. Slowly, he came to his feet to greet them. A smile lurked around the corners of his mouth but outwardly he appeared solemn.

"Pritchard? Is it really you?" Crowley shouted joyfully. He threw his arms around the white-haired, white-bearded man and lifted him from his feet as he hugged him. Halt stood ready nearby, waiting for his chance to hug his old mentor.

"Yes. It's me," he said calmly. "And if you're not careful, it'll be me with half a dozen broken ribs."

"Sorry!" said Crowley, instantly releasing him so that he dropped awkwardly back to the ground. Then, just as instantly, Crowley seized him in another great bear hug. Pritchard looked over his shoulder at Halt, meeting his eyes with a bemused gaze and pointing at his former pupil with both hands.

Halt stepped forward and tapped Crowley's shoulder. "Crowley, let go of him. Now!" he ordered.

Crowley released his second bear hug of the day and stepped

back, beaming delightedly. As soon as he relinquished his hold on Pritchard, Halt stepped in and threw his arms around the old Ranger in his turn. Then, as Pritchard emitted a grunt of surprise and pain, he instantly released him.

"What are you doing here?" Halt asked. He heard the shuffle of horses' hooves behind them as the rest of the group caught up and stared at them with obvious interest. Halt heard the name Pritchard whispered among the others, in varying tones of surprise.

Pritchard made a pretense of examining his ribs and arms for possible damage from the exuberant greetings of his two former students, then he smiled at them, looking from one to the other with obvious pride in what he saw.

"I kept hearing rumors about two madcap youngsters who were recruiting former Rangers with an eye to confronting Morgarath," he said. "Apparently, one of them is a grumpy Hibernian and the other is a redheaded prankster. Imagine my surprise when I heard it was you two."

The Rangers sitting their horses behind the group of three men all laughed.

"So I decided I'd better come and see if you needed a hand," Pritchard finished.

Crowley shook his head in amazement. "But you were in Hibernia! How did you get word there?"

Pritchard tapped a forefinger against the side of his nose in a knowing gesture. "Oh, I have my sources of information still. Not much goes on in Araluen that I don't hear about."

Berrigan gave vent to a meaningful cough, which seemed to conceal the word rubbish inside it.

Pritchard looked up at him with a smile. "Oh, and of course,

I received a pigeon mail from Berrigan a week or so ago, telling me what you're up to."

Halt and Crowley both swung round to look at the occasional jongleur.

He shrugged. "Didn't I tell you we keep in touch from time to time?" he asked, indicating Pritchard with a nod of his head.

"No. Egon said he did. But I don't recall your mentioning it," Crowley replied.

Berrigan thought for a second or two, then said, "Pritchard and I keep in touch from time to time."

"Highly amusing," Crowley said, giving Berrigan a withering look. Berrigan managed to survive without being too withered.

Unable to keep his delight in check, Crowley turned back to Pritchard, the huge grin returning to his face. "So now you're here! Will you join us?"

"Of course," Pritchard replied and the other Rangers indicated their pleasure at the news. Pritchard was a renowned figure in the Ranger Corps. His dismissal from the Corps and departure from the Kingdom some years prior had been a source of great distress among his peers.

"Then you'll assume command?" Crowley said, indicating the line of horsemen facing them. It was typical of his friend, Halt thought, that he had no hesitation in offering the command to Pritchard, no regret at handing over his position of authority. But Pritchard was shaking his head.

"The men elected you," he pointed out.

Crowley dismissed that with a wave of his arm. "Then they can unelect me and elect you in my place!"

Pritchard, however, continued to shake his head. "No. You're the commander and you'll do a good job as commander. I know that because I trained you." He glanced at Halt, who had been watching the proceedings with an interested look. "And young Halt here will make an excellent second in command for you." He smiled again. "I trained him too, after all."

"But . . ." Crowley was momentarily lost for words. His confusion showed on his face. Before he could proceed, Pritchard spoke again.

"I'm too old for the job, Crowley. This is going to be a hard battle. Morgarath is not going to relinquish his power too easily. Command of this group is a young man's job. It needs a young man's energy and determination. I'd probably fall asleep halfway through a battle," he added, jokingly.

"You're not old!" Crowley scoffed. "You're still fit as a fiddle and I wager you still ride and shoot as well as you used to."

"Well, yes. My accuracy is still pretty good. But I have to admit, at the end of a hard day's riding, I tend to groan and grunt when I climb down from the saddle. I ache in places I never knew existed. I am old, Crowley." He fingered his short white beard with his forefinger and thumb. "My hair and beard aren't white because I got caught out in the snow."

"But . . ." Crowley still wouldn't concede the point. He turned to Halt. "You tell him," he said.

But the Hibernian shook his head thoughtfully. "I think he's right."

Crowley was scandalized. "How can you say that? He taught you all the skills of being a Ranger!"

Halt nodded. "He did. And he taught me to recognize the truth when I hear it."

Pritchard smiled at his former pupil. "Well said, Halt. I can see I trained you well." He could tell that Crowley was still prepared to argue the point, so he cut him off. "Besides, Crowley, I can be of more value to you in another capacity."

Crowley put one hand on his hip and stood straight, his body language challenging the older man. "Oh, really? And how's that?"

"This white hair and beard, along with the aching, creaking joints, make me appear less threatening to the enemy. It'll be easier for me to infiltrate Castle Gorlan and find where they're keeping the King. People don't take notice of an old, white-haired, bent-over man."

Halt scratched his beard. "How did you know Morgarath has the King prisoner?" he asked.

Pritchard regarded him evenly. "I told you, I have my sources," he replied. "And Berrigan may have mentioned it," he added, before Berrigan could utter another of those meaningful coughs.

"You're not bent over." Crowley tried one more sally. But Pritchard merely stooped in front of him, holding one hand to the small of his back and groaning. It was a perfect picture of an old, harmless man. The assembled Rangers couldn't keep themselves from laughing. Even Crowley cracked a smile.

"Well . . . maybe you're right . . ."

"I am right," Pritchard said, and finally, Crowley conceded. He held out a hand.

"Very well. I'll stay as leader and you can be our geriatric secret agent, and break into Castle Gorlan to see what's what."

"Of course, I may need someone to push me in a wheelchair when I do break in," Pritchard said with a smile. Then he became serious. "But we're wasting daylight. We could still put a few kilometers behind us before we stop for lunch and share out that turkey pie."

Once again, Crowley regarded his former teacher with surprise. "How did you know about the turkey pie?" he asked.

For the second time, Pritchard tapped his forefinger along the side of his nose. "I told you. I have my sources."

They rode on for another hour and a half before Crowley called a stop for the midday meal. There wasn't a lot of talk as they ate. Even served cold, chef Chubb's turkey pie was still a masterpiece, and it was quickly reduced to a small pile of pastry crumbs, many of them finding their way onto the Rangers' jerkin fronts.

Leander sighed happily as he wiped his slightly greasy fingers on the hem of his cloak. "Morgarath would have done better kidnapping Arald's cook rather than the King," he said, and several of the others agreed with him.

Farrel glanced up at him. "Chubb was one of the reasons I nearly didn't join you," he said.

Reluctantly, they rose to their feet, draining the last of their coffee and brushing crumbs off their shirtfronts. Some, like Leander, used their cloaks as napkins.

The horses responded to their riders' whistles and calls and trotted into the clearing where the group had stopped to eat. They all spent a few minutes tightening saddle girths, then prepared to mount.

"Should we break up into three groups again?" Egon asked.

Crowley considered the question, then shook his head. "We're close to the border of Gorlan Fief now, so I think we're better off staying together. But we'll put out scouts. Halt, you take the point. Stay about half a kilometer ahead of us and keep your eyes peeled for patrols. Farrel, you take the rearguard position. Keep the same distance and make sure nobody comes up behind us without your seeing them."

The two Rangers nodded and swung into their respective saddles. Pritchard had watched the exchange, noting Crowley's decisive response to Egon's question. He nodded his head quietly. Crowley had the makings of a good leader, he thought. Halt mounted his horse and trotted out to the road, heading northwest. Crowley waited several minutes, then signaled for the others to mount and follow him. Farrel mounted but kept his horse reined in. He'd let the main party get ahead of him for five minutes or so, then take up his position as rearguard.

They held that position for the rest of the afternoon. On two occasions, Halt sighted small parties of soldiers ahead of them and halted the column until they were out of sight. There was no sign of anyone following them. Farrel had a relatively easy afternoon.

That night, as they sat around the campfire after dinner—a meal in which several of them bemoaned the lack of turkey pie—Crowley called for their attention. They gathered round as he spread a map of the Kingdom out on the ground before him.

"We need to start getting our plan together," he said. "First order of business is to find out where the false Duncan is operating. We'll set up a base camp here . . ." He indicated a spot some kilometers northwest of Castle Gorlan with the tip of his throwing knife. "Then we'll all fan out north and northwest to the border and locate him."

"Shouldn't be too hard if he's continued raiding," Halt said grimly.

Crowley looked at him. "True. He certainly doesn't try to hide his light under a bushel. Once we know where he is, the rest of you will go after him and secure him. Farrel, you'll be in command."

The heavily built Ranger from Redmont nodded. His eyes were scouring the map, as if he might see some sign of the counterfeit prince there. Unconsciously, his hand touched the head of the battleax by his side.

"In the meantime, Halt and I will make our way to Castle Wildriver and get Duncan away from his captors."

"Just two of you?" Egon queried.

Crowley nodded. "We won't be using force. We'll be using stealth. So two will be plenty. On the other hand, the rest of you will be facing an armed company of soldiers. You may have to fight your way out with the phony Duncan, so you'll need the numbers."

"Makes sense," Egon agreed.

"The important thing will be timing," Crowley said, looking round the small group to drive home the point. "If we act too early, word may well get to Morgarath that Duncan is on the loose and his copycat Duncan has been taken. We need to take both men no earlier than two days before the tournament is due to begin."

There was a mumble of agreement and understanding from the Rangers.

"In addition, I want you, Jurgen, and you, Berwick, to cover our back trails once we've got Duncan free and the others have captured Tiller. Intercept any messengers coming through from Castle Wildriver or from wherever this character Tiller might be."

"Tiller?" Pritchard put in.

Crowley turned to him. "That's the name of the false Duncan,"

he said, and couldn't resist adding, "I'm surprised your sources"—
he mimicked Pritchard's tapping his nose—"hadn't told you that."

Pritchard grunted, but said nothing.

Crowley waited several seconds, to see if there were any questions. Then he clapped his hands together in a gesture of finality.
"Right, let's get some sleep. It'll be an early start tomorrow."

"It's an early start every day," Samdash said and several of the
Rangers smiled.

Crowley rolled the map up and stood, dusting the dirt from
his trousers. "Who has the first watch?"

"That'd be me," said Lewin.

Crowley looked around the group. "Who's second?"

"That'd be you," Lewin told him, with a hint of good-natured
malice.

"Oh . . . good," Crowley said. He'd been hoping for a night of
uninterrupted sleep.

"I'll take it," Halt said. "You've got a lot of thinking to do, and
I know how that exhausts you."

Crowley smiled beatifically at his friend. "Normally I might
take umbrage at that remark," he said. "But the prospect of six
hours' uninterrupted sleep makes up for a lot of umbrage."

29

"I FOUND HIM," BERWICK SAID AS HE DISMOUNTED STIFFLY. IT was late afternoon. He'd been riding all day and his muscles ached.

Crowley and Halt rose from their seats by the fire and walked toward him. Halt took the reins to Berwick's horse and began to unsaddle the animal, prior to rubbing him down. The horse had been traveling hard. He was streaked with foam and his head hung low.

Berwick smiled tiredly. "Thanks," he said. He would have tended to his own horse, but he was glad to relinquish the task to Halt. He stretched, rolling his shoulders to work the kinks out of his back muscles and groaning in pleasure as he did.

Crowley waited patiently until he had eased the cramps and stiffness. "Where is he?"

Berwick jerked a thumb toward the northeast. "In a village called Haller's Rill, a few kilometers this side of the border."

They had been scouring the countryside along the border for the past three days. Crowley had led them north to a spot where they could set up a semi-permanent camp. Then he assigned a search area to each man and sent them off find to Tiller and his band. He and Halt had remained in the camp to coordinate the search, and to await word of the impostor's whereabouts. Half of the Rangers were still out searching. The others had returned with no current news. Samdash and Berrigan had brought word of where Tiller had been in the past two weeks, but he had already moved on from both locations. Berwick was the first to bring a positive location.

"Haller's Rill?" Egon asked, joining them as Berwick sank gratefully to the ground beside the fire. "What kind of name is that?"

Crowley poured Berwick a cup from the ever-present cof-feepot and Berwick took a deep draft.

"A rill is a small run of water," Crowley said. "Like a stream but smaller. A spring, really."

"Why not call it Haller's Spring then?" Egon wanted to know.

Crowley shrugged. "I guess they thought Rill sounded pret-tier—more poetic."

Egon sniffed disdainfully and Crowley turned back to Ber-wick. The other Rangers in camp had moved quietly to join them, forming a semicircle around the fireplace where Berwick sat, reclining against a large log.

"How many men does he have?" Crowley asked.

"I counted twenty," Berwick said. "Three mounted warriors and seventeen foot soldiers."

"Then you'll be outnumbered," Crowley said, glancing at Farrel. The ax-wielding Ranger would lead the party to capture Tiller. He pushed out his bottom lip in an expression of unconcern.

"Not after the first volley," he said succinctly, and Crowley nodded. Nine Rangers, all expert marksmen, would quickly lower the odds. He and Halt would not be there, of course, and Pritchard had already left them to infiltrate Castle Gorlan, disguised as an old beggar. "The longer I'm there," Pritchard had said, "the less notice they'll take of me when the day comes."

"How do you plan to take Tiller?" Halt called, from where he was rubbing down Berwick's horse. The horse nudged him reproachfully as he stopped rubbing and he quickly started again.

"I think subtlety will be the key," Farrel replied. "After we've shot a volley or two, I'll point out that his force has been seriously degraded and invite him to come with us. If he refuses, I'll hit him with my ax."

"You have a strange idea of subtlety," Crowley said, hiding a grin.

Farrel regarded him, deadpan. "I plan to use the flat of my blade. Not the edge."

Crowley nodded. "That's subtle, in its way," he said. "Once you've got him, you can disarm and scatter the others. I doubt they'll go back to tell Morgarath what's happened."

"Just to make sure, you can point out that he doesn't like hearing bad news. He usually kills the bearers," Halt put in.

Farrel acknowledged the point. "He does have that reputation."

Crowley glanced at the sun, where it was hovering over the trees that ringed their campsite. "The others should be back tonight, or tomorrow morning at the latest. Once we've briefed them, you lot can set off for Haller's Rill. I'll leave the exact plan to you, Farrel."

He knew that Farrel or, indeed, any of the other Rangers, would be capable of producing an effective plan of action once they reached Haller's Rill. There was no need for Crowley to tell them their business and, besides, they'd have the advantage of seeing the terrain and the situation in which they'd be working.

Berwick yawned. "Well, if we're heading out tomorrow, I'll take the opportunity to get some rest." He rose from his seat by the fire with a low groan and headed for his small tent. He glanced at his horse and saw that she was rubbed, and brushed and was grinding contentedly away at a small bag full of corn and oats.

"Thanks again, Halt," he said. He resisted the urge to check more closely on his horse. The bearded Hibernian would have done a good job looking after her, he knew, and if he checked, he risked insulting his comrade.

Halt nodded and Berwick crawled into his tent, sighing happily as he rolled himself in his blankets and stretched out on the bed of soft leaves and branches. Dimly, he heard Halt and Crowley discussing the coming day. It seemed they were talking from a long way away.

"We'd better get moving tomorrow as well," Halt said. "Time we got a look at this Castle Wildriver."

"Any ideas how we might get Duncan out?" Crowley asked.

"I thought you could go in after him while I surround the castle," Halt said.

Crowley suppressed a smile. "Sounds like a good plan," he said.

Then Berwick fell asleep and heard no more.

"So that's Castle Wildriver," Halt said.

They were crouched on a high bluff opposite the castle—a position that was as high as the castle itself and barely fifty meters away. From their position, they could look down upon a small terrace outside what looked like a set of rooms. A sheer drop fell from the terrace to the rocks lining the racing water some twenty meters below.

The castle was set on an elongated island that separated the fast-flowing river into two halves that rushed around it. The island and the castle were barely thirty meters from the bank below them. The bluff they were on sloped away from the river, adding another twenty meters to the distance that separated them from the castle.

The narrowness of the channel on their side gave a false sense of accessibility to the castle. At first glance, it appeared that it would be easy to slip across the twenty-meter gap. But the very narrowness of the channel added to the difficulty of the approach. The river was already a fast-running body of water. Where the island split it, the water accelerated considerably. The water running through the twenty-meter gap surged wildly, building up in a smooth hump at the top of the channel where it was first constricted, then racing in a wild maelstrom between the bank and the island. The bank itself was a narrow, rock-strewn path barely two meters wide, soaked by the constant spray the river threw up. There was no footing on which a bridge might be built, and any attempt to swim the channel would result in the swimmer being dragged under by the current and swept far downstream.

"So, how do you plan to get across?" Crowley asked Halt.

The Hibernian looked sidelong at him. "I thought I was surrounding the castle while you went in?"

Crowley shook his head gravely. "Now that I see it, I've decided to change our job assignments. You go in and I'll keep watch."

Halt opened his mouth to reply but Crowley laid a hand on his arm to silence him, leaning forward eagerly to scan the terrace opposite them. The door to the inside room had opened and a figure emerged onto the terrace. He was tall and broad shouldered, and moved with the grace of a natural athlete. The lower half of his face was covered by a blond beard but he seemed young, perhaps in his early twenties. He wore a red surcoat over woolen trousers, tucked into knee-high tan leather boots. He walked to the battlements and, placing both hands on the wall, leaned slightly over to study the roaring river far below.

"It's Duncan," Crowley breathed.

As they watched, two armed men emerged from the door and moved quickly to stand beside the prince, as if worried that he might be contemplating hurling himself over the battlements to the rocks and river below. One of them put a restraining hand on the prince's arm and tugged him back from the wall. Duncan looked up at him angrily and shrugged the hand aside. He spoke to the man but the roar of fast-running water in the gorge below drowned his words.

The guard gestured toward the door and Duncan reluctantly went back inside, pausing in the doorway for one final look at the freedom outside his prison. The two guards followed him and shut the door behind them. Faintly, the watchers heard the dull clunk as it closed.

"So now we know we're in the right place," Halt said.

Crowley nodded eagerly. "All you have to do is get across the river, scale that wall and bring him back with you."

Halt turned to him, one eyebrow raised. "All I have to do?" he said. "If it's as easy as that, perhaps you should take care of it after all."

But Crowley was shaking his head before he finished. "Out of the question. I can't swim."

"I've seen you swim," Halt replied, but Crowley was untroubled by the statement. He pointed to the raging water thundering through the gap.

"I mean I can't swim in that," he said.

"Nobody could swim in that," Halt pointed out.

Crowley nodded. "There you are. And besides, I have no head for heights. If I tried to scale that wall, I'd fall for sure."

"It's a sheer wall," said Halt, who had been studying it. "I'm not sure anyone could scale it."

"You'll find a way. I have confidence in you."

"I'm touched," said Halt.

Crowley considered the statement. "You'd have to be, to consider climbing that wall."

Halt glowered at him. "You're no great help," he said.

Crowley spread his hands in a gesture of humility. "True. But I know you'll find a way."

This time, Halt chose not to reply. He was staring across the gorge to the small terrace, and the door that led to Duncan's quarters.

"I'm sure I will," he muttered, although right then, he had no idea how he might go about it.

30

THERE WERE STILL FIVE DAYS BEFORE THE TOURNAMENT WAS
set to begin. Halt and Crowley had three days to wait before
they could make the rescue attempt. Between them, they had
come up with a plan of action. Crowley sat now, working on an
arrow he had taken from his quiver.

He was binding two small iron rings to the shaft, just behind
the warhead, pulling the rawhide thong tight, then fastening it
with a quick series of half hitches. He tested the firmness of the
binding, saw that the rings were securely held in place, and nodded. The rawhide thong was wet, having been soaked in water
for some time before he tied it in place. As it dried out, it would
shrink and the binding would become even more secure.

Halt took the finished product from his hands and turned it
round, inspecting it keenly. The rings were set either side of the
shaft, at right angles to the razor-sharp warhead.

"Two rings?" he asked, although he thought he knew the
answer.

"For balance," Crowley said. "We only need one, but that
would throw off the balance of the shaft and make it more difficult to hit the mark."

Halt inclined his head. "I could hit it with an hour's practice," he said. "And this adds twice the weight."

"The extra weight won't be significant. You're only shooting over a range of thirty meters or so. Might as well keep the shaft balanced as much as we can."

"I suppose so." Halt watched as Crowley took two more rings and a second length of saturated rawhide and began to make another identical arrow. The redhead sensed his gaze and looked up.

"Just making a couple of spares. Inconceivable as it might seem, you could miss."

Halt grunted. "Remember, you'll also be shooting one from the top of the bluff to the terrace. Better make three or four spares."

Crowley ignored him. As he worked, his companion began to study the coils of rope they had brought with them. Even without seeing the castle, they had known that they would have to cross the river and scale the walls—and those tasks would require plenty of rope. They'd purchased two large coils, and an equal amount of light twine, in a village they had passed on the way to Castle Wildriver. The iron rings came from a smithy in the same village and they had also bought an extra saddle horse—a long-legged young gelding with strength and speed in his lines. Duncan would need a good horse when they escaped. Once they reached the tournament grounds, Arald would supply him with a trained battlehorse.

Crowley grunted slightly as he heaved the second rawhide thong as tight as he could, then quickly knotted it. He tested the firmness of the knots, then set the arrow aside so that the rawhide could dry.

"Once they're dry, we should try a few shots to get used to the different weight," he said.

Halt nodded, then reached for the coffeepot standing to one side of their small fireplace. "Just time for a mug of coffee in the meanwhile."

Crowley was already beginning to work on a third arrow. "Good idea," he said. Then he frowned as a thought struck him. "Have you noticed that Leander puts milk in his coffee?"

Halt grunted. "The man's a savage."

Crowley raised an eyebrow. "This from the man who laces his coffee with honey?"

"Honey is natural," Halt told him. "Milk is little short of an abomination."

For the next three days, they observed the castle, paying particular attention to the lack of sentries. What few guards there were tended to remain in the shelter of their guardhouses, well back from the parapet. Every hour or so, they would make a brief patrol around the walls, occasionally glancing down into the gorge beneath them, where the river thundered through the gap.

"They're complacent," Halt observed critically.

"The castle hasn't been attacked in the past twenty years," Crowley replied. "I suppose they think the river forms enough of a barrier. It would take hours to get an assault party across it. And then they'd be facing a sheer granite wall. Still, it's all the better for us."

On the fourth day, immediately after one of the infrequent patrols, they moved down to the riverbank to a spot opposite the base of the castle. The roaring water shot past them, only a few meters away. Spray hung in the air and Halt kept his bow under his cloak, to prevent the bowstring becoming soaked and useless.

Idly, he twirled one of the specially prepared arrows between the fingers of his right hand. Crowley had done a good job. The arrow felt a little head-heavy compared with a normal shaft, but its balance was true and it turned evenly in his fingers. He looked up at the battlements, towering high above them. There was no sign of any guards keeping watch. They're overconfident, he thought. Crowley had told him that it had been years since there had been any assault on the castle. Apparently, the inhabitants felt the raging water was sufficient protection. Only a madman would consider crossing it.

"Like me," he muttered to himself.

Crowley touched Halt's arm and pointed across to the far bank. "There," he said. "The tree stump."

At some time in the past, a massive tree had been cut down, close by the base of the castle wall. Possibly the castle's defenders thought it posed a threat, providing a way for attackers to climb the wall and gain access to one of the lower windows or turrets. They had sawn through the tree on an angle, so that when it fell, it would drop away from the castle and into the stream. Now, only a stump just over a meter tall remained, with its angled top facing them—a pale oval of dense hardwood.

Halt nodded, eyeing the smooth face of the stump, gauging the shot. The distance was less than thirty meters, but he knew the arrow would drop faster than a normal arrow.

"Get the line ready," he told Crowley, as he uncovered his bow and nocked the arrow to the string.

Crowley took a length of light line from under his cloak and ran its end through one of the iron rings behind the arrow's broadhead. The broadhead itself was heavy iron and razor-sharp, designed to punch easily through an enemy's shield and chain mail.

He moved to one side, wrapping one end of the line around his wrist and letting the rest of it lie on the riverbank in smooth coils, ready to run out when the arrow was under way. There were a few twigs on the riverbank and he carefully removed them, making sure nothing would snag or impede the line. There was at least sixty meters of line in the coiled rope, enough to bridge the river twice. The end was fastened to a small sapling behind them.

"Keep the line clear," Halt said, his eyes still fixed on the target as he saw, in his mind, the path of the arrow and its trailing length of line.

Crowley checked one more time. "It's clear," he said. "Just make sure you don't tread on it with your big, clumsy feet."

"Clumsy yourself," Halt muttered. But he checked carefully as he set his feet in a balanced stance, making doubly sure the line was nowhere near them. He began to draw the bow back to its full draw. The string and wood creaked loudly under the eighty-five-pound strain but his face showed no sign of the massive effort it took.

Crowley moved to stand a little ahead of him, holding the line clear.

"Stop jumping around," Halt told him.

Crowley decided it was better not to make a sarcastic reply, but to let his friend concentrate on the shot. It wasn't a difficult shot by any means, but Halt's life would be depending on it.

"I won't move," he said calmly. Halt snorted, then drew in a deep breath, sighted, exhaled half the breath and released.

The arrow flashed across the river, dead on line for the tree stump, the arc of the twine following behind it as it unwound smoothly out of the coils on the ground between them.

The arrow slammed into the tree stump, three centimeters from the center, and buried the barbed iron head deep into the hardwood.

"You missed," Crowley said.

Halt glanced at him, unsmiling. "There's a crack in the center of the stump. I aimed to miss it." He set his bow to one side and reached for the coil of heavier rope that they had brought with them. Quickly, he tied it to the end of the light line that now stretched in a double loop across the river, and tested the knot.

"Haul it in," he told Crowley.

The redheaded Ranger began hauling the light line in, feeling it running smoothly through the greased iron ring on the arrow. Before long, the heavier line began to jerk out across the river in pursuit of the lighter line. Halt held the second rope as high as possible, maintaining a light tension on it to keep it clear of the racing water.

As the heavier line reached the ring, there was a moment of resistance as the knot joining the two lines jammed slightly. Crowley gave it a little slack, then tried again. This time, the knot ran through smoothly, and the thicker rope began its return journey across the river, pulled along by the light twine.

Once they had the end back on their side of the bank, they secured the double line to a solid tree trunk behind them and tugged on the rope to test that the arrowhead was firmly set. There was no sensation of movement or looseness. Crowley surveyed the rope, sagging in an arc so that it was a meter above the river's surface.

"I think you're good to go," he said.

He helped Halt into a harness they had fashioned from a few meters of rope. It had loops for his arms and ran round his chest, fastening at the front. He took the loose end and formed a loop over the rope spanning the river, tying it off with several half hitches. He tested the knots for security and stepped back, satisfied.

"Are you sure I'll need this?" Halt asked doubtfully.

"You'll need it. If you let go of the rope, you'll be swept five hundred meters downstream before you can draw breath— although breathing might be a problem in itself. You'd be hard pressed to keep your head above water in that current," Crowley told him.

"I wasn't planning on letting go of the rope," Halt said.

Crowley raised an eyebrow but said nothing. Halt stepped toward the river's edge, treading carefully on the wet, uneven rocks. Crowley steadied him as he stepped into the water at the edge of the bank. He was wearing only his shirt and trousers, and had left his boots on the riverbank.

Halt cursed as the water rose to his knees.

"What is it?" Crowley asked, instantly concerned.

"It's cold," Halt told him.

Crowley shook his head in relief. "Of course it's cold. It's fed by snowmelt. That's why I wanted you to do this part."

Halt glared at him and stepped farther into the river. The bottom shelved steeply and with one more step he was chest deep. He gasped as the cold water rose round his body, then he pushed off into the stream.

Instantly, he was engulfed by the racing, ice-cold water. His feet were swept from under him. He gasped again, then the violent current forced him under and his hands let go of the rope. With the gasp, he released most of the air in his lungs and found himself twisting violently underwater, held by the harness around his chest, and with no air. He had been turned onto his back and he reached wildly behind him for the rope. But his reach was restricted by his position and his hands grasped uselessly at the water. He was blinded by the wild rush of the water against his eyes and he felt his lungs bursting as he tried desperately to get his head above water for air. Water forced its way up his nostrils and he coughed once, unable to prevent the reflex action. Immediately, he swallowed more water. He thought he heard Crowley call out but he couldn't make out the words. In any case, he couldn't answer his friend. The urge to take a breath was becoming unbearable, even though he knew he was underwater and any such action would spell the end for him.

After all the dangers he had faced in his young life, he thought this was a particularly useless way to die—twisting and turning on the end of a rope in a river, like a hooked trout. In spite of himself, he allowed a little water to force its way into his mouth, instantly coughed and gagged and swallowed more water. His chest was bursting with the need for air. He knew he couldn't last much longer. Then he managed to twist onto his side and his flailing left hand touched something.

It was the rope! He twisted his hand so that he wrapped a loop of the rope round his wrist and heaved himself back against the force of the current. He tried to open his eyes but the battering water kept them closed. Then his searching right hand closed over the rough texture of the rope and he gripped it fiercely. With both hands on the rope, he had better purchase and he hauled himself forward and up against the current. He felt his head break clear of the water and took in a huge, shuddering breath, feeling the burning pain in his chest abate.

He slid his right hand farther along the rope, loosened the loop around his left wrist and began to haul himself toward the far bank a meter at a time. His head was constantly submerged and he learned to breathe quickly in the brief moments during each pull when he was above the surface.

Doggedly, he continued to drag himself through and under the water, amazed by the sheer force of the current as it buffeted his trailing body. He knew that if he lost his grip on the rope again, he would never regain it. He wouldn't have the strength. Once, he thought he felt the rope move slightly, as if the arrowhead holding it had loosened. His heart rose into his mouth at the thought of being cast adrift in this pummeling, freezing water. But the arrow held and he continued his slow, breathless progress.

Working blindly, he crabbed his way into an eddy behind a large rock on the far side. The current suddenly lessened and his legs, for the past desperate five minutes stretched out horizontally by the force of the river, sank slowly down again until his bare feet touched the rocky bottom.

He heaved himself out of the river on his stomach, sprawling on the rocks of the riverbank, too exhausted to move.

After several minutes, retching and gasping, he rolled over onto one elbow and looked back to where Crowley was watching anxiously. He waved one hand to signify he was all right, then let it drop wearily. He needed more time to recover from the wild passage across the river.

Correctly interpreting the signal, Crowley waved in encouragement, then pointed to the top of the bluff. Halt nodded, exaggerating the movement so that Crowley could see it clearly.

Crowley waved once more, then set off for the slope leading upward to the bluff. He would shoot a line across the chasm from there, so that Halt could climb the castle wall.

Halt, sprawled on the wet rocks, feeling the spray soaking over him, watched him go.

"Take your time," he muttered.

31

HALLER'S RILL WAS A TYPICAL SMALL VILLAGE, APART from its namesake. The rill, a small spring that fed a narrow stream, was located at the far end of the village, in a common grazing ground where villagers could run their pigs and sheep and cattle. A swiveling derrick was built on the bank, supporting a large wooden bucket over the stream. Obviously, the villagers would fill their household containers with fresh water from this source, although most houses also had large water butts standing under their eaves, where they would catch rainwater.

The main street was empty, even though it was late morning. There was no sign of the usual bustle of movement that might be expected in a prosperous little village like this.

"People are staying indoors," Berwick remarked. He and Farrel were concealed in a small copse of trees ten meters before the beginning of the high street. From here, the road sloped down into the village, where it leveled out once more. The other Rangers were camped fifty meters back in the trees, well out of sight. Berwick and Farrel had come ahead to survey the village and plan their next moves.

"Can't say I blame them if Tiller and his gang of thugs are still here," Farrel replied.

"Sounds as if they are," Berwick remarked. They could hear raised voices emanating from the inn, even though it was some seventy meters away. "When I saw them last, they'd taken over the inn for their own use."

Farrel glanced at him. "They sleep in there, do they?"

Berwick nodded. "Tiller and his three senior men do. The others bunk down in the barn next door."

Farrel rubbed his chin reflectively. "And from the row they're kicking up now, I imagine they sleep pretty soundly. That might be our chance to take him prisoner—wait till they're asleep and capture him then."

Berwick grinned at him. "I thought you were planning to go in and bash him with your ax."

Farrel grunted. "That's plan B. We'll go to that if he annoys me."

They settled down for the next few hours to watch the inn. The sounds of singing and shouting and, occasionally, fighting continued through the afternoon, but there was no sign of Tiller. Once, one of his men lurched out of the door of the inn and relieved himself in the middle of the road.

"Charming," said Farrel as the man clumsily refastened his breeches and staggered back inside the inn.

"But encouraging, in the light of what we've got planned," Berwick replied. "If he's typical, they'll sleep the sleep of the dead tonight."

"Let's hope so," Farrel said.

After another half hour, Farrel rose cautiously to a half crouch, staying below the level of the underbrush around them. "I'll go and bring the others up," he said. "Keep an eye on things here."

Berwick nodded assent and Farrel ghosted back through the trees, moving smoothly from one piece of cover to the next so that his progress was barely discernible. Berwick glanced back to watch him once. For a big man, he thought, Farrel moved with remarkable grace and stealth. Then he shrugged. It wasn't really so remarkable. Farrel was a Ranger, after all, and stealth and silence were a Ranger's stocks in trade.

Stealthy as he might be, Farrel's approach to the Rangers' temporary camp didn't go unnoticed. He had slipped past a large fallen log, covered in secondary growth and vines, when a low voice stopped him.

"Welcome back."

He spun round, searching for the source of the voice. Then his eyes settled on a figure lying beside the fallen log, among the vines and bushes. The only reason he saw him, he realized, was that the hidden Ranger moved a hand in greeting.

"Just letting you know that your approach has been noted," said Norris, smiling.

Farrel shook his head admiringly. The other Ranger was no more than five meters away, yet he had gone entirely unnoticed. "I remember you now," he said. "You were always good at staying unseen."

Norris stood and moved forward to join him. "I'll admit I've practiced it a lot," he said. "What's happening at the village?"

Farrel gestured toward the campsite, visible through the trees twenty meters away. "Come on in and I'll brief everyone. Tiller's there, so far as we can tell, and he and his men are doing a lot of nonstop drinking."

"Good," said Norris, falling into step beside him.

The other Rangers looked up as Farrel and Norris entered

the small clearing where they had pitched their tents. They gathered round and Farrel quickly brought them up to date on events in the village, and their plan to abduct Tiller that night.

Samdash frowned as he heard this. "You're planning to go barging in there without any idea of the layout?" he asked doubtfully.

Farrel acknowledged the point. "Not completely. Berwick and I will go in there this evening and ask for rooms. If my guess is right, Tiller will send us packing. But at least we'll get a look at the downstairs part of the inn. Then later, we'll just have to play it by ear. I imagine Tiller will have taken the best room—which in most inns is the one facing the street. We'll try that first. If he's not there, we'll look in the other rooms until we find him."

"They'll have sentries out at night, surely?" Lewin said.

Farrel nodded. "Almost certainly. We'll take care of them. They'll probably still be half drunk anyway. Then we'll find Tiller, knock him out and carry him downstairs, where the rest of you will be waiting."

"I take it we'll be there to discourage any possible pursuit?" Lewin said.

"Exactly," Farrel said. "We'll try to do it quietly so there's no alarm raised. But if it all goes pear-shaped, I figure half a dozen archers can do a good job of discouraging anyone who might be following us."

He looked around the circle of faces. There were a few nods, and no sign that anyone had an alternative to offer. It was a simple plan, but they had all learned over the years that simple was best.

"Pack up the camp here," he said, sweeping an arm around the circle of tents. "We'll move up to the edge of the village while it's still light. That way, you can get a look at the place—and keep on eye on Berwick and me when we go to the inn."

As one, they turned away to begin breaking camp, striking their small tents, then folding them ready to tie behind their saddles. There had been no fire, so there was little else to do. One by one, they moved to where the horses were waiting in a larger clearing some distance away.

Satisfied that things were in hand, Farrel nodded to Norris. "Bring them forward when they're ready," he said. Then he headed back through the trees again.

Farrel and Berwick, minus their longbows and distinctive Ranger cloaks, walked down the middle of the high street, making no attempt to conceal their approach to the inn. There were no sentries visible, but that wasn't to say that there weren't watchers at the inn's windows. They both carried stout oak staffs and Farrel had left his ax behind at the edge of the village. They wore plain brown woolen cloaks. Each of them wore his saxe, with the second, smaller scabbard containing his throwing knife concealed under his jerkin. The double scabbards, like the mottled cloaks, were unique to Rangers.

The other Rangers, split into two groups, moved stealthily down the back roads on either side of the high street, stopping some thirty meters short of the inn and standing ready to lend a hand if their two companions found themselves in trouble. Unlike the two walking down the main street, they all carried their longbows and each man had a full quiver slung over his shoulder.

Farrel strode up to the inn door and pushed it open, stepping inside with Berwick a pace behind him.

The small room was crowded with armed men, drinking and talking noisily. The usual bar ran along one wall—a heavy plank set on wooden kegs. More kegs were held in racks behind the bar, lying on their sides. At least half of them, Berwick saw, were already tapped, with spigots set in the bungholes. Spilled ale and wine puddled on the floor in front of them, and on the bar and tables where drinkers sat. The innkeeper, a harried-looking man with receding hair, and his two equally harried serving girls, were kept busy filling and refilling tankards for their guests.

"And who the devil might you be?" demanded a rough voice from a table close to the fire.

32

By the time Crowley was in position, Halt had recovered his breath and was ready for the next phase of the operation. He could see Crowley moving around at the top of the bluff. He moved along the steeply sloping bank until he was opposite his friend's position.

Checking that Halt was ready on the bank below him, Crowley nocked another of the line-carrying arrows to his bow and threaded the light line through the ring behind the arrowhead. He fastened the free end to a branch behind him, and laid the rest of the line out in carefully arranged coils.

There was a heavy wood table on the castle terrace opposite and slightly below him, with chairs set around it. He had marked it out as a target several days ago. If it had been moved in the meanwhile, he would have targeted the wooden frame of the doorway leading to the tower rooms, but he preferred to avoid the noise of the arrow hitting the doorjamb. Any solid piece of wood would do as a target. This arrowhead didn't have to support anybody's weight. He simply needed a firm anchor point for it on the terrace.

Standing, he checked one more time that the line was ready

to run freely, then he drew the arrow back, sighted quickly and smoothly, and released.

The arrow, trailing the light line behind it like a smoke trail, flashed across the gorge and slammed into one of the solid legs of the table. As before, he attached a heavier line to the free end and began to pull in on the guideline. A few meters past the point where the two ropes joined, a solid branch, a meter and a half long, was attached to the heavy rope as a crosspiece. Crowley pulled in the light line carefully, and watched the heavier rope beginning to snake out over the chasm, the piece of wood sitting at right angles to the line.

He maneuvered the rope carefully, flicking it in a long loop, and taking a few paces to the side until the branch was positioned over one of the crenellations on the wall, then he slowly released the tension so that it sank into the gap. As soon as it was in position, he pulled gently on the heavy line until the branch was wedged across the gap in the battlements, firmly anchored in position. He tugged on the line more forcefully to make sure the branch was set solidly, and nodded with satisfaction.

He glanced down to the far bank at the foot of the castle wall and saw the pale oval of Halt's upturned face as the Hibernian watched him. He signaled that all was well, then looped the heavy line round a sapling to keep tension on it and keep the branch firmly wedged in the gap in the battlements.

Checking once more that Halt was ready, he tied a large rock to the free end of the rope and moved to the edge of the bluff. He swung the weighted end of the rope several times, allowing it to gather momentum, then released it, sending it curving out and down over the gorge to where Halt was waiting to receive it.

The rock bounced on the bank a few meters from where Halt

stood and he scrambled forward to secure it before it could slide off into the river. He seized it firmly and took up the slack, then signaled to Crowley to release it from the far side of the river. Crowley unhitched the rope from the sapling and let it fall as Halt quickly hauled in the slack.

This was the crucial point. As the tension came off the rope, the branch wedged between the battlements fell loose onto the flagstones of the terrace. Then Halt carefully began to take up the slack once more. He felt the branch riding up the stone wall, then it checked as it wedged in the crenellation again. Halt tugged on it to test that it was firmly set. Feeling the resistance on the line, he tugged harder, letting his feet come off the ground to test it with his full weight. No point in getting halfway up and having it come loose, he thought.

But the rope held firmly and he moved close to the wall, took a bight around his upper body, then seized it firmly in both hands and heaved himself up, setting his feet against the rough stone wall so that his upper body hung back, at a steep angle from the wall—almost perpendicular to it.

With the aid of the rope, it was a simple matter to scale the wall. The roughly cut blocks of stone gave his bare feet plenty of purchase and he walked up the wall, heaving in on the rope with each step. The thick branch held firm and supported his weight easily, and he made rapid progress upward.

On the bluff opposite, Crowley watched his friend moving smoothly up the castle's side, looking like a giant spider as he ascended. He divided his attention between Halt and the door leading into the tower room where Duncan was held, making sure there was no sign of anyone coming onto the terrace to investigate the thud of the arrow into the table leg or the occasional scraping sound of the branch wedged in the crenellation. But so far, there was no sign of movement.

Halt had reached a point three meters below the terrace where the wall bulged outward slightly to provide defenders with a vantage point from which they could hurl down rocks or other projectiles. He leaned his body even farther back over the abyss and walked himself up over the reverse slope. The going was more difficult and his progress slowed.

Crowley chewed his lip, his eyes flicking from Halt to the doorway into the tower room. "Come on, Halt," he muttered.

But Halt moved slowly and carefully past the obstruction. This was no time to rush and risk slipping. As the wall returned to the vertical, he straightened up and, with a few more carefully placed steps, heaved himself into the gap in the battlements, dropping lightly onto the flagstones of the terrace and releasing the rope so that it hung back down the castle wall to the bank of the river below.

He looked across and up at Crowley and signaled all was well. Then he dusted off his hands and flexed his shoulders—which were aching from the strain of the climb. He gave himself a few moments for his breathing to steady, then moved, soft footed, across the terrace toward the door leading inside, drawing his saxe as he went.

Gently, he tried the handle. It came as no surprise to find that it was locked. Leaning his ear against the rough wood, he listened for a few seconds, hearing muted voices inside.

He turned around to face Crowley once more, and mimed knocking on the door. He saw Crowley nod in assent, then draw an arrow from his quiver and nock it to the bowstring.

Halt raised the saxe and scraped its hilt across the wood of the door. The voices inside fell silent. He repeated the action, scraping the hilt on the metal door handle for good measure, making a soft metallic shriek. This time, the voices from within were louder and more easily understood.

"What was that?" a man's voice asked.

Another replied, with considerably less interest. "What?"

"There was a noise—something's at the door."

"Probably a bird," said the disinterested one. Halt waited but conversation had lapsed. He scraped the hilt of his saxe on the door handle again, a little harder this time, so that the squeal of metal on metal was louder and more distinct.

"There it goes again. That's not a bird!" said the first voice.

"Well, go and see what it is," said a third voice, with a distinct note of irritation perceptible.

Halt frowned. Three of them. He half turned back to Crowley and held up three fingers. Then he stepped to one side as he heard a key turn on the other side of the door.

He flattened himself against the wall as the lock clicked and the door began to open. A helmeted head emerged through the doorway, turning to peer from side to side. Unfortunately for its owner, it peered first in the direction opposite to where Halt stood.

He grabbed the man by the scruff of the neck and heaved him out through the door, pivoting on one leg to spin him around and slam him face-first into the stone wall beside the doorway. The soldier let out a strangled grunt. The short sword he had been gripping fell from his fingers and clattered on the flagstones. A few seconds later, the soldier followed it as Halt heaved him backward, then released his grip. The man crashed to the ground, his helmet rolling free, then lay there, groaning.

Halt stooped quickly to retrieve the sword. He felt a rush of movement behind him and threw himself to one side as a second soldier emerged, swinging his sword in a vicious arc that just missed Halt's head. Halt hit the flagstones on his shoulder and rolled clear before the soldier could recover. He came to his feet in one smooth motion, sword in his left hand, saxe in his right, and faced the sentry.

This man had a long sword and he swung it up to deliver a clumsy overhand stroke. Halt blocked it with the two shorter blades locked together, then brought up his right foot and kicked out at his opponent, hitting him in the midriff and sending him staggering, to slam back against the open door.

The soldier cursed him and started forward again, the sword sweeping back for a round-arm cut, when something hissed viciously past Halt's ear and an arrow thudded into the man's chest. The man looked down at it in surprise. His sword arm dropped to his side as he staggered back several paces. Then the weapon dropped from his fingers as he hit the wall beside the door and fell, sprawling against it. His head sagged forward.

Halt leapt over the still body and went through the doorway, dropping the sword and holding his saxe ready.

The third sentry had been resting on a narrow cot by the far wall. He was busy untangling himself from his blankets as Halt burst into the room. He tried to rise to stop the intruder, tangled his feet in the blankets and tripped as he came out of the bed, falling to his knees. He reached desperately for a scabbarded sword leaning against the foot of the cot. Halt swept his saxe around in a short arc, slamming the heavy brass pommel into the side of the sentry's head. The man's eyes glazed, and he collapsed to the floor.

Halt glanced quickly around the room. There was nobody

else visible. There was another door leading to an adjoining room. He noted that there was a key in the lock.

"Prince Duncan!" he shouted.

"Here!"

The voice came from behind the locked door. Quickly, Halt turned the key and threw the door open. He found himself facing a tall man not much older than himself. His blond hair and beard were long and unkempt. He was wearing a red surcoat, with a stooping hawk emblem. The surcoat was wrinkled and grubby. He looked at Halt, who was barefooted, still soaking wet, dressed in only a shirt and trousers and with a gleaming saxe in his hand.

"Who the blazes are you?" he asked, more than a little confused.

"My name's Halt. I'm here to get you out of here," Halt told him. He stripped the two unconscious sentries of their belts and used them to lash their wrists to their ankles, hauling the leather as tight as he could manage. He studied the result critically.

"That should keep them out of mischief," he muttered. Then he gestured for the prince to follow him. "Come on."

Duncan hesitated. "That isn't the way out," he said, but Halt grabbed his arm and dragged him toward the terrace.

"It is now. Get moving," he ordered. He half dragged the reluctant prince out and through the room that led to the terrace. Duncan took in the sprawled figure by the bed, then raised his eyebrows as they emerged into the open and he saw the man slumped by the door, an arrow in his chest.

They raised even farther when he saw the original sentry sprawled on the ground as well. He was moaning weakly.

"Did you do this?" he asked.

Halt shook his head. "I did two of them. He did this one." He gestured to the man by the door, then to the bluff opposite, where Crowley was standing, waving to them. Duncan recognized the mottled cloak and the longbow.

"That's a Ranger," he said, a note of wonder in his voice.

Halt continued dragging him toward the battlements. "So he tells me," he said.

But Duncan was still looking at the distant figure. "I didn't think there were any Rangers left," he said.

Halt reached over the wall and pulled a loop of the rope up toward him.

"There are a few of us," he said. "Now grab this rope and get going down the wall."

Duncan backed away a pace. "It's a long way down," he prevaricated.

Halt raised an eyebrow. "Castles tend to be that way. They build them high. Now get going."

But Duncan had paled at the sight of the drop below them. "I don't have a head for heights," he said. "I don't think I can do it."

Halt sighed in exasperation. "What is it with you Araluens? Are you all afraid of a little fall?" He began hauling the rope up, coiling it over his shoulder as it came.

"It's not the fall that bothers me," said Duncan. "It's the sudden stop at the end."

"Be that as it may, this is the way we're going." Halt had retrieved all the rope now and he quickly tied a loop in the end. "Put your foot in this, hang on tight and I'll lower you down." Then, as an afterthought, he added, "Can you swim?"

"No," said Duncan, as he slipped the loop over one foot and moved to the gap between the battlements.

"Then I hope you can hold your breath," Halt said. He shoved the table up against the wall and belayed the rope around one of its legs. He wrapped the free end round his shoulders, seized onto the rope and leaned back, ready to take the strain. "Away you go."

Gingerly, Duncan lowered himself backward over the drop, holding tight to the rope as Halt began to pay it out. He used his free leg to fend off from the wall as he went. Halt grunted as the prince's weight came onto the rope, but the bight around the table leg gave him a mechanical advantage and he let the rope run out smoothly and slowly.

After several minutes, he felt the line go slack and he moved to the edge of the wall, peering down. Duncan was on the river-bank below, looking up and waving as he saw Halt's face appear over the battlements. His relief at being back on firm ground was evident in his body language.

"You're all smiles now," said Halt as he reset the wooden crosspiece in the crenellation, then lowered himself backward over the edge. "Wait till your backside hits that freezing river."

33

FARREL LOOKED AROUND THE INN TO FIND THE MAN WHO
had spoken. His face was set in a scowl and he wore a red surcoat, smeared with stains and grease. In the center of the surcoat was a crude representation of a red hawk in a white circle.
Farrel, who had met Prince Duncan on several occasions, had
to admit that there was a surface resemblance to the prince. But
it was as if he were looking at an imperfect copy, with the lines
blurred and inexact.

Tiller was holding a flagon of ale in one hand and a joint of
mutton in the other. As Farrel watched, he tore a strip of meat
off the bone with his teeth, set the bone down and absentmindedly wiped his greasy hand on the front of his surcoat. That
explained the stains, Farrel thought. The seated man continued
to survey the two new arrivals as he chewed the tough mutton,
his brows furrowed as he waited for an answer. Eventually, he
lost patience.

"Well?" he demanded. "Who the devil are you, I said."

Farrel nodded his head deferentially and raised a knuckle to
touch his forehead. Berwick mirrored the action.

"We're honest foresters, my lord, looking for work with the

local squire. My name is Farrel Molloy and this is Berwick of Gladstone."

He glanced around the room as he spoke, feigning nervousness but using the opportunity to study the room and its occupants. There were at least a dozen men in the room in addition to the fake Duncan. All of them were armed with an assortment of swords and maces, and they all had heavy war daggers in their belts. Most of them were drinking and several had their heads resting on the table—in one instance in a pool of ale. The room was redolent with the smell of stale ale, cheap wine and too many unwashed bodies. The gaze they turned on Berwick and Farrel was decidedly hostile. This was a group that didn't welcome strangers, Farrel thought.

Tiller snorted scornfully. "I've yet to meet an honest forester. In any case, there'll be no work for you here. Now get out."

Farrel bowed his head in an obsequious movement. "Begging your pardon, my lord, but we've traveled long and hard to get here—"

"Not my problem," Tiller interrupted, but Farrel persisted, head still bowed.

"We thought we could find lodging here in the inn, my lord," he said.

Tiller made an imperious gesture. "The inn is full!" he snapped. "My men and I have all the rooms."

Farrel allowed his glance to slide sideways to the innkeeper, who was watching the byplay with an anxious expression. He shook his head warningly at Farrel.

It was a small movement, but Tiller noticed it. "Don't look at him! I'm telling you the inn is full."

"Yes, sir," Farrel replied, rubbing his hands together nervously. "But perhaps we could bed down in the barn—"

Again, Tiller cut him off. "My men are in the barn. They don't want you in there with them, waiting for a chance to steal their purses!"

"My lord, we're not thieves—" Farrel began.

"You're foresters," Tiller said scornfully. "It's much the same thing."

Farrel tried one more time, looking hesitantly around the crowded taproom. "Perhaps we could bed down here, by the fire, sir?" he suggested. "It's bitter cold of a night in these parts."

"Did you hear me?" Tiller said, his voice rising in anger. There was a petulant ring to it now. He was accustomed to ordering people about, but he had no natural authority. Any authority he had came from fear, and the fact that he had twenty armed men to back him up. "There's no room here. Get out. You're foresters. You can sleep in the forest."

Several of his men chuckled at that sally but he ignored them. His eyes, burning with anger, held Farrel's.

"But, my lord," Farrel whined.

"I said get out. Do you know who I am?" The counterfeit prince stood abruptly, knocking his bench over backward and jabbing a thumb at the hawk crest on his chest.

"I . . . er . . . no, my lord," Farrel admitted.

"I am Prince Duncan of Araluen, son of King Oswald and heir to the throne. And I will not sit here and bandy words with a thieving forester. Now get out!" He turned to four of his men sitting nearby. "Throw them out!" he ordered.

As the soldiers began to rise clumsily to their feet, Farrel and

Berwick turned and beat a hasty retreat from the inn. Behind them, as the door closed, they heard a burst of rough laughter.

The two Rangers, maintaining their charade of fear, half ran back down the high street until they had put a safe distance between them and the inn. Berwick glanced back. There was no sign of any pursuit.

"We're clear," he said softly and they slowed to walking pace.

Farrel glanced down one of the side alleys and caught a brief glimpse of several hooded and cowled figures keeping pace with them.

"Well, he's a charmer, isn't he?" he said.

Berwick shrugged. "Not what I'd call courtly manners," he replied. "Pity a few of them didn't come after us. I would have enjoyed seeing the lads use them for target practice."

But Farrel shook his head. "We could have cut their numbers down, I suppose. But that would have put them on the alert and made our job tougher tonight."

"True," Berwick agreed. "But I hope friend Tiller, heir to throne of Araluen as he is, shows a little resistance tonight. I'd enjoy smacking him in the chops."

Midnight had come and gone. The moon had slid in a low trajectory across the sky before slipping below the western horizon.

Farrel, hunched beside a tree in the small copse, pulled his cloak tighter around his shoulders. The night was chilly, as he'd told Tiller it would be.

"Time to go," he said softly. There was an almost imperceptible rustle of movement from the darkness around him as the assembled Rangers rose to their feet and began to move toward the road leading downhill to Haller's Rill.

Nine dark figures, swathed in their cloaks, emerged from the tree line and flowed down the hill, staying either side of the road and moving through waist-high grass. To an observer, they would have appeared like a small, dark stain spreading across the ground—dim and indistinct and difficult to focus upon. But there was no observer. Tiller and his men, having drunk themselves insensible, were lying snoring in their beds. The two sentries Tiller had detailed sat on a bench, leaning against the wall of the inn, eyes closed, breathing deeply.

As the Rangers reached the first buildings of the village, they slipped quietly into the side alleys between the houses and disappeared from view. Berwick and Farrel made their way along the high street, staying in the shadows under the eaves of the houses. The other seven men moved to the back lanes parallel to the high street and kept pace with them. They stopped several buildings short of the inn and made their way to the high street to rejoin their leader.

They had discussed their tactics earlier, so there was no need for talk now. Farrel made a few peremptory gestures and the seven Rangers spread out in a line, bows ready, cloaks pulled clear of their quivers. They crouched, ready to shoot on a moment's notice. Silently, each of them selected an arrow from his quiver and nocked it ready to the bowstring. Farrel glanced along the line of dark figures. He wouldn't care to come charging out of the inn looking for trouble, he thought. With seven archers of this caliber, trouble would be exactly what Tiller's men would find.

Farrel started across the empty main street. There was no point crouching to avoid being seen. If anyone were watching, he'd be all too visible. Better to move as quickly as possible to get across the open space. Berwick shadowed him and the two of them slid silently across the street, disappearing into the shadows under the eaves of the house next to the tavern. They paused there, listening, every sense alert.

They heard a strange, low-pitched droning sound. The two Rangers exchanged a puzzled glance and moved silently to the end of the house, peering round it to view the entrance to the tavern.

The droning continued, then was broken by a sudden snuffle and coughing sound. As he heard that, Farrel recognized the droning for what it was. He turned to Berwick, put his mouth close to the other man's ear and breathed the word:

"Snoring."

Berwick nodded. He had recognized the sound in the same moment Farrel had. The two men reached inside their cloaks and each produced a short, heavy wooden club. The heads of the clubs were wrapped in rags. They had no wish to split the sentries' skulls—they simply wanted to knock them out.

Silent as a pair of wraiths, they slipped round the end of the house and crossed the narrow alley to the tavern. The two sentries were sprawled on a bench by the front door. Their weapons were on the ground beside them and they leaned in on each other, snoring heavily.

Berwick wrinkled his nose. "Wouldn't care to smell that breath from close to," he murmured. Farrel frowned at him and put a finger to his lips. They stood by the two sleeping men, clubs ready, and hesitated.

Somehow, it seemed unsporting to knock two sleeping men over the head. Berwick looked at Farrel and shrugged uncertainly.

Farrel frowned, then leaned forward and placed his hand on

the nearest man's shoulder, and shook him. "Oy!" he said softly. "Wake up!"

The sentry's eyes flicked open. His mouth hung open as well and he looked up at the two dark figures standing over him. He had no idea where he was or what he was supposed to be doing.

"Wassa matter . . . ," he began.

Farrel, seeing he was awake and so fair game, brought his club down on his head with a muffled thump. The man let out a little groan and slid sideways on the bench, jostling his companion, who opened his eyes in turn, staring owlishly around him.

Farrel made a permissive gesture to Berwick. "Be my guest," he said.

"Who're you?" the sentry said blearily, and with a dull THUD! Berwick laid him out in his turn. He lowered the man off the bench onto the ground, looking up at Farrel.

"Do we need to tie them up?"

Farrel shook his head. "They'll be out for hours. Let's go."

He tried the door handle and wasn't surprised to find it was unlocked. After all, why lock a door when you have two sentries outside it? The hinges creaked softly as he pushed the door inward and they stepped into the darkened taproom.

Berwick took the lead. While Farrel had been pleading with Tiller earlier that day, the second Ranger had used the time to fix the layout of the room in his mind. He pointed to the right-hand corner, beyond the fireplace where remnants of the day's fire still glowed, casting an uncertain half light over the empty room.

"Over there," he said, and led the way to the staircase. The stairs went up eight risers to a landing. Then another eight steps went off to the left. They moved carefully upward, setting their feet on the very edge of the stairs, where there was less movement that might cause the boards to creak.

They took the second set of eight steps in the same manner and found themselves in a low-ceilinged hallway. Berwick glanced around, letting his eyes become accustomed to the gloom. There was a small, dirty window to their right, which let in a little starlight. On either side of the hallway were doors to two bedrooms. And the end of the hall was a third door, to a room that seemed as though it took up the entire width of the upper story. That would be the main bedroom and that's where they expected to find Tiller.

The air was full of the rasping sound of half a dozen men snoring. Occasionally someone coughed, then resumed the snoring again. As they listened, someone let go a long and resounding fart.

"Delightful people," murmured Berwick.

They soft-footed down the hall and paused outside the door, listening. From inside came the sound of one man snoring. They exchanged a look, nodded to each other, and Berwick eased the door open for Farrel to slip inside.

The window was uncurtained, and even without a moon, there was enough ambient light for Farrel to make out the tall form of Tiller spread-eagled on the bed. He was wearing a nightshirt. His surcoat and trousers were tossed over the end of the bed. His boots were lying on the floor where he had discarded them. Although the two Rangers moved noiselessly, something must have penetrated his dulled, drunken senses. His eyes flicked open and he sat up, staring at the two dark figures standing over him.

"Who are you?" he said, his voice thick and slurring.

"Prince Duncan says hello," Farrel said softly, then hit the fake prince with a short, hard right hook to the point of the jaw.

Tiller's eyes rolled up in his head and he went back down onto the bed, stone-cold unconscious.

Farrell dropped his brass striker, which he had held in his right fist, back into an inner pocket. He shook his hand once or twice to relieve the pain. Even with the striker to support his fist, the punch had been a painful one—albeit more painful for Tiller.

Berwick watched him curiously. "Why didn't you use your club?"

Farrel gave him a fierce grin. "It was more fun this way," he said.

34

FARREL BENT OVER AND SEIZED HOLD OF THE UNCONSCIOUS impostor's hands, pulling him upright in the bed and forward from the waist.

"Give me a hand to get him up," he said quietly.

Berwick leaned in, dragging Tiller over his companion's shoulder. Farrel got both his hands around the back of Tiller's thighs. He paused a moment, then heaved up with his legs and lifted the unconscious figure off the bed.

Tiller was heavier than he expected, and he staggered for a pace or two, then regained his balance. He glanced around the room.

"Grab his pants and boots," he said and Berwick moved quickly to comply. Then Farrel nodded toward the door and Berwick slipped past him to open it, clearing the way to the hallway.

Farrel grunted softly as he stepped slowly out into the hallway. The floorboards creaked under the additional weight he was carrying. He paused, but then figured that the slight noise they made would be hidden by the thunderous snoring from the other two rooms.

He shrugged Tiller's limp body into a more secure position

and continued toward the stairs. Berwick brought up the rear, his saxe drawn and glittering in the dull light of the hallway. They passed the doors to the two bedrooms. Berwick half turned, shuffling sideways so that he could keep an eye on the source of possible trouble.

Farrel reached the top of the first flight of stairs and paused, getting his balance and his breath back. He stepped cautiously down onto the first stair, settled himself again and brought his back foot down to match the front one. Burdened as he was, he wouldn't be striding down the steps. He'd need to take them carefully, stepping down one at a time with both feet.

He took the second stair. One foot, then two. He swayed, leaning against the wall for balance, then stepped down to the third stair.

Which was loose, and turned slightly under his foot.

He hadn't noticed the loose board on the way up. They had been putting their weight on the very edges of each step, and there had been no sign of movement. Now, he didn't have that luxury. He had to step down onto the middle of each riser, where there was more movement. He hastily brought his second foot down to try to regain his balance, but it simply exacerbated the problem. The extra load made the step tilt even farther and he felt himself losing his balance. Berwick, behind him and facing back up the staircase, didn't notice his companion's predicament. Farrel threw out his left arm to grab at the wall, trying to prevent himself from falling, but he had already tipped too far past his balance point and he couldn't recover.

It seemed to happen in slow motion and that gave him time to consider his two options: to fall with Tiller, or to get rid of the unconscious man and let him fall by himself down the staircase.

He chose the latter, slipping Tiller's body free of his shoulder and letting him go, while he threw himself backward, bending his knees to regain balance.

Tiller crashed down the stairs, a tangle of arms and legs. He hit on his left shoulder, more by luck than good management, and rolled, his feet cannoning off the walls. Then he somersaulted, so that his feet went over his head, crashed into the stairs below and dragged him, crashing and banging, after them.

"What are you doing?" Berwick hissed. He hadn't seen Farrel lose his balance, and turning quickly, it seemed to him that his companion had simply hurled their prisoner headlong down the staircase.

"Shut up!" Farrel replied, rising to his feet and taking the stairs two at a time to get to the fallen man.

Strangely, the series of violent impacts, which might have rendered Tiller even more deeply unconscious, served to rouse him. He lay sprawled halfway down the stairs, head jammed against the wall where the stairs made a right-angle turn, and bellowed in pain and shock.

Above them, they heard a scramble of movement as his men were wakened by the row. Bare feet hit the floor and it seemed everyone was shouting at once. There was a crash as two of them, still half drunk from the night before, collided with each other in the hallway and went down in a tangle of arms and legs. Reaching Tiller, Farrel grabbed him by the scruff of his neck, hauled him to his feet and dragged him down the next flight of stairs. As they reached the taproom, Berwick caught up with them and seized hold of Tiller's arm from the other side. Between them, they half dragged, half carried the dazed man to the door.

Above, they heard doors banging and feet pounding on the stairs. Someone was trying to blow a blast on a horn, to alert the troops in the barn. But his mouth and lips were dry and the first few efforts emitted only a strangled squawk. Then he got it under control and a shattering blast sounded through the inn.

"That's torn it," Berwick said as he shouldered the door open and dragged Tiller through it, Farrel following behind them. The impostor, now more fully aware of what was happening, began to struggle, resisting their efforts. Berwick glared at him.

"My turn," he said, and hit him with a savage left hook. Tiller's knees sagged once more and his head lolled. He was a dead weight again but it was easier for the two Rangers to drag him out into the street. Farrel stepped on one of the unconscious sentries and stumbled, throwing more weight onto Berwick, who staggered, then recovered.

"Watch your clumsy great feet!" Berwick hissed.

"I'm not doing this on purpose!" Farrel replied, then he called in a louder voice, "Rangers! Alert!"

There was no need for the command. The noise they had made exiting the inn was enough to wake the dead. The seven Rangers were ready and waiting in a long line, bows raised, arrows nocked and ready.

"Clear our shot!" Jurgen called urgently. Berwick and Farrel realized that they were directly in line with the waiting Rangers and the inn itself. Hastily, they altered their direction, crabbing to one side to leave Jurgen and the others with an unimpeded shot.

They weren't a moment too soon. The inn door banged open, disgorging four of Tiller's henchmen onto the street. A second later, another half-dozen armed men pounded out of the stable-yard gate to join them, forming up in a rough line.

One of them pointed his sword at the three figures hobbling down the high street. He hadn't noticed the Rangers opposite, ready to shoot. "There they are! Get them!"

"Don't move!" It was Jurgen again and now the soldiers turned their attention to the single rank of dark-cloaked figures to their right. For a moment, they hesitated, then, with a roar of anger, they surged forward in a ragged charge.

Instantly, six of them went down, arrows through thighs, calves or arms. Jurgen and his men hadn't aimed to kill, simply to stop the charge. The impact of the arrows at point-blank range was staggering—literally. Those at the rear of the charge stopped as they saw their comrades sprawling on the ground, crying out in agony. Several more reinforcements exited the stableyard gate, took in the situation and withdrew immediately. There'd be no help from that quarter.

The wounded men lay on the ground, sobbing in pain and shock. Their four remaining companions watched in horror and began to back toward the tavern door. Then one of them, perhaps drunker than the others, perhaps in a fit of bloodlust, lost control and charged after the retreating figures of Farrel, Berwick and Tiller, his sword drawn back, ready to strike.

Norris, an arrow nocked and drawn, swung with the running man and released.

There was no time to aim to wound. The arrow hit the man in the ribs and the force of it flung him sideways, so that he crashed into the wall of the house adjoining the tavern and slid to the ground, lying there silent. The sword clattered and rang on the hard ground as it fell from his fingers.

Jurgen stepped forward from the shooting line and faced the wounded men on the far side of the street. "Don't try to follow us," he ordered, his voice cold. "Next time, we'll shoot to kill."

The wounded men looked up at him, faces contorted with pain. None of them, he knew, would be anxious to face the seven archers once more. His words were aimed at the men back in the inn, and in the stableyard.

"We're King's Rangers!" Jurgen called loudly, and was surprised at the small surge of pride it gave him to use the title. "Tiller is under arrest and will hang for his crimes. Any of you want to join him, you're welcome. But if you try to follow us, you're dead men. Get back to whatever hole you crawled out of and lie low. That way, you might have a chance to survive. If you keep raiding, we'll come looking for you."

He made a quick gesture to the other Rangers and they began to trot down the high street after Farrel and Berwick, catching up to them and relieving them of their burden.

Norris, Jurgen and Samdash stopped after thirty meters, standing in the middle of the street and facing the inn, ready to deal with any sign of pursuit.

After a few minutes, the inn door opened and the three Rangers raised their bows in a warning gesture. Several men emerged, holding their hands up to show they were carrying no weapons, and began to help their wounded comrades back inside. The door closed behind the last of them and Jurgen turned to his companions.

"That's it," he said. "Let's get out of here."

35

THE TOURNAMENT GROUND OUTSIDE THE WALLS OF CASTLE Gorlan was a cheerful riot of noise and color and surging humanity. Flags and pennants flew on all sides, flapping in the breeze. The turf, which had been mowed by an army of scythe-wielding peasants, was rich, lush and green.

The long, rectangular tournament field was divided down the middle by a meter-and-a-half-high wooden fence called the tilt, which defined the jousting ground. At either end stood the varicolored pavilions of the competing nobles and knights. Their shields were mounted on poles outside the pavilions, the bright enameled colors of their insignia adding to the glitter and excitement of the setting.

Each baron had his own roped-off area, inside which a main pavilion served as his headquarters for the duration of the tournament. These pavilions, decked out in the barons' personal colors, were surrounded by smaller tents, accommodating the barons' followers—knights, battle-school students, armorers, horse masters, cooks, servants and various other supernumeraries. In the case of the larger fiefs, like Redmont, there could be up to a dozen tents, so that the area resembled a small canvas village.

Morgarath's pavilion was at the opposite end of the field to Arald's. His enclosure had only three tents, including the main pavilion, as most of his men would be accommodated in the nearby castle. His black shield, with its golden lightning-bolt insignia, was mounted on a tall pole outside his main pavilion— which was also finished in black and gold.

The shields outside each pavilion were not merely for decoration. Young knights or squires wishing to make a name for themselves could challenge the senior knights and barons by striking a lance against the mounted shield. Those who were challenged could accept the invitation to joust or not.

Not all the barons in Araluen had traveled to the tournament. For some, the distance was prohibitive—as was the cost. If a baron lost in a challenge joust, he would have to forfeit his horse and armor. Many of the smaller fiefs could ill afford such an expense—particularly as the barons were less than skillful in their weapons drill. Others were simply too old to be competitive, and had elected to remain at home. As a result, only thirty-two of the fiefs were represented here.

The tilt was aligned in a north–south direction. On the western side, where the late afternoon sun wouldn't strike into the eyes of its occupants, was a covered grandstand with separate sections laid out for the nobles and their followers. The seats in this grandstand were comfortable and padded with cushions. In the center was Morgarath's section, which was only fitting as he was the sponsor of the tournament. There was a small separate section within this part of the grandstand to accommodate the King and his servants. But Morgarath had let it be known that King Oswald was indisposed and would not be attending.

At either end of the grandstand were common areas, where

jugglers and musicians performed and where cook fires were lit, preparing roasted meats, ears of corn or spitted, spiced river fish. The delicious smell of grilling meat and the sizzle of fat dripping onto red-hot coals set mouths watering. There were half a dozen tents selling ale and wine.

These vendors supplied the needs of the junior knights and squires. In the space behind the grandstand, the barons' servants prepared their food for them.

On the opposite side was the commoners' seating area. It wasn't enclosed or covered against inclement weather and the seats were simple wooden benches, rising in tiers. It was nowhere near as comfortable, but it was said there was more fun to be had here than in the august—some might say stuffy—presence of the nobles and knights opposite. More food stalls and sideshow tents were arrayed in the open spaces beside the tiers of benches. There was no wine on sale here. Ale was the drink of the common people and there was plenty of that on hand. Several tents were set up with large barrels mounted on their sides, ready to be tapped. Each had long rows of wooden tankards hanging from pegs. Already, the ale sellers were doing a steady trade, even though the actual combats wouldn't begin till the following day.

On the tournament field itself, half a dozen squires were exercising their masters' battlehorses, and an equal number of lesser knights, who couldn't afford retainers, were getting a feel for the ground as well.

The tournament rules were simple enough. Each combatant would wear chain-mail armor and carry a shield. His head would be protected by a full-face jousting helmet. The jousting lances they carried would be made of lightweight wood—usually pine—instead of the heavier iron-tipped oak that made up a war lance. The jousting lances were designed to shatter and splinter in the event of a direct hit on an opponent's shield. An indirect or off-center strike would leave the lance undamaged. A knight gained a point for each lance shattered in this way, with a maximum of five lances being used for each encounter.

A dead-center strike on a shield could result in one's opponent being hurled from the saddle, or in extreme cases, the horse being thrown down as well, in addition to the lance shattering. With the lightweight lances that were being used, it required a particularly skilled and exact eye to perform such a perfect strike.

If a warrior was unhorsed in this way, his opponent was declared the automatic winner of the bout—unless the vanquished horseman indicated that he wished to continue the fight on foot. It was the winner's prerogative to accept or refuse such a challenge. He could continue to fight from horseback, discarding his lance and continuing with his sword. Or he could, as a matter of sportsmanship, choose to dismount and face his opponent on foot. If he vanquished his opponent once more, he was awarded a double penalty and double points were added to his tally. Swords were, of course, blunted.

The tournament was due to begin the following day. The first two mornings would be set aside for elimination bouts between lesser knights and final-year battle-school students, hoping to win their way into the main draw.

In the hour after lunch, younger, less experienced knights would be able to issue challenges to their more senior and experienced colleagues—the barons, senior knights and battle masters. Those challenged could choose to accept or refuse the contest. Most would opt to accept, seeing a chance to get in some worthwhile practice against less dangerous opponents. The tournament was, after all, basically a fun event.

Personal contests between the senior knights and barons would be held in the afternoon.

On the third day, jousting would be postponed and the Grand Melee would be held, beginning at eleven o'clock in the morning. This was an opportunity for every combatant entered in the tournament to win prize money. The fighters were divided into two teams, wearing red or blue kerchiefs round their upper arms. They fought on foot, with blunted tournament weapons— swords, maces or axes. The objective was to seek out an opponent and force him to yield. Losers were tallied by heralds and referees, and their weapons and armor would be forfeited to those who had defeated them. As the numbers reduced, the more successful fighters usually retired from the field, taking their booty, and their captives, with them. At intervals, the teams were reassigned to keep the numbers more or less even, so it was possible to fight for an hour or so with another knight as an ally, only to find oneself facing him as an enemy as the numbers were adjusted. Technically, each combatant was supposed to fight as an individual, but loose alliances were often formed and it was hard to police the practice, given the wild, unstructured nature of the melee.

Even though weapons were blunted, the melee was highly dangerous and serious injuries often occurred. The barons and senior knights generally refrained from taking the field.

On the fourth and fifth day, jousting would resume and a series of elimination bouts would decide the eventual grand champion of the tournament.

Baron Arald of Redmont sat at a long table set up in one of

his service tents. It was normally used by his armorers, and racks holding chain-mail shirts and leggings, as well as various helmets and other fittings, lined the interior. Today, however, there was no sign of the armorers. The tent was being used for a secret council of war. At the table with Arald was Prince Duncan, Crowley and Halt, Mistress DuLacy from Arald's Diplomatic Service, and Sir Rodney, the young battle master from Redmont Fief.

Arald had elected to use this tent for the meeting as it was less conspicuous than his main pavilion, set out in the open where all could view it. The armorers' tent was pitched back among the cluster of other, lesser tents and it was easier for those meeting here to make their way to it unobserved.

As Arald drummed his fingers impatiently on the table, the final member of the council entered, pushing back his ragged cowl as he came.

"Sorry I'm late," Pritchard told the assembled group. "Had a little trouble getting away from the castle without being noticed."

"Have you found my father?" Duncan asked, the strain in his voice obvious.

Pritchard nodded. "Yes, my lord. There's a high-ranking prisoner being kept in the eastern tower's turret room. I've made friends with one of the serving girls who takes him his meals and it's pretty obvious that it's King Oswald."

"Is he all right? Is he in danger?" Duncan wanted to know.

Pritchard hesitated. "I won't lie to you, sir. It sounds as if he's in very poor health. The girl has told me he's feverish and dispirited and he has long periods where he's semiconscious. It sounds to me as if he's being drugged."

Duncan slammed his hand on the table. "Then we have to

get him out of there!" he snapped, but Pritchard held up a hand in warning.

"It would be a mistake to act too soon. Morgarath doesn't know you're here. And he doesn't know we're aware of the King's situation. We need him to show his hand before we act."

"But—" Duncan began.

Arald interrupted him. "Pritchard's right, my lord. We need to pick our time carefully. There's no concrete proof against Morgarath—"

"No proof? He had me held prisoner in Castle Wildriver!" Duncan said heatedly. "And he's holding my father prisoner now!"

"There's nothing to tie him to the fact that you were held prisoner," Arald told him. "He's sure to deny any knowledge of the fact. As for your father, he claims he's protecting him— against you."

"What about the impostor who was raiding across the border?" Duncan demanded.

Crowley answered him this time. "Again, there's no proof that Morgarath had a hand in that. Oh, we may get Tiller to confess, but it'll be his word against Morgarath's. It's going to come down to an accusation against him before the Council of Barons. And Morgarath has a lot of support there."

Arald turned to Pauline DuLacy. "Speaking of which, what is the situation, Pauline?" he asked.

The blond woman glanced down at a pile of notes in front of her. But she was merely gathering her thoughts. She had no need of written notes.

"It's close. A majority are on our side—probably thirty-five of the Council. But not all of them are present. On the other hand, most of Morgarath's supporters are here. They've probably been warned that he's planning some kind of grab for the throne. If we confront him here, we won't have the numbers to find him guilty." She glanced apologetically at the prince. "We need at least two-thirds of the Council to side with us, and they have to be present."

Duncan sat back from the table, his frustration all too evident. "So what can we do?"

"Our best witness against him is your father, the King," Pritchard said calmly. "But right at the moment, it's impossible to get him out of Gorlan. Morgarath's attention is focused on him and nothing short of a full-scale attack could get to him. On the other hand, once the tournament begins, it'll be a different matter."

"How so?" said Arald.

Pritchard turned to face him. "Morgarath's attention will be distracted. He'll be looking to whittle down our numbers. I've heard whispers through the castle that he plans to attack as many of his enemies as possible in the Grand Melee. His henchman Teezal will lead a group of warriors, targeting specific opponents. You can bet they'll be either people already on our side, or tending to favor our position. Most of them won't be senior knights, but if they're put out of action it will weaken our forces."

"Against the rules, of course," said Crowley. "But that's never bothered Morgarath in the past."

"Perhaps we can turn the tables on him, with a group of our own men, targeting the targeters," Halt suggested. Crowley and Arald smiled at him.

"Not a bad idea," said Arald.

Pritchard cleared his throat. "There's another thing, my

lord," he said to Arald. "Morgarath is almost certain to challenge you. And he's almost certain to try to bend the rules his way so he can kill you. If you're out of the way, our position is seriously weakened. You're the focus for our campaign against him. You can bring enough of the Barons' Council on board to defeat him."

Arald shrugged. "Let him try," he said. "I've fought him before."

"My point is," said Pritchard, "that once he's involved in the tournament, it's going to be easier to rescue the King. I could lead a small group into the castle. I know the layout now and I know where they're keeping him. If we can set him free, he can denounce Morgarath as a traitor."

"Of course, Morgarath will demand a hearing before the Council of Barons," said Arald. "He's a stickler for proper procedure, when it suits his purpose to demand it. And it'll take months to assemble the full council."

"But at least the King will be free, and we'll have stopped Morgarath's attempt to discredit Duncan and seize the throne." Pritchard paused, then added, "We'll have only one chance to confront him and we want to be sure he doesn't wriggle out of it. We have to make it stick. King Oswald is the key to that."

Duncan looked around the table. It was obvious that he was still frustrated by the lack of immediate action, but he could see the sense of the arguments that had been raised.

"Very well. We'll wait. Crowley, are your men ready?"

Crowley smiled. "They're scattered among the crowds, sir, disguised as ordinary workers and yeomen. But they'll be ready the moment you need them."

Duncan studied him for a few seconds, then nodded. "Good. And in the meantime, Arald, you are to do your best to prevent Morgarath killing you."

Arald smiled. "I did plan to do something along those lines, sir," he said.

36

MORGARATH REACHED ACROSS TO REFILL BARON PELLER'S goblet.

"More wine, Lord Peller?" he asked, giving the gray-haired Baron a winning smile. Behind the smile, he nursed the sarcastic thought that Peller was unlikely to ever refuse the offer of more wine. The network of veins on his nose and cheek bore testimony to his love of, and dedication to, more wine.

"Why, thank you, Lord Morgarath!" the nobleman replied. He hastily took a deep gulp of the wine remaining in his goblet, then pushed it forward so that his host could top it up. He regarded the brimming goblet contentedly, and raised it to his lips.

Morgarath was entertaining three of the barons who were favorable to his cause, although not yet fully committed. They were seated at a laden table in his sumptuous pavilion. The tent flaps were raised to allow a cool breeze to enter and they had dined on roast pork, a spectacular game pie and a wide assortment of vegetables. The remains of the meal lay in front of them and they were now setting themselves to the task of finishing off the fine wine that Morgarath had provided. He was an accomplished host and was known to provide excellent fare for guests. The three barons, Peller, Meagher and Cordell, had accepted his invitation eagerly.

"How is the King, Lord Morgarath?" inquired Meagher.

Morgarath shook his head and assumed an unhappy expression. "Not well, I'm afraid," he said sadly. "His health deteriorates every day and his spirits are lower than ever. I fear his son's actions in the north are behind it. He is vastly disappointed in Duncan and that is affecting his attitude and, in turn, his health. He's not been strong since the assassination attempt. The poison took a lot out of him, physically and mentally."

"We're all lucky that you got wind of the attempt in time to save him, my lord," said Baron Cordell.

Morgarath gave a deprecating shrug. "I simply did my duty. Any of you would have done the same."

"I've heard rumors, my lord," Peller said ponderously, "that the King is thinking of disinheriting his son."

Morgarath raised his eyebrows in apparent surprise—although those rumors had been started by himself. "That would be a most serious circumstance, Lord Peller."

Peller shrugged. "No more than Duncan's actions deserve, some might say."

Cordell and Meagher murmured agreement. Morgarath shot a shrewd glance at the two of them. He had staged this banquet to gauge their reactions to such an event. He felt a warm glow of satisfaction. His three guests did not represent major fiefs in terms of manpower or troops, but they did wield considerable influence with many of the other barons, particularly those who were so far uncommitted to either side in the obvious struggle for power going on in the Kingdom.

"But if the King were to take such a step, he would have to name a successor in Duncan's place," Morgarath said mildly.

Again, Peller couched his reply in those ponderous tones that were his trademark—particularly when the wine level in his goblet had been lowered several times. "I could think of no better candidate than yourself, my lord," he said to Morgarath.

But the Baron of Gorlan Fief waved the suggestion aside. "Me? I have no business being King. Nor any wish to become one. I'm content with my lot."

"I believe there are many among us who would disagree, Lord Morgarath," said Cordell. "We would be happy to support your candidature for the position. After all, you are the foremost knight in the realm. Many of us look up to you."

Again Morgarath shook his head, smiling reluctantly at the idea. But inside, he felt a surge of triumph. Now that the matter was out in the open, raised by someone other than himself and greeted with approval by these three, he could progress his plan to the next stage. He had doubts that King Oswald would publicly denounce Duncan as his heir, but if the matter were already being discussed as a fait accompli, he could use a written proclamation, marked with the King's seal, to bring the matter to a head. Such a proclamation would need to be ratified by the Council of Barons, but he sensed that he would be able to gather a majority there.

"Let's hope it doesn't come to that, my lords," he said easily. "I'm sure that if we put our minds to it, we can resolve this problem with Duncan."

The three men mumbled agreement, although they sounded less than convinced. Morgarath smiled to himself. The resolution of this problem might well be to have Duncan killed, he thought. But before that, he would need Oswald to put Morgarath's name forward as his successor.

He was about to speak when someone approached the entrance to the dining section. He glanced up and saw Teezal standing expectantly.

"What is it?" he snapped, anger creeping into his voice. He had left explicit instructions that his banquet was not to be interrupted.

"My lord, I have news," Teezal said nervously.

Morgarath frowned. Teezal wasn't stupid and he was aware of Morgarath's instructions that the luncheon not be interrupted. Therefore, what he had to say must be important. Still, the interruption gave Morgarath an opportunity to further ingratiate himself with his guests.

"It can wait," he said coldly. "I am entertaining honored guests." He turned to smile at the three barons. Morgarath was a blackhearted killer, but he was capable of exuding enormous charm—just as a viper might lull its victims before striking.

He saw the looks of gratification on their faces and turned back to Teezal. "Wait outside," he said curtly.

His lackey turned and stepped outside the pavilion. "Yes, my lord," he said as he withdrew.

Morgarath turned back to his guests, smiling expansively. "Now, my friends, some more wine? Or perhaps some fruit?" He gestured to the table, but already Cordell and Meagher were rising from their chairs. Peller followed suit, after a reluctant glance at the quarter-full wine jug on the table.

"Really, my lord, we've taken enough of your time," said Cordell, and the others instantly concurred. Morgarath feigned disappointment.

"But we were just beginning to enjoy ourselves," he said, although the real reason for the luncheon had been accomplished, as far as he was concerned.

"No. We'd best get away. You have much to do as the host of this excellent tournament, Lord Morgarath, and we're grateful for the time you've given us," said Meagher, leading the way toward the doorway. The others followed, and as Morgarath ushered them out, maintaining his expression of disappointment at their departure, Peller turned back to him and tapped the side of his nose with one finger.

"Remember what we discussed, my lord," he said.

Morgarath nodded, his expression serious and concerned. "I will, Lord Peller. But I doubt that anything will come of it. After all, the rumors about Oswald's intentions are just that—rumors."

"Nevertheless," Peller intoned, "these are troubled times and in such times we look for a man to take firm control."

"Perhaps," said Morgarath. "But let's not make any decisions in haste."

Peller nodded and followed the other two barons out into the sunlight and bustle of the tournament field. As he waved them good-bye, Morgarath turned and surveyed the anteroom to his private dining space. Along with several of his servants and his clerk, Teezal was waiting patiently, sitting on a stool. As his lord's gaze fell on him, he rose to his feet. Morgarath jerked a thumb at the inner room.

"Inside," he said and, as the servants moved to enter to clear the table, he stopped them. "You wait here."

They stepped back and he followed Teezal into the inner

room, once again taking his seat at the head of the table. He gestured to the wine jug and one of the glasses left empty by his guests. "Have some wine if you like. It'll go to waste otherwise."

Teezal accepted this rather dismissive invitation eagerly. He knew that Morgarath would have provided the finest wine from his cellars for the day's luncheon. He poured a glass and sipped appreciatively.

Morgarath waited a few seconds. "Well, what's this important news that you've discovered?"

Teezal set the glass down reluctantly. He knew that after he delivered his news, there'd be no more time for wine drinking. "My lord," he said, "I'm sorry I interrupted—"

But Morgarath waved the apology aside. "No matter. I was finished with those three self-important bores anyway. Gave me an excuse to be rid of them. Now what did you have to tell me?"

"My lord," Tiller said warily. He knew Morgarath's violent temper only too well. "It's Tiller. He's here."

"Tiller?" Morgarath's face was blank. For a moment, the name meant nothing to him.

"Tiller," Teezal repeated, emphasizing the name. Then, seeing Morgarath's brows come together in anger, he elaborated. "The false Duncan. The impostor who's been raiding across the northern border. That Tiller."

Morgarath's face cleared, anger being replaced by curiosity. "You say he's here? Here at Gorlan? What does he want? I told him never to show his face near me!" Momentarily, he assumed that Tiller had come of his own volition.

Teezal quickly disabused him of that idea. "He's not here

willingly, my lord. He's a prisoner. He's being held in Arald's compound."

"Arald? May the Fates curse the man! Must he always interfere in my business? How does he come to have Tiller as a prisoner?"

Teezal shrugged. "I have no idea, my lord. I was keeping an eye on Arald's compound, as you ordered, when I became aware that someone was being held prisoner in one of the smaller tents. I saw food being taken in, but whoever was being fed never came out. So I managed to get a look inside and there he was—Tiller. He's chained up and can't move more than a few meters in any direction. But it's definitely him."

Morgarath stroked his chin reflectively. "Why would Arald have brought him here?" he wondered.

"He could be planning to contest your plans for the throne, my lord," said Teezal. "After all, they depend on Prince Duncan being discredited and disowned. If Arald produced Tiller, and had him swear he was impersonating Duncan on your orders, that could complicate things."

"True. But how has Arald got wind of my plans?" Morgarath was thinking aloud rather than asking questions. But Teezal replied nevertheless.

"The rumors are all over the tournament, my lord, that the King plans to disinherit Duncan. It wouldn't take much for Arald to guess that you were behind them, and were planning to replace him."

"True," said Morgarath thoughtfully. "Very true. But how did Arald get hold of him?"

"I can make inquiries, my lord. I'm sure I . . . ," Teezal began, but Morgarath waved him to silence.

"Time enough to do that later. If we start asking around,

Arald might get wind that we know Tiller is here. No. I have something more urgent for you to do with friend Tiller."

"What's that, my lord?" Teezal asked.

Morgarath turned to look at him. Not for the first time, Teezal was reminded of the eyes of a snake about to strike.

"Kill him," Morgarath said.

37

PRITCHARD PEERED ROUND THE DOORWAY INTO THE MASSIVE kitchen in the basement of Castle Gorlan. For the moment, the giant roasting pits and huge iron ovens weren't in use. But one of the kitchen maids was preparing a meal on a tray—as she did every day around midday.

Having watched her for the past week, Pritchard knew the tray would be going to the isolated room in the tower—where Oswald was being held prisoner.

He watched as the girl placed a bowl of thin broth onto the tray, then turned away to prepare a small plate of sliced chicken and green vegetables. The portions were never large. Morgarath had no intention of letting Oswald regain his strength and Pritchard had noticed that the girl stirred a small quantity of white powder into the soup each day, pouring it from a small bottle she kept in her apron pocket. He was convinced that Oswald was being kept sedated, although he had overheard the girl being told by the kitchen master that the powder was a tonic. She was a good-hearted lass and he knew she would have no willing part in keeping the old man in the tower drugged.

Pritchard stepped down the three steps into the kitchen and moved toward her. She sensed him coming, looked up and smiled. She liked the ragged old man who had taken to loitering round the kitchen looking for scraps and handouts. He was invariably polite and courteous to her, and always thanked her profusely for the tidbits she gave him. And he had a delightful twinkle in his eye, she thought.

"Good morning, Belmore," she said now. That was the name he had given her.

"Good morning, mistress. How are . . . ?" Pritchard stopped in mid-sentence and put his hand to his forehead, shaking his head. He staggered, regaining his balance by seizing the kitchen bench, and stood, swaying uncertainly, bewilderment and fear in his eyes.

"Are you all right?" she asked anxiously and he made a dismissive gesture, taking his hand away from his forehead to do so.

"Just a little dizzy," he said, his voice quavering. "I didn't eat yesterday."

The previous day, he hadn't appeared in the castle kitchen. He'd been meeting with Arald and Prince Duncan.

"You should have come to see me!" she scolded. Forgetting the tray, she turned back to the worktable and quickly sliced him a slab of bread from a fresh loaf, buttering it thickly, then poured a beaker of water for him. She placed the bread and water on the table and gestured to it.

"Here, sit and have something to eat!" she said.

Pritchard moved cautiously toward the chair she indicated, keeping his balance with one hand on the workbench. Then he sat heavily and began to eat hungrily, washing the mouthfuls of fresh buttered bread down with cool water. "Ah!" he said. "That's better! The gods bless you, mistress!"

The girl smiled at him, relieved to see he was obviously over the fainting spell that had seized him. "You have to look after yourself, Belmore. You're not a young man anymore and you know there's always plenty to spare in the kitchen. If you're hungry, just find me. I'll always get you something."

He smiled at her. "Thank you, mistress. You're too kind," he said. He felt a slight twinge of conscience over the fact that he had deceived her and taken advantage of her kindly nature. As she had turned away to fetch him food and drink, he had quickly slipped a folded scrap of parchment under the soup bowl.

She patted his shoulder now, smiling at him. "I must be about my work," she said. "You sit here and eat your bread until you feel better."

"I'm feeling better already, thanks to you," he replied warmly. She gathered up the tray and headed for the door out of the kitchen.

"Take all the time you need," she said. "Nobody will bother you."

Pritchard waited, listening to the sound of her light footsteps as she crossed the flagstones of the vast central hall and began the long climb up a series of winding stairways to the eastern tower. In spite of her best efforts the broth would be little more than lukewarm by the time she delivered it, he knew.

Once he was sure she had gone, he wolfed the last of the bread—which was fresh baked and warm and quite delicious. Then he hurried out of the kitchen by a side door and made his way out of the castle grounds. He had become a familiar sight around Castle Gorlan over the past week and was able to come and go virtually unhindered. In fact, he thought, the guards and sentries probably didn't even notice him as he passed under the massive portcullis and made his way across the drawbridge.

King Oswald glanced up from his chair as he heard the door of his turret room open. The sound of the large key grating in the lock was a reminder that he was a prisoner here in Gorlan. He sat at a table in his nightshirt—the only garment he had been given. A blanket was draped round his shoulders because the sentries would allow no fire in the turret room.

"Can't have you burning yourself, your majesty," they'd sneered when he'd requested some warmth in the chilly room. High above the surrounding countryside like this, the turret room was subject to constant chill winds whistling round it and finding their way in through the gaps in the shutters.

He managed a wan smile as the kitchen maid appeared with his meal. At least she was pleasant, he thought, and was constantly solicitous of his health.

He coughed, the action racking his body. He felt weak and totally lacking in energy. He was sure they were putting something in his food to keep him drowsy and dispirited, but he didn't know where they were putting it, or what they were giving him. And, truth be told, as each day went by, he cared less and less. He could feel his will to live, his will to resist Morgarath's constant demands that he disinherit his son, diminishing.

Morgarath had made no bones about Duncan's current fate. King Oswald knew his son was being held prisoner by Morgarath's allies. And he knew that Duncan's life depended on his, Oswald's, doing as Morgarath commanded. He sighed unhappily. There had been a time when he had trusted

Morgarath, but that time was long past and now he realized he had been a fool to do so.

He also knew that the minute he signed any proclamation naming Morgarath as his heir, Duncan's life would be over. Morgarath couldn't afford to let him live, and possibly rechallenge for the throne at a later date. All Oswald could do was continue to resist.

Although each day, his will to do so became weaker and weaker.

"Here you go, my lord," said the kitchen maid cheerfully. "A nice bit of chicken there, and some greens. Eat 'em up. They'll do you good."

In spite of his situation, Oswald smiled tiredly. Her cheerful prattle reminded him of his old nanny when he was a boy. His nanny had been fond of telling him to "eat up, it'll do you good."

He picked up the chicken leg and took a nibble. But the maid scolded him good-naturedly.

"Have the soup first," she said. "Before it goes completely cold."

She touched her hand to the side of the bowl, checking the temperature. "There's still a bit of warmth in it," she said. "Just what you need in this drafty old room."

He nodded and picked up the clumsy wooden spoon. Morgarath had forbidden him the use of any iron implements, lest he try to fashion a makeshift weapon from them.

He took a sip. The broth was tepid and thin, without much nourishment in it. But he nodded his thanks to the girl. It wasn't her fault, after all.

"Thank you, mistress. You're too kind."

She grinned at him and bobbed down in a curtsy. "Wish I

could give you something more substantial," she said. "But Lord Morgarath's healers say you need to keep to a low diet to prevent fevers."

"I'm sure they do," he said dryly, taking another sip.

Content that he was eating, she turned away and knocked on the door to be let out. The guards outside opened the door and she departed. Oswald heard the key grate in the lock behind her. He looked at the watery broth and the small chicken leg. What was the point, he thought.

"Keep your strength up," he said. He noticed that he'd taken to talking to himself over the past week or so. He thought that might be a bad sign. Then he shrugged the thought away. Bad sign or no, it made little difference to his situation.

He dipped the spoon into the bowl once more and let the soup fill it. As he did so, he accidentally pushed the spoon against the far side of the bowl, moving it a few millimeters on the tray. He frowned as he saw the edge of a piece of parchment revealed under the soup bowl. He set the spoon down and moved the soup bowl to one side, revealing a small square of parchment that had been hidden underneath. There was writing on it.

He picked it up and held it angled so that the light from the shuttered window fell on it. His lips moved as he made out the five words written there, and he felt a dull glow of hope in his breast. He read them again, to make sure he wasn't hallucinating, and this time he said them aloud.

"'Duncan is safe. Hold on.'"

38

"THERE'S A CHALLENGE!"

Word ran round the tournament ground like wildfire and people rushed to line the jousting ground fence where they could get a good view. The crowd buzzed with expectation. This was the first of the challenges to one of the senior knights or barons. The challenger was a young knight seeking to build his reputation.

Such combats were always a source of excitement for the spectators. There was a strong element of the unknown about them. The young challenger could well be a champion in the making, and could succeed in defeating his more experienced opponent.

Or he might simply be a hopeless optimist whose confidence far outweighed his ability and he might well be dispatched into the dust of the jousting field in the space of a few passes. Either way, it made for exciting viewing—and an excellent chance to place bets on the outcome.

The crowd watched as the young knight, his green-painted helmet and shield shining, his mail polished till it shimmered in the sunlight, completed a circuit of the field, as was laid down in the challenge procedure. It was done this way to enable the crowd, and the gamblers, to get a good look at him and assess his chances.

"Who is it?" The question was on a score of lips, but only a few knew the answer.

"Wallace of Belconnen," came the reply. "He was knighted six months ago."

"Is he any good?" Arald asked. He had come to the entrance to his pavilion to watch procedures. He glanced up. His blue-enameled shield was displayed on a tall pole beside his pavilion.

Sir Rodney, the young battle master of Redmont Fief, replied. "He's won a few minor tournaments in the past months, so he's good. But I doubt he's any threat to you, sir."

Arald was aware that he could well be the subject of the challenge. After all, he was the reigning champion. He glanced to one of his squires, standing watching.

"Make sure my gear is ready," he said and the man knuckled his forehead and dashed for the arming tent.

Sir Wallace, his circuit of the jousting field complete, now began a slow progress around the pavilions at Arald's end of the field. Again, this was part of procedure. The challenging knight must ride past all potential opponents' pavilions before selecting one. It was a piece of theater, of course, but an effective one.

His battlehorse, a high-spirited young chestnut, clip-clopped nervously as he held it in, resisting its inclination to prance and curvet. They passed the pavilions closest to Arald's, and seemed to slow as they came closer to the blue shield mounted high above the blue-and-gold-striped tent. Wallace had his visor up and he made eye contact with Arald as he approached. He was a clean-shaven, good-looking young man.

Arald tensed to receive the challenge. He had already decided to accept.

The young knight nodded a greeting and Arald responded. Then the challenger set his spurs to the chestnut and cantered past, heading for the far end of the jousting field.

This time, he didn't do a circuit of the assembled pavilions, even though protocol said he should. He rode straight for the black-and-gold pavilion in the center, raising his lance so that it struck Morgarath's shield with a ringing clang.

The challenge was issued. Now it remained to be seen if it would be accepted.

Having struck Morgarath's shield in a challenge, Sir Wallace reined in his horse and waited for a response from the tournament host. His pulse was racing, although he tried to appear calm and unperturbed. Morgarath was perhaps the most skilled knight in the tournament—with the possible exception of the young Baron Arald. Wallace knew he was risking serious injury by challenging him, but he was determined to advance in the world, and contesting with the best was the quickest way to do it.

Besides, it was a tournament, not a real battle. If he lost, he might suffer some bad bruises or even a broken bone or two. But a joust like this was rarely a matter of life and death.

The canvas flap that closed the entrance to the pavilion was pulled aside and Morgarath stepped into the open. Wallace had previously only seen him at a distance and he was a little surprised by Morgarath's height. The lord of Gorlan stood just under two hundred centimeters tall and was an impressive, and somewhat disconcerting, figure. He was slim in build, but well muscled, with long arms and legs. His height and long reach had made him a formidable opponent in duels over the years. He was dressed entirely in black—thigh-length black boots over black trousers, and a belted black leather doublet marked with the yellow lightning-bolt insignia on the breast. His face was pale and long, with a prominent nose. His hair was white-blond and lank—a startling contrast to his all-black attire.

He regarded the young knight on the nervous battlehorse, his lance raised to the vertical, its weight supported in a small leather cup on the saddle's right stirrup. Wallace had his visor up still and Morgarath sneered as he studied the young face, fresh and unmarked so far by any scars of battle.

We'll soon change that, he thought to himself.

"What do you want, boy?" he said, his tone dismissive and bored.

Wallace went to speak, found his throat was dry with nerves. He swallowed twice, then managed to force the prescribed words out. "I stand here challenging you to a joust, Lord Morgarath. This is my right and privilege as a knighted warrior of the realm."

Morgarath sniffed sardonically, allowing his gaze to travel over the carefully polished arms and armor worn by the young man. There was not a dent or a scratch visible. Never seen a real fight, the Baron thought.

He didn't answer immediately, allowing the silence between them to stretch to an almost unbearable length while he kept his sardonic gaze on the young man.

"Is it indeed?" he said finally.

Wallace was a little taken aback. He had been expecting either acceptance or refusal. The question had no part in the set dialog for such occasions.

"Er . . . yes," he said.

Morgarath muttered a reply in a low voice—so low that

Wallace leaned forward in the saddle, frowning uncertainly. "I beg your par—"

"I said I accept, you young idiot!" Morgarath roared at the top of his voice. The young battlehorse started at the sudden noise and took several nervous paces backward before its rider brought it under control. Wallace, by now thoroughly confused, wasn't sure how to proceed.

"Then . . . ," he began, and faltered.

"Thirty minutes. In the lists. Don't keep me waiting," Morgarath snapped. Then he turned on his heel and plunged back into his pavilion, calling for his armorers. Once out of sight, he smiled cruelly. He had successfully wrested the initiative from his young challenger and sowed a seed of uncertainty in his mind. All this was part and parcel of the mental game that one played in a challenge like this, and over the years, Morgarath had played that mental game more times than he could remember.

Morgarath sat unmoving astride his dead-white battlehorse, Warlock, at the head of the tilt—the long meter-and-a-half-high board fence that separated the jousters as they thundered toward each other. His visor was down and he looked enormous and menacing in his glittering black armor and surcoat, relieved only by the lightning bolt in yellow on the breast of the garment. The same device was evident on his black-enameled shield. His helmet was plain and rounded at the top, with no ornamentation that might provide purchase for an opponent's lance.

The shield was a specialized tournament shield. Whereas a battle shield would often be slightly convex in shape to cause an opponent's sword or lance point to glance off, those used in tournaments were concave, designed to allow a lance head to stay in contact with the shield and so facilitate the shattering effect that was sought after. Even a slightly off-center hit would tend to slide toward the middle of the shield.

A well-directed center hit would, of course, deliver maximum impact to the shield, and could throw an opponent from his saddle, even while the light wood shaft shattered into splinters.

Morgarath watched impassively through the slits in his visor as his green-armored opponent approached the far end of the list. One of Morgarath's attendants brought over a lance and passed it up to him. He hefted it, testing its weight. Alone among the jousters, Morgarath had his jousting lances bound at intervals along the shaft with lead bands, to approximate the weight and balance of a heavier war lance.

"Is this all right, my lord?" the attendant asked nervously. "Or did you want the other—"

"Shut up, you fool!" Morgarath snarled, his voice echoing dully inside the helmet. The attendant backed hastily away, bowing his head obsequiously, cringing before his master's anger.

Morgarath balanced the butt of his lance in the leather cup on his right stirrup and waited. Wallace was having some trouble with his horse, he noticed. The young chestnut was prancing nervously, sensing the tension of the occasion. That probably meant his rider was nervous as well, Morgarath thought. Battlehorses were highly attuned to their riders' moods. If a rider was nervous or uncertain, that would often communicate itself to the horse, who would behave accordingly.

Warlock, of course, a veteran of hundreds of combats, stood steady as a rock beneath the ominous, all-black figure astride him.

Finally, Wallace seemed to gain control of his horse, although the chestnut still pawed the ground with his front hooves and looked ready to burst out of control at any minute. The marshal standing close by him said something to the young knight. Morgarath saw him nod.

There was another marshal standing at Morgarath's end of the list. He looked up now at the sinister black figure, towering above him.

"Are you ready, my lord?" he asked.

"Ready." Once again, Morgarath's voice rang inside the steel helmet. He tossed the lance up and caught it at the balance point, behind the fluted handguard. The butt of the lance was thicker and heavier than the long shaft, to provide better balance. He tucked the butt under his right arm and held the lance at forty-five degrees. The marshal raised a flag, the action mirrored a few seconds later by the marshal at Wallace's end of the field. Both riders were ready.

In the center of the western grandstand, a herald raised a long trumpet to his lips and blew an ascending series of triple notes. As the last note died away, both riders clapped their spurs to their horses and started forward.

Battlehorses were not racehorses. They didn't leap forward, reaching full speed in a few strides. They were heavily muscled animals, bred to carry the enormous weight of an armored man, and to resist the thundering impact of another horse and rider's charge.

Warlock gathered speed steadily, reaching his top speed within fifteen meters. He powered toward their opponents, his hooves thrashing the earth beneath them, sending torn clods of dirt and grass high into the air. Morgarath leaned forward slightly in the saddle and began to lower his lance. Forty meters away, he saw Wallace doing the same. But the young knight's horse was crabbing slightly to the right, losing speed and forcing Wallace to correct him with his knees instead of concentrating on where his lance would go.

With ten meters to go, the young challenger got his horse under control and his lance point steadied, zeroing in on Morgarath's black shield.

The two combatants crashed together with a thunder of wood on metal. Morgarath's lance hit dead center on Wallace's shield. Wallace's was slightly offline, and hit with reduced impact. Both lances bent alarmingly, then shattered into splinters, hurling slivers of white wood high into the air around them. Then the two warriors were past each other, their horses now at full tilt, their momentum carrying them on, in spite of the savage impact.

A gasp rose from the watching crowd.

Wallace, taking the full force of Morgarath's lance before it shattered, had been sent reeling back in his saddle. The high rear cantle saved him from being hurled to the ground, but he slipped sideways, for a moment hanging out over the earth whirling past beneath him. Then he recovered, and the crowd let go a relieved sigh as he regained his seat, slowed his horse and cantered to the end of the list.

Morgarath had been unmoved by the impact. Wallace's lance shattering against his shield had caused him no more apparent concern than a faint movement to one side—almost imperceptible.

He cantered to the far end of the list and turned Warlock to face back the way they had come. The imperturbable warhorse stood ready and unmoving. Each combatant had attendants waiting at the opposite end of the list with spare lances. Morgarath's servant ran forward now and passed him a new lance.

He watched as Wallace reached the opposite end and received a new weapon as well. But now the young knight's battlehorse was thoroughly disturbed. He had felt his master being hurled backward and sideways by Morgarath's strike, felt him struggling to regain his balance. And now he sensed the fear that had begun to take hold of the young knight. Never before had Wallace felt anything as devastating as that center hit upon his shield. For the first time, he began to appreciate the gulf between his level of skill and Morgarath's. As he accepted his new lance, trying to calm his horse, he realized that he was seriously outclassed.

Morgarath, on the other hand, was furious. The lance strike had been perfect—centered exactly on Wallace's shield. Morgarath had felt the overwhelming force of the impact transmitted back through the lance and into his arm and body before the shaft had shattered. The young knight should have been hurled ignominiously into the dirt. But somehow, he had retained his seat. Morgarath had even heard some among the crowd cheering as the upstart managed to stay in the combat. That infuriated him. He was used to being the crowd's favorite.

Now Wallace would be taught a lesson.

He raised his lance to the forty-five-degree point and nodded to the marshal below him. The man raised his flag, a few seconds before his opposite number did the same. The long trumpet was placed to the herald's lips and the signal to charge rang in the air.

Warlock began his measured, lumbering run. Once again, he slowly accelerated to top speed, his hooves thundering on the torn grass beneath them. As his horse's gait steadied into a full gallop, Morgarath lowered his lance point, again seeking Wallace's shield. He could see a mark in the green paint where his first stroke had hit. Wallace lowered his lance in turn, but Morgarath could see it wavering as the young challenger tried to keep it aimed at his shield.

Then, in the final five meters, with exquisite timing and precision, Morgarath raised his lance point to aim for Wallace's helmet.

There was a ringing crash. The lance point snagged in the bars of Wallace's visor and the young knight's head was thrown back. His lance fell from his nerveless fingers as his body followed and he was hurled out of his saddle. At the very last moment, just before he lost consciousness, he had the instinct to kick his feet clear of the stirrups. Then he was driven several meters through the air by the savage impact, before he crashed to the turf. He lay still, half on his side.

A horrified silence fell over the crowd. Watching from the grandstand, Arald shook his head in recognition of Morgarath's skill. It had been a brutal stroke, but it was perfectly legal and expertly executed. There were few knights in the Kingdom with the skill to pull it off.

A murmur of relief swept over the crowd as Wallace slowly began to move. He rolled onto his stomach, then got hands and knees beneath him and started to rise to his feet, swaying unsteadily, grasping at the central fence for support. Dirt and torn grass stained his tunic and armor. Someone cheered, then applause swept over the crowd, only to die away when they saw Morgarath rein in at the far end of the list and drop lightly to the ground, drawing his massive, two-handed longsword from the scabbard on Warlock's saddle.

The marshal stepped forward. "My lord, what are you doing?" he said urgently.

Morgarath shoved him aside and began to march toward the tottering figure of his opponent.

"He hasn't conceded," he said. "The fight continues."

"He doesn't need to concede!" the marshal shouted after him. "You unhorsed him!"

"He must concede or the fight continues!" Morgarath shouted.

Both marshals were shouting now, but he ignored them. A killing rage was on him. Wallace turned to see the tall, black-clad figure striding toward him. He staggered. His eyes wouldn't focus properly but it seemed to him that Morgarath had his sword in his hand. Dazed and confused, Wallace reached for the sword he carried at his waist, not sure what was happening but sensing the need to defend himself.

He heard feet pounding on the turf as Morgarath was almost up to him. The Baron of Gorlan swung his huge sword back for a horizontal stroke as Wallace fumbled to draw his own sword, which had somehow become tangled behind his back.

Then a blue-clad figure came into sight and shoulder-charged Morgarath before he could begin his forward stroke. Morgarath, his peripheral vision restricted inside the jousting helmet, never saw Arald coming.

Arald's shoulder drove into Morgarath's ribs with a sickening impact. Even beneath the chain mail, Morgarath felt the force of Arald's charge. He lost his balance and crashed over into the dirt. As he tried to rise, he felt his sword pinned to the ground by Arald's foot.

He struggled furiously, but to no avail. And now Arald had

his own sword clear of the scabbard and its point at Morgarath's throat.

"It's over, Morgarath!" Arald said coldly. "Let the boy be!"

And now they were surrounded by marshals and officials, including Baron Naylor, the grand marshal of the tournament.

"My lord, what are you doing?" he cried, aghast at Morgarath's unknightly behavior. At last, the lord of Gorlan gained control of himself. He released his grip on the sword, allowing one of the marshals to help him to his feet. He pushed his visor up and shook his head in mock bewilderment.

"My apologies, my lords," he said. "I thought I heard the boy shout continue."

There was a general chorus of understanding. Naylor nodded wisely.

"These things can happen in the course of a combat," he said. "But no harm done and all's well that ends well." He gestured to the surgeon's attendants to take Wallace into their care. Then he nodded approvingly at Arald. "Just as well Baron Arald was thinking quickly. He saved us from a certain tragedy."

Arald curled his lip as he and Morgarath locked eyes. Then Arald mouthed a single word:

Liar.

Morgarath leaned forward, pretending to embrace his fellow baron in gratitude. But as his mouth came close to Arald's ear, he whispered his reply.

"I'll kill you for this."

39

"There's little doubt now that Morgarath will challenge you," Halt said.

Arald shrugged casually. "There never was. I can take care of myself."

"Still," said Duncan, "he's a snake in the grass and he'll do his best to kill you."

Again, Arald was unfazed by the comment. "He might find I'm a tougher nut to crack than young Wallace," he said. "And even he wouldn't dare to try and claim a misunderstanding like the other day."

"Keep an eye on him, nevertheless," said Crowley.

They were seated once more in the armorers' tent in Arald's compound. Duncan, Pritchard, Halt, Crowley and Farrel were present, discussing plans for the melee later that morning. Arald regarded Farrel. The burly Ranger had constructed a wooden replica of his battleax to use in the melee. Only practice weapons were allowed and an ax, even with blunted edges, was considered too dangerous to use in the event.

"Are you ready?" Arald asked Farrel.

The Ranger nodded. "Don't worry. We'll definitely cramp Teezal's style."

"How many of you?" asked Arald.

"Just two. That'll be enough to take them by surprise. A bigger group might draw attention. We could be disqualified by the marshals. And the more of us there are, the more chance of Teezal realizing what's going on."

Arald nodded. He had a good idea who would be assisting Farrel in the melee, but he decided to say nothing.

At that moment, Mistress Pauline entered the tent.

"Teezal and his group will be fighting in the blue force," she said, placing two scarlet armbands on the table. "I've had you two registered with the reds."

Arald wasn't surprised when Farrel retrieved the two armbands and handed one to Duncan.

"You're sure about this, my lord?" Arald said.

Duncan nodded. "I owe these people a few bruises," he said grimly. "And with the possible exception of yourself, I'm the best fighter we have. We need to thin Teezal's group out quickly, then get off the field."

"So long as you're not noticed and recognized," Crowley put in.

Duncan turned his gaze on him. "I'll be wearing a full-face helmet," he said. "And it's been a long time since I've had one of those knocked off my head."

They heard a rustle of canvas as the outer door screen was pulled aside, then replaced. Then the inner screen opened in turn. The double screen had been Crowley's idea, to prevent spying eyes from seeing into the tent when they were conferring.

Martin, the Baron's secretary, entered, a worried expression on his face.

"My lord, serious news," he said and Arald gestured for him to continue. Martin glanced around the table to make sure everyone was listening, then announced: "Tiller is dead."

There were startled exclamations from the assembled group. Duncan held up his hand for silence.

"Dead?" he queried. "How did this happen?"

Martin shrugged uncomfortably. "It appears that he took poison, my lord."

"Took it, or was given it?" Crowley put in.

"There's no way of knowing that, sir," Martin said unhappily. He felt that Tiller's death reflected badly on him. He was in charge of the Redmont camp's administration. "He could have had the poison concealed on him all this time."

"Surely he was searched?" Duncan said.

Crowley interjected. "My men searched him for weapons. But poison could have been concealed anywhere on his person or in his clothes."

"Still, it's something of a coincidence that he managed to get his hands on poison just when we were about to use him to denounce Morgarath," said Halt.

The others muttered agreement, but Lady Pauline disagreed with the general view around the table.

"It's really no great loss," she said. "His evidence wouldn't have been conclusive. Morgarath could always claim that we'd recruited him and coerced him into the accusation. He would have provided useful corroborating evidence of Morgarath's guilt, but that would have been all."

The others looked at her, realizing she was right.

Pritchard was the first to speak. "The key witness is still going to be King Oswald," he said. "That's always been the case. And now this feud between Arald and Morgarath will give us our best chance to set him free."

"How so?" asked Arald.

"Your interference in his fight with young Wallace has infuriated him. He's fixated on making you pay for it. And that means his attention will be distracted from Oswald. Your duel will provide a perfect opportunity for us to get into the castle and release him. You can be sure his own followers will be distracted by the event too. Security is sure to be slack."

"Assuming, of course, that he does challenge you," Pauline said.

Arald smiled at her. "Oh, he will. And if he doesn't I'll challenge him."

Outside, they heard the brazen note of multiple trumpets sounding from the jousting field.

"That's the first call for the melee," Arald said. He glanced at Duncan and Farrel. "You two had better get ready. And for pity's sake, be careful!" he added, looking directly at Duncan.

Farrel smiled. "Don't you want me to be careful, my lord?"

Arald treated him to a mock scowl. "I can always get another Ranger," he said. "Round here, they're as thick as fleas on a stray dog. But we only have one heir to the throne."

The dividing fence down the center of the jousting field had been removed for the Grand Melee. The two sides, each wearing their distinctive colored armbands, formed up in three rows at either end of the field.

Already, the crowd was buzzing with excitement. The Grand

Melee was a popular event with the spectators. It was a guaran-
teed source of violence and action. The individual fights that
took place gave spectators ample opportunity to wager on their
outcomes, and there was always the attraction of wagering on
either the red or the blue side to be triumphant at each stage of
the melee.

On the blue side, Teezal mustered his six fighters around
him.

"Remember who we're targeting," he said.

They had been briefed on a dozen knights whom Morgarath
wanted removed from contention and they had spent the morning memorizing their crests and individual insignia. The six
men, clad in chain mail, wearing pot helmets and carrying an
assortment of drill swords, clubs and maces, all nodded.

One, however, raised a hand in doubt. "Sir David of Holder
and Morris of Norgate are on the blue side," he pointed out.
"Aren't they our allies in the melee?"

Teezal regarded him scornfully. "We're here to get rid of
them. If they're wearing blue, they'll be that much easier," he
said. "They won't be expecting us to attack them. Just get behind
them and hit them hard and fast. Nobody'll notice in the
confusion."

The trumpets rang out, sounding the one-minute-warning
signal. Teezal set his shield a little more firmly on his left arm
and drew the weighted wooden sword from his belt.

"One minute to go," he said. "Get ready!"

A minute later, the trumpets blared long and loud and, with
a roar, the two sides charged across the field at each other.

As the first ranks crashed into each other and weapons
began to rise and fall, Teezal found himself behind Sir Morris

of Norgate. Teezal glanced quickly around to make sure nobody was watching, but the blue force were all intent on the enemy facing them. Quickly, he brought his sword down onto the warrior's helmet. Morris staggered, looking round in alarm. He hadn't realized that an enemy had got behind him. He saw a black-clad fighter a few meters away, then saw the wooden sword swinging toward his forearm. The bone cracked as the blow landed and Morris cried out in pain and anger. Then the black-clad man backhanded the pommel of his sword into Morris's face and he went down under a surge of trampling feet.

"Come on!" Teezal yelled to his small force, and they followed him through the struggling mass, forming a wedge behind him as they sought their next victim.

"There!" Farrel yelled, pointing with his ax at the little formation forcing its way through the melee. In a series of disorganized individual combats, it was easy to see Teezal's group, working together as they surrounded one of the red fighters. Farrel recognized their target as a warrior from the fief of one of Arald's supporters and he shoved his way through the fighting mass of men to get to him.

"Take them from behind!" Duncan yelled and they swung in behind the six men, who were surrounding the knight as he desperately tried to defend himself. But there were too many attackers and he was taking blow after blow from the wooden weapons.

Duncan slammed his shield into the side of one of Teezal's men, sending him flying. The man stumbled and fell to his knees, where an enthusiastic member of the red force, seeing his chance, brought a wooden mace crashing down on his head.

Duncan didn't bother to see what happened to his first

victim. He went at the rest of Teezal's group like a battering
ram, his heavy wooden sword flashing from side to side, beating
down his opponents' defenses, finding the small gaps left
unprotected by their shields and delivering crunching, crushing
injuries. They went down before him like wheat before the
scythe. Some turned away, nursing broken limbs. Others crashed
to the turf, unconscious. Duncan was a master warrior, powerful,
fast and pitiless, while Teezal's men were, for the most part,
semiskilled bullyboys accustomed to striking from behind and
with overwhelming numbers in their favor.

Too late, Teezal realized that his troop had been cut down
by the terrifying red-clad knight, who moved through them like
a hurricane, his sword rising and falling, sweeping and thrusting
almost too fast for the eye to follow its blur of motion.

He turned to see if any of his men had survived these first
violent few minutes and found himself facing a grim, heavy-set
man in chain mail and a surcoat bearing Arald's blue and yellow
colors. The man smiled at him and brandished his heavy wooden
ax.

"Didn't turn out quite how you planned?" he asked.

Morgarath's henchman realized that he had been outwitted.
Instead of targeting Arald's followers, he and his men had been
targeted themselves by these two fighters. With a scream of rage,
he swung an overhand blow at the man.

Farrel's drill ax was fashioned like his real one. The cutting
edge of the blade was a crescent of hardwood, with a supporting
center strut connecting it to the long haft. The ends of the crescent extended past the center strut, giving him a large striking
surface, without the prohibitive weight of a solid blade. As a
result, there was a gap between the top quarter of the blade and

the haft of the ax. He used this now to his advantage, trapping the descending sword blade in the gap and twisting savagely to spin the sword out of its owner's hand.

Teezal looked aghast as his weapon flew through the air. Then the flat of Farrel's ax slammed against his head. He was wearing a helmet, but it did little to stop the concussive force of the blow. His eyes glazed and his knees sagged as he sank to the ground.

Above him, he was dimly aware of the red-clad knight dropping his hand onto the axeman's shoulder. He heard the words he said as if the knight were a long way away.

"They're done. Let's get out of here."

As Teezal sank into unconsciousness, Farrel and Duncan shoved their way back through the ranks of the red force, stripping off their armbands as they went. A group of brown- and gray-cloaked men were standing ready by the rail to the public viewing area. As the two fighters scrambled under it, the Rangers bundled them in cloaks and spirited them away, out of sight.

40

Teezal slumped in a chair in Morgarath's pavilion, his head heavily bandaged, his temples still throbbing with the headache he had suffered all night.

Before him, the lord of Gorlan paced furiously, unable to stand still as a terrible rage swept over him. He stooped before his wounded servant, thrusting a pointing finger in his face.

"I don't know if I explained this," he said sarcastically, "but the whole idea was for you and your men to injure and incapacitate as many of Arald's allies as you could. That way, some of those barons who are wavering in their decision would have been driven over to my side. Was that so incredibly hard for your tiny mind to grasp?"

"No, my lord," muttered Teezal, shrinking away from the shouting voice as it set his head throbbing even worse than before.

"But instead, you've made me a laughingstock! You allowed yourselves to be ambushed by two men. Two men!" He screamed the last two words as he repeated them.

"They were working for Arald, my lord," Teezal said miserably.

But his words had no soothing effect on Morgarath. Rather, they had the opposite result.

"Well, *of course* they were working for Arald!" he roared. "Who did you think they were working for? The Great Badger of Bumbleberry?" He named a beloved creature from a well-known children's story.

Teezal guessed, correctly, that it would be wise not to respond.

"I've had to pay out a small fortune to have you and your idiot men released. Did you think that was my plan?"

"No, my lord," Teezal whispered. Even though Farrel and Duncan hadn't taken Teezal and his helpers prisoner, there were other fighters in the red force who had taken advantage of the situation, claiming the unconscious, injured men as their prizes and dragging them from the field.

Morgarath stopped pacing and held his clenched fists up to the sky, shaking them with impotent rage. The number of Arald's allies who were to be captured or defeated had never been the real issue. The point had been to show those uncertain barons that Morgarath's arm was long and merciless. Instead, he sensed a wavering in the resolve of several barons and knights who had previously been favorable to his cause. He had been outwitted, and it had been done in public.

Even worse, his force of seven men had been routed by two warriors. One of them, he recognized as Farrel, the Ranger from Redmont Fief whom he had tried to have discredited. The other was a tall man in a red tunic over silver mail. There was something familiar about him, Morgarath thought. But so far, he had been unable to place the man.

Now he would need to take drastic action to restore his

position and preeminence among the ranks of the barons. Fortunately, that drastic action would match something he already planned to do.

He glared at the pitiful figure in the chair before him. "Get out of here!" he snapped. "Send in my armorers. I'm going to have to take care of the situation myself—as ever!"

Teezal looked up warily as he rose from the chair. He crouched slightly, fearful of what Morgarath might do to him. "My lord, what are you going to do?" he asked, his voice quavering.

Morgarath fixed him with a basilisk stare that sent a shiver of dread down his spine. Never before had he seen such hatred in a man's eyes.

"I'm going to challenge Arald. He's the one who's behind all this. He's the one my opponents are gathering around. He's the one who gives them the courage to defy me. So I'll challenge him and then I'll kill him."

"But . . . how? It's a tournament, after all. There are rules . . ."

"And accidents do happen. I'll challenge him to fight, stipulating *à résultat final*. He won't dare refuse—he'd lose too much respect in the eyes of his followers if he did."

"But even so . . . ," Teezal began. *À résultat final* was a Gallican phrase that translated as "to the final result." It meant that, even after a combatant was unhorsed, the duel continued on foot until one of the fighters had overwhelmed his opponent. Usually, that meant until one of the combatants surrendered and admitted defeat. But sometimes, it meant to the death.

And that was how Morgarath planned it to be.

Arald was relaxing in his pavilion. The previous day, he had accepted a challenge from a young, untried knight looking to boost his reputation by contesting with the current tournament champion.

Arald had accepted. There had been no malice in the challenge and he felt it was his duty—and that of the other senior knights in the tournament—to give such young men a chance to prove themselves, and gain valuable experience in the profession of arms.

They had conducted five passes, with lances shattering on each. Arald could have unhorsed his young opponent at any time he had chosen, but that wasn't the purpose behind the challenge system. Afterward, he sat with the young man and provided a critique of his technique and advice on how to improve it. The tyro knight had departed gratefully, well aware that the champion had gone easy on him.

The door flap was open, admitting a pleasant breeze. Gorlan was a beautiful fief, Arald thought, in a part of the Kingdom blessed with a most benign climate. Winter was never too cold, although around Yuletide there would sometimes be a picturesque scattering of snow on the trees. And summers were never too hot.

It was a shame that such a beautiful spot was under the control of a blackhearted killer like Morgarath.

Still, he thought, maybe that wouldn't be the case for too much longer.

His head nodded on his chest and he dozed quietly.

"My lord!" a voice said urgently, snapping him awake with a start. He looked up and saw one of his battle-school apprentices pointing toward the far end of the tournament ground.

"Well, what do we have here?" he murmured. Riding across the jousting field toward him was the black-armored figure of Morgarath, astride his massive battlehorse, Warlock.

Slowly, Arald stood. He had no doubt as to who was about

to be challenged. As Morgarath came to the end of the jousting field, he reined Warlock down from a canter, until the tall white horse was walking toward the blue-and-gold pavilion.

There was something ominous in Warlock's steady gait. No curveting. No nervous prancing. No pulling at the reins. The huge white horse paced steadily and inexorably toward Arald. Morgarath's face was hidden behind his lowered visor—a breach of protocol, Arald thought. Challengers were supposed to reveal their faces to their erstwhile opponents.

Morgarath brought Warlock to a halt in front of the pole bearing Arald's shield. There was no sign of any command or action that stopped the horse. Arald knew it must have been accomplished by a minor pressure of the legs. Then Morgarath's lance struck the shield hanging high above them.

Again, protocol had it that a knight merely touched the shield of an opponent with his lance. But Morgarath contrived to put a vicious thrust behind the action, sounding a ringing clang as the lance head struck the metal shield.

Arald was aware that there was a small crowd watching proceedings. Some had hurried after Morgarath across the jousting field. Others had emerged from tents clustered nearby.

A few muttered in surprise at the force behind Morgarath's blow to the shield. But the muttering quickly died away as they waited for the coming byplay between the two champions.

"Arald of Redmont, I challenge you to single combat." Morgarath's voice echoed inside the helm.

Arald shrugged and leaned against the pole supporting the front of his pavilion. "And who might you be, you great black bird of evil omen," he replied easily. A few of the bystanders tittered, then fell silent as the black helmet turned toward them to mark them down for later reference.

"You know well who I am!" Morgarath snapped. "I am Morgarath, lord of Gorlan and knight of the realm, a loyal follower of King Oswald of Araluen."

"Then I'd best accept," Arald said.

The onlookers grew silent. Some had expected him to reject the challenge. As the reigning champion, that was his right. He could have avoided combat until the final day of the tournament, when he would be obliged to defend his title against whoever qualified to fight him.

"The duel will be *à résultat final*," Morgarath continued and the buzz of conversation sprang up again. Nobody had any doubt that Morgarath's idea of *à résultat final* would be final indeed.

"I wouldn't have it any other way," Arald replied, smiling grimly at his challenger.

41

THERE WERE STILL SEVERAL HOURS TO GO BEFORE THE DUEL between Arald and Morgarath was due to begin, but already people were streaming into the tournament ground looking for the best seats in the grandstands. The combat between the reigning champion and the three-time former champion promised to be an epic trial of arms, and nobody—noble or commoner—wanted to miss it. Aside from the expected quality of the bout, the two barons had polarized opinion over the past few days.

Morgarath had a strong following among the barons. Among the common people, he was less popular. He had a reputation as a cruel and haughty nobleman, who cared little for the castle staff who served him or the serfs and farmworkers who tended his lands. But he was a superbly skilled warrior with lance and sword and there were many who would forgive his personal failings for the privilege of watching him fight. A champion was always worth seeing, no matter how unpopular he might be.

Arald, on the other hand, was a more cheerful and approachable person. He was considerate of the needs of those who worked his estates and made sure they were looked after. Plus he had an irrepressible sense of humor and a ready smile. He was well liked, and as far as his skill as a warrior was concerned, there was little to choose between him and Morgarath. Many of the spectators felt they were watching a changing of the guard, with the younger Arald poised to replace Morgarath as the acknowledged champion knight of the realm.

The steady tide of people flowed down the hill from Castle Gorlan to the tournament ground, growing thicker with each passing minute. They carried pillows and picnic hampers and some even had small casks of ale balanced on their shoulders.

As Pritchard had foreseen, the castle was virtually empty, with everyone who had no urgent work to do that day heading for the tournament ground. He suspected that, while the majority of people from the castle would support Morgarath, there would be a considerable number who were secretly hoping to see the tall, black-armored knight thrown down into the dust. Keeping his head down and trying to look as inconspicuous as possible, he worked his way up the hill against the traffic, slipping unnoticed across the drawbridge and under the portcullis.

Moving quickly, he crossed the inner courtyard to the main keep. But, instead of entering via the door that led to the great hall, he turned down a small flight of stairs to one side and entered the service area of the castle.

This was where the kitchens, storerooms, sculleries and laundry were situated. Pritchard had familiarized himself with these below-stairs areas over the past week and now he made his way, head down and face concealed, to the huge laundry complex, where the castle staff had their uniforms washed and cleaned.

The massive vats were empty today, and the grates over

which they hung were unlit and filled with gray ash. The laundry workers, like so many of the others in the castle, had taken the duel as an excuse for a holiday. They had left the piles of unwashed linen and uniforms in their hampers, and the neatly folded items of freshly laundered clothes lying in stacks on the long pine tables that ran the length of the room.

Pritchard hurried to a pile of linen surcoats, finished in a checkerboard pattern of Morgarath's heraldic colors—black and gold. These were the everyday uniforms worn by the castle staff—servants, housekeepers and administrative assistants. He grabbed three of them from the stack, bundled them under his ragged cloak and made his way quickly out of the laundry.

He hurried back down the hill, now borne along by the people headed for the tournament field. He gradually worked his way to the edge of the press of hurrying humanity and darted off to the side, heading for a gardener's toolshed set outside the tournament area.

Glancing around to make sure nobody was watching, he elbowed the door open—he had unlocked it earlier that morning—and stepped inside. Halt and Crowley were waiting for him. He tossed them two of the tunics and, pulling off his ragged cloak, donned the third one himself.

"Did you bring the hamper?" he asked.

Crowley indicated it—a food hamper with a crumpled tablecloth, several linen napkins and half a dozen wooden platters and goblets. There was also a large serving platter and a domed cover—the type used to keep food warm. Rounding out the collection of table items was an empty wine cask. If they were challenged on their return to the castle, they would claim they had been sent for extra refreshments by Morgarath's castle chamberlain. It was highly unlikely that they would be asked what they were doing, but it never hurt to have a story ready. And it always helped if you could invoke the name of an important person in that story.

Pritchard checked his companions, leaning forward to adjust Halt's tunic where the collar had rolled over and was inside out.

"You always were a snappy dresser," he said. Halt ignored the comment.

Satisfied that the two Rangers looked like castle servants, Pritchard jerked a thumb toward the door. "Let's go," he said.

The traffic heading downhill was gradually petering out and they made good time back to the castle. The sentries on the drawbridge glanced idly at the empty hamper, and the wine cask Halt was carrying on his shoulder, then went back to discussing the coming contest. They were sour faced over the fact that they had to remain on duty, but at least they had managed to place wagers on Morgarath as the likely victor. They had seen their Baron in battle and had no doubts about his ability on the field.

As before, once they crossed the courtyard, Pritchard led Halt and Crowley to the side door and down into the service area of the castle. This time, however, he made his way to the kitchens. He peered round the doorway and ascertained that there was nobody working inside. Today, meals for Morgarath and his senior retainers would be prepared in the field kitchens behind his pavilion. If anybody else wanted food, they'd just have to wait till the fight was over.

Hastily, Pritchard tipped the contents of the hamper onto a wide pine table. Below the other items, in the bottom of the hamper, was a wooden serving tray. He proceeded to set up the tray with the serving platter, its domed cover in place, a goblet and a small wine flask, and one of the smaller platters. He folded a napkin and set it beside the small platter. Then, glancing round, he saw a wooden spoon on the next table and set that on the tray as well. He gestured at Halt.

"Pick it up," he said.

The Hibernian complied, balancing the tray, with its empty platters and flask, and followed Pritchard out of the kitchen and across the great hall to the eastern staircase. Crowley brought up the rear, glancing back from time to time to make sure nobody was observing them.

As they hurried up the steps, their soft-soled boots making little noise, Halt whispered to his old mentor, "Won't they be expecting the usual serving girl to bring the food?"

Crowley nodded. "That's why we've planned our little byplay when we get to the tower," he said. "It'll keep them distracted."

"We hope," Halt said heavily.

Pritchard nodded. "Yes. We certainly do."

Behind them, Crowley dropped his hand to the hilt of the saxe underneath his black-and-yellow tunic.

The problem with castles, Halt thought as he continued upward, was that they were full of stairs. If someone could only design a castle that was all on one level, it would save a lot of effort. But he continued upward, moving quickly as he took the stairs two at a time.

"One more flight," Pritchard whispered behind him.

Halt paused at the landing, gathering his breath and his thoughts. Pritchard moved closer to him.

"We'll wait at the entrance to the hallway," he said in a lowered tone. "You go on with the tray. The door to Oswald's room is on your right, ten meters away. There'll be two guards."

Halt nodded. He was tempted to ask, *What if there are more than two?* but he sensed that Pritchard's reply would be simply: Improvise. Then he set out, heading up the remaining dozen steps at a more sedate pace. He could hear the faint sound of his friends moving up behind him, then he was at the top and was stepping out into the corridor, turning right. He saw the two guards where Pritchard had said they'd be, sitting on straight-backed wooden chairs on either side of a solid wooden door, bound with iron reinforcing strips. They wore chain mail under their black-and-yellow tunics and short swords in their belts. Neither wore a helmet and their mail coifs were pushed back off their heads, lying in thick folds around their necks. Two halberds were leaning against the wall, one on either side of the heavy, ironbound door.

The man nearest to him began to rise from his feet, frowning at him. His hand dropped casually to the hilt of the sword in his belt, but he made no movement to draw it.

"Hullo, what are you doing?" he asked. "Where's Nelly?"

Halt guessed that Nelly was the serving girl who usually brought Oswald's meals. He pulled a wry face.

"Said she was sick," he replied. "Ask me, she's skived off to the tournament to watch Lord Morgarath beat the tar out of fat Arald of Redmont."

The other guard was on his feet now. Any change in the daily routine was to be treated with suspicion. He'd served Morgarath for fifteen years and had learned that lesson the hard way.

"Nobody told us . . . ," he began, but then he was distracted, looking toward the staircase doorway, where a furious Pritchard had emerged from the stairs, puffing heavily from the effort of climbing to the tower and pointing an accusing finger at Halt.

The guard noticed that the newcomer wore the chain and medal of a senior servant around his neck—an item Pritchard had spent the previous evening fashioning.

"You!" Pritchard yelled. "Where are you going with that tray? Come back here at once!"

Halt turned to face the angry white-haired man, his voice and face sullen. "Bringin' the prisoner his meal, is all."

Pritchard waved his arms angrily as he advanced along the hall. Crowley emerged from the staircase door and followed him.

"I told you!" Pritchard raged. "Lord Morgarath left orders that the prisoner wasn't to be served today!"

"Man's got to eat," Halt said stubbornly.

But Pritchard snapped his fingers at Crowley and pointed to the tray.

"Ridley! Take that tray from him!"

"Yes, Master Wildom," said Crowley, moving to stand closer to Halt and, coincidentally, to the two guards.

The guards were now exchanging grins, enjoying the sight of a squabble between the palace servants. Morgarath's soldiers held the serving staff in mild contempt. They had a soft, easy life, with ample opportunity to augment their rations with choice pieces from the kitchen. And they suffered no hardship or danger. There was little love lost between Morgarath's soldiers and the castle servants.

"You tell him, grandpa," one of them said.

Crowley reached for the tray, but Halt snatched it away, out of his reach.

Crowley glared at him. "Hand it over!" he demanded.

"Stop messing about!" Pritchard yelled, his voice cracking into a higher register. "Hand it over, Massey!"

Halt glared at the other two. "You want it so bad, you can have it!" he said to Crowley, and hurled the tray onto the flagstones of the corridor. The platters and the dome flew in the air as the tray hit the ground, then fell back, rattling and rolling. The two guards burst out laughing at Halt's display of petulance. Then one of them noticed that the platters were all empty.

"Hey," he said, "there's no food—"

That was as far as he got. Halt swung a savage left hook at him, catching him on the point of the jaw and sending him down like a poleaxed steer. The other guard, confused and alarmed, reached for the hilt of his sword, but Crowley, pivoting on one heel, drove his elbow into the man's belly. Then, as he doubled over with an explosive whoof of released breath, the Ranger brought both hands, clenched together, down onto the back of his exposed neck. The guard joined his companion on the floor, facedown.

Halt didn't wait to see the result of Crowley's work. Once his own man was down, he stepped quickly to the door. The large key was in the lock. That made sense, he thought. No need to hide it with two armed guards outside the door. He twisted it quickly, feeling the well-oiled lock click open, then pushed the door inward and went into the room.

Crowley and Pritchard were close behind him.

They found themselves in a large, dimly lit tower room, where the windows were barred with wooden shutters and only thin streaks of daylight made their way through the wooden slats. A pine table and straight-backed chair were in the center of the room and on the far wall was a narrow bed. An elderly man, his hair and beard untrimmed and matted, was sitting up on the bed, watching them with alarm in his eyes. He looked a little dazed, Halt thought.

Crowley stepped past Halt, approaching the elderly man and dropping to one knee beside the bed. He took one of the thin, wrinkled hands in both of his and spoke quietly and soothingly to the prisoner.

"Come on, your majesty. We're King's Rangers and we're getting you out of here."

42

THE TWO CONTESTANTS SAT THEIR HORSES AT EACH END OF the tilt. Their visors were lowered and neither man moved. They resembled metal statues, Morgarath in his all-black armor, relieved only by the patch of yellow on his breast and shield, and Arald in his dazzling blue, with the gold boar's head on his shield that was his personal insignia.

As they had ridden out to their starting positions, a hush had fallen over the crowd. Baron Naylor of Taft strode out to a position halfway down the tilt, and stood facing the western grandstand.

He nodded to a herald who had accompanied him. The brightly garbed man raised his long trumpet and blew an echoing blast on it—the signal for silence—although, with the sudden hush that had fallen over the spectators, the signal was unnecessary. Still, it was part of the ceremony of the joust and so it was carried out.

Naylor had a penetrating voice—one of the reasons he had been selected as grand marshal—and now he used it to its fullest extent.

"Milords, ladies, noble knights and citizens of the Kingdom

of Araluen! This will be a single combat, a challenge between Morgarath, Baron of Gorlan Fief, and Arald, Baron of Redmont Fief." He paused, gathering his breath, then continued.

"The challenge has been issued by Lord Morgarath, and accepted by Lord Arald. Both men have agreed that this passage of arms will be *à résultat final.*"

Now a buzz of excitement ran through the crowd—particularly those in the public grandstand on the eastern side. Although many had heard rumors about the details of the challenge, this was the first time they had heard it officially confirmed.

Naylor frowned. He was a somewhat pompous man and he didn't like being interrupted. He turned and faced the eastern grandstand and its noisy inhabitants. Like a flock of starlings at sunset, he thought. The undercurrent of conversation continued in spite of his withering glance. He gestured impatiently with his grand marshal's mace to the herald beside him. Again, the trumpeter blew a shattering blast, which finally brought silence to the crowd.

Naylor now looked to the end of the tilt where Morgarath sat astride Warlock. The white horse was as unmoving as his rider.

"Lord Morgarath, are you ready for combat?"

Morgarath's face was covered by his helmet. Knowing that his voice would be muffled, he chose to signal his readiness by raising his lance vertically in his right hand, then allowing it to drop back into the socket on his right stirrup.

Naylor turned to Arald's end of the field. "Lord Arald, are you ready for combat?"

Arald mirrored Morgarath's signal, raising his lance, then lowering it again. His battlehorse, Barnaby, flicked his tail at several errant flies, and trembled a muscle on his left shoulder. Otherwise, he too was unmoving.

Naylor nodded and paced toward the western grandstand, leaving the field of combat clear for the two barons. He turned to face them and raised his mace toward the three additional heralds who were standing ready.

Three trumpets rose to three sets of lips, and the strident notes of the signal to begin rang out over the field. As the last note died away, both warriors drove their spurs into their horses' sides and thundered forward. In the same second, a massive cheer rose from the crowd. Individual cries could be made out, here or there, encouraging either Morgarath or Arald, but for the most part, the crowd simply gave voice to a wordless shout of excitement.

The thunder of the two horses' hooves rose in intensity and huge clods of torn turf were hurled into the air behind them as the massive beasts strained every muscle and sinew, striving for the maximum speed and power as they charged.

The cries intensified as the two lances came down from their forty-five-degree angle to the horizontal. Some in the crowd had bet that one or the other of the riders would be unhorsed in the first pass and they leaned forward eagerly now as the collision was imminent.

It came, a thundering crash of wood and metal as the horses hurled themselves at each other on either side of the wooden fence that separated them. In this first pass, neither rider tried for anything more than a centered hit on the other's shield. This was a moment when they would assess each other's strength and timing and balance. As they came together, each lance was trapped by the concave shape of the opponent's shield. Both bent like bows until, in the same instant, they both shattered into hundreds of splinters, showering down on the riders as they crossed.

A groan rose from those who had bet on the first pass being decisive. Then their voices were drowned by a swelling tide of cheering as the crowd, nobles and commoners alike, roared their encouragement.

As they met, Arald had felt the shuddering impact of Morgarath's lance against his shield, and the inexorable force trying to hurl him back out of the saddle. He thrust forward against it, gripping his horse with all the strength of his thigh muscles to retain his seat, feeling the same savage pressure on his own lance as it locked on to Morgarath's shield.

It had been a year since he last faced the black-clad Baron on the tournament field and he had forgotten the timing and power of the man's lance stroke. For a second, he thought the sheer force of the impact would hurl him back out of the saddle and onto the ground. Then both lances shattered at the same time and he lunged forward, the backward pressure suddenly relieved. He shook his head. That had been a close call, he thought. But he felt that his own strike on Morgarath's shield had been nearly as forceful.

Morgarath, for his part, cursed inside his helmet. Arald had hit him hard—harder than he'd expected. In the past year, Morgarath had dueled occasionally, but never with a knight as accomplished or as skilled or as determined as his current opponent. For the first time, he felt a flicker of concern. Not fear, but simply the realization that he must not take Arald too lightly. That had been his mistake in the past.

He knew he had hit Arald with a near-perfectly centered

strike. A hit like that would have thrown most men out of the saddle. Yet he had felt no movement from the blue-and-gold knight. He might need to change tactics, he thought. He tossed the shattered stump of his lance to one side. Behind him, Arald was doing the same. Then they both checked and turned their horses at the end of the tilt.

Arald's black horse reared onto his hind legs as he turned, but the Baron of Redmont sat him easily. He calmed the horse and waited till his attendant ran forward and passed him a new lance. The assistant marshal stationed at this end of the tilt stepped close to Barnaby's shoulder and called up to Arald.

"Are you ready?"

"Ready," called Arald, his voice muffled and echoing strangely, sounding like someone else. He stared past the slightly blurred bars of his visor to the other end of the field, where he saw Morgarath answering the same query. Both marshals raised their batons, and the heralds blew the signal to charge once more.

Again, the cheering swelled with the thunder of horses' hooves as the two straining animals churned the soft ground in an attempt to put as much force behind their charge as possible. Arald could hear his own breath rasping hollowly inside the helmet, above the background of his horse's pounding hooves. His eyes were set on Morgarath's lance point as they approached and it came down to the horizontal. Then he saw a slight waver. He suspected that Morgarath would try to end this combat quickly, that he would use his undoubted skill and precision to achieve a decisive blow with the lance. Even as he had the thought, he saw the tip of Morgarath's lance suddenly rise and center on his helmet, with only a few meters still separating them.

Nine times out of ten, the ploy would have been successful. But Arald's premonition had prepared him and his reflexes were lightning fast. Keeping his lance trained steadily on the center of Morgarath's shield, he swayed slightly to the right, allowing the black warrior's lance point to slide over his left shoulder. A fraction of a second later, Arald's lance hit Morgarath's shield and, once again, shattered with a splintering crack.

Morgarath, slightly unbalanced after his own thrust met no resistance, swayed visibly in the saddle before he recovered and galloped on.

Now the spectators shouted even louder. In a normal joust, such a pass would have put Arald at an advantage. His lance had shattered; Morgarath's had not. That would put Arald a point up. But this was to be fought *à résultat final*, so it really had no significance. It was a moral victory for Arald, but that was all.

He slowed Barnaby, who was puffing and grunting with the effort of the two passes, and wheeled him at the end of the tilt, throwing his broken lance aside and taking a new one from his attendant. At the far end of the field, he saw Morgarath discarding his lance and he frowned, a little puzzled. Morgarath's lance was undamaged. Why change it? Morgarath's attendant passed him a replacement. The black-clad warrior tested the heft and balance of the new weapon, then tossed it aside, gesturing for another.

Maybe I've rattled him, Arald thought. He wondered if he might try a helmet strike himself this time, then discarded the idea. Morgarath was too wily an opponent and he would probably be expecting such a move. Stay with what you're doing, Arald told himself. Two good hits on the shield have unsettled him. Another one might do the trick.

"Baron Arald! Are you ready?" It was the marshal beside him and he realized he'd already been asked the question and had given no answer. Stop woolgathering, he told himself angrily.

"Ready," Arald replied.

At the far end of the field, Morgarath finally seemed to be satisfied with the feel of his lance. He brandished it several times, testing the weight and the balance. Then, as the marshal asked him, he signified that he was ready for the next pass. Warlock had begun to toss his head and paw the ground at the delay. Morgarath tugged his head around and calmed him. The battlehorse's blood was up and the excitement of combat was making him agitated and eager to charge.

Again the two batons were raised. Again, the trumpets blared out. And once more, the two combatants set off toward each other, digging in with their spurs and urging their massive steeds on to an even greater effort than before.

The ground on either side of the tilt was torn and muddied now, after the horses had churned it in the two preceding passes. Their ironshod hooves had worn a track in the grass, leaving it more earth brown than green. Clods and divots of turf littered the ground to either side. But that didn't diminish the enthusiasm or energy of the two horses. They pounded toward each other, not needing their riders' hands to aim them at each other. These were battlehorses, bred, born and trained for the role, and they were each totally intent on one thing: destroying the other, smashing him down, leaving him screaming with pain and frustration in the dirt.

Once again, Arald was conscious of the roar of his own breathing—and the accelerated pounding of his heart beneath the chain mail. He leaned forward, gripping with his thighs to guide Barnaby.

Thunder of hooves. Roaring of the crowd. Morgarath, seen through the blurred bars of the visor, coming closer and closer, his lance point lowering. This time there was no wavering. This time, Arald knew his shield would be targeted and he braced himself for the impact, ready to thrust back as hard as he could.

This time, he thought, I'll have him!

They smashed together, with that same terrible, rending sound of wood and metal colliding. Arald felt his lance bend and then shatter. He heard splinters raining down on his helmet.

Then, a fraction of a second later, as Morgarath's lance hit his shield, Arald realized that something was wrong—terribly wrong.

43

In his time, Arald had fought in hundreds of bouts—
practice rounds, friendly tournaments and deadly serious bat-
tles to the death. He instinctively knew the difference between
a strike with a tournament lance, designed to shatter on contact
and fitted with a rounded wooden practice head, and a war
lance, designed to penetrate and kill.

Morgarath was using a war lance.

There was a large puff of dust as the molded clay ball disguis-
ing the iron tip disintegrated. Then the iron head struck and
held, biting deep into his shield, lodging there and gouging a
jagged hole in the thin metal covering the wooden framework.
The heavy oak shaft didn't bend and splinter as a tournament
lance would have. It held firm, barely flexing, and driving the
lethal iron warhead deep into the shield, hurling Arald back, the
massive power of the strike driving his horse down onto its
haunches as Morgarath rose in his stirrups, using his own weight
and strength and momentum to drive the lance home even
harder.

Arald tried to kick his legs clear of the stirrups. Barnaby
screamed in rage and pain and crashed over onto his side,

trapping Arald's right leg underneath his massive body. Barnaby struggled to rise, but he was badly winded by the fall and the weight of his rider and saddle. Added to that was the fact that Barnaby had badly strained a fore shoulder muscle as he was sent twisting to one side, leaving him kicking and struggling helplessly on his side, his rider trapped beneath him.

Desperately Arald tried to shove himself clear of the struggling horse, but the weight was too much. His left arm still retained the torn shield, and he held the horse's reins in his left hand. Realizing that if Barnaby made it to his feet, the threshing, ironshod hooves might well put an end to his life, Arald took the reins in both hands and held the horse down as he struggled to extricate himself. Time enough to let Barnaby up when he was clear, he thought.

He craned round to see where Morgarath was and saw the black-clad knight rounding the far end of the tilt and trotting his horse back toward him. He still had a few moments, he thought, thrusting despairingly with his left leg against the saddle to try to slip his right leg free.

Morgarath was swinging down from the saddle. He drew his two-handed longsword from its scabbard with a ringing hiss of steel on leather. He shook the black-and-yellow shield from his left arm, discarding it on the grass. Then he turned to face the western grandstand.

"À résultat final!" he shouted, reminding those watching of the agreed conditions of the duel. Then he began to run toward the stricken figure on the ground, raising the huge sword above his head in a two-handed grip as he went.

Arald realized he had misjudged badly. Too late, he released his grip on the reins. But Barnaby was exhausted now by his struggles, and by the thundering charges he had delivered during the duel, and he lay, snorting and groaning, and refused to try to rise.

The huge sword came down, hissing through the air. Arald, lying helplessly, his own sword trapped somewhere under his body, had only the light jousting shield with which to defend himself. Desperately, he threw it up into the path of the descending longsword and felt the heavy blade bite into the metal, tear through it and shatter the wood beneath it. The force of the blow drove the shield down against him. Morgarath struggled briefly to free the blade from the tangle of splintered wood and torn metal. With a final tug, he jerked it clear, breaking the shield's leather arm straps in the process and sending it spinning across the field.

Now Arald lay at his mercy. Morgarath brought the sword back again and swung it in a forty-five-degree arc, aiming to shear through Arald's shoulder where his neck joined his body. Arald saw it coming and shut his eyes, waiting for the end.

But the blow never landed.

Morgarath felt a jarring vibration up his arm and heard a ringing crash of steel on steel as something intercepted his stroke, stopping it cold. He looked up from the helpless man trapped under the horse and saw another warrior had joined the battle—a tall man wearing a red surcoat and glittering chain mail. A flat-topped, cylindrical helmet was set on his head, with a broad nasal reaching down to protect his nose and face—and conceal his features.

His sword, a heavy-bladed cavalry sword, had intercepted Morgarath's killing stroke. His iron wrist had blocked the long blade, stopping it dead in midair, even though it had all of Morgarath's strength behind it.

Morgarath screamed in rage and stepped back, pointing accusingly at the interloper.

"You have no right!" he screamed. "This is a duel of honor and you cannot interfere!"

"There's no honor here," the other man replied. "You broke the rules of the tournament. You used a war lance with a killing head."

His voice carried clearly to the grandstands on either side and the crowd, which had grown silent at his intervention, began to buzz with comment. They had seen how Morgarath's lance hadn't shattered, how it had driven deep into Arald's shield, sending his horse staggering and falling. Now they understood why it had happened that way.

But Morgarath wasn't about to give in easily. He turned and screamed toward his pavilion.

"Crossbowmen! Shoot him down!"

Tournament rules stated that two crossbowmen should always be on duty in case a combatant was seen to break the rules during a bout. Striking at an opponent's horse, or turning to attack an opponent from behind after a pass was completed, were two of the situations that would result in the transgressor's being shot. Another rule forbade a third party taking a hand in a duel, as had just happened. Since Morgarath was the host of the tournament, the crossbowmen were his soldiers. Now, they stepped forward and leveled their weapons at the red-clad knight facing their Baron.

"Rangers!"

Morgarath looked round, confused, at the cry. He saw a group of men, all wearing the distinctive mottled cloaks of the Ranger Corps, all with massive longbows, stepping clear of the public grandstand.

"Drop the crossbows!" The same voice carried across the field and the crossbowmen hesitated. They had heard the word Rangers. Now they saw eight men in mottled-green-and-gray cloaks, each one with a massive longbow leveled.

These men, they realized, were real Rangers, not the ineffectual pretenders that their lord had been appointing over the past months.

"Do it now!" the voice added and the crossbowmen set their bows down on the grass at their feet, backing away from them, their hands held in the air.

"You cowards!" Morgarath screamed. "Shoot him down! I order you!"

The two men exchanged a glance, then turned and ran.

"He's broken the rules! He must die!" Morgarath ranted after them. But the red-clad stranger interrupted him in a voice that was audible around the field.

"You can't break the rules of the tournament, then invoke them to suit yourself," he said.

His voice was vaguely familiar and Morgarath regarded him through slitted eyes. "Who are you?" he demanded.

The knight smiled at him, a grim smile totally devoid of humor. Plunging his sword point into the ground, he reached with his right hand toward his shield. Morgarath realized now that the shield was covered with a thick linen overlay. The stranger released the retaining cord and the linen fell away, revealing a red-enameled shield. In the center, in a white circle, was the figure of a stooping red hawk.

Prince Duncan's insignia. There was a gasp of surprise from the onlookers.

"Duncan!"

"Actually, that's Prince Duncan to you," Duncan told him.

For a moment, Morgarath was taken aback. Then his devious mind found a way to turn the situation to his advantage. He pointed accusingly at the prince.

"Then I name you traitor to the Kingdom! You've been raiding across the border into Picta, looting and killing and endangering our treaty with our northern neighbors! Lay down your sword and surrender, you traitor!"

Duncan shook his head slowly. He took hold of the sword, standing point down in the turf, and drew it clear.

"Not going to happen, Morgarath," he said.

The black-clad Baron leapt toward him, swinging his vast sword in a horizontal stroke at rib height. It smashed into Duncan's shield with a ringing crash.

But this was a war shield, not a light wood-and-metal piece designed for friendly tournaments. It was thick metal set over a solid hardwood frame, with a slightly convex shape to deflect an opponent's blows. The sword blade shrieked against the shield as it slid off, leaving a scar in the paint and a faint dent in the surface.

And then Morgarath found himself fighting for his life.

Duncan rained blow after blow on the tall Baron, one stroke blending into another in a continuous barrage. Morgarath had no shield and the longsword was a heavy and cumbersome weapon. It took all his mighty strength to position it for each parry and he was left with no time to attempt a counterstroke. He gave ground slowly, backing away from the relentless storm of blows, seeing Duncan's sword as a glittering wheel of light, striking at him first from one direction, then another. His breath was coming in short gasps and fear struck deep in his heart as he realized that he was outmatched. For the first time, he was facing a swordsman who was just as powerful as he was, but faster and more skilled.

They moved back along the tournament ground, their swords clashing in a continuous ringing, shrieking din. Then, as Morgarath had backed almost all the way toward his own pavilion, Duncan caught him with his sword momentarily lowered and struck down at it, beating it from Morgarath's grasp and sending it thudding to the turf.

The black-clad knight held up both hands in a gesture of surrender.

"Wait!" he shouted, expecting Duncan to simply continue with a coup de grâce. But the prince stopped, his sword pointing at Morgarath's throat.

"What is it?" Duncan said.

Morgarath heaved a shuddering sigh of relief. He looked around to the grandstand. The barons assembled there had risen from their seats. Some had even begun to move toward the tournament field itself. Morgarath's next words were pitched to the onlookers.

"I still call you traitor, and I demand the right to speak in front of the barons assembled here." He raised his voice and beckoned to the nobles in the grandstand. "My lords! Join us, please! We have vital business to discuss!"

As the various noblemen began to descend from the grandstand and make their way to the end of the tournament ground where Morgarath and Duncan faced each other, Duncan realized the moment was lost. A second ago, he could have killed Morgarath and claimed it was done in the heat of battle. Now, after Morgarath's appeal to the assembled nobles, such an act would be regarded as cold-blooded murder.

Morgarath glanced round and saw Teezal hovering nearby. He beckoned him closer and whispered, "Get the proclamation."

He had been planning to reveal the proclamation after his bout with Arald. Now, he realized, it could still be a deciding factor for him. Teezal nodded and turned away, but Morgarath's hand on his arm stopped him. The Baron of Gorlan leaned closer and said in a lower tone, "And assemble our men."

As Teezal hurried away, Morgarath turned back to face the group of nobles. Behind them, members of the general public were also streaming onto the field, crowding around the group of barons and knights, jostling for a better view. That suited Morgarath. He was a skilled rabble-rouser, and the fake Duncan's exploits had eroded the prince's popularity and credibility with the common people.

Duncan saw that most of the barons present had gathered around them. He decided not to wait for Morgarath. He sensed that the man had some stratagem in mind.

"Morgarath, I accuse you of breaking the rules of your own tournament and attempting to murder Baron Arald of Redmont," he said in a firm, clear voice.

"And I counter-accuse you, Prince Duncan, of attempting to murder your own father, King Oswald, and of raiding and murdering in the north. I accuse you of breaking our treaty with the people of Picta and risking all-out war. I accuse you of treason against the crown and demand that you face the death penalty."

44

THERE WAS A SHOCKED BUZZ OF REACTION FROM THOSE assembled, nobles and commoners alike. A royal prince was being charged with treason and threatened with the death penalty.

Duncan ignored the muttering from the crowd and made a dismissive gesture. "All of these charges are false, Morgarath. The raids in the north were carried out by an impostor, sent by you to discredit me, while you held me prisoner at Castle Wildriver."

"*I* held you prisoner, Duncan? *I* did this?" Morgarath said with a sarcastic smile.

"You arranged it," Duncan said.

Morgarath followed up quickly. "And you have proof?"

Duncan realized he was on shaky ground. "The castle was commanded by Sir Eammon of Wildriver," he said. "A well-known supporter of yours."

"And Sir Eammon is here to swear to that? To swear that he held you on my orders?" Morgarath made a show of looking around, then looked back to Duncan, his hands held wide in a gesture that said *show me*.

Duncan set his jaw and said nothing.

"Then perhaps," Morgarath continued in the same mocking tone, "you can produce this impostor you say I hired to impersonate you? Is he here to speak up?"

"He was," Duncan said shortly. "But he was killed."

"How very inconsiderate of him," Morgarath said. Several people in the crowd behind the barons tittered. Duncan flushed angrily. "And how very inconvenient for you."

Duncan decided he should counterattack and try to regain some lost ground by dealing with the one matter where there was concrete proof.

"The fact remains," he said, addressing the crowd, "Morgarath broke the rules of the tournament, the rules of honor, by using a war lance and trying to murder Baron Arald."

Sir Rodney, Baron Arald's battle master, stepped forward, holding the lance. He had retrieved it from the jousting field. He passed it to Duncan, who held it up for inspection.

"See? An oak shaft, not pine. And see the iron point—a killing point." He looked at Morgarath. "I suppose you concealed this behind clay or plaster, painted to look like a wooden jousting tip."

Morgarath pursed his lips and shrugged. "I had no knowledge of this, I swear. Obviously, one of my followers took matters into his own hands. But if so, he did it without my approval. I'll find out who did this and he will be severely punished, you have my word." He had addressed the comment not to Duncan, but to the barons gathered around them. He noted with satisfaction that several of them nodded. Others looked less convinced, but he had sown the seed of doubt that would be vital to his defense.

Duncan hefted the oak shaft once or twice. "And you're telling us you didn't notice the difference in weight?"

Again, Morgarath spread his hands in a gesture of innocence. "I have all my jousting lances weighted with lead so that they feel the same as a war lance. You know the saying, practice as you plan to fight."

There was a murmur of concurrence from the barons standing around. Morgarath's habit of weighting his lance with lead bands was well-known.

Morgarath saw Teezal approaching through the crowd, carrying a roll of parchment. He turned to his henchman and beckoned him forward.

He sensed that he was gaining the upper hand in this battle of words. This came as no surprise. Duncan was young and inexperienced in matters such as this. And Morgarath knew the prince had no concrete proof of the charges he was laying. He had bluster and indignation and unsubstantiated accusations. Given time, of course, he might be able to prove that he had been held captive. But here and now, his case was weak, and it was seen to be so. Now was the time for Morgarath to present his most conclusive argument.

Behind the crowd of spectators, Morgarath could see files of his soldiers taking up their positions, ready to attack on his command. He estimated that Teezal had managed to assemble approximately fifty men, which would be more than enough for the current situation.

Teezal stepped forward and handed him the rolled piece of parchment. Morgarath took it, then leaned close to his assistant and spoke softly.

"Go to the castle. Kill Oswald and get rid of the body."

Teezal lowered his head in a quick bow. "Yes, my lord." He turned and hurried away through the crowd.

Duncan watched him go and wondered what Morgarath was up to. But Morgarath's next words caused him to forget the hurrying figure.

"My lords, and people of Araluen, I have a most unpleasant duty to perform here—one which I am reluctant to carry out. But in the light of the false accusations against me, tendered without proof or evidence of any kind, I feel I must bring this matter before you."

He brandished the rolled parchment above his head. Silence fell over the crowd as they looked at it, wondering what it was.

"What trickery are you planning now?" Duncan asked angrily. But several voices from the crowd admonished him.

"Let him speak!"

"We'll hear him!"

"You've said your piece, Duncan. Now let Morgarath speak!"

Morgarath waited, letting the moment stretch while the interjections grew and more people took up the cry. Duncan noticed that those calling out were barons who favored Morgarath's cause. That was to be expected, he thought. But among the others, those as yet uncommitted, several were nodding their heads in agreement. Defeated, he took half a pace back and gestured for Morgarath to continue.

Holding the parchment high, Morgarath allowed it to unroll. The crowd could see it was covered in ornate writing, and a large seal was fixed in red wax at the bottom.

"This is a proclamation from King Oswald!" he shouted. "In it, the King disinherits Duncan, on account of his disloyalty and of his brigandry on the northern border. In his place, the King names me as his heir."

Uproar broke out among the crowd. Some protested that the

proclamation was false. Others cheered Morgarath's elevation to the position of royal heir. Duncan frowned as he estimated that the differing reactions were about equal.

Morgarath handed the parchment to Baron Naylor and raised his voice above the shouting crowd. "Let Baron Naylor read and confirm what I have said!" he shouted.

The bickering, catcalling, cheering and protests died away. The crowd waited as Naylor scanned the document. He was an irritatingly slow reader and his lips moved to frame the words as he read. The crowd waited on tenterhooks. Then he looked up.

"It's true," Naylor declared. "King Oswald has disinherited Duncan and named Morgarath as his rightful heir." There was a note of satisfaction in his voice. It was clear where his loyalty lay.

Pandemonium broke out, with everyone speaking or shouting at once. Morgarath threw a triumphant glare at Duncan, then raised his hands for silence. Gradually, the noise died away. He took the parchment from Naylor and brandished it, pointing to the large seal on the bottom.

"And this proclamation bears King Oswald's royal seal!" he shouted triumphantly. He turned from one side to the other, showing them the seal.

Then a thin voice broke the silence.

"But not my signature."

There was a commotion at the rear of the crowd, as three figures pushed their way through to confront Morgarath. Flanking the central figure were Halt and Crowley. The man between them pushed back the cowl on his ragged cloak and revealed his features.

Word ran round the crowd in a startled series of exclamations. "The King!"

Oswald faced Morgarath, pointing a trembling, accusing finger at the Baron.

"The proclamation is a forgery, Morgarath. You took my seal and fixed it there. I would never name you as my successor."

"The proclamation is true!" Morgarath shouted angrily. "You're simply recanting now that your son is back with a cock-and-bull story about impostors and being held prisoner."

"Just as you held me prisoner, Morgarath," accused Oswald.

But the tall Baron shook his head violently. "I held you for your own protection!" he declared. He pointed at Duncan. "This man—your *son*"—he put a sneering emphasis on the word—"tried to kill you, remember? You were glad enough for my protection then, if you recall?"

Oswald shook his head doggedly. "I was mistaken."

"And now you're not?" Morgarath said sarcastically. "It seems our royal family are continually changing their mind as the situation suits them. One minute Duncan is a brigand and a traitor, next he's a captive, being held against his will on my orders. And our good King seems to look for my protection one minute, then claim I've taken him prisoner the next."

Several voices were raised in agreement. Morgarath's efforts currying favor among the barons were bearing fruit.

But Duncan stepped forward angrily. This war of words had gone on long enough and he was amazed at the way Morgarath could sway the sentiment of the crowd.

"Arrest him," he said to Crowley. The Ranger leader made a gesture and his eleven companions stepped forward, bows ready and arrows nocked.

At the same moment, Morgarath shouted an order. "Gorlan!

To me!"

The fifty soldiers Teezal had summoned now shouldered their way through the crowd and stood by their lord. Swords drawn, they faced the grim-visaged line of Rangers.

"Say the word, Duncan, and we'll start shooting," Crowley said.

But the King raised a hand. "No," Oswald said. "Innocent people will be killed if we fight now."

Morgarath smiled grimly. He knew he had won this round and bought himself valuable time. He raised his voice and addressed the King.

"I will answer to your charges," he said. "And I'll bring my own against Duncan. But I'll do it before the full Council of Barons, as is my right."

"The King himself has accused you!" Duncan shouted angrily. "You'll answer to him!"

Morgarath eyed his enemy and said, in scathing tones, "The days are long gone when kings could be judge, jury and executioner," he said. "We have a rule of law here in Araluen now. And that law says I can demand to face the council of my peers."

"It'll take months to assemble the full council," Crowley protested.

Morgarath allowed himself a bitter smile at the Ranger. "And I will await the assembly in my own castle," he said. "Not in some dungeon at Castle Araluen, where Duncan and his backsliding father can plot my *accidental* death."

"You'll surrender yourself to me now!" said the King, his face white with fury.

But Morgarath shook his head. "As I've said, I'll await the

Council's summons in Castle Gorlan," he said. He turned to the commander of his force. "Captain! We're going back to the castle."

"Yes, sir!" the captain snapped, saluting. Then he turned to his men. "Form a phalanx around the Baron, men!" he said. "Prepare to withdraw in force."

Morgarath's soldiers had been well drilled. Quickly, they formed a protective circle around him, with all of them facing outward, swords drawn and ready to meet an attack from any direction. Slowly, they began to withdraw toward the castle, shoving aside any who were slow to move out of their way.

Duncan watched, frustration mounting, as the group withdrew, in a shuffling gait designed to maintain their formation and conform to the slowest among them—those moving backward.

"Can't we stop them?" he said furiously.

The others shook their heads. Morgarath was on his home ground, with all of his soldiers, men-at-arms and knights at his disposal. That totaled over one hundred men, a well-organized force trained to act together. None of the other barons had brought a full retinue to the tournament. Arald had the largest group and that amounted to less than twenty men. Given time, they could probably muster a force of around a hundred men, but right now they didn't have time. Morgarath was in control of the situation.

In addition, there was a strong possibility that a good number of the barons, sympathetic to Morgarath's cause, would refuse to lend men to fight him.

"We can contain them," Pritchard said. "We can muster enough men to bottle them up, but not enough to storm the castle. By the same token, he doesn't have enough men to fight his way out."

"So it's a stalemate?" Crowley said.

Pritchard nodded. "Until the council has assembled, that's the situation. We can't get in. He can't get out."

Halt watched the shuffling mass of soldiers as they moved in a steel-bristling formation toward the castle. He could see the tall figure of Morgarath in the center, standing head and shoulders above his men. Acting on an impulse, he unslung his bow from his shoulder and began to move toward the exit to the tournament ground.

Duncan caught up with him and stopped him with a hand on his arm.

"Where are you going?" he said.

The Hibernian faced him grimly. "I'm going to put an arrow through that blackhearted swine and finish this once and for all."

But Duncan shook his head. "That'll be murder," he said. "I won't have it done on my account, or my father's. We'll leave Morgarath to the Council."

Halt dropped his gaze, knowing Duncan was right. "Even so," he said, "I can't help thinking we're making a big mistake."

45

A MONTH LATER, HALT RETURNED TO CASTLE GORLAN TO observe the situation and report back to Duncan and Oswald, who had taken up residence in Castle Araluen once more.

He rode into the camp, noting with satisfaction that the haphazard accommodations that had been in place when he left were now replaced by ordered lines of tents and a small group of command pavilions. Central among these was Arald's blue-and-gold tent. The Baron of Redmont had taken command of the force left to keep watch on Morgarath and his men. Initially, it had been a hastily thrown together group of knights and men-at-arms, gleaned from the retinues of the barons present at the tournament. As Duncan had feared, several of the barons had refused to provide troops to the force, withdrawing to their own castles with their men.

Now, things looked more organized, with regular drafts of troops arriving from all corners of the Kingdom each day. He studied the rows of tents keenly. He estimated that there were over a hundred men encamped outside Gorlan's walls.

The tournament field was bare of all decoration. The flags and pennants were long gone and the tilt had been dismantled.

The grandstands were bare. The canvas coverings, comfortable chairs and brightly colored cushions were all gone. On the jousting field where Arald and Morgarath had met in combat, a troop of spearmen were drilling, under the command of a sergeant.

Above the fluttering canvas of the tents, Castle Gorlan loomed, its beauty and symmetry now seeming to bear an air of gloom and malevolence. He shook his head. He was being fanciful, he thought.

Baron Arald stepped out of his command tent and came to greet Halt as he dismounted.

"Welcome, Halt," he said. "You're a sight for sore eyes. What's the news from Castle Araluen?"

Halt frowned. "Not all good, I'm afraid. King Oswald's health is very poor and he's growing weaker every day. I don't think he's going to be with us much longer."

Arald shook his head. "That's sad news indeed. How is Duncan taking it?"

"He's very worried for his father, of course. Oswald has appointed him Regent, so he can take most of the strain of command off his shoulders. That might help a little. But he's kicking himself for the way he let Morgarath out-talk him and twist his words at the tournament. He wasn't ready for the way Morgarath muddied the water with his barrage of allegations and accusations."

Arald shrugged. "Not his fault. He's only young and Morgarath has years of experience in that sort of intrigue and obfuscation. Duncan will learn. In any event, once the King appeared and accused Morgarath, he knew the game was up. He had to act quickly and barricade himself in the castle where we couldn't get to him. And that was as good as an admission of guilt."

"Duncan had better learn," Halt said. "He's summoned the Council of Barons, as you know, so he'll be making his case before them. He's also reinstated the Ranger Corps as it was. Crowley has been appointed Commandant—he'll have authority over the entire Corps, not just the dozen of us who've been with him so far. He'll have to recruit new apprentices and locate as many of the former Rangers as he can. He's moved into quarters at Castle Araluen."

"Sounds like he'll have his hands full," said Arald. Then he tilted his head at Halt. "What about you?"

"Duncan has ratified my commission as a Ranger," Halt said. "Although Crowley tried to convince him that I still needed extra training as an apprentice."

Arald laughed. That was typical of Crowley, ever looking for an opportunity to pull Halt's leg.

"So he wanted you to revert to a bronze oakleaf?"

Halt nodded. "Fortunately, he was convinced otherwise."

Arald's grin widened. "By whom?" he asked innocently.

Halt replied, straight-faced. "By me, mainly. I presented a most eloquent case against demotion. I threatened to shove the bronze oakleaf up his left nostril."

"That sounds eloquent indeed."

Halt turned away and studied the castle. Even at a distance, he could see the heads and shoulders of the sentries on the walls. One of them was leaning against the wall of a small fighting turret that projected above the battlements.

"Anything happening here?" he asked.

Arald shook his head. "Nothing. They watch us. We watch them. Haven't seen or heard from Morgarath in over a week now. But I feel he's going to have to make a move sometime soon.

With every day that passes, his position grows weaker. We've got new troops arriving every week. Eventually, we'll outnumber him and have enough men to storm the castle and take him prisoner."

"Hmmm," said Halt thoughtfully. "Pritchard said something along the same lines. Have you seen him lately? He was heading here to check up on a rumor he'd heard. Didn't say what it was. You know how Pritchard can be."

"He came through here four days ago. Stayed the night, nosed around, then must have headed out. He hasn't been back since."

Halt nodded absentmindedly. "He'll turn up sooner or later."

"You know him better than I," Arald said cheerfully. "Are you staying with us tonight? I'd welcome the company at dinner and I have a tent you can use."

Halt glanced at the sky. The sun was sinking low to the horizon, through a screen of heavy clouds. It had rained the last few nights, heavy soaking rain, and it appeared that tonight would be no different.

"That'd be most welcome," he said.

"I'll see you at dinner then," Arald said, turning back to his own pavilion. "Right now I have to write out my night orders for the new troops."

As he entered the tent, heavy raindrops began to thump down on its canvas roof and sides.

Halt pulled his cowl over his head and looked up at the castle again. Lights were beginning to show in the windows of the towers, coming on one after the other. Braziers along the battlements began to flare as well, screened from the rain by wooden roofs. He could make out the form of a single man moving along the battlements, carrying a torch and moving from one beacon to another, lighting them in turn. The oil-soaked firewood they held flared quickly into life.

He felt a touch on his arm and turned to see a young page, dressed in Arald's blue-and-gold livery and staring at him with some awe. "Your pardon, Master Halt," said the boy nervously. "The Baron said as how I should show you to your tent."

"Then lead on, young man," said Halt, smiling at him. "But first show me where the stables are, so I can tend to my horse."

He slept fitfully that night, kept awake by the drumming of rain on the canvas. Around three in the morning the rain died away and he fell asleep. But at five thirty he was awake again, listening to the crowing of a rooster somewhere in the camp.

Reluctantly, he decided that he was unlikely to fall asleep again. He rose, washed in the leather basin in his tent, and dressed.

The cook tent was already in action and he made his way to it, striding through the long, sodden grass. He snared a small loaf of bread, tore it apart and filled it with hot bacon, wolfing the food down hungrily. There was fresh coffee in a pot and he poured himself a mug. Then, cup in hand, enjoying the rich hot drink in the chill of the morning, he strolled up to study the castle once more.

He frowned. Something was odd, he thought. Something was wrong. But the castle was unchanged. The sentries were still visible on the battlements, still in their positions. The man he had noticed the previous evening, leaning against the turret, was still in the same spot.

Then it hit him. *Nothing* had changed. Nobody had changed positions in eleven hours. That was what was wrong.

Unslinging his bow from his shoulder, he began to walk purposefully toward the castle. As he came closer, he saw a line of white-painted stakes driven into the ground. One of Arald's men stood just outside the line. He called a warning to Halt.

"Careful, sir! These pegs mark the maximum range of their crossbows. Young Billy Creek was shot by the one of the swine just a week ago."

Halt ignored him and continued to walk toward the castle. His eyes scanned the battlements keenly, looking for the first sign of movement that would indicate a crossbow being trained on him. He stopped at a point a hundred paces from the moat, looking up at the dark figure of the sentry leaning against the turret wall. The man had shown no sign that he had noticed Halt's approach.

Halt drew an arrow, nocked it, and casually took aim.

Still the man didn't move—although he must have seen the Ranger on the sodden ground below the walls.

Halt released. The arrow hissed away, in a fast-moving arc toward the figure high above. Still no sign of recognition or reaction. Then the arrow struck home and the figure was thrown backward by the impact. Faintly, Halt heard a clatter as it stuck the flagstones.

But no cry of pain.

He ran back to where the sentry was watching, a puzzled look on his face.

"Get me a long rope," Halt said. "I'm going over that wall."

The castle was empty, except for half a dozen servants who had been left behind to light the lamps each night. The battlements had been manned by mannequins—dummies dressed in cloaks and helmets, left leaning against the walls to create the impression that the castle was still occupied.

Arald and Halt faced one of the servants, a sniveling, frightened man who was convinced they were going to kill him.

Halt did nothing to disabuse him of that notion.

"Where is Morgarath?" he snarled, his face close to the other man's. The servant tried to look away but Halt grabbed him by the chin and forced him to look into his dark, burning eyes.

"He's . . . g-g-gone," the man stammered.

Halt allowed his anger at the inane reply. "When? And how?"

"Four, mebbe five days ago. They all left. There's a tunnel."

"Where?" thundered Arald and the servant looked at him in terror. The usually affable Baron of Redmont was furious. He had been tricked and he was in no mood to treat the man well. The servant gulped.

"There's a tunnel," he repeated. "In the basement under the kitchens. They went out through it . . ."

Halt and Arald exchanged a look. "Let's go!" the Ranger said, and led the way to the kitchens.

It took them five minutes to find the tunnel. The departing troops hadn't bothered to close the entrance behind them. It gaped in the south wall of the basement, dark and forbidding.

"Get some torches," Arald told one of his men, and the soldier departed at a run.

"This isn't new," Halt said as they made their way through

the tunnel, the darkness pushed back by their flickering torches. The tunnel was wide, with room for two men moving abreast, and the walls were lined with brick and stone.

"He's had years to build it," Arald replied. "Makes sense, I suppose, to have a bolt hole like this. I should do the same at Redmont."

"Are you considering bolting?" Halt asked.

Arald thought about the question for a few seconds. "Not really. But you never know when it might come in handy."

As they walked farther through the passage, Arald gestured with his torch at the water that was running down the walls and pooling on the floor. "We must be under the moat," he said. They stepped through it and continued.

Halt sensed that the tunnel was beginning to slope upward. "We're getting close to the exit." For some reason, he lowered his voice, although the likelihood that Morgarath or his men would be waiting for them was slim. Then a glimmer of light showed ahead of them, rapidly growing into a lit rectangle as they got closer.

They stepped out into the open air. The tunnel mouth was just inside the edge of the woods, concealed within a tangle of vines and brambles. Halt peered closely at them, seeing where they had been cut away in the past few days. The muddy ground around the exit had been churned by dozens of feet. But the tracks quickly died out as they moved across the thick grass, soaked by the rain of the preceding four days.

"Tracks are washed away," Halt muttered. "But this is where they came out, all right."

"Question is," said Arald, "where have they gone?"

Halt shrugged. "They could have gone in any direction."

"North, maybe?" said Arald. "After all, that's where he had Tiller raiding across the border, so he might have some kind of base there."

"Maybe," Halt said. He was unconvinced. "But as I say . . ."

His voice trailed off. He had caught sight of something in the trees about twenty meters away. It wasn't easy to see. It was mottled green and gray and blended into the forest background. But the wind had stirred it and the movement had caught his attention.

"Oh . . . no . . . ," he said softly, in a stricken voice. He began to run through the trees toward it.

Pritchard was lying on his back, eyes wide-open. There were half a dozen gaping wounds on his body. He had obviously been attacked by three or four men. His bow was lying nearby, snapped in half. They must have emerged from the tunnel, catching him by surprise. Then they killed him and left him to lie here. The flutter of movement Halt had seen had come from a corner of his cloak.

He dropped to one knee beside his old teacher, the man who, years ago, had replaced his own father in his affections. He felt hot tears forcing their way through his eyes and running freely down his cheeks.

Vaguely, he was aware that Arald had followed him and was standing a few paces back, unsure of what to say or do.

Halt bowed his head and said in a broken voice: "I'd only just found him again. And now he's gone."

He remained kneeling, head bowed, beside his old friend

and mentor for some minutes, thinking of the time they'd spent together in Dun Kilty, and of the sheer joy he had felt at their recent reunion. Finally, he wiped the tears away with the back of his hand, leaving a smear of dirt on his cheeks. Dry eyed, he rose to his feet and looked up into the morning sky.

"You'll pay for this, Morgarath. I swear on Pritchard's life, you'll pay for this."

EPILOGUE

The Mountains of Rain and Night

THE CAVE WAS SMOKY AND DRAFTY BUT AT LEAST IT WAS DRY. Outside, the rain blew in almost horizontal sheets across the rock-strewn plateau.

Morgarath sat, hunched over by the fire, facing the terrifying beast he had lured to his cave. It had taken months to find the Wargal, and now he had finally begun to win his confidence. The Wargal was the leader of a tribe of similar beasts. He had cajoled it with gifts of fresh meat—treasured by the Wargals for its scarcity in these cold, dripping mountains.

And it had taken days after that to establish a pattern of dominance over the primitive creature's mind. It had been a slow process. Morgarath had begun by emptying his mind of all conscious thought, allowing it to be open to receive messages from outside. That in itself had taken days to achieve. Then, on one memorable occasion, he had seen an image growing in his mind—even though his eyes were shut.

It was hazy and unfocused at first, and when he tried to concentrate on it, it receded. He realized that he mustn't try to focus with his conscious mind. And when he cleared his mind of conscious thought, the image returned—clearer and sharper this time.

He realized, with a start, that the image was himself. He was seeing what the Wargal chief was seeing.

He began to try to form an image of his own—difficult to do when he had to keep his conscious mind at bay. He envisaged himself sitting on a high throne, and the Head Wargal was bowing down before him, placing its head under his hand in submission.

Then he switched tack. He imagined Duncan, terrible in his red surcoat and glittering mail, cutting and hacking at a group of Wargals, killing and maiming them.

Morgarath had been doing this for a week now, always projecting the same image. But today he felt a slight jolt in his consciousness—an impression of repellence.

The Wargal had seen what he was projecting, and was disturbed and frightened by it.

Morgarath half opened his eyes and saw the creature's lips draw back from its fangs in a snarl.

He closed his eyes again and added to the image. Now a black-clad figure, with long white-blond hair, strode in front of the Wargals to protect them and to face Duncan. His long, two-handed sword swung in a gleaming arc to block Duncan's blade as the red-garbed warrior tried to kill another helpless Wargal.

The sword flashed quickly up and down, severing Duncan's head from his shoulders and sending it spinning among the rocks. The headless torso remained standing for a moment, then slowly toppled over.

The surviving Wargals swarmed around the black-clad

figure, bowing before him in gratitude and submission. Morgarath held the image in his mind for several minutes.

Then he felt a rough touch on his hand and he opened his eyes slowly.

The Wargal chieftain had moved closer and was kneeling before him. It took Morgarath's right hand in both its savagely clawed upper paws and placed it on its own head, bowing before Morgarath.

The former lord of Gorlan smiled grimly, allowing his hand to rest on the bowed head before him.

"Oh yes, my ugly friend," he crooned. "I think we're going to get on very well indeed."

COMING SUMMER 2016!

BROTHERBAND
BOOK 6

The Herons take to the high seas in their
next pulse-pounding adventure!

From John Flanagan,
author of the international phenomenon

Also by John Flanagan

THE RANGER'S APPRENTICE EPIC
BOOK 1: THE RUINS OF GORLAN
BOOK 2: THE BURNING BRIDGE
BOOK 3: THE ICEBOUND LAND
BOOK 4: THE BATTLE FOR SKANDIA
BOOK 5: THE SORCERER OF THE NORTH
BOOK 6: THE SIEGE OF MACINDAW
BOOK 7: ERAK'S RANSOM
BOOK 8: THE KINGS OF CLONMEL
BOOK 9: HALT'S PERIL
BOOK 10: THE EMPEROR OF NIHON-JA
BOOK 11: THE LOST STORIES
BOOK 12: THE ROYAL RANGER

BROTHERBAND CHRONICLES
BOOK 1: THE OUTCASTS
BOOK 2: THE INVADERS
BOOK 3: THE HUNTERS
BOOK 4: SLAVES OF SOCORRO
BOOK 5: SCORPION MOUNTAIN

About the Author

JOHN FLANAGAN grew up in Sydney, Australia, hoping to be a writer, and after a successful career in advertising and television, he began writing a series of short stories for his son, Michael, in order to encourage him to read. Those stories would eventually become *The Ruins of Gorlan*, Book 1 of the Ranger's Apprentice epic. Now with his companion series, Brotherband Chronicles, the novels of John Flanagan have sold millions of copies and made readers of kids the world over.

Mr. Flanagan lives in the suburb of Manly, Australia, with his wife. In addition to their son, they have two grown daughters and four grandsons.

You can visit John Flanagan at
www.RangersApprentice.com
www.BrotherbandChronicles.com